STORIES FOR BOYS

STORIES for BOYS

Selected and edited by
LEONARD GRIBBLE

HAMLYN
LONDON · NEW YORK · SYDNEY · TORONTO

Published by
THE HAMLYN PUBLISHING GROUP LIMITED
London · New York · Sydney · Toronto
Hamlyn House, The Centre, Feltham, Middlesex, England
© Copyright The Hamlyn Publishing Group Limited, 1961
Seventh impression, 1972
ISBN 0 601 8631 7
Printed in Czechoslovakia by Svornosť, Bratislava
51103/7

CONTENTS

IN THE TRACKS OF COLUMBUS
Peter Dawlish

The crew of the *Golden Duck* had fallen foul of Sir Percy Bertram's temper in the past, for they were Devon men and Sir Percy was a rascally Devon landlord. Peter Moone, who tells this rousing sea story of Elizabethan days, had been cheated of land by Sir Percy, who had vowed vengeance on those who had worsted him. Captained by Nat Berryman, the *Golden Duck* is refitted after an encounter with a Spaniard, and then sails westward in the tracks of Columbus. The further adventures of the crew of the *Golden Duck* are related in *Aztec Gold*, from which this story is taken.

We beached the *Golden Duck* on a smooth, sandy beach of Africa. Like some wounded animal crawling to shelter, the ship slid her forefoot in the sand and clung there by the anchors we carried out through the white surf. Then we threw ourselves on the hot beach and sought relief from our weariness; until Nat roared at us to return and toil again. We hated his voice, and scowled, but we obeyed. In the last two days we had learned to obey that harsh voice even as our bodies seemed to have melted with tiredness.

It had been a grim and bitter struggle to save the ship. The explosion that had blown the Spaniard into pieces had shaken the *Golden Duck* in her every timber. Water poured into her from sprung hull-planks and from gaps left where the oakum had been blasted. She was dismasted, with her bulwarks gone, and imbedded in her starboard side, half in and half out of her planking, was the iron barrel of a Spanish gun. Hardly a foot of her but was scarred or torn by the tremendous bombardment.

We manned the pumps and kept manning them. We raised and dropped the handles until our backs ached, then ceased to ache because we were past pain. Nat oathed and bullied, not hesitating to beat men with his fists when they lagged. He was everywhere, a roaring terror to the weak, a stinging challenge to the strong. There was little remaining of the jolly mariner who had come to our farm.

Driven by him, led by him, men crawled into the water-filled hold and brought out spare sails to drag under and round the ship's bottom so that the water poured in less dangerously. Cables were wound round her and hove tight to hold her weakened frames together, binding her like some bandage. Yet she still took much water, and we had to keep pumping. We never ceased to pump.

Nat drove us mercilessly. He spared neither wounded nor wearied. He was tireless, and did not leave the deck nor rest in those two awful days. The mast that had been cut away still floated near, and with the boat blown to pieces, Young Morgan and Joe Worrel swam to it and carried a line to drag it back alongside. It was parbuckled over the side and raised against the stump left in the deck, lashed there and the rags of what canvas remained sewn into a square sail and hoisted. What was left of our mizzen-mast became a yard.

The rudder had been broken from its fastenings, and men were lowered over the stern on ropes to secure it as best they could.

Then we headed for the distant shore and the gleaming yellow beach. The slight breeze gave us bare steering-way, so Nat had deck-planks torn up and shaped into rough sweeps and men were set to work these; while others, pumped, pumped and pumped. The weight of water held her close into her water like some dead thing, and we never got it less than halfway up her hold's depth. Yet she floated, and, while she floated we had hopes. Nat cursed us and jeered. He laughed and said we would live to hang. He set Young Morgan and others who could swim to diving into the flooded hold to seek out food, and they brought up sacks of sodden biscuit, and rescued the floating casks of ale and wine. And slowly the land rose and the beach became larger, until we were in the shallows and among the surf that was mercifully slight. As she touched, some of us leaped over the side and scrambled on shore, carrying kedges, grapnels and anything that would hold her fast.

'We've done it, my hearties,' Nat shouted. 'And now to work.'

'Let us sleep,' a man cried desperately.

Nat pounced on him and shook him brutally.

'What if the wind rises and raises the surf to smash her completely?' he demanded. 'No, you will toil night and day to make her seaworthy, and then you will sleep.'

He set us to work. As the tide dropped and the water left her, spouting from her sides in fifty places, we went into the hold to start unloading stores. Everything must come out of her so that we could discover the damage. Nat sent Joe Worrel and two others along the beach to seek a more sheltered haven. We others brought up sodden and ruined food, shot and ammunition, spare ropes and gear, tools and the hundred other objects that had been stowed so neatly. Powder was dried and men armed to stand sentry and watch for natives who might attack us.

Even the bullying of Nat Berryman could not hold back weariness for ever, and he was forced to put the men into watches. He sneered at us for our weakliness, and when he told me to go on shore with the watch off duty, I growled that I would keep pace with him or his like. We eyed each other like savage beasts and then he laughed.

'Ye hate me?' he demanded.

'I scorn you,' I told him, 'as one who betrayed his comrade.'

He nodded, his eyes become sombre.

'That I accept,' he said, 'and if ye would choose another captain I'll work wi' the mariners.'

I shook my head.

'It is done,' I said. 'If we fail in what we set out to do I shall not forgive you. But you are Captain.'

He heaved a great sigh.

'Then to it. You will take one watch. The bosun commands the other. Go you and rest.'

I obeyed him. I took my men on shore, and we lay under the bushes near the beach and slept. Two hours later we were shaken from our sleep and relieved the others. Nat still toiled, and I thought he must be made of iron.

The ship emptied and the stores and arms piled on the beach, we examined the hull. It was in a sad state. Her sheathing on one side had been torn clean from her and exposed the hull-planks beneath. At her ends, planks were sprung from their fastenings. Her ribs had been loosened at futtocks and floors. But her stout keel was firm and sound.

'We'll bind her again,' Nat cried jubilantly. 'Give us a week of fine weather and we will have her afloat.'

Joe and his companions were back with news of a small island not four miles distant, and we planned to make temporary repairs that would carry the ship to that haven. Among us were men skilled as shipwrights, and these directed the work. They took others into the forest and chose the hardest trees. These were felled and parts chosen for bends to double at our strained frames and for tree-nails to drive into the sprung planks. Not until this work commenced, five days after the disaster that had struck us, did Nat Berryman rest. How he kept awake and toiled as he did I do not know. Perhaps his guilt prevented sleep; perhaps he was made of iron. I saw him return from helping to choose the timber we would need, and he strode upright, swaggering as ever. He reached the edge of the beach, and suddenly he turned and faced me. He grinned, his face gaunt and pale.

' 'Twas a fool's trick, Peter,' he said. And he dropped like a log and lay there.

I dragged him into the shelter of a bush and called Morgan to watch over him. He slept for twenty hours, then awoke and cursed me for allowing him the respite. By then we had cut and dragged our chosen timbers to the ship and our men skilled with the tools were shaping them with saws and adzes. My task was to take the straight-grained pieces and with a hand axe to shape them into tree-nails, eight sided and some two feet long. New holes were bored in the sprung planks and the planks bent back into place so that the tree-nails could be driven home and the end secured. Others set the doubling pieces to the frames into place; others teased out rope for oakum and beat it between the planks, or melted down pitch to pour over the caulking.

In five days we had the hull seaworthy, and then we reloaded our stores and hauled the ship into deep water. We had made great sweeps, and with these we moved her along the coast until we reached the small island. It was a hump barely half a league long and less in width, but it would shelter the *Golden Duck* from any storms that came. We had discovered the hull made only a small amount of water on her short passage, but we beached her in a sheltered cove to finish our task.

We were cheerful now. Nat still drove us hard and was less his reckless self, but he still laughed and joked. To me he was blunt and without humility, treating me as he treated his other officers. I knew he was the true leader among us, and though

I hated him for imperilling the voyage, I obeyed him. In turn I drove my men without mercy, yet saw to it that they rested and were well fed.

The work on our vessel proceeded. No large trees grew on the island, so we built a raft of wine-barrels and short lengths of timber and floated it to the mainland. With half a dozen men well armed and keeping watch for natives, though we sighted none all the time we were on that coast, we sought out a tall straight tree and felled it. Our adzes trimmed it roughly, and we hauled it to the beach and floated it to the island. There it was shaped to a mainmast. What had been our mainmast was trimmed down to become a new mizzen-mast. We set up sheerlegs on the deck and hove out the stump of the old mainmast and set up the new.

We had been ten full days at work when our look-out on the island's top height hailed us and announced a sail. I was with the blacksmith, shaping new rudder gudgeons and pintles over an open fire, and at the look-out's hail I looked up. The man who worked with me voiced my thoughts.

'Is it that thieving knight?' he asked.

We dropped our tools and started for the hill, until Nat's voice halted us.

'Would ye let them find us?' he demanded. 'Our new mast will show above the island and the smoke from your fire betrays us. Aloft there, some of you, and fasten bushes to the mast so that it merges against the forest. Douse that fire and set up guns to command the channel.'

We obeyed him. Men shinned up the new mast, and others brought bushes and branches to be hauled aloft and fastened to the bare pole. I smothered the fire with earth, and then helped to sling a murdering piece on a pole to carry it to the end of the island. The others worked hastily, and within two hours we had placed guns at either end of the island and the mast was hidden by bushes and leaves. Then we crawled to the top of the hill, each armed with musket or bow and arrow, and peered over the edge.

The ship was within a mile of the shore, and we could see plainly her great green-and-white Tudor flag and a long pennant hanging from her mainmast. She was a ship of fully eighty tons, and well armed. Behind her she trailed a pinnace with two men seated in it.

'I have seen her before,' a man near me growled. 'She is the *Black Swan* of Dartmouth, a pirate ship.'

'Ye are right, Thomas,' another man called. 'I saw her lurking off Poole a year since, and her commander was that famous rogue Giles Kingsley. He took her from the Frenchmen in the Channel. A fast and strong vessel, as Frenchmen are.'

We watched her, muttering among ourselves and speculating if she were Sir Percy's ship now. She sailed past, making a full five knots to the breeze that carried her. My heart sank as I saw her pass, for I was sure that she carried our enemy, and he was ahead of us. She went on and came abreast of a headland five miles to the south, and then we saw her come round and head for the land.

'She has sighted us,' a man cried.

All of us believed she had, and we watched her anxiously. We saw her topsail drop as she disappeared behind the headland, and then we gazed at each other in horror. Nat's voice brought us to action.

'We sail tonight,' he roared. 'There is five hours before darkness, and in that time we must be out of this trap. Aye, if we sail on an upright oar.'

'We are not yet ready,' a man protested.

Nat turned on him savagely.

'The masts are set up,' he declared fiercely. 'An hour will complete the rudder. Most of our stores are on board and now we must make a hasty job of what is left. I tell you we sail tonight, and before these rogues return along the shore or by boat to destroy us. They will have twice our number.' He waved an arm and hurried down the hill. 'Come, lads, to it.'

We followed him. We raced to the beach and were detailed to our several tasks. The blacksmith and I finished our repair to the rudder and it was floated to the ship and the foot weighted to slip the pintles into the gudgeons. Young Morgan dived repeatedly under the surface to guide in the hangings and to cut loose the weight on the foot when the rudder was in place. Others brought the guns back to the ship, and those most skilled bent on the spare sails and sent them aloft on their yards. There was a spring on the island, and we filled our waterbutts and floated them off to be hove on board. Stores that had been on shore we tossed into the hold to be stowed later and an hour after nightfall we were ready. A man stood forward to cast the lead and find us deep water, while Nat conned the ship into open water. The guns were loaded, and we who manned them stood ready to fire.

We left our haven cautiously and by using our sweeps. Morgan Cliff and two other younkers were on the mainyard, ready to cut away the sail lashings, and one man stood by the mizzen smiting line to break it free. Nat had taken ten men from Sir Percy's crew, and we were manned enough to handle our task.

With only the creak and rub of the sweeps and the chanting of the leadsman to be overheard, the *Golden Duck* crept out of the narrow channel. We by the guns peered anxiously at the glistening, star-lit sea, seeking an enemy. The linestocks were glowing, but the glow was hidden close under the bulwark rails. Now and then I could hear Nat giving an order to the helmsman, to port or to starboard his helm, and I had time to admire our commander. To me there was only darkness, and yet he gave his orders quietly and surely.

'We are clear,' a voice said near me, and I heaved a sigh of relief.

Then the leadsman shouted in alarm, and as he did a voice challenged us from seaward and there loomed up, seemingly over us, a ship.

'Larboard guns... Fire!' Nat roared, and our well-trained gunners tugged clear their linestocks and thrust their glowing ends at the guns. In the flash of the three guns I saw the ship that lay across our course and heard the shouts of her crew. I fancied I recognized the shrill voice of Sir Percy Bertram, but it was drowned in Nat's cry to 'Cut! Cut! Haul aft lee braces, forward the bowlines... Helmsman, we pass under her quarter. Master Gunner! Her rudder! Fire!'

The *Golden Duck* spun. Men hauled on ropes, and those manning the sweeps lay back on them strongly. Above me the raked stern of the other ship appeared, and there was a splintering sound as our sweeps were shattered against her and something fell on the deck beside me. Then our port side guns roared and crashed into her stern and we were clear.

'Up, up your helm, Quartermaster!' Nat roared. 'Ease her off and run. Bosun, square away and bring the wind aft. Cast overboard those linestocks else they betray us. Now all be silent. Hold her so, Quartermaster, with the wind on the port quarter. Trim your sail to it, Boatswain.'

We were speeding along the coastline now, the wind astern and the mainyard squared. Nat laughed softly.

'We surprised them, mates. What carried away from her?'

I stooped and found what had dropped on our deck and discovered a short spar.

'Her outliker,' I told him.

'Then we have caused some damage,' Nat cried. 'Is she chasing us?'

Men peered aft, but could see nothing.

'Our last shot struck her rudder,' the Master Gunner declared. 'I saw it shatter as the shot struck clean against its head.'

'Let us pray you saw truly,' Nat answered, 'but we will know by dawn.' He laughed then as though he enjoyed it all. 'By King Harry,' he cried merrily, 'now we will see how our *Golden Duck* swims against a lousy Frenchman. To it, lads. We must have more canvas. Send up the topsail and square the spritsail. Tomorrow we will see if our bold ship will carry a third sail on her mainmast. John Hawkins claims our ships are under-canvassed, and we will test his claim; even if she leans over until the yardarms lick the sea. It is a race.'

A race! We had not the strength to fight the larger ship, and so we showed her our heels. The men argued on our chances as we worked through the night to stow the hold to give her her best sailing trim and to shape the new sail Nat meant to carry. Some swore a third sail on the mainmast would turn us over; others argued that John Hawkins was a master seaman and was fitting the third sail on his ships. They declared we would gain a full knot at least, for our bottom was newly cleaned and graved with grease, while the *Black Swan* had sailed from England and would be foul with weed. All night they argued and I listened, grasping at the hopes of those who would have the *Golden Duck* the speedier ship and glowering on the pessimistic.

The dawn swelled up, to find us anxiously scanning the sea astern. It was empty and we gave a cheer for our brave little ship. Nat called us aft and from the stern castle he looked down on us.

'Lads,' he announced, 'we have escaped that villain for the time. Did we do him damage?'

'I planted a shot near his rudder; that I swear,' the Master Gunner boasted again.

'Aye, but did it harm him?' Nat demanded. 'For if it did not he will be after us, and he is too strong for us to fight.' He watched us keenly for a time while our men murmured among themselves.

'But we have outpaced him,' a fellow cried, 'so we have the heels of him.'

Nat shook his head and pointed astern.

'Have ye looked?' he asked, leaning over the rail. 'Have ye not noticed there is no land in sight?' He stood upright and went on: 'In those last hours we have steered west, lads,' he told us. 'Hauled to seaward. That is why you do not see that pirate.'

The muttering increased then and the men looked at Nat wonderingly.

'Out wi' it, Nat Berryman,' the Master Gunner challenged. 'What is in your mind?'

'This, mates,' Nat answered grimly. 'We dare not encounter the *Black Swan* again, for we were lucky tonight and have escaped more by luck than anything else. Those French crafts are speedy —— as speedy as our little bark. If we did not damage the *Black Swan* she will be seeking us even now and to the southward.'

Our fellows were uneasy now. They looked astern and to port and scowled. Some declared they could fight and master the *Black Swan*, but others were less sure. Nat watched them steadily and suddenly he clapped a hand on the rail of the stern castle and spoke.

'So, mates,' he said, 'we must change our course. We'll leave the coast and sail straight for the river. We'll cut a corner and let the *Black Swan* search for us in vain.'

I was amazed at the men's reactions to this proposal. To me it seemed our only sensible course, but yet these reckless mariners gazed at Nat and at each other with something like horror in their eyes. Nat folded his arms and looked at them scornfully. One fellow, bolder than the others, stepped forward.

'We are in no condition to sail into this unknown ocean, Nat Berryman,' he protested. 'Our bark is not staunch as she should be and our food is low. It is a thousand leagues of open water and has never been sailed. You carry us to our deaths.'

'Columbus the Italian sailed it,' Nat retorted, 'and we will find food before we attempt it. The Canaries lie ahead of us and we will seek food there.' He glowered on us and went on: 'I had thought ye bold and reckless men. Does open water frighten ye?'

'Unknown ocean!' the fellow who had protested cried. 'We have heard fearsome tales of that vast space. Of parts where winds never blow and ships lie motionless until they rot, of a sea of weed that grasps a ship and holds her for all eternity.' The man shivered. 'I think I would risk Sir Percy Bertram's mercy rather than that.'

Nat's scorn was biting as he replied.

'That is the talk of a craven,' he cried. 'We are already in the latitude of the trade winds, and they will carry us sweetly to our destination.' He swung an arm as though to gather us closer together. 'But we will vote on it. Who is for the route to the southward and the destruction of all our hopes of wealth if we meet the *Black Swan?* And who will sail with this bark across the unknown ocean and have a peaceful voyage?'

I turned to watch the men. One by one they raised their arms to vote for the southern route. Nat counted them. They were twelve. He laughed and shouted for us who would sail by a straight course to show ourselves, and we cheered and shouted. Nat rubbed his hands together.

'Then so it is, comrades,' he declared. 'We'll make for the Canaries and find stores, and then we'll head our little bark into the unknown.' He grinned at me and winked slyly. 'And no piracy,

Peter Moone. We'll have little to pirate where we shall sail.'

I saw the great chart that night. Nat called those of us not on duty into the cabin and explained what we would do to reach the river.

'Look you,' he said, laying a fingertip on the upper part of that great swelling bulge of Moorish Africa, 'we made the land here at Cape Cantine and we coasted down to where we met that Spaniard. Our island was Mogador.'

We watched him, one man holding a lighted candle to illuminate the chart. He spread the chart open and exposed the coast of the Americas and laid his finger on the narrow Isthmus of Panama that joins the two great masses of the continent with its slender length. Where this isthmus widened at its northern end and the land named Florida appeared and stretched to the east to form a great bight, Nat touched a part of the coastline.

'Here is our river,' he said.

'We must penetrate into the Gulf of Mexico to reach it,' John Davis said doubtfully.

'I sailed out of it,' Nat retorted, 'and can sail in again. Now I point out to you that we plan to steer from these islands close against the coast of Africa —— the Canaries —— to the Bahamas that lie athwart the entrance to the Gulf of Mexico.'

'I pray we steer truly,' John Davis said, 'for it seems a feat of navigation.'

'I can do no more and no less than others who have crossed unknown seas,' Nat said humbly enough, 'but I have listened often and carefully to navigators who know these oceans well and I have learned to check our compass and to lay a course.'

'Then with God's aid we will make our landfall,' the Master Gunner acceded, though grudgingly.

Nat nodded soberly and drew his finger back across the chart to the coast of Africa.

'Here is our position now,' he said. 'We run along the thirty-second parallel of North Latitude, and we pass between the island of Madeira and those of the Canaries. When we are well clear of these we will haul a little to the southward, and that should take us to our destination.'

'A curse on Sir Percy Bertram!' Davis complained. 'I would have preferred to follow the known track and to hold the coast to Cape Blanco, and then to make for Cape Verde Islands, as is done by all experienced navigators. It lessens the distance across open water, and we could replenish our water and food at those islands.'

'We have decided against it,' Nat retorted firmly, 'and take the shorter route, though it makes a longer open-water voyage.'

We left the cabin and sought our sleeping-places in the hold and under the forecastle. Mine was in this last shelter, for I could not abide the stench in the hold, and I had a lingering fondness for the manger, since I had found solace there with our animals. I lay on the bare planks with a length of cable as a pillow and slept.

The next day we sighted the highlands of the Canaries far to the southward, but hauled away to keep out of sight. England was not yet at war with Spain, but that did not prevent ships of both nations fighting if they encountered each other. We had no fancy to battle with more Spaniards.

At noon that day our look-out on the masthead cried a sail, and Nat scrambled aloft to watch it. He stayed aloft for a full half-hour, then descended and called us together.

'Lads,' he announced, 'I shall close yonder ship.' He looked at me and smiled mischievously. 'Nay, not to challenge her, Peter. I am done with such tricks for the time. But to buy from her what food we need.' He raised his hands to his neck and tugged from his doublet a thick chain of gold that I had seen him wear when he first came to our farm. 'I have this,' he announced, 'and some of ye will have other pieces to offer.' He lifted the chain from his neck and tossed it on the deck. 'Who will add to the muster?' he demanded. 'We shall be well rewarded.'

There was a general search and then a shower of small objects of value. I tossed into the pile a ring that had been my father's, and Joe found a bauble he had had from a wench. Nat looked on the small pile and grinned.

'It will buy us enough—if that ship carries something to spare.'

The look-out sang out to tell us the distant ship had swung from us and was headed into the land, and Nat roared at us to

send up our new sail. He conned the *Golden Duck* in pursuit of
the other ship, and soon we knew we were overhauling her speedily.
Her hull rose into view, and by late afternoon we could see her
as a tub-bellied trader. Our eyes sought her nationality, and some
declared her Spanish and others English. Nat, who knew every
ship afloat, seemingly, declared she was the *Rose of Avon* and
a Bristol ship trading between that port and the Canaries. Sure
enough, when we were a bare half-league from her she sent up
a great Tudor flag, and we could see her guns run out and manned.

'The sturdy rogues,' cried Nat. 'They would fight.'

'You promised...' I began and Nat laughed.

'Content yourself, Peter,' he assured me. 'There will be no
bloodshed today.'

We wore the English colours, and now Nat swung the *Golden
Duck* to run alongside the trader, but beyond range of her guns.
We drew ahead of her, and laid ourselves between her and the
distant land, and Nat ordered our topsails down. Next he sent
the younkers aloft to furl the great course, and we lay into the
wind to our mizzen. The move was neatly done, for Nat had laid
us so close ahead of the trader that her clumsiness did not permit
her to haul far from us, and as she passed a bare two cables away
twenty-five lusty English throats hailed her.

Her master and crew heard, and knew that we were not Spaniards nor Frenchmen, and knew also we could overhaul them
with ease. To our great relief, she dropped her topsails, brailed
up her course and hove to. Nat had our course dropped again,
and we sailed closer to the other ship. We saw that her crew
stood by her guns and were armed, but none of us wore any
weapon, and Nat had ordered the guns drawn inboard. A shrill
Welsh voice hailed us and demanded our business, and Nat
climbed to the rigging to ask that we might buy food and what
wine they could spare.

'Come no closer,' the Welshman ordered, 'and I will send a boat,
for I see you have none.'

We had twelve sacks of flour that had gone somewhat musty,
a mass of salted fish, fresh fruits such as I had never seen before,
and six butts of good sack in exchange for our small pile of valu-

ables, and the Welshman promised to send word of our condition to my mother and others. As the stores were transported from ship to ship, the trader's men watched us carefully, and I think they parted from us with relief. Her Master—the stout little Welshman—said his ship was indeed the *Rose of Avon* and of Bristol, as we had guessed. We warned him of Sir Percy and the *Black Swan*, and had his promise to disclose our whereabouts to none but those whose names we gave him. Then we parted, each crew cheering the other, and we saw no other ship for nearly forty days.

The *Rose of Avon* had told us our position, which was fifteen miles northward of the Island of Palma, and when we had parted company, Nat had set our course to the Bahamas. Now we should have no enemy, or friend, except the ocean and the winds, and see no living thing but fish and a few strange birds.

It was the last day of June when we parted company with the *Rose of Avon* and laid our ship on the course the Italian, Columbus, had followed on his first voyage of discovery. On the eighth day of August, thirty-eight days later, like Columbus, we saw a cloud that became land, and we knelt on our ship's deck and thanked God. Our prayers were the more fervent because of the horrors of our voyage and our present condition. Most of our men were afflicted by the dread disease of scurvy that rots the flesh so that teeth fall out and scabs cover the skin; our food was almost gone; our water had become foul scum; and only their weakness prevented some from rising against Nat's leadership, and only his indomitable strength gave the rest of us hope.

For myself, I had learned why men feared this huge ocean, and knew that I would fight a dozen Sir Percys before attempting another such voyage.

We began our long passage cheerfully enough, though some grumbled and whispered among themselves. But the wind blew steadily and the *Golden Duck* made good speed. Nat said we would have found the wind stronger nearer the Equinox, but we were satisfied. Sir Percy was far from us, and we would reach the river before he did. Meantime we sailed on steadily, and I learned a little of the mariner's arts each day. Nat confessed himself no great navigator, but he could find the ship's latitude by the cross-staff when the sun was in its zenith at noon, and could check his compass by the Guard Star, which should bear within a degree or so of north. Each day he brought his cross-staff——a wooden instrument consisting of a slender squared stick marked in degrees and with another piece that slid back and forth on the main length like a movable sword-hilt. Nat laid the end of the staff to his eye and moved the shorter piece until the sun appeared on its uppermost tip and the sea horizon at the lower tip. When the sun ceased to rise in the sky, as it does at noon, he read the angle between it and the horizon by taking the degrees marked on the staff where the cross-piece rested. Then by a simple calculation he knew his latitude; and for his westing he took the ship's speed by the log and had what he described as a 'near enough' position to prick on his sea-card. He laughed, and swore worse than he had found their landfall by these simple means, and there was always Young Morgan to check his figuring. Morgan, indeed, became more skilled in this clerkly task than Nat himself, and I got enough of the art to satisfy my thick skull.

The work of the ship was perhaps too easy, for we hardly had need to touch a rope for days, and Nat, now that no danger threatened us, was not so strict as he had been. He remained our leader, but he joked with the men and joined them in their rough sport at times. He also kept their greed alive by telling of the fabulous wealth in the Aztec city and how they would all become rich. He even argued with those who still declared we should have taken the longer and known route, and who said we were missing many rich prizes by sailing this lonely and empty ocean. I soon learned that many of our fellows had joined the adventure as much for what rich prizes we might encounter on the way as for the greater prize of the Aztec city. None of them, except Nat, Joe Worrel, Young Morgan and myself, had come to rescue my unfortunate brother.

When we were what Nat reckoned was half-way across the ocean, the winds began to fail us. There were times when the ship lay with sails flapping and rolling heavily to a long, lazy swelling of the water. The sun's heat increased, and we could see the pitch boil from the deck seams, and we gasped for air. Our water was getting foul now, though few drank it while the wine lasted, but it gave another complaint to the grumblers. They cursed the heat and the lack of wind, and they cursed Nat when he was out of hearing. I laid two fellows on their backs who kept this complaint going in my hearing.

But I was worried. Joe had charge of the food stores, and he said they were lowering too fast. He told Nat, and our allowance was reduced. The lack of fresh vegetables brought the first sign of the dreaded scurvy, and then the grumblers became more outspoken and demanded that Nat head south and to waters where we could find others ships.

'We shall lie here and rot,' they swore, and Nat laughed at them and set them to tasks to keep their minds occupied.

Yet I saw that he spent more time over the sea-card and came from it looking troubled. Where he had been satisfied to stream the log-chip at the end of every watch to discover our speed, he must now have it done twice in a watch, and though he swore he did this to keep our lazy hands occupied, I saw he was worried by our lack of progress.

Such worries and our everlasting desire for food, the lack of wind, and the heat tormented us and began to make us ill-tempered with each other. There was snarling and quarrels, and poniards were drawn, and we who held to our sanity had to use brutal means to stop murder being done. Joe and I took turns in sleeping beside the food where it was stacked in the cabin, for Nat used the open deck for a bed in the hot weather. The whole ship lived in an uneasy, watchful enmity, and we soon discovered that there were certain of our fellows who would attempt to take the ship from us if our troubles continued.

I marvelled that Nat, who must have heard the mutterings that went on, did not descend on the rebels and handle them as he had handled others earlier in the voyage. I spoke to him of this and he shook his head.

'It is always the same, Peter,' he told me. 'For it seems the nature of mariners to grumble. While they make no move to attack me I shall let them have what small pleasure there is in their complaining, for indeed they have much to complain of.'

So he still went among them, good-natured, cheerful, seemingly oblivious to their scowls and mutterings.

'I am no lofty gentleman, Peter,' he joked, 'but a common tarpaulin like them, even if I have a smattering of tricks they do not possess. Let them curse me. They will follow me just as heartily when the time comes.'

I did not argue. After all, I was only a youth, and Nat was a grown man; though indeed there were times when I doubted this last fact, for, with all his experience, he was in many ways more youthful than I. A first-class mariner in the handling of a ship, possessing a smattering of the higher art of navigation and being, when he cared to assert it, a forceful commander, he still remained the reckless importunate tarpaulin who would sooner settle an argument with his fist or a roar of laughter than by a stiff and aloof dignity. Maybe that is why our fellows did not rise against him on that weary voyage. He was more one of themselves than an officer. Also, without him they would have been quite lost; for nobody amongst us, except perhaps Young Morgan, who had learned the trick quickly, had the slightest knowledge of navigation. And they feared the stength in his huge fist and the thunder of his rages when he was aroused. Those of us who had no need to fear him got to love him, for he was the most lovable of men in his simplicity.

So on that wearisome, cruel voyage across the unknown ocean he heartened the weaklings, laughed at the dangerous and earned the fierce loyalty of others. And when that cloud took shape as land, he ran thick fingers though his long hair and grinned.

'I' troth,' he exclaimed ruefully, 'I had almost given up hope of this myself.'

'You mean,' I demanded, 'you were not sure of your navigation?'

He nodded, chuckling.

'That's what I mean, Peter,' he confessed, 'but tell no one. By my reckoning we were either in mid-ocean or had sailed a hundred leagues into the jungles of America——the cursed figures would not sort themselves.' He winked at me and said in a hoarse whisper: 'Young Morgan had it better than I, for he assured me that we'd be lifting the land this very day.'

I was aghast, and stared at him in amazement.

'And do you know which land this is we have sighted?' I demanded.

He scratched his head.

'If my latitude is right, Peter,' he told me, 'these are the Islands of the Bahamas that lie athwart the straits of Florida. But I'll not swear to it. We'll close and find out.'

'And perhaps be welcomed by a Spanish garrison or war galleon,' I said worriedly.

He nodded without any sign of anxiety.

'True enough, Peter,' he agreed, 'so if ye'll call Master Davis to me, we'll have the guns loaded, and those able to stand upright will stand by. But land we must, for our food is gone and we must find some.'

So in this haphazard manner, and in no condition to meet a strong enemy, we sailed close to the land, and discovered it to be an island some ten miles in length, with, beyond it, other islands. A man stood on the wale to swing the handlead, and the ship was conned close to the shore. We anchored in a small cove where the shores were thickly clustered with trees, and we disturbed a flock of coloured birds with the noise of our anchor striking the water's surface. By then it was dusk, and Nat announced we would remain on board until the following morning, and then attempt to lay the ship against the shore, as we possessed no boat to make a landing. He heartened everyone by bidding Joe bring forth what food remained and to serve a full meal. Tomorrow, he declared cheerfully, we should find food. It seemed to me an improvident step, but it achieved miracles among the men, for they ate and drank, and their spirits returned, so that to hear them one would have believed our adventure was over and we were in Plymouth harbour with the hold crammed with treasure. They sang and joked, Nat the heartiest among them, and I sat and watched them, and marvelled at this childishness in all mariners. Twenty-four hours ago they had been in the lowest misery and depression; they might even now be lying a musket-shot from powerful enemies;

26

Nat had no true knowledge of where we were; yet they made merry, like children at a feast. Even Joe Worrel sat there, flushed with wine and merriment, and it seemed the only sensible person on board ship was myself. I left them to their feasting and sat on the forecastle, and was determined to keep watch all the night. I, at least, would not be careless in this unknown world. Then I woke up to the shaking of a vigorous hand and groaned a protest.

'Wake up, Peter,' Young Morgan was whispering urgently into my ear. 'A craft has sailed past our anchorage, and I must call Nat.'

I sat up and discovered it was daylight and the night had gone. Where it had gone I had no idea, but all my fine intentions had gone with it, for I had been sound asleep. Then I remembered Morgan's voice, and leaped to my feet. From aft came Nat's voice, roaring to the men to get under way. He strode among the prostrate figures, poking them with his foot.

'A prize, lads!' he bellowed. 'Slip and buoy the cable, for we have no time to bring it inboard. Ho, Boatswain, cut and run! Our breakfast has just sailed past our noses, and we must after it.'

The fellows might never have been weak, so smartly did they obey his orders. A small keg was fastened to the anchor cable, and the end slipped outboard to be recovered later. Morgan was already aloft, knife in hand to cut away the ribbands. Others swarmed to join him. Silas Pierce was in the waist, clearing ropes and bullying the mariners, and in a second, seemingly, the *Golden Duck* was moving out of the cove to a breeze that sent her ahead prettily. By then I was at work, seeing to it the guns were primed and linestocks glowing. Others brought up muskets and loaded these and set them inside the bulwark rail. Grapnels were put ready, their chains and lines coiled, and the fellows were laughing and promising each other the finest meal ever eaten. I asked Morgan what manner of ship had passed, and he said she seemed smaller than ourselves, but he had caught only a glimpse of her as she had disappeared beyond the cove.

We sighted her as we cleared the cove, and our fellows laughed their scorn at our prize. She was a bare mile ahead of us, and was little bigger than a canter. But she seemed deeply laden, and would give us some return. Nat shouted to the Master Gunner to lay a shot ahead of her when we were within range, but to do her no harm until we had boarded. We were overtaking her fast, and she seemed unaware of our intentions. In less than an hour we were abreast of her, and we could see half a dozen figures on her deck. Our shot landed a half-cable ahead of her, and at once she came into the wind and her solitary sail dropped in submission. I blushed for the fuss we had made to master such a prize, and then it occurred to me that I had not protested at what was no other than piracy. But I felt the hollow in my stomach, and forgave myself this once.

I will pass quickly over the next hour. We lay alongside the smaller craft, and three Spaniards and a dozen Indians watched us stolidly. To Nat's questions, spoken in awkward Spanish, we discovered the craft carried a cargo of maize and wines and a root much eaten in America. This was a prize greater to us than gold at this moment, so Nat ordered the craft to sail back to our cove ahead of us and to anchor. We followed her and picked up our anchor cable again, and bade the Spaniard bring his bark alongside. Then we transferred his cargo to the *Golden Duck* and took possession of a stout boat the craft had been towing behind her. The Spanish captain accepted this thievery without protest, and informed Nat that our island was indeed one of the Bahamas, but farther south than Nat had reckoned by almost sixty leagues.

'I think,' Nat announced when we had taken the Spaniard's cargo, 'we will engage our prisoner as pilot. He may be lying as to our whereabouts, and if we carry him he must be truthful. If the says rightly, we are near to a channel between the island of Cuba and another, and we will discover this if the Don has been truthful. We can land him on the coast of Cuba and his boat can follow and pick him up.'

Fourteen days later we sailed the *Golden Duck* into the river the Spaniards called the River of Cannibals, and which lies within the Tropic of Cancer. If I give no clearer direction, it is because I have no wish to send others seeking this place, and would leave the Aztecs to find what peace they may until the Spaniards who are rapidly covering that land discover their hidden town.

MURDER IN CAMERA
Morgan Hall

Murder in one of the Lancewood Television studios during the broadcast of a thrilling serial drama — that was the problem Jeremy Grant, the programme's assistant producer, had to solve. But he did not arrive at the answer until he had learned why someone had rewritten a final scene to include the payment of a personal debt — permanently.

'We must apologize,' said the soothing voice of the television announcer, 'for the fading of your picture at the end of our serial play. This was due to a camera fault...'

Everyone in Studio Y knew that the "camera fault" was Roland Kane—and he was dead. Even in those few panic-stricken moments between the fadeout and the announcement, each one of the cast had time to experience two paradoxical emotions — relief and fear. They waited in a kind of petrified silence for the producer to make the next move. They all knew why—but this is Jeremy Grant's story. Let him tell it...

I joined the Lancewood Television Studios about two months before the death of Roland Kane. I'd been aware of him, of course, as an actor, before that time, in my job as assistant producer with Merrivale Films. I was one of the fortunate few from Merrivale who came to Lancewood when the film company closed down.

I knew Roger Whiteman, TV producer with Lancewood, and he took me on as his assistant. I hadn't done any 'live' shows before, but as my engagement coincided with the beginning of rehearsals for the new serial, I thought I had a little time to settle down before we went on the air.

But it wasn't so easy to settle down. There was an undercurrent of tension in the studio. It was nothing to do with 'camera nerves.' It was something deeper, sinister, like the fictitious atmosphere Whiteman was trying to generate into the serial play. I'm not sure when I sensed the first disturbing ripples; but it was after the transmission of Episode One that Whiteman dropped the first pebble into the millpond of my mind and I became consciously aware that the ripples were there.

The control room staff had gone, and cast and technicians were leaving the studio. I was reading the script of the second episode when Whiteman entered. He was a slightly built man with a pinched, sensitive face. Full of nervous energy, he drove himself to extremes—as well as those who came under his direction.

'Well, Grant,' he said slowly. 'What's the verdict?'

'O. K.,' I answered. 'Settled down nicely after those rather shaky rehearsals, I thought.'

31

'You're easily satisfied, and that won't do for me,' he frowned. 'Maybe it's different in films. A poor performance gets by because of the wide scope for action, impressive background, and so on. In TV, performance is everything, for it's mostly close up. And I only want the best.' He looked at me curiously. 'Tonight was a poor show.'

Well, maybe it wasn't anything to rave about; but I couldn't agree that it had been bad.

'Who was it falling down, then?'

'All of them,' he murmured without hesitation. He sat down wearily. 'There's something wrong somewhere... with the whole cast. I've been feeling it in the past few days... a kind of atmosphere. Haven't you noticed anything?'

I thought back over the rehearsals.

'Well — yes. There's been a bit of temperament, a show of "nerves", but I didn't take it in. I put it down to the usual reaction of starting a new play.'

He shook his head. 'It isn't that. It's something quite different. As though they were on edge — waiting for something to happen.'

'You're not questioning their ability?'

'No. Something that's sapping it. And if we don't do something about it, this serial won't run for three weeks let alone six. We can't change the whole cast in the middle of it.' He stood up. 'Well, sleep on what I've said, and tomorrow you can take on an extra duty.'

'What do you want me to do?' I asked.

'Just watch them,' he said. 'Very closely.'

Back in my room I sat up drinking cups of coffee while the cast of the serial paraded on the screen of my mind. There was Mickey West, a good actor in a minor part with which he seemed dissatisfied. Was he jealous of Roland Kane, the rather pompous young man who played the hero?

Talented Steve Melton was also moody and disagreeable. Was he jealous of Kane's "meatier" part when he knew him to be an inferior actor? Then there was Lucille Maitland, a young girl whose bouts of nerves and temperament puzzled me. Was it because they were jealous — jealous of Kane? His leading role, his expensive car, his ingratiating manner that gave him a veneer of success?

Considering him seriously, I reached the conclusion that he was a bit of a "ham", and I couldn't understand why Whiteman had given him the lead in the programme. As far as I could remember the other two members of the cast, young Dick Hartley and John Stokes, were both easy-going and smooth performers, and I'd seen nothing unpleasant from either of them. But it was early yet; we'd only worked together for one week...

The next morning being Saturday I knew I should find none of the cast in the studios, but I went down just the same in the hope that Bob Ridleigh would be around. As I turned into the studio drive, Kane's car almost bowled me over.

He grinned at me, but I was more intent on looking at the white-faced young man in dark glasses at his side. It was not a bright day, and I couldn't see the point of the glasses. As I made my way along to Studio Y I wondered where I'd seen him before.

Ridleigh was our genial studio manager, and as I entered his small office his eyebrows lifted in surprise.

'Hullo, Jeremy. Forgotten it's Saturday? Thought you were going fishing for the weekend.'

'I am — in a way.' I sat down, staring at him soberly. 'I met Kane leaving as I came in. He nearly ran me down.'

'That must have been fun for Kane.'

'I wasn't looking at him,' I said. 'His passenger interested me. Thought I'd seen him somewhere. Young chap in dark glasses.'

He nodded. 'He's the old man's son.'

'Who — Lancewood?' I must have looked surprised, but Ridleigh seemed to take the friendship of Kane and the managing director's son as a matter of course.

'Sure,' he said. 'They're as thick as thieves. Trust Roland Kane for skimming the cream.'

'You don't like him?' I suggested.

'Like him? Who does? Every time he's in the studio I feel like ramming the mike down his throat.'

'How come he's so friendly with young Lancewood?'

Ridleigh shrugged. 'Like the death-watch beetle, he's got a way of crawling into the most sacred places. I don't know how it happened but he seems to have some hold over the youngster. That puts Kane O. K. with the old man, and that's why we have to put up with him strutting about here as the star of the show.'

'Do the rest of the cast feel like you?'

'I'd say all of them.'

'Then why doesn't Whiteman do something about him?'

Ridleigh's expression was quizzical. 'What would you do? The man who pays the piper and all that. Old Lancewood does the paying. What he says, goes.'

'Then why doesn't Whiteman tell the old man that Kane's having a bad effect on the others?' I frowned.

'Maybe he has told him,' Ridleigh said. 'Or maybe, perched up there in his control box, he hasn't noticed.'

'He's noticed something all right. He told me so last night. He wasn't satisfied with the show. He thought there was something radically wrong with the whole cast.'

Ridleigh was pensive.

'I wouldn't go as far as that,' he returned slowly. 'They may be "het up" with Kane's pomposity, but they wouldn't let their feelings ruin the show.'

'Well, Whiteman thought something was doing just that.'

Ridleigh gave me a sidelong glance. 'How long have you known Whiteman?' he asked, quietly.

'I met him about three years ago,' I answered, surprised, 'But I hadn't seen him for eighteen months prior to meeting him accidentally at a club three weeks ago. Merrivale had just closed down and he offered me the job of assistant.'

Ridleigh nodded. 'He wants a good assistant to take his place. He's on the short list for Controller of Programmes. The vacancy's coming up in about two months. He's been going flat out for it since he returned from his illness.'

'He drives himself too much. He doesn't look well now.'

'It takes time to recover from nerve trouble. He had a breakdown about three months ago and if he doesn't ease up he'll be back in hospital.' He paused, leaning back in his chair. 'Honestly, Jeremy, what did *you* think of the performance last night?'

'Well — O. K.; but when he started talking about it afterwards,

I did realize that in the past week there had been an undercurrent of — well, friction, but I thought it was just a question of everyone settling down. Remember, I haven't been here long. I don't know anything about Kane or the others.'

He nodded. 'Whiteman doesn't know much about them either. We've used three of them before — Melton, Stokes and Hartley, who introduced Miss Maitland. None of us know much about Kane except what we can see for ourselves, and we don't like what we see.'

'It seems to me,' I said, 'that he ought to be put in his place now, once and for all.'

'Who's going to do it if Whiteman can't?' he smiled weakly. 'I told you what the set-up is — no one can touch him. He's wormed his way in too far with the old man's son, and the old chap's a yes-man where his son is concerned.'

He rose, and patted me on the shoulder. 'I shouldn't worry about it too much, Jeremy. Just concentrate on the job. I'll keep everyone smooth on the floor.' He grinned. 'We may have our difficult moments, but I don't think there'll be any fireworks.'

But the fireworks were there all right. Waiting to explode.

In the days that followed I became acutely aware that under the surface the fuses were smouldering and that before the end of the serial real trouble would blow the production to pieces.

I watched the cast closely at every opportunity. Off the set their hostility towards Kane was obvious, but if he noticed, he rode it calmly. He seemed to revel in the fact that if they wanted their jobs they'd have to put up with him. There was no shaking him off. He gave the impression that he was "carrying" them all; that the success of each episode depended on his talents. I found myself disliking him as intensely as the others.

'There's only one thing troubling the cast and it's Kane,' I told Whiteman a few days later on one of the few occasions when we were alone.

'I know,' he admitted wearily. 'I've been watching too.'

'Surely Lancewood can be persuaded to do something about him?'

Whiteman shook his head helplessly.

35

'I've talked to him,' he said. 'He told me to have patience. To give Kane time to settle down to my direction.'

'Was his son present?'

'Yes. He had the audacity to tell me I'd got to get used to Kane's particular kind of genius!'

'I've never heard such rot,' I retorted.

'Everyone knows he's a "ham". What kind of spell has he spun round young Lancewood?'

'Goodness knows,' moaned Whiteman. 'Some sort of hypnosis, it must be.'

'What are you going to do?'

'I don't know.' His hands clenched on the desk. 'If only we could get something tangible on him; some concrete proof that would expose him to Lancewood and his son as the frightful sham he really is.'

I was doubly vigilant in the days that followed, searching for some sign or clue that might lead me to the source of Kane's secret and sinister power. Most of the rehearsals had been little short of nightmares, but somehow the other members of the cast had rallied for the transmission, and two more episodes had gone out.

During a rehearsal of the fourth episode Lucille Maitland had broken down. She wouldn't admit what the trouble was, but Dick Hartley, who took her home, told me as he went out that he thought it had been caused by Kane.

The next day I knew Hartley was right. Whiteman had decided on some last-minute alterations in Lucille's lines, and I went along to her dressing-room with the revised script. I was about to knock on the door when I noticed it was ajar, and a man's voice... Kane's voice... issued from within.

'Well, my dear,' he said, in cold, silky tones, 'either you do this little service for me or I hand over the letter. You can have it which way you like, but if you're sensible you'll do me the favour. It's a harmless enough request.'

'Then why don't you do it yourself?' Lucille's voice quivered in anguish. 'I know you,' she added bitterly. 'You're nothing but a cheat and a blackmailer! I'll go to the police.'

'Be sensible, darling,' he answered soothingly, 'if only for old times' sake. You know very well you've got nothing to go to the police with. All I'm asking you to do is a simple little errand. I've told you I've got another engagement on that night, and —'

'Oh — give me time. Give me time to think,' Lucille broke in desperately.

'Surely, my dear, surely. Time enough. I shan't need you till the thirteenth. Think it over...'

I retreated quickly a few steps along the corridor, and then walked boldly up to the door. As I reached it Kane emerged, grinned, and strode away. I went in.

Lucille was sitting before the mirror combing her hair. Her eyes were red, as though she'd been crying.

'Was Kane troubling you?' I asked.

'No more than usual,' she smiled, weakly.

I looked at her and she turned round to the mirror again.

'You're sure about that?' I persisted.

'Of course,' she answered, quickly. 'He doesn't get much change out of me. I don't treat him any easier than the others do.' Her smile broadened. She turned and noticed the script in my hand. 'Do you want me?'

On my way back to the studio I wondered why I hadn't tackled Kane or said more to Lucille; but before I reached it I knew the reason. Wasn't this the answer to Whiteman's prayer?

Kane was meddling in something and was somehow blackmailing Lucille into keeping an appointment for him. If she acted on his instruction and I followed her, might I not find something tangible, something that would put him on the spot, once and for all? The thirteenth, Kane had said. The thirteenth was a Thursday, the night before the last episode in the serial.

The days ticked slowly by. Rehearsals and transmissions were accomplished somehow; but instead of slanging matches between Kane and the rest of the cast, his jibes and sneers were met with tight-lipped, ominous silence.

Lucille, too, managed to keep herself under control. Her face gave no hint of her feelings. As soon as work finished for the day, she hurried off with Dick Hartley, whom I'd thought all along had paid her a good deal of attention.

Even Whiteman seemed to have accepted the inevitable. I was sure he wasn't really satisfied with the productions; but he made no further comments to me. He seemed moody, withdrawn, as though he were living on his nerves again. Ridleigh alone appeared to remain his old optimistic self, and he certainly did his best to sweeten the atmosphere in the studio.

Although I hadn't been able to discover whether Lucille had accepted Kane's offer, I was prepared when the thirteenth arrived. I arranged to leave immediately rehearsals were over, and I had a taxi waiting in a convenient spot outside the studios.

Lucille left as usual with Hartley, and I followed his car at a safe distance in the taxi. She lived in a small house in Chelsea with her mother. Hartley went in with her, stayed about half an hour and drove off. I waited.

An hour passed. Daylight was fading when she came out again. She walked up the street to the King's Road and got a taxi. I followed her through the West End. Near Cambridge Circus her taxi turned off, went through a maze of back streets and stopped.

She paid off the driver and began walking. I told my driver to wait, and followed her on foot. She turned down a dingy street, walking slowly. She stopped suddenly and looked into the window of an antique shop. Then she went quickly inside.

I peered through the glass door. She spoke to a youth lounging behind a small desk. He disappeared, and a few moments later came back with a stout, middle-aged man of foreign appearance. The youth went back to his desk and Lucille handed the dealer an envelope. He nodded and beckoned her to follow him through a curtained arch at the rear of the shop.

I looked at the name over the doorway and read: *M. Nicolajos, Antique and Fine Art Dealer.* He was foreign all right and he obviously had another line as well as arts and antiques. I went inside.

The shop was large and low-ceilinged; the walls were festooned with all kinds of objects, both antique and arty. On gnarled oak pillars hung small, miscellaneous curios.

The youth dragged himself away from what I now saw was a novel on the desk.

'Just browsing around,' I said casually, turning to examine what looked like a Chinese vase. 'I'm a collector.'

He nodded. 'We close in ten minutes, sir,' he informed me, went back to his book and forgot I was there.

I edged my way round to the archway. I could almost touch one of the curtains when I heard someone enter the shop. I was partly screened from the entrance by a pillar, and at my side, waist-high, was a roughly made display stand, its top covered with bric-a-brac. I bent down and looked through this assortment of objects at the two men in the well of the shop.

'Mr. Nicolajos about?' inquired the first man pleasantly.

'Yes, sir,' answered the youth. 'He's out at the back — who shall I say it is, please?'

'Detective-sergeant Reed,' he smiled, encouragingly.

I moved into the shadow of the pillar as the boy came round and went through the arch. Keeping my head down, I crept after him, beyond the dimly lit stone passage. He opened a door on his right and went in. I hurried past it and flattened myself against the wall, hoping that in his agitation Nicolajos wouldn't look in my direction when he came out.

A moment later he and the youth appeared and went into the shop. I ran into the room. Lucille was standing, nervously clutching a chairback. She stared at me incredulously.

'Jeremy Grant!' she gasped. 'What are you—?'

'No time to talk now,' I cut in briskly. 'We've got to get out of here. It looks like a raid — the police are in the shop.'

I grabbed her arm and led her into the passage, along it towards the back of the premises. We turned a corner, opened a door and found ourselves in an alley. 'Can't go back to the front,' I told her, 'a police car may be there. Come on, I've got a taxi waiting.'

In the taxi she told me her story. How she had met Roland Kane while still at her finishing school in Switzerland, and had written him several foolish letters, only to find out afterwards what a rogue he was. She'd never seen him again until a few weeks previous, when Hartley had brought her to the studios.

Kane had tried to renew their acquaintance, told her about the letters, threatened to pass them to Hartley and break up their friendship. He had cut off the address on the notepaper and had added a recent date. He had scared her into the assignment with Nicolajos.

'Blackmail is only one thing against him,' I said. 'What's his connection with Nicolajos?' I told her what I'd overheard outside her dressing-room door and why I had kept it to myself.

'Everyone would like to see the great Kane behind bars.' She looked out of the window. 'Where are we going?'

'Whiteman's place,' I said. 'We'd better tell him all we know and let him decide the next step. You don't know what this assignment tonight was about? I saw you give the dealer an envelope.'

'Yes,' Lucille agreed. 'I was supposed to collect something — a package — in exchange. When he opened Kane's envelope there was a written note and a bunch of five-pound notes. He never had time to get whatever it was he should have given me because the boy came in and said he was wanted.'

'Did Nicolajos say anything?'

'Yes, when he'd read the note. He made a sneering remark about Kane — though he didn't call him by that name. He said something like — "So, what's wrong with Mr Mulgrave? Getting cold feet, or are they too big for his boots now?" They may not have been his exact words; he was difficult to understand, his accent was so strong.'

We reached Whiteman's flat without incident; but he was not at home.

'I think we should go to the police,' I said.

Lucille looked frightened again.

'No, don't do that, not tonight. There are good reasons — and a few hours won't make all that difference.' She stared at me. 'Remember, the last episode goes out tomorrow night. We've stuck Kane up to now, it's only fair to tell Whiteman and let him decide whether to ruin the serial by informing the police straight away.

'Twenty-four hours will save us throwing Lancewood studios into an uproar and probably finishing Whiteman's career. He was

A moment later he and the youth appeared and went into the shop

banking on that Controller's job, you know. There's another reason,' she admitted, coyly. 'Dick will have to know now. I'd rather tell him quietly myself, than have him read it in a police report. We're hoping to be married soon.'

First thing next morning I made a point of getting Whiteman alone. I told him the whole story — everything. He nodded solemnly. 'All right, Grant,' he said when I'd finished. 'I'll take care of it. You've done your duty.'

'You're going to get the police?'

'Of course — tonight, after the show.' He smiled grimly. 'For the sake of a day, we can't let Kane disappoint his public now.'

When we went to lunch Whiteman took me aside. 'There's a job I'd like you to do, Grant,' he said. 'That film sequence we were going to use tonight — you know, the exterior shots of the wharf and barges?'

I nodded. I knew that none of the cast were in it. It was just a few shots strung together for the opening of the last episode.

'Well, the one we've got,' Whiteman continued, 'is not quite strong enough; there's too much daylight in it, for one thing. But there's a similar sequence, much more impressive. Taken at dusk in wind and rain. I want to use that; but the film department here tell me that particular reel is down in the library.'

'You want me to get it? I've never been down to the library before. It's at Lancewoods' film set-up at Varley, isn't it?'

He nodded. 'Here's the serial number. Take my car.'

Twenty minutes later as I went across to the parking lot, I met Kane leaving his car.

'Looks stormy,' he commented, gazing at the sky. 'Just put my hood up.'

I nodded, wondering how much Lucille had told him of our escapade the night before. She'd promised to tell him as little as possible until she had got Whiteman's advice, and I'd seen the producer talking to her just before the mid-morning break.

I reached Varley a few minutes after three, and found the small block of studios on the outskirts. The librarian seemed to take hours looking out the film. When I finally drove out of the gates it was a quarter to four.

I knew the first fifteen miles were the worst. They were winding secondary roads, and the uneven surface rattled and bumped the car, forcing me to keep down the speed. After some twenty minutes of this rough treatment, the engine began to splutter at intervals, and then, quite suddenly, stopped altogether.

I tried the starter. Nothing happened. I turned the ignition key on and off. Not even the gauges worked. It seemed like a complete electrical failure. I lifted the bonnet and peered at the engine. The loose wire I found looked important. I couldn't identify it, or to what it should have been connected, but a bright indentation close to where it had parted suggested that it had been weakened — perhaps with a file.

Who might have tampered with it? Who wished me out of the studio for the rest of the day? I suddenly thought of Kane. He'd been in the car park. Had Lucille or Whiteman told him of my part in the conspiracy against him?

I looked round at the undulating countryside. There was not a house to be seen. The road was deserted, and I tried to calculate how far along it was to the lonely garage I'd remembered passing soon after I'd left Varley.

I looked at my watch and was staggered to find it was four-thirty. Transmission started at seven! Angry and uneasy, I plodded back the way I had come, the film wedged under my arm.

It took me the best part of an hour to reach the garage. The proprietor was sympathetic and arranged to tow the car in without delay. But time was pressing so much by then I knew I couldn't wait.

'Look,' I told him as we walked to the breakdown van. 'I'm in a difficult spot. I've simply got to be in London before seven. I daren't hang on for the car. Have you any suggestions?'

'Seven, eh?' he muttered. 'You've cut it a bit fine, mister. Tell you what I can do though. Take you across to Wilminster. There's a good train service from there. You might do it.'

I had ten minutes to wait on Wilminster station for the next London train. I bought an early edition of a London evening paper, and marched impatiently up and down the platform.

When the train came in, I found an empty compartment, and looked through the paper in an effort to forget the nagging fears in my mind. As I turned over the page, two paragraphs, halfway down a centre column, suddenly attracted my attention. I stared at the heading; but it was the name that seemed to swell up and hit me between the eyes — *Nicolajos*.

I read the brief story twice. It revealed that Nicolajos, a Greek antique dealer, had been taken into custody the previous night on a drug trafficking charge. It seemed he had acted as agent, and had long been receiving quantities of heroin for distribution to various contacts. The statement added that, to help the police in furthering their inquiries, they were anxious to interview a Mr Mulgrave... and Roland Kane was Mr Mulgrave! What was it the Greek had asked Lucille? Was Mr Mulgrave getting cold feet? Of course he was. He was afraid the police were on his trail. So he'd blackmailed Lucille into collecting the next consignment.

Supplying drug addicts — that was the main source of his income; that accounted for his expensive car, his irritating pomposity — with a little blackmail on the side!

That could account for his influence in the studios, his friendship with young Lancewood. Young Lancewood... spouting Kane's genius, persuading his father that Kane was the top, insisting that he got the top roles... wearing dark glasses — hiding the dreaded secret his eyes might reveal? Was young Lancewood one of his victims — a confirmed drug addict?

The train arrived late, and by the time I'd got a taxi and it had rushed me down to the studios, it was seven-fifteen. I went in and up the staircase outside the studio to the control room. The dim light from the five television screens above the control panel silhouetted the two people in the room.

The slight figure of the vision-mixer, a girl who selected, on the producer's instructions, which picture from the four cameras the viewers should see, sat at one end of the control desk. Whiteman leaned back in his chair, an intense look on his face. The small room was filled with the sound of the actors' voices.

I held out the film can and shrugged helplessly. Whiteman stared at me for a moment and then nodded, turning back to the screens. Fingering the newspaper in my pocket, I moved to the window overlooking the studio.

As I looked down on the scene below — the three different sets, the four cameras and their crews, the boom microphones, the crowd of technicians, and moving in and out just behind the cameras, Ridleigh, earphones clamped to his head, receiving intermittent instructions on his tiny portable radio from Whiteman — I suddenly realized there was something wrong with the last scene.

The empty set which Camera 2 was covering was right enough — it was the office of private-detective Maloney — played by Kane — — with all the appropriate props. But when Lucille, in the role of Maloney's secretary, came into shot she was carrying something that was not in the script.

It was a bottle. She put this on the desk and took a glass out of the cupboard, standing it next to the bottle. Maloney entered the scene and sagged into his chair. He reached for the bottle and glass.

A wave of cold fear swept over me as I swung back into the room. I heard Whiteman give instructions through his desk microphone to close up Camera 2, as I snatched up the script. The last two pages had been deleted, two new sheets of typescript added. The final scene had been re-written. One line of directions stood out from the rest — *Maloney takes long drink from glass...*

Whiteman was watching me curiously.

'You — you — re-wrote — this?' I managed to say.

'I thought it improved the ending.' There was a hint of triumph in his voice; and I suddenly knew why I'd been sent to Varley, why the car had broken down, why I was meant to be delayed. He thought I would interfere. Kane might be rotten to the core — but this was murder! I had to save Whiteman from himself.

I sprang up and rushed to the window, raising my foot to send the glass panes shattering down into the studio; but Whiteman was anticipating such a move. He jerked me away in a vice-like grip and thrust me gently into a chair.

'Don't be a fool!' I gasped. 'Don't be a fool, man!' But watching the screen, I knew nothing more could be done. Kane was drinking...

'I thought you hated him like the rest of us.' Whiteman's voice was icy-calm.

'Not enough to poison him. You — you — can't take the law into your own hands just like that.'

'Look at him,' he urged smoothly. 'Giving the performance of his life. He's not shamming now...'

I stared in fascinated horror at the screen as Kane, coughing and choking, his face contorted, staggered from his chair. He jerked a few steps, and then crumpled to the floor.

'Fade it!' Whiteman snapped at the bewildered, trembling girl. The transmission screen became a blank.

I was trembling, my mind a void, like the screen.

'You're crazy, Whiteman!' I whispered. 'You've ruined yourself — finished...'

'I was already ruined, Grant,' he answered in a level voice. 'Kane finished me — like he finished so many others...' He turned and spoke into the microphone, instructing Ridleigh to warn the announcer.

'You mean — you and — Kane's drugs?'

He shook his head. 'Not drugs. Blackmail. Some time ago I got heavily in debt. In trying to get out of the mess I did a foolish thing and was sent away — to prison. I came here to make a fresh start. I was doing well till Kane came and found out my past.

'When I mentioned him to Lancewood a few days ago, Kane heard my report, came down and threatened if I ever crossed him again he would reveal my whole sordid story. I couldn't go on like that.' He smiled, and seemed contented, at ease. 'You know what to do, Grant,' he went on softly. 'You wanted to get on to the police. Well, now's the time. Get them. I'll go quietly.'

I stared at him, dazed. Slowly, reluctantly, I reached for the phone. As I picked it up a voice from the loudspeaker swelled up and filled the room with clear ringing tones... Like Kane, Whiteman had played his act to the last...

'We must apologize,' said the soothing voice of the announcer, 'for the fading of your picture at the end of our serial play. This was due to a camera fault...'

JAGUAR MAN
S. C. George

There are dangers in being a witch-doctor, as Iso discovered after
he had failed to keep a promise. But Iso was full of cunning,
and this was his undoing, for no man can control treachery any
more than he can control the striking power of a deadly, silent
bushmaster snake, the kind known to white settlers as the dumb
rattler.

El Bravo — The Tough Guy — was worried. He had begun life as Luiz Velez, a poor boy in a wretched *adobe* hut. By natural ability and unswerving determination he had carved from the virgin forest a ranch that was the envy of the province, earning his nickname during its achievement.

Nevertheless he was a good man, and he regarded as his major triumph his patient pacification of the savage tribe of Indians upon whose friendship the existence of his ranch depended. He was blood-brother to the *cacique*, a well-meaning but weak chief under the thumb of Iso, the tribe's witch-doctor. Iso hated El Bravo whose influence undermined his power.

Iso was a jaguar man, and his people believed he could turn himself into a jaguar at will. El Bravo knew of this, and when wild beasts began to make lightning night-strikes at his cattle and sheep he sought out the witch-doctor.

'It is the drought,' Iso said, blandly. 'Otherwise the beasts would stay in the forest.'

'Your people seem to have had good hunting,' El Bravo said significantly, glancing at the well-nourished Indians who watched them from their huts.

'They travel far and have been lucky,' Iso smirked.

'Whenever there has been famine, I have fed them. This time they have not sought my help,' said El Bravo. 'I give willingly, but I suffer thefts badly.'

49

Iso shrugged. The *cacique* looked uncomfortable.

'Tell your friends, the jaguars, that I shall post guards who shoot straight.' El Bravo warned him. To the *cacique* he added. 'We are blood-brothers, you and I. Since when has a brother refused food to his kinsfolk?'

The *cacique* dropped his gaze and shuffled his toes in the dust.

Having made his point, El Bravo returned to his *estancia* where twenty thousand famished sheep were eating the burrs from each other's wool, and getting thinner and dying daily, for only hard *pasto duro*, coarse tufted grass with little nutritious value, was left for his stock.

El Bravo had cause to suspect the Indians. Wild cats would have jumped on the sheep's backs and killed them by eating the soft cartilages of their noses, but they had not died that way. On the night following his veiled threats to Iso, Perez, his foreman, was killed. The claw-marks of a jaguar streaked his cheeks. El Bravo made a systematic search that led him to a depression in the forest where a small pool was all that remained of a water-hole. The surrounding grass had been nibbled away. Various beasts had left their pads in the soft mud, but he found no trace of a jaguar.

Thoughtfully he followed a game-track to the Indian village. The drought had pressed its harsh hand on the forest: withered undergrowth, bare baked earth, a deep hole at the foot of a tree whose scarred roots had been torn by the desperate foraging of a famished peccary, a limp panting iguana with a loose skin. Everything was dry and parched; even the trees seemed to gasp for moisture.

By the side of the track a coiled bushmaster lay in its favourite spot, drowsy after a meal. The rough pointed scales along its back were like armour-plating; it was nine feet long, tan in colour, and its tail terminated in a brown spine that vibrated sharply when it moved. It had no rattle, and the Spaniards called it *La Cascebela Muda* — The Dumb Rattler.

There was no need for special caution, and El Bravo walked carelessly. The bushmaster sensed his approach through the two small pits between nostrils and eyes. The sinister head lifted, its

50

cold eyes shielded by bony plates, revealing distinctive brown stripes that passed through the hinge of the jaw, through the eyes, into the lighter coloured snout. It sensed from the smell and the heat radiation of El Bravo that a warm-blooded animal was approaching, and from his noise that he was too large to be swallowed. In any case, it was gorged with food and had not had time after its recent strike to renew its position. The wicked head dropped again, and El Bravo passed, unaware of his danger.

Naked men with matted hair and slivers of bone stuck through their noses and ear-lobes came out from the crude shelters of leaves and bark, and in sullen silence watched his progress to Iso's hut. The witch-doctor did not bother to rise when El Bravo stopped before him. His blood-shot eyes, sunk deep in a painted face, glittered insolently. He wore a necklace composed of bits of bone, jaguar's teeth and claws and other gruesome objects.

'There sits madness,' thought El Bravo. Aloud he said, 'I lost a man last night, Iso.'

'So,' Iso grunted woodenly.

El Bravo touched the claws on Iso's necklace while the Indians crowded round.

'Perhaps you forgot to warn the jaguars.'

'Why did not your man shoot? Besides, what has it got to do with me?'

The Indians pressed nearer.

'You claim kinship with them,' El Bravo said. 'I never sought their enmity, but for a man-killer there is only one end.'

'Take care that he does not kill you first.'

'It would be better if you warned him to leave this part of the forest,' said El Bravo, for he did not wish to risk provoking a war between the gauchos and Indians that would inevitably result in many deaths. 'My gauchos are more impetuous than I.'

'They must blame the drought,' Iso laughed openly.

'You pretend to be a rainmaker. Stop the drought, or admit to your people that you are powerless.'

'If rain is all you want, why did you not ask before?' Iso demanded. 'You shall have rain after two days if you dare come alone at midnight to the water-hole to see me make it.'

'Why should I?'

'So that you will never doubt my powers again.'

'And your people?'

'They will not harm you,' Iso said, guessing El Bravo's thoughts. 'Are you not the *cacique's* brother?'

'I shall be there,' El Bravo said curtly, departing.

He had already sensed an almost imperceptible change in the temperature. Iso might be mad, but he was wise in Nature's ways. Rain was coming, and, by demanding that Iso should produce it, he had rashly provided the witch-doctor with a means to add still further to his reputation.

Moreover, if he failed to keep his promise, and the rain failed, he would be blamed for it; and if he did keep the appointment he might not live to see the rain, for he knew that Iso was the murderer, and Iso was aware of it. One of them must die, and he could not refuse to walk into the baited trap.

From the first there had been antagonism between them. It had been a long, weary task to wean the ignorant Indians from their suspicions and persuade them to help with the seasonal work on the *estancia*. Iso had watched with a jealous eye their dawning independence and the lessening of his authority which exceeded that of the *cacique* himself. He had adopted his own methods to end the situation. Sickness had broken out among the gauchos until El Bravo had caught Iso slipping into the cookhouse during the cook's temporary absence and had kicked him off the *estancia*. Iso never forgot the humiliation. El Bravo had fallen sick himself, but he could never prove anything against Iso.

When the Indians withdrew their labour he guessed that Iso had thrown the fear of death into them. An Indian who was not a friend was likely to become an enemy. Thereafter, El Bravo kept a close eye upon them. More than once, when the drums throbbed in the forest, he had stolen out to watch their secret ceremonies. Despite his blood-brotherhood with the *cacique*, discovery would have brought him a sudden and violent death, but all his life he had accepted risks. Thus he learnt that Iso was a jaguar man, and that this was the mainspring of his power.

Primitive peoples widely believe that man can transform himself into an animal — bears and wolves in Europe; tigers, leopards or hyenas in Asia and Africa, jaguars in South America. The cult becomes an instrument of terror, especially as it is employed to wipe out old grudges, and seldom indeed is it that anyone can be prevailed upon to testify against them.

El Bravo secured his own evidence. Always careful to examine his bedding before retiring at night, he had uncovered a fourteen-inch horned viper; the snake, green, spotted with pink and yellow and orange, had been killed by him before it could strike. Now the horned viper prefers to live in trees. El Bravo's minute examination of his blanket revealed a few jaguar hairs. For some nights the drums had been calling more insistently than usual, and the deep hoarse cry of the jaguar had been heard around the *estancia.*

El Bravo said nothing to anyone, but took his gun, and with a long knife stuck through the back of his silver-embroidered belt, disappeared into the forest. He found the men of the tribe dancing around a circle of sweating drummers. The flames of a huge fire flickered on their shining bodies; their eyes rolled wildly with excitement and *chicha,* their potent drink. Their dancing suddenly stopped, and they sank to the ground as there dashed through their ranks half a dozen men with steel claws strapped to their wrists and with jaguar tails dangling behind them.

Leaping and capering, and imitating the jaguar's cry, the roused the spectators to a frenzy. It was then that Iso made his dramatic appearance. Below the head-dress of a jaguar his cheeks were hideously painted; a necklace of jaguars' claws lay on his bedaubed breast, and bracelets of its teeth clicked on his arms. A jaguar's tail swung about him as he sprang into the circle. The other dancers withdrew.

The drums began to beat again, at first slowly, then rising to a crescendo as he imitated a jaguar stalking its prey. So realistic was his performance — the mighty leap with which he sprang on his imaginary victim, the snarling and clawing with which he simulated its destruction — that for one horrifying moment El Bravo found himself seeing Iso as the beast itself. The effect upon the credulous Indians must have been overwhelming.

El Bravo knew his danger when he accepted Iso's challenge; he withdrew.

That was why he was so sure that Perez had been murdered. Had his men suspected it, they would have taken their guns to revenge him. They would have burnt the Indian village; they might have killed innocent people; it was more than likely that Iso would escape. Certainly they could not have captured him without meeting resistance, and, blood having been shed, the restoration of friendly relations would be almost impossible. This was a personal matter between Iso and El Bravo, but something far deeper than a mere feud between two men; it was a clash between barbarism and the encroaching civilization.

El Bravo knew his danger when he accepted Iso's challenge, he anticipated treachery: perhaps Iso intended him to be a sacrifice to the Rain-god; but he guessed that Iso, for the sake of his reputation, would attend this encounter single-handed. As before, El Bravo went out, armed but alone.

The two days were up, hot parched days, each with its mounting tally of dying animals. No more had been killed, though the jaguar roars at night were fraying the nerves of the gauchos. The sun, a molten copper disk, set in a yellowish sky. Night came in one giant stride, a hot breathless night that brought no easement. For the first time, the drums were silent; the roosting birds were still; no breeze stirred the dry leaves; an ominous quiet brooded over the forest. El Bravo moved stealthily, partly from caution, partly from the awe which its immensity always inspired in him.

He reached the track leading from the village to the water-hole and turned down it. Ahead of him the bushmaster waited hungrily. On an impulse, El Bravo left the path, for here, if treachery were meditated, it would be found.

Despite the full moon little light filtered through to the forest floor, but he had developed an eerie sense of direction and had not far to go. Long ropes of creepers hung from the trees, ready to cascade into flower at the first kiss of rain. The water-hole was little more than a sheet of mud gleaming in the moonlit clearing like a silver breastplate. El Bravo approached cautiously, and

It was then that Iso made his dramatic appearance

listened. All was still, but he continued standing there as motionless as the tree into whose lower branches at last he climbed after satisfying himself that it held no snakes. There he would be inconspicuous, even to Iso with all his cunning.

Heat still rose fiercely from the baked ground. The surrounding forest, made even darker and more mysterious by the silence and the silvered patch of ground, held an air of expectancy. Opposite him, across the tiny pool, lay the track by which Iso would approach. The knife at El Bravo's back and the gun in his hands were more comforting to him than he could have supposed.

The brooding stillness was broken by a distant rumble of thunder that at first he mistook for drums. It would not be long now before the drought broke, and Iso would take the credit for it. A little later, rainclouds obscured the moon and darkness blotted out the clearing. El Bravo strained to catch the rustle of dry grass or the cracking stick that might betray his enemy, for he knew that Iso would come with the stealth of a jaguar and that the *cacique* would be too weak to save him.

And behind Iso, at a respectful distance, would be the Indians, waiting to see their witch-doctor's magic culminate in a human sacrifice to the Rain-god. The thunder was nearer now, but Iso would arive before rain fell, or the sacrifice would be meaningless. El Bravo's heart beat faster; insects bit him, but he dared not move.

He had not wanted to kill Iso, nor would his death now solve the problem, for the Indians would believe he wanted to prolong the drought by interfering with Iso's witchcraft and would react accordingly.

When he had left the *estancia* he was still uncertain what to do when they met, but suddenly he knew. He must surprise Iso and keep him immobile until the rains broke. Iso knew the power of a gun; to save his life he would order the Indians not to attack. They would have believed Iso that a human sacrifice was necessary to appease the Rain-god. When the rain fell without one, they would know that he had lied, and maybe Iso's power would be broken and friendship could be restored between the gauchos and the tribe. Justice could then take its course with Iso. Should he be acquitted Iso would bear him a deadly hatred, but that would be a private quarrel whose outcome he did not fear. El Bravo was taking a desperate chance, and knew it.

The moon swam from the clouds and the clearing was visible again. Suddenly the forest came to life. Mosquitoes whined; a tree porcupine scuffled along a branch, dislodging a pattering shower of dried fruits; cicadas chirped; night birds began to sing; monkeys hooted; a jaguar roared and El Bravo decided that it was neither Iso nor one of his jaguar men; a frog plopped into the shallow pool, and a hairy armadillo stole down to drink only to scuttle away as two collared peccaries charged through the undergrowth. Then it was dark again.

Towards midnight, Iso came stealthily down the track clad in the full regalia of a jaguar man, wicked steel claws strapped to his wrists, his face painted.

Before him, in its favourite haunt, waited the bushmaster, hungry, restless in the sultry heat, the flicking tongue in its swaying head tasting the sour forest air for the flavour of a warm-blooded animal.

Iso paused with the same idea that had occurred to El Bravo. He had no doubt that his enemy was already at the appointed place, waiting for him to step into view. He, too, would abandon the trail and circle round to the water-hole. A flash of lightning and a closer crash of thunder changed his mind. He must get there before the rain fell. He would advance nearer yet before turning off the trail and approaching the pool behind El Bravo whom he guessed correctly would be concealed in the lower branches of the tree that faced the trail. He slavered as he imagined El Bravo's shocked horror as the steel claws dug into his neck and dragged him down.

With redoubled caution he went on. Behind him, the following Indians squatted down to listen for the jaguar-howl of triumph that would tell them the kill had been made.

The sensitive pits in the bushmaster's head detected the approaching prey. Deceived by the absence of noise that would have indicated an animal too large to be swallowed, it began to uncoil, for the bushmaster does not strike like a rattlesnake. The front third of the body lifted, its remaining six feet tensed in deep S-loops behind the poised head. Iso's smell and warmth reached the waiting reptile's brain in strengthening waves of radiation. Coldly the bushmaster waited, judging the distance. Then, like lightning, the loops straightened, propelling the vicious head that slapped its curved fangs into Iso's thigh. The powerful folds constricted round him as the hinged fangs pressed against their swollen glands, squeezing out the virulent poison that ran down the grooved teeth into the wounds. Iso's scream of terror reached El Bravo a moment before a tremendous crash of thunder. This, he knew, was no trick to deceive him. He dropped from the tree and ran, guided by the weakening cries of the bushmaster's victim. Lightning flashed almost continuously now. Iso still struggled feebly, but the coils held him powerless. The snake's head was lacerated where the steel claws had first tried to rip the head from its deadly anchorage. El Bravo dared not shoot in the flickering gloom for fear of killing Iso, of whom he now thought only with pity.

The Indians arrived as he whipped the long knife from his belt, hurled himself upon the writhing mass, and severed the bush-master's head. The headless body continued to jerk convulsively about the dying man. El Bravo stood back, trembling now and drenched with sweat. The heat of the forest had gone; a cold breeze rustled the dry leaves; the first heavy drops of rain fell.

'The Rain-god has had his victim,' El Bravo addressed the *cacique*. 'Iso did not bring the rain and he has been punished for his presumption and his wickedness.'

The Indians drew aside to let him pass. He hurried down the track that was already becoming a river as rain slashed the parched world, drowning even the rolling thunder with its torrential violence.

The *cacique* thrust Iso aside with his foot. His power was restored. Iso's jaguar men felt his wrath and fled, their courage drained from them by what they had seen. The *cacique* overtook El Bravo and splashed just ahead of him on the track, a vulnerable position that an enemy would not have taken.

'We are friends, my brother,' he shouted over his shoulder.

ESCAPE ROUTE TO EXETER
John Elsworth

Kidnapped on Dartmoor in a fog by a red-bearded stranger named Denning, Richard Henderson was taken by car to a house in London, where he saw the gardener of Admiral Burnaby. The Admiral was the uncle of his friend Michael, with whom he had been trying to trace buried treasure in Devon. But before the treasure can be found Richard has to escape, a problem that presents numerous obstacles to a youngster on his own and with little money in his pocket. The adventures of Richard and Michael are told in *The Mysterious Orchard*, from which this story is taken.

I had made up my mind that when we came into London I would keep my eyes open and try to find out, if I possibly could, where it was they were taking me, so that afterwards I should be able to describe it to the police. I remembered our journey down to Devon with the Admiral, and I supposed we should come in by Hammersmith and Kensington High Street and Piccadilly. But we kept on taking turnings and short cuts, and soon I hadn't the faintest idea where we were.

'Never mind,' I said to myself, 'I'll look out for the name of each street we turn into. One of them must be the street where we're going to stop.'

But I wasn't allowed to do that. I suppose Denning saw what I was up to, because sometimes we were past a street sign before I could spot it, and I had to turn in my seat to see where it was. Anyhow, after a while he took a big handkerchief out of his pocket and began folding it in the shape of a bandage.

'I'm sorry about this,' he said. 'But I'm sure you'll understand that it might be inconvenient for me if you were able to direct anyone afterwards to the place where I'm taking you. As soon as we get indoors I'll take this off. Until then——' He leaned across and tied the handkerchief round my eyes.

'Well, that's that,' I thought.

I must say I felt pretty miserable at that moment. I felt sure that if Michael had been in my place, he'd have thought up some way of doing these people in the eye and getting free, but I couldn't. All I could do was to wait, and to hope that some chance would turn up.

The car stopped about a quarter of an hour after Denning had blindfolded me, and my guess was that we were right in the middle of London. It was a quiet street, though I could hear the noise of traffic in the distance. Denning took my arm and hurried me across the pavement, through a gate and along a short garden path.

'Six steps up here,' he said.

When we reached the front door, I heard him put a key in the lock and open it. We passed across a hall with a stone floor and into a room. As Denning closed the door behind us he took the handkerchief from my eyes.

The room was very brightly lit and, after being blindfolded, my eyes were dazzled for a few seconds. Then I saw that there were two people in the room besides Denning and me. One was a woman in a red dress. The other was Hacking, Admiral Burnaby's gardener, who had run away after Michael and I had caught him prowling about the garden at night.

The woman just stared curiously at me as though she wondered who I was, but Hacking looked really startled. He jumped to his feet.

'What's this mean?' he demanded.

Denning motioned me to a chair, and sat down himself.

'What does what mean, Hacking?' he asked.

'Why, bringing that boy up here. I'm not going to have anything to do with kidnapping, and that's a fact.'

'My dear Hacking, what a word to use! I've brought my young friend up to spend the night here as my guest. Tomorrow he will return to Devonshire and continue to enjoy his holiday. No harm will be done to him or to anyone else.'

'That's all very well, but it's kidnapping, and there's no use calling it anything else. And if it's found out— —'

'But it won't be found out.'

'How do you know it won't? How do you know you haven't been followed? If I'd known, when Baxter rang up and told me you were coming, that you were doing this, I wouldn't have been here when you arrived. And I'm not staying now.'

He started towards the door.

'I wouldn't go if I were you, Hacking,' said Denning.

He spoke quite quietly, but there was a sort of threatening note in his voice which stopped Hacking all right. He hesitated, turned, and then flung himself into an armchair.

'Well,' he muttered, 'get on with it. What's it all about.'

'Really, Hacking,' said Denning, 'I don't think you're behaving very well.'

The calm, contemptuous way in which he said this seemed to infuriate Hacking. He went scarlet in the face, and looked as though he wanted to get up and sock Denning on the jaw.

'Never mind how I'm behaving,' he growled. 'What do you want?'

But Denning seemed determined to delay as long as possible before coming to the point. He turned to the woman.

'Stella, my dear, we've had a long journey and it's a warm evening. I'm sure our guest would like a glass of lemonade. And if you have any cake, so much the better.'

She smiled——she looked rather a nice person, as a matter of fact——and went out of the room.

The lemonade was good and so was the cake. I remember wondering whether I ought to be accepting food and drink from these people now that I knew they were crooks. But I decided that nothing much mattered as long as I didn't let *them* get anything out of *me*.

When we had all finished, Denning got up and stood in front of the fire filling his pipe. There was a look on his face as though he were deciding how to put what he had to say, and I knew that at last we were going to get down to brass tacks.

'Well, Mr Henderson,' he began.

I smiled to myself. The first time we met he had offered me a sweet, as though I were about eight years old, and now he was calling me "Mr Henderson"!

'I'm sure,' he continued, 'you must be wondering what this is all about?'

I didn't answer. I had *suspected* what it was about ever since we started, and as soon as I saw Hacking I felt absolutely certain. But I'd decided that the best way to be sure of giving nothing away was to open my mouth as little as possible.

Denning struck a match and lit his pipe.

'I've brought you up here,' he said, 'because I want your help. You may think it odd that I, a perfect stranger, should need the help of a boy like you. But, you see, you're staying in a house that holds a certain secret — a secret I very much want to know. You may already know it, in which case I want you to tell me what it is. If you don't know it, I want you to find it out for me.'

'Why did you have to bring me all the way to London if you wanted me to find something out for you in Ponscombe?' I asked.

He smiled, and stroked his lower lip with his forefinger. This was a habit he had; I'd noticed it before.

'Because the cottage where I took you first is too near your friends at Ponscombe House. They might have found us before we had finished arranging our business together, and that would have been awkward for me. But you needn't worry about that. As soon as you've agreed to help me you can go straight back to Ponscombe again. What do you say?'

'No,' I said.

'I don't think you will when you hear what the reward is. I'll give you a hundred pounds.'

'I still say no.'

Denning sat down in an armchair, crossed his legs and looked thoughtfully up at the ceiling.

'You know,' he said softly, 'when I said you would be able to return to Ponscombe tomorrow, I was expecting we should have been able to come to a satisfactory arrangement by then. But if you're going to be difficult — well, I'm afraid there may be a bit of a delay.'

'You won't get anything out of me,' I said, 'if you keep me here six months.'

'We shall see,' he replied.

At that moment Stella, who had been sitting quietly in a corner with some sewing, suddenly stood up.

'Do you see what the time is?' she asked. 'Nearly twelve o'clock. The boy looks tired out. What's the use of keeping on at him like this? Let him go to bed, and talk to him again in the morning.'

'Not just yet, my dear. I quite realize he's had a very tiring day, and I don't want to keep him up any longer than I can help. But I must just explain what it is I want of him before he goes to bed. It will give him a chance to think things over, and perhaps by tomorrow morning he will have changed his mind about helping me. It won't take long to say what I have to say.'

With a shrug of her shoulders she sat down again. Denning turned to me.

'Now,' he said. 'You remember that piece of parchment your friend found under the floor at Ponscombe House the other night? Never mind how I know about his finding it. I not only know about it, but I've got it — here in this house. In case you don't believe me, I'll show it to you.'

He got up, crossed the room and unlocked a desk.

'Here you are,' he said.

It was the parchment all right; the one that had been stolen from Admiral Burnaby's desk. When I had had a good look at it, Denning put it back and locked the desk. While he was doing this I was thinking very hard. I felt sure he was going to ask me if we had found out anything more about the treasure. If I refused to answer he would think we *had* found out something more, and this would make him all the more determined to keep me there until I told him what it was. But if I said we hadn't, he might tell me something I didn't know — something which might help us to find the treasure. I decided to speak, and say we hadn't.

Denning came back to his chair and sat down.

'As of course you've guessed, the lines that are written on that parchment refer to hidden treasure. But there's another thing about it that I know. I know there's another clue that will help anyone who's looking for it. Did you know that?'

'No,' I said, 'I didn't.'

'I see. Well, I'll tell you about it. The treasure, by the way, is something that belongs to my family. It disappeared many years ago, and we've never known what happened to it. It was only recently that I stumbled on a clue that led to Ponscombe House. So, you see, it's not just a case of my having heard about the treasure and wanting to get it before anybody else does. It *belongs* to me, and once I can lay hands on it I can prove it.'

He paused, watching me closely, as though he wanted to see what effect his words were having on me. I felt absolutely certain he was lying, but I tried not to let my face show that I didn't believe him.

'As I said just now,' he went on, 'that piece of parchment isn't the only clue. There's another, *and it's somewhere in Ponscombe House.*'

Still I tried to show nothing in my face, but I felt my heart give a leap of excitement. I knew that this time he *was* speaking the truth, and I felt it was worthwhile being kidnapped and brought to London to get this piece of information.

'I haven't the pleasure,' Denning went on, 'of knowing Admiral Burnaby, and I'm afraid that if I called at Ponscombe House and told him what I've just told you he wouldn't believe me. So I had to think of some other way, and I thought the best thing I could do was to get you to help me out. All I want you do to is to find that clue. I can see you've got your wits about you; you'll manage it all right. When you've found it I want you to write and tell me what it is. When you've done that I'll send you, by registered post, a hundred one-pound notes.'

He stood up.

'And now, as my wife said just now, you must be feeling very tired. I'm sorry to have kept you up so late, but I thought I had better explain matters. Think it over. Think what a very small thing, after all, I'm asking you to do. And think what you could do with a hundred pounds. And then we'll talk of it again in the morning. Stella, my dear,' he added, turning to his wife, 'perhaps you would be so good as to conduct our guest to his room and see that he has everything he needs?'

As I went out of the room I glanced at Hacking, who hadn't spoken a word since Denning began talking to me. He was slumped down in his armchair, staring straight in front of him, and he didn't look at me as I passed. He looked scared; as if he had found himself let in for something more than he had bargained for.

Denning's wife led the way up two flights of stairs and along a passage, at the end of which she opened a door.

'This is your room,' she said.

Like Hacking, she didn't seem to want to meet my eye. She turned down the bed, showed me a pair of pyjamas that had been put under the pillow, and then, with a murmured "good-night", went out of the room, shutting the door behind her. I heard her walking away down the passage.

It was quite a nice, cheerful sort of room. There was a comfortable armchair by the fireplace, and I sat down in it. In spite of all that had happened, I didn't feel a bit tired; I began to think things out.

It was pretty clear that Denning knew more about the hidden treasure than we did. He must know that it was very valuable, or he wouldn't be so jolly keen to get hold of it. I now felt certain that Hacking must have been snooping through a gap in the window-curtains when Michael made his discovery under the floorboard in the Admiral's study, but how Denning knew there was another clue somewhere in the house I couldn't imagine. And I didn't waste much time thinking about it. What I had to do was to plan some way of getting out of the tight spot I was in.

I knew I shouldn't get back to Devon next day just by trusting Denning to let me go. When I refused to help him — and of course I was going to refuse — he would at least keep me a prisoner in this house, even if he did nothing worse to me. But supposing I *did* promise to help him? How did he know I wouldn't just go back to Ponscombe and break my promise? The more I thought about it, the more sure I felt that there was a jolly sight more in this kidnapping of me than just an attempt to get me to promise to help Denning to find the treasure. In some way or other he was going to make it impossible for me *not* to help him — or thought he was. Even if I were to tell him I would help him, my troubles wouldn't be over — not by a long way.

'I must get away,' I thought. 'I must get away somehow.'

Easier said than done. I pulled aside the curtains and looked out. No hope there. It was a sheer drop of about twenty feet to the ground. I crossed the room and tried the door. As I expected, it was locked. They weren't taking any chances.

'I may as well go to bed,' I thought. Up to now there had been a certain amount of excitement to keep me going, but now, all alone in this strange room in this strange house, I was beginning to feel pretty fed-up. If only I hadn't been such a fool as to go with Denning to that cottage on the moor! But there was no use crying over spilt milk. If I was to be on the alert tomorrow, ready to seize on any chance that came along of getting away from these people, I must get some sleep. It was one o'clock in the morning.

I undressed and got into the bed. It was a comfortable one, and I don't think I had been there more than ten minutes when I fell asleep.

When I woke up it was broad daylight. For a moment I stared round the room, wondering where on earth I was. Then I remembered. I got out of bed and went over to the door. It was still locked.

I looked at my watch. It was a quarter past nine. Anyhow, I'd had a good night's sleep, and things didn't seem so bad as they had the night before. There was a basin in the corner of the room with hot and cold water, so I had a wash and put on my clothes. I was just ready when I heard a knock on the door.

'Come in!' I said.

The key turned in the lock and in came Denning.

'Good morning,' he said. 'Slept well?'

'Yes, thank you.'

'That's good. I looked in half an hour ago, but you were fast asleep, so I didn't disturb you. Breakfast's on the table, so, if you're ready, we'll go down.'

I followed him downstairs to the room we had been in the night before. His wife was already at the table, and she too asked me if I had slept well. I thought she seemed relieved when I said I had. After that she never spoke at all and hardly looked at me, though she kept on passing me things, as if she wanted to make sure I was having enough to eat.

Denning began by talking a lot about the weather and all that kind of thing, but when he saw that neither I nor his wife was taking any notice of him he shut up. The rest of the meal passed in silence.

When we had finished, Mrs Denning got up and went out of the room. Denning went over to the fireplace and began filling his pipe. I stayed at the table, wondering what was going to happen next. After a pause, Denning spoke.

'When we talked last night,' he said, 'I told you of the other clue at Ponscombe House which will lead to the hidden treasure. I asked you to find it and tell me what it is, and I told you that if you agreed to help me in this way you could go home today. You refused, but I gave you time to think it over. I hope you've decided to be sensible.'

I sat silent.

'Are you going to help me?' he asked.

'No,' I answered. 'I'm not.'

'Why not? Don't you want a hundred pounds?'

'I wouldn't lift a finger to help you in your rotten game for a thousand pounds.'

He frowned angrily.

'Not so much of the "rotten game", young man. I told you the treasure belongs to my family. There's nothing so very rotten about trying to get your own property back, is there?'

'There's something pretty rotten,' I replied, 'about kidnapping me and then bribing me to help you take something out of Admiral Burnaby's house.'

'He's never known it's been there all these years,' said Denning, 'so he won't miss it now. However, I'm not going to argue the matter. If you want to get back to Devonshire and have a very good chance of winning a hundred pounds into the bargain, you know what to do. You've only got yourself to blame if I have to keep you here.'

He got up out of his chair.

'We'll speak again this afternoon, and see whether you've changed your mind. And now I must ask you to come back to your room.'

So I was to be shut up in one room, like a convict!

'I've had some books put here,' Denning said when we got upstairs, 'so I hope the time won't hang too heavily on your hands.' With that he left me, locking the door behind him.

The bed had been made and the room tidied up. On a table by the fireplace there was a pile of books, but I didn't feel in the mood for reading. I was beginning to realize what a serious position I was in. Evidently Denning was a determined man, and he certainly wouldn't be taken in by any such trick as my promising to help him, in order to get back to Ponscombe, and then going back on my word or giving him away to the Admiral. He'd have thought all that out, and would have some scheme ready for making it hot for me if I double-crossed him. In any case, I jolly well wasn't going to promise him anything, let alone carry it out.

But I saw quite clearly that my refusal put paid to my getting back to Devon — unless I escaped. And I didn't see how I could possibly escape. I looked out of the window, and the drop to the ground looked even higher by daylight than it had looked in the dark. There was a little garden, then a wall about eight feet high. Outside the wall was a road, and beyond that some waste ground. The road didn't have much traffic or many people on it. Occasionally I saw somebody pass, but that didn't do me any good. If I shouted to them I should be heard in the house, and if they tried to come to me they'd be seen. In fact, those passers-by were no more good to me than if they'd been walking along a road a hundred miles away.

No, if I were to escape it would have to be by my own efforts, without any help from anyone. I must keep my eyes open for a chance, for any slackening in Denning's guard over me. And of that I didn't feel very hopeful.

He came up at one o'clock and took me down to lunch. We had it alone; there was no sign of his wife. Afterwards he again asked me the question he had asked in the morning, and I answered him with the same refusal. Before two o'clock I was locked in the bedroom again.

As time went on I picked up one or other of the books and turned over the pages, but I didn't feel like reading. I had too much to think about.

There was just one possibility that had been in my mind all day. Once Michael and I had had to get out of a bedroom window, and we had done it by tying together sheets from the beds for a rope. I had hung on to one end while Michael let himself down. But we knew there was a ladder outside, and as soon as he was down

Michael got the ladder for me to come down by. There was no help like that for me here. Also, in that room there had been two beds, and therefore four sheets, but there were only two sheets here. I had a look at them and tried to calculate how far they would stretch tied together. There was a heavy chest standing near the window, and I decided that if I tied one end to one of the legs of this it would just about hold my weight, but tying it would use up a good deal of its length, which would end ten or twelve feet short of the ground. Well, I should have to jump the rest, that was all, and if I broke my leg it would be just too bad! It would be a drop on to grass, and if I landed with my knees bent I ought to be all right.

It would be useless to try during the day; I should be spotted at once from one of the ground-floor windows. But I made up my mind that I would have a crack at it that night, late, when everybody in the house would be in bed. I might fail; the chest mightn't be heavy enough to hold my weight; I might hurt myself when I dropped to the ground; but anything was better than just doing nothing.

At about three o'clock, from the window, I saw Denning's wife come in, and at four she brought me up some tea. She didn't speak a word, though just before going out she hesitated and looked at me as if she wanted to say something. It was a splendid tea; I cartainly wasn't being starved!

For supper I was taken downstairs again. Denning and his wife and I had it together and, as at breakfast, Denning did a lot of talking at first, but talked less and less as he found that neither of us was taking much notice of him. I thought Mrs Denning loaked pale and worried.

Rather to my surprise, Denning said nothing about the treasure. It was a relief in a way, though I wondered why he didn't. I wondered whether he'd got some other scheme up his sleeve. It made me feel a bit uneasy; I was glad that in a few hours I was at least going to have a shot at getting away.

It was getting very dark when I went up to my room again. In another hour it would be quite dark enough for my purpose, but I wasn't going to make my bid for freedom until much later.

I didn't want to run any risk of Denning walking into the room and finding me tying sheets together! About two o'clock in the morning would be my time, when it was pretty certain that everybody in the house would be asleep. For all I knew, Denning might be one of those late birds, so it wouldn't do to make it any earlier.

There was a long time to wait, so to pass the time, I picked up one of the books and began to read. The book was *Greenmantle*, by John Buchan; I'd read it before, but I managed to get fairly interested in it — enough to keep me awake, anyhow.

Just before ten o'clock I heard footsteps coming along the passage. They stopped outside my door, the key turned, and Mrs Denning came into the room. She was carrying a cup of cocoa and a plate of biscuits. She put them down on the dressing-table.

'Thank you,' I said.

She stood and looked at me. It was a queer, meaning sort of look.

'I hope you'll get on all right,' she said, and went out.

I sat staring in front of me. What a strange thing to say! It was almost as if she knew what I was planning. But of course she couldn't know. Then what on earth did she mean?

Greatly puzzled, I got up from my chair to fetch the cocoa and biscuits from the dressing-table. But before I reached it I suddenly knew what Mrs Denning meant.

She hadn't locked the door. I remembered quite clearly that there was only the click of the latch as she closed it behind her, no sound of the key being turned. Why this hadn't registered in my mind until now I didn't know.

I crossed to the door and gently turned the handle. It opened at once. I was as free to walk out of that room as out of my own bedroom at home. But once outside in the passage — what then? I closed the door quietly and, sitting down again in the arm-chair, thought hard.

I had never been left in that room with the door unlocked before. Had Denning's wife just forgotten to turn the key this time? No, of course she hadn't. Although she had said nothing to me and very little to Denning at meal times when we were together, it was pretty obvious from her manner that she hated the whole business of my being kidnapped and kept prisoner in this house, and that she was scared stiff of it being discovered. And now she was trying to give me a chance to escape. That was what she meant by saying she hoped I'd get on all right. And I suddenly realized that if I was going to do anything about it I'd better get cracking. At any moment Denning might come up and discover the unlocked door.

Stooping down, I unlaced my shoes and took them off. Most houses nowadays just have Yale locks on their front-doors, which simply means turning a knob. But there might be a bolt as well. I knew how jolly hard it was to draw bolts without making a noise about it. I reminded myself that I probably shouldn't get as far as the front-door anyhow, but that I should be a fool if I didn't have a good try. If Denning caught me on the stairs — well, I shouldn't be any worse off than I was now.

I tied the ends of my shoelaces together—in a bow, so that I could untie them again quickly. Then I crept to the door, opened it and listened. The house was absolutely silent. I shut the door behind me and made my way along the corridor. There was a light on, so there was no danger of my making a noise by bumping into anything, but it meant that I should be spotted at once if anyone came out of one of the rooms. When I reached the top of the stairs I listened again. All I could hear now was a murmur of talk coming from the sitting-room.

I think the stairs in that house were a bit on the old side! The creakings and crackings they made as I went down them made me feel sure every second that I should be heard. But I got to the bottom at last. I had a bad moment when I passed the sitting-room; I felt sure I heard someone moving towards the door. But it was a false alarm.

There *was* a Yale lock, and the door wasn't bolted. In a couple of seconds I was out in the garden, putting my shoes on. I could hardly believe my luck! I hadn't the least idea what I was going to do next, but the great thing was that I was out of that house!

I was halfway to the gate when I had an idea. Why shouldn't I have a shot at hearing what the others were saying? It was a warm night; one of the sitting-room windows would be sure to be open. With a bit more of the luck I seemed suddenly to be having, I might pick up something useful before I left.

I turned and made my way round the corner of the house. Yes, a window was open; what was more, there was a gap between the curtains, and I could see right into the room. Denning was sitting in an armchair, and his wife was standing in front of him, her hands on her hips, looking down at him. The first words I heard came from her.

'I tell you you're a fool.'

'Thank you, my dear,' replied Denning, in his usual calm, polite voice. 'And just why am I a fool?'

'Why, keeping that boy here. It's a crazy thing to do. Have you thought of what would happen to you if he was traced here?'

'He won't be traced here. You can take my word for that.'

'I can't take your word for anything. Besides, what are you going to get out of it? That boy's got courage; he'll never give way. And even if he did — even if he promised to help you in order to get away from here — he'd tell the whole story as soon as he got home. How else could he explain his absence? The whole idea's mad, I tell you!'

Denning stroked his lip. There was a smile on his face that made me feel very, very glad I had got out of his clutches.

'I think you're right there,' he said. 'I thought the amount of money I was offering him would be enough to get him on my side; if it had, we could easily have cooked up a story for him to tell when he got back. A hundred pounds is a fortune to a schoolboy. But I see now that he will always put his stupid ideas of loyalty to old Burnaby before his own interests, so it's no good. However, I've always had an alternative plan with regard to that young man, and now I'm going to put it into operation.'

'What do you mean?'

'I should think that old man down at Ponscombe House would be ready to pay a good deal to get him back again. And if he won't, the boy's parents will.'

'So that's it, is it?' she exclaimed angrily. 'You know what'll happen to you if you try that game and get caught, don't you? Kidnapping's bad enough, but—'

Denning was sitting in an armchair

'That'll do,' interrupted Denning roughly. 'I've made up my mind what I'm going to do, and all your talking won't stop me. And now you'd better go up and see that he's all right. No, I think perhaps I'll go.'

'There's no need,' she said. 'It's only about ten minutes since I took him a cup of cocoa, and he was all right then.'

She spoke nervously, and her face had gone white. Denning noticed it, and a suspicious look came into his face.

'Now I wonder,' he said softly, 'why you're so anxious to stop my paying a visit to our young guest?'

'I'm not anxious. It's only that — that there's no point in it.'

'Isn't there?' His voice was grim. 'All the same, I think I will, if you don't mind.'

He got up from his chair, and I legged it for the garden gate as hard as I could go.

When I won the under-sixteen quarter-mile at school I suppose I may have run faster than I did that night, but not much. I felt I'd stayed listening to the conversation of Denning and his wife just a bit too long. It would only be a matter of seconds before he found out that I'd escaped, and then things would move all right! Denning looked like a chap who could get over the ground if he gave his mind to it, and if he caught me I didn't think it was likely that my bedroom door would be left unlocked a second time!

I sprinted to a corner, crossed the road, and headed down a side turning. In another twenty yards or so there was a turning to the left, and I took it, my idea being to go by as zig-zag a route as possible, to throw Denning off the trail if he was following me. I suppose I must have taken half a dozen more turnings when I came out into a wide road with lots of people about. I felt sure Denning couldn't have trailed me here, so I stopped and leaned against a wall to get my breath. Before leaving that bedroom I had put on the overcoat Denning had lent me down in Devon, over my shirt and shorts, and the sweat was pouring off me in streams. I was glad I had the coat, though, because I should have looked a bit odd going about London at that time of night in nothing but my shirt and trousers!

When I had got my breath back I began to walk slowly on.

I was wondering what to do next. All the money I had on me was a fifty pence piece and a penny, which would have been quite enough for tea and a bus home if Michael and I had finished our day as we had intended, but it wouldn't take me very far on the journey from London to Ponscombe. Aunt Dorothy was up in Scotland, and I didn't know anyone else in London. I realized that what I ought to do, after what had happened, was to tell the police; but what was I to tell them? I had been in such a tearing hurry to get away from Denning's house before he caught me that I hadn't seen the name or number of it or the name of the street or anything. And now I couldn't possibly find the way back to it. Still, I suppose the obvious thing to do, when you've escaped from a kidnapping, is to tell the police; and I was just going to ask somebody the way to the nearest police station when something happened that made me change my mind.

I was passing a café at the time. I had noticed it from some way away because it was the only shop in the street that wasn't in darkness. It was full of people. As I came level with the entrance a man came out and crossed the pavement to where a big lorry was drawn up by the kerb. Struck by a sudden idea, I went up to him.

'Excuse me,' I said, 'but would you mind telling me which way you're going with your lorry?'

The man turned and stared at me for a moment. He looked rather a nice chap, I thought.

'Where am I going? Exeter. Why? Want a lift?'

'Yes, please!' I said. I could hardly believe it!

'Where are you bound for, then?'

'A place called Ponscombe, thirty-five miles beyond Exeter. If you *would* let me go with you I'd be awfully grateful. Only—'

'Only what?'

'I'm afraid I can't pay you. You see, I'm stranded in London with very little money. But if you give me your address I can send it.'

'Go along with you!' said the man, with a laugh. 'I don't want money for giving you a lift. Glad of the company. Hop in!'

I climbed up to the seat beside him, he started the engine and off we went.

I still couldn't believe it! Half an hour before I had been sitting in that bedroom in Denning's house wondering what on earth was going to happen to me, and now, out of all the millions of people in London, I had run across somebody who could give me a free lift back to Devon! If I didn't believe in luck before, I jolly well believed in it now!

In spite of its being so late at night, there was a lot of traffic about, and for a while the man beside me gave all his attention to his driving and didn't talk. But presently we were in an almost deserted road and he turned and looked at me.

'You all right, mate?' he asked.

'Yes, thanks. I'm fine.'

'Stranded in London, you said, didn't you?'

'Yes.'

'How did that happen, then?'

'If I told you,' I said, 'you wouldn't believe me.'

'Wouldn't be the first queer story I'd heard. You meet all sorts on this lorry-driving lark, and that's a fact.'

'All right, then. I was kidnapped.'

'Go on!'

'I said you wouldn't believe me.'

'I believe you all right. Who snatched you?'

And so, as the lorry rumbled out of London into the dark country, I told him how Michael and I had started out for our day's hike, how I had lost him in the fog, how Denning found me and then brought me up to London, how I had escaped. Bill Hutchings (he told me his name afterwards) listened in silence until I'd finished. Then—

'But what did he do it for?' he asked. 'What's his game?'

I told him about the hidden treasure. He was so interested that he kept turning to look at me, and I was afraid he'd ditch the lorry!

'Well, I don't know,' he said when I had finished. 'I've heard some things in my time, but this beats the lot! But I reckon you ought to have gone to the cops as soon as you got free.'

'I was just going to when I met you. But I hadn't much to tell them. You see, I came away in such a hurry I didn't see where the house was.'

'Which direction had you come from when you met me?'

I told him, as nearly as I could.

'That'd be Paddington way,' he said. 'You came up to me in the Edgware Road. I reckon you ought to have gone to the cops,' he repeated, 'even if you couldn't tell 'em much.'

'Yes, I suppose I ought. But Admiral Burnaby'll soon get on to them.'

'Who's he?'

'He's Michael's uncle. We're staying with him at Ponscombe.'

'If he's an admiral,' said Bill Hutchings, 'he'll know what to do all right. Good old Navy! I was with 'em in the war. But look here,' he added. 'What about letting him know you're safe? I reckon he must be worrying himself sick about you.'

'I know. I'll ring him up when we get to Exeter.'

'And leave the poor feller lying awake all night wondering whether you're alive or dead? I wouldn't leave it as long as that, if I was you. In another three or four miles there's an all night place where I stop for a cup of tea. They've got a telephone. Ring him up from there; that's what you ought to do. Will he hear the bell?'

'Yes, he's got a telephone by his bed.'

'There you are, then. And if you haven't got enough money to pay for the call, tell 'em to reverse the charges. That means he pays for it instead of you. I reckon he'll think it's worth it, too!'

Ten minutes later we stopped at a wayside café at the top of a hill. 'Unless the chap at the exchange is asleep,' said Bill Hutchings, 'it won't take you long to get through at this time of night.'

He was right. The operator told me to hold on, and it wasn't more than a few seconds before I heard the Admiral's voice saying he'd pay for the call.

'It's me, Admiral Burnaby,' I said. 'Richard.'

'Richard! Are you all right?'

'Yes, I'm all right.'

'Thank God, my dear boy! Where are you? What happened to you?'

'I'm about thirty miles from London,' I answered, 'on the way back to Exeter.'

'Thirty miles from *London?* How the dickens did you get there? I've only just got in from searching the moor for you. Half Ponscombe's been out. We thought you'd fallen into a bog. Thirty miles from *London?*'

'I was kidnapped on the moor,' I said, 'and taken to London in a car. I managed to escape, and a chap's taking me back to Exeter in his lorry. Is Michael all right?'

'Yes, right as rain, but worried to death about you. He's just come into the room. I suppose he was awake and heard the telephone-bell.'

'Well, tell him it was the red-bearded chap.'

'What red-bearded chap?'

'He'll tell you. And I'll explain about it when I see you.'

'You'd better. And then I'll get hold of this red-bearded chap and wring his neck. Kidnapped you, by Jove! And we were out all night and all today searching for you. The police were out, too. I'd decided to cable your father in the morning. Have you told the police in London?'

'No, I haven't. I was going to, but then I had the chance of getting this lift back to Devon, and I took it.'

'Quite right. We'll put the police on to this fellow when we hear all about it. What time will you get to Exeter?'

'About nine, I think.'

'Good. Now listen. When you get there ask someone to direct you to Pearson and Symes' office. They're a very well-known firm of solicitors, near the Cathedral. Everybody knows them. When you get there ask for Mr Robert Pearson. I'll telephone him first thing in the morning, so he'll be expecting you. He'll fix you up with money and see you're all right. Don't forget the name — Mr Robert Pearson of Pearson and Symes, near the Cathedral. Got that?'

'Yes, sir. I've got it.'

'That's right. And now Michael'll be tearing this receiver out of my hand if I don't let him speak to you. Good-night, my dear boy. Thank God you're safe and sound!'

'Hello, Richard!' said Michael's voice.

'Hello, Michael! Here we are again!'

'Been having some fun, haven't you?'

'Not so bad. I ran into that red-bearded bloke in the fog and he dragged me up to London. But I slipped him.'

'Good for you! What was he after? The Treasure?'

'Yes.'

'I guessed as much. Got any clues?'

'One cracking good one. Tell you about it when I get back.'

'O. K. Well, be seeing you.'

I hung up the receiver and joined Bill Hutchings at his table. He'd ordered me a cup of tea and some cake, and wouldn't let me pay for it. I don't usually think much of tea as a drink, but I enjoyed it that night. I was pretty tired, and it bucked me up. Soon we were on the road again. I think Bill saw how tired I was, because he rummaged about in the back of the lorry, produced a cushion for me to put behind my head and a rug to cover over my knees, and very soon after we started I was dozing off. Of course, I didn't sleep soundly; the lorry was too noisy for that. But altogether I think I must have slept quite a lot, because I remember how surprised I was, after what seemed a very short time, to open my eyes and find it was daylight.

Soon after that we had another cup of tea, and then I felt as fresh as a daisy. It was a lovely morning, and my adventure with Denning seemed like a bad dream. Bill told me about his experiences in the Navy during the war, and jolly exciting they were. He'd been pretty well everywhere, and finished by being wounded off the Normandy beaches on D-Day and getting the Distingushed Service Medal. I wished he and the Admiral could have met; they'd have liked each other.

We reached Exeter at quarter past nine. I was sorry to say good-bye to Bill Hutchings; I felt as though I'd know him a long time. He gave me his address and asked me to let him know when we found the treasure and when Denning was caught. I thanked him for driving me down, and he said he'd enjoyed it as much as I had. Then we parted, and at half-past nine I turned into a narrow little street by the Cathedral and saw, on the door of an old-fashioned sort of house, a brass plate with "Pearson and Symes, Solicitors," on it.

THE SECRET
Gordon Shirrefs

Gene Russell, deputy-sheriff, had the makings of a good lawman. He was not only observant, he could use his observations to prove an argument. When he took the trail to discover how an accident occurred to Uncle Harry Forbes he did not know what he would find. But at the end of that trail he had uncovered a startling truth and brought a killer to justice.

Don Forbes reined in his buckskins and looked back at his elder cousin, Gene Russell, who was farther back on the trail. 'Here's Uncle Harry's old ranch house!' he called. The old adobe stood beside a dry wash in the shallow New Mexican valley. Its front door gaped open, and one corner of the earthen roof had fallen in. There was a brooding loneliness about the place.

Gene stopped beside Don and shoved back his hat to wipe the sweat from his face. 'Whew! I never realized what a long ride this was from your father's ranch.' Gene was twenty-two, four years older than Don, and had just finished his first year as deputy-sheriff, after three years in the military police. He had been visiting at the Forbes' ranch on the Pecos.

'I haven't been up here since last year,' said Don soberly. 'That's when dad and I found Uncle Harry dead.'

Gene scratched his jaw. 'When I heard he had accidentally shot himself, I could hardly believe it. He taught me all I know about firearms. Ballistics was one of his hobbies. It just doesn't figure.'

Don touched his horse with his heels. 'No. It doesn't. That's why I wanted *you* to come back in here with me. To make sure it *was* an accident.' He guided his horse down into the valley. Uncle Harry had lived there for years raising a few cattle, guiding hunting parties into the Guadalupes, but most of the time he was away in the blue haziness of the mountains hunting for the legendary lost gold mine called the Secret of the Guadalupes.

Gene caught up with Don beside the dry wash. 'Then you don't think his death was an accident?'

'No. Uncle Harry had quite a reputation as a treasure hunter in the Southwest. Many men knew about his work. I think he *had* found something of importance and someone knew he had.'

'You mean — ?'

'Yes. Someone made it look like an accident.'

Gene whistled. 'Now I know why you asked me to spend my vacation at your place. Me thinking I'm up here on a nice quiet camping trip and all the time my young cousin is looking for a criminal.'

'It was the only way I could get someone to come in here with me. You've been through the MP school, and the whole state knows about that gang of bank robbers you tracked down and caught last year with your modern crime detection methods. I couldn't think of anyone better able to help me.'

Gene slapped Don's shoulder. 'Listen, kid, I would have come whether or not I had any experience.'

Gene took care of the horses while Don took their gear into the old adobe. It hadn't changed much. For a moment he had a strange feeling that Uncle Harry would come in, start a fire in the beehive fireplace, and then begin one of his interminable stories about lost treasure. Don remembered all of the old man's tales. The Treasure of Fort Ramirez, the legendary Lost San Saba once seen by the almost legendary Jim Bowie, The Engineer's Ledge, Yuma's Gold, The Lost Breyfogle, the fabulous Lost Adams Diggings, and many others, clouded in years of lies and contradictions. Uncle Harry had heard the owl hoot in many strange and lonely places. He had been a dreamer, called by many a ne'er-do-well, but he had never lost faith in his dreams. He had never harmed anyone, and Don's father had said he justified his existence by the fabulous stories he could tell.

After they had eaten, the two cousins sprawled on their blankets and looked into the dancing flames licking over the sweet-smelling pinon wood. Don half-closed his eyes. Gene rested his chin on his forearms and looked sideways at Don. 'There's something I'd like to know, Don.'

'Yes?'

'You said Uncle Harry had found something important and someone knew it.'

'Correct.'

'What made you think that?'

Don got up and went to the back of the room. He pulled aside a heavy bench and groped behind it. He pulled out a hide-covered box and hauled it toward the fireplace. 'Uncle Harry kept his odds and ends in here. Last time dad and I were in here we were too busy getting his body out to bother with anything else. Dad sent a man up here to close up the place, but he overlooked this.'

He threw back the lid and began taking things out of the box. There were several charts, *derroteros*, Uncle Harry had called them. One of them was in blue ink on the scraped hide of a javelina. There were worn maps of every state in the Southwest, marked here and there with red crosses and cryptic symbols. There was part of a cartridge reloading outfit and a few shells. There were many mineral specimens neatly labelled in Uncle Harry's crabby handwriting. Don looked away. It was almost as though he could see the old man's gnarled hands fondling his treasures, probably the only treasures he had ever found for all his years of chasing El Dorado.

'What's this?' asked Gene, as he held up a lump of wax from which protruded four wicks at right angles to each other.

'Uncle Harry got that from a *brujo*, a Mexican wizard, in San Antonio. It's supposed to reveal the direction in which treasure lies.'

'How?'

'First you get three other superstitious characters and wait for a windy night. Then the four of you take that trick candle out, light each of the wicks, and each of you holds a wick at its base. The wick that burns the longest is supposed to point out the way to the treasure.'

Gene grinned. 'You mean Uncle Harry actually *believed* in things like this?'

'No. He just liked to have things like that around.' Don poked about in the box, throwing out a peach switch which was used for divining precious minerals. He held up a large plugged brass cartridge shell, to which was attached a string. 'Here's another gadget. It's filled with a little gold dust, opium, some powdered black rock, and various powdered minerals. The user hung it from his forehead and followed the way the cartridge oscillated.'

'You seem to be looking for something.'

'I am. Something that isn't here.'

'Maybe someone took it out of the box?'

Don shook his head. 'No. It wasn't in the box when Uncle Harry was still alive. It was a piece of smooth board. He was burning a map on it.'

'A map?'

Don nodded. 'Every time he went into the mountains he made additions to it. I always looked at it each time I came to visit him. The last time I saw him alive, I noticed the board was not in the box. I asked him about it, and he winked and said it was getting too valuable and that he had hidden it. He told me it would be ours if anything happened to him. Almost as though he expected something to happen to him.'

'What did it look like?'

'It was full of funny little symbols such as mule shoes, arrows, triangles. Uncle Harry didn't know where the Secret of the Guadalupes was, but he always claimed a patient man could find it by locating certain signs left by the old Spanish miners. My guess is that he was finding those signs and recording them and that he was pretty close to finding the mine when he died.'

Gene looked up quickly. 'And someone did away with him, took the map, and found the treasure.'

'I don't think so. I think he had already hidden the chart.'

'So where is it?'

Don got up and looked out of a window toward the shadowed Guadalupes behind the cabin, their tips silvered by the moon. A panther screamed harshly, far up a canyon. 'That's why I wanted to come back in here,' he said quietly. 'Somehow I think it will tie in with Uncle Harry's death, providing we can find it.'

Gene stood up and walked thoughtfully around the room, tossing two cartridges in his hand. He studied the layouts for a while, then said, 'We'd better get some sleep. Tomorrow morning we'll turn this place upside down looking for that map.'

Sometime during the night Don opened his eyes. The moonlight streamed through the windows, forming silvery patches on the beaten earth floor. Gene was sleeping soundly. Don listened. He was sure he had heard his buckskin nicker. Suddenly he sat upright. The horse had nickered again. Don got up and took his Winchester from the corner. He padded quietly to a window and, standing back in the shadows, eyed the valley. His horse was at the far side of the old peeled pole corral looking upstream toward a willow motte. The dry wind was the only sound. Don waited for ten minutes and then went back to his blankets, but he kept his carbine close by his side.

After breakfast the next morning, the two stood outside the adobe. 'Where do we start, Don?' asked Gene. 'This is your show.'

'Where would you hide a valuable map, Gene?'

Gene shrugged. 'The least likely spot anyone would look for it. It wouldn't be easy.'

Don eyed the corral and then the old shed that stood behind the adobe. He crossed to it and opened the door. A few rusty tools lay on the floor amid a litter of rotten sacks. A broken saddle hung from a peg. Don scratched his jaw. Gene poked his head in through the doorway. 'In here?' he asked sceptically. 'It looks like this place has been gone over!' Don left the shed and looked at the back of the adobe. Suddenly he ran to the back door. It was formed of thick boards, crossed by diagonal braces. The door had been patched by a short board, silvered by the sun. He drew out his hunting knife and began to pry at it easily until it came loose. He turned it over. He whistled softly. The smooth under-surface had been marked by a red-hot wire. It was the map. There was no mistaking it.

Gene ran up beside Don. 'How did you figure out that was it, Don?'

Don touched the door. 'There always was a patch on this door. But it had a large knot at one end. I guess most people wouldn't have noticed it, but I was here when Uncle Harry nailed it on two years ago. He nearly blew his top because he couldn't drive a nail through the knot.' Don held up the board. 'Do you see any knot in *this* board?'

Gene slapped Don's shoulder.

'Nope. Your new name is Hawkeye in my book, kid.'

Don took the board in through the back doorway of the adobe. He placed it on the battered table. 'It's pretty obvious this is a map of a canyon west of here. Rough country. Used to be a Mescalero Apache camp in there years ago. I can tell by this mark.' He placed a finger on an Indian pipe burned into the wood.

Gene rested his chin on his right fist and studied the map. 'You were right about the markings on the map. But what do they all mean?'

Don pointed them out as he named them. 'An arrow without feathers *can* point toward a treasure or water or it *may* mean there are other signs farther on. A horizontal mule shoe means you are en route to treasure; keep travelling. A Spanish gourd means water ahead. That's all I know.'

'Then this map isn't any use at all. Unless we know the symbols, we can't read it.'

Don nodded. 'Uncle Harry knew them all by heart. He told me once he had copied them from an old document he had studied in a mission library in Hermosillo.'

'That doesn't do us much good.'

Don stood up. '*He meant* for us to have this map. If he thought we'd ever use it, he would have provided a key to these symbols.'

Gene glanced up at him. 'I'm beginning to think you're a genius, kid.'

Don waved a hnad. 'Naturally. Now, where is it?'

Gene leaned back in his chair, steepling his fingers on his chest. '*You're* the genius, cuz.'

Don sat down on the box in which Uncle Harry had kept his personals. He slapped it. 'Where could it be?'

Gene looked at the box. 'That lid is covered with javelina hide. Maybe there's something under the hide.'

Don snorted, 'Yeah. The lid.'

Gene got up and pulled Don from his seat. He unsheathed his knife and worked it carefully under the heavy brass tacks that held the hide to the wood. He loosened one end and then worked his way all along the edges, peeling the hide back. The wooden lid was bare of any markings. Gene examined the hide. It was coated on the underside with red and yellow paint.

'Ochre,' said Don. 'Indian paint.'

Gene placed the hide flat on the table and scraped it gently with his knife. Don looked over his shoulder. He whistled sharply. 'Look!' Where the paint had been removed there were markings, done in indelible ink on the smooth hide. Don held the hide taut while Gene worked carefully to remove the rest of the paint. In half an hour they could read a list of symbols with their meanings opposite them, painstakingly lettered on the hide. Gene looked up at Don.

'This is it!'

'Now what?'

Don looked out of the window towards the hazy mountains. 'Uncle Harry meant for us to have that treasure. Are you game to try for it?'

Gene sheathed his knife.

'Look, kid. I'd like to find it as much as you would, but I thought we were interested in solving Uncle Harry's death.'

Don turned. 'Don't you see? If he was murdered for that map, the murderer never got it. Whoever did it is still around somewhere, hoping he'll get his hands on it. I'm willing to bet someone saw us come in here. If we hunt for the mine, he, or they, will probably follow us.'

Gene nodded slowly. 'It's a long chance, Don.'

'I'm willing to risk it.'

'O. K., let's saddle the horses.'

It was still early morning when they rode up the valley towards the west. The sun had not yet begun to beat down. As they passed the motte of willows, Don glanced into them. Suddenly he drew rein. Gene circled his horse on the forehand and looked at Don. 'Well?' he asked.

Don slid from his saddle. His buckskin shied a little. Gene swung down from his claybank and came up beside Don. An empty Bull Durham bag was caught on a twig. Gene parted the brush and studied the ground. He pointed at several hollows in the sandy earth. 'Looks like a man was lying here. See the depressions of his elbows and knees?' Looking toward the 'dobe' Gene circled about. He touched some of the lower branches of the willows. They had been chafed, and many of the lower leaves were missing. 'Tethered horse,' he said quietly.

Don rubbed his jaw. 'My buckskin was nervous last night. He was looking toward this motte. I didn't see anything though.'

They went back to their horses. Suddenly Gene gripped Don's shoulder. He pointed to a butte which overlooked the valley. Something flashed in the sun.

'What is it?' asked Don.

'The sun reflecting from shiny rock or from a *tinaja*, a rock water hole. Or, it could be from field glasses.' The two cousins looked at each other and then swung up on their horses.

Hours later they were in a high-walled canyon which held the heat like a great trough. Don pointed at a mule shoe sign chiselled horizontally into a rock slab. 'That jibes with the chart, Gene.'

Gene gingerly picked a cholla needle from his boot. 'That's the third such sign in the last two miles. How much farther, Don?'

Don shrugged. 'Until we find a marker that tells us the distance, we've got to keep moving.'

Gene glanced back down the canyon. 'You know I haven't seen anything yet, but I'll swear we're not alone in here.'

Don nodded soberly. 'I've had the same feeling.'

The canyon narrowed as they went on. They led their horses through dense clumps of catclaw and prickly pear. Brittle bush and ocotillo blocked their way, forcing them to use their machetes. Don dropped on a rock after an hour of rough going and wiped his face. Gene studied the map and then the symbols on the javelina hide. 'According to this, there should be a symbol somewhere in here. Something like a reversed 3. Means change direction.'

'You're loco. Where can we change direction in this canyon?'

Gene hacked at some brush at the side of the canyon. 'Here it is. On this rock.' He pushed into the brush and suddenly was gone from sight. His voice came faintly back to Don. 'Come on! Bring the horses!'

Behind the huge rock a narrow passageway appeared, winding its way deep into what had looked like a solid wall from the canyon. Their feet clashed on shale, and the floor of the passageway began to rise. Gene slapped his hand against a smooth spot on the wall. A chiselled arrow pointed upward. The passageway narrowed still more, so that the horses could just get through. Then it widened again and Don caught sight of a symbol beneath an overhanging ledge. A sunburst. He gripped Gene's arm. Gene studied the javelina hide. 'Mine close by,' he said quietly.

They worked their way up the loose rock, slipping and sliding, until the canyon broadened into an area surrounded by towering rock walls. A hawk glided off before the wind. Just beyond the narrow passageway was a ring of blackened rocks. Don ran forward. 'That's from the old Mescalero camp, Gene. They used to roast *sotol* in those things.' He glanced at the map. 'An Indian pipe. Look for other signs.'

Gene swung his machete against the brush veiling a rock slab. 'How will a snake sign do?'

'Pointing which way?'

'Head downward.'

Don swallowed quickly. His eyes met his cousin's. 'We're supposed to measure the distance from the tip of the tail to the ground. Step off that distance ten times, straight out. Treasure will be there or there will be another sign.'

Gene pulled a rawhide thong from his pocket and measured off the distance. He lined up with a bush on the far side of the area and then bent down to measure it off. Slowly he placed the thong length down ten times, ending up atop a flat slab of rock. He looked back at Don. 'Nothing here, kid.'

Don ran forward and looked at the rock. He swept away the

thin film of sand that covered it. He looked at the surface closely. There was a six-inch line in the centre of the rock. It was not a crack but a chiselled mark. He looked at the hide. 'Straight line means we measure off fifty or one hundred more lengths.'

Gene groaned and bent to his work. He got to thirty measurements away from the rock and stopped short beneath a sheer wall. He looked back at Don and wiped the sweat from his face. 'There's something wrong here.'

Don scratched his cheek. Suddenly he looked up. 'How long is that thong?'

'Six feet.'

Don grinned. 'Feet? We don't want *feet*. We want *varas*!' That's an ancient Spanish measurement. Thirty-three and a third inches. You went about one hundred and eighty feet. Try it at one hundred and fifty feet.'

Gene paced it off and looked about. He dropped to his knees and brushed away the sand from a rock. 'Capital G,' he said, looking up at Don.

'Gold short distance away,' Don said with a catch in his voice.

Gene cast about. Suddenly he ran to the edge of a slope and stared at a rock. 'Mule shoe! Toe down! Three dots inside the shoe in an up and down line!'

Don ran to his cousin's side. 'Look for a cave or a shaft.' He glanced at a pile of rock which was against a sheer wall. A bracket sign was chiselled into a flat rock to one side of the pile. He didn't have to look at the hide chart.

'What is it?' asked Gene.

For a moment Don's voice failed him. 'A tunnel! This is it! The Secret of the Guadalupes!'

'What are we waiting for?' Gene began to lift rocks and throw them to one side.

Two hours later the sun was dipping low to the west. Gene was sitting on a rock with his carbine across his lap watching the narrow passageway while Don took his turn at the pile. Don pulled at a large rock. It slid to one side. A draught of air poured about him. Beyond the opening was a dark tunnel. Gene pushed up beside Don. 'Well?'

Don wiped his lacerated hands on his shirt. An icy finger seemed to trace the length of his spine. He picked up his Winchester and thrust a leg through the opening. 'Hand me some of those *sotol* stalks we cut,' he said quietly. He worked his way cautiously into the hole and took a *sotol* stalk from Gene. He lit it. It flared up into light. Gene wormed his way through the hole. 'Look!' he said, pointing at something which showed whitely in the flickering light. Don thrust the stalk forward. The uncertain flame alternately plunged parts of the tunnel into darkness and light. A skull was propped against the wall, the hollow eye sockets staring back at them. Don swallowed. 'Wonder who it was?' asked Gene. 'It's been here a long time, Don.'

'*Patrone*,' answered Don quietly. 'The dead man left to guard the treasure. No one has been in here in about two or three hundred years, I'll bet.'

Gene nodded.

Don walked slowly into the tunnel. It widened into a room. At the back of the room was a hole with a deeply notched log ladder protruding from it. Beside the hole lay several ancient hide bags which the miners hung from their heads and shoulders, to take out the ore. 'Do you see anything, Gene?' he asked his cousin over his shoulder.

'Something like a pile of wood over here. Bring the light.'

Don turned quickly. Gene was squatting beside a pile of what looked like billets of wood. Don ran to him, handing him the *sotol* stalk. He drew out his knife and then swept away the dust of centuries from the billets. He scraped at one of them with his knife. The cut showed up brightly. 'Gold,' he said softly. He turned away. In the moment of discovery he thought of Uncle Harry, whose sun-faded eyes had never seen the will-o'-the-wisp for which he had hunted for so many years. 'Let's get out of here,' he said.

Long shadows moved over the canyon, and a chill wind moaned through the rocky pinnacles. Gene looked toward the passageway into the canyon. Don glanced at him. 'Should we hide the mine entrance?' he asked.

Gene shook his head. 'No. There will be a good moon tonight. I want it to be seen.'

'Think someone will come?'

'Yes. Lead the horses up the canyon and picket them. Bring back some chow, the canteens, and your rifle. We're going to sit this one out.'

Hours later the two crouched behind some rocks a hundred yards from the mine. The moon silvered the open area, showing the mine entrance in sharp contrast to the light-coloured rock. Suddenly Gene leaned forward and gripped Don's wrist hard.

The wind moaned through the canyon. Don stared at the passageway until it seemed as though the shadows were dancing. He closed his eyes and then opened them again. A shadow *was* moving. It crept along the canyon wall. A man, trailing a heavy rifle.

Don crouched lower. The stock of his Winchester was greasy with sweat from his hands. From far down the canyon came the mournful cry of a coyote. The man padded forward. He halted in the open area and looked about. A tall man. Suddenly he stared at the mine entrance and then he ran forward to it. He clambered over the rocks and felt in one of his pockets. He lit the stub of a candle and leaned his rifle against a rock. Then he worked his way into the hole.

Gene waved Don up. 'Now!' he said. They left the shelter of the rocks and moved toward the mine, placing their feet carefully. Gene cocked his Winchester. Feet scuffled in the mine. Don swallowed hard and stepped to one side, raising his carbine. Gene picked up the man's rifle and placed it behind a ledge. He glanced at Don. 'You! In there!' he called. 'Come out with your hands up!'

Suddenly feet clashed against rock. The man appeared, bent over, plunging through the tunnel entrance with a cocked revolver in his hand. Gene leaped back, hitting a rock, and went over backwards. He shouted. Don ran forward, thrusting his carbine between the man's legs, spilling him forward. The revolver spat flame, the slug whining off into space. The man rolled to one side and leaped to his feet. Gene came up in a crouch, holding his rifle in his left hand, and swinging his right fist. With a crack it sent the man back on his shoulder blades. He raised his revolver, but Don swung his carbine, the barrel landing on the gun wrist. The revolver clattered to the rock. The man lashed out at

The man appeared, bent over, plunging through the tunnel entrance

Don. Don went under the blow. Gene stepped in close. His right fist shot out in a jab, catching the man on the point of the jaw. He went down, rolled over, and then lay still. Don grabbed the revolver.

Gene wiped his face. 'Thanks, kid. That was too close for comfort.' He took the rawhide thong from his pocket and swiftly bound the unconscious man's wrists together. Don went for his canteen and splashed some of the water on the man's face. He spluttered and then opened his eyes to stare at them. He was a big man, hard of face and burned by the sun. A short black beard covered his chin but did not conceal a twisted scar running from the tip of his chin up to his left ear. 'Cass Fitch,' said Don.

'You know him?' asked Gene.

'He used to ride for dad some years ago. He left the ranch after a scrap with Uncle Harry. That's where he got the scar. He got rough with Uncle Harry's horse, and Uncle Harry didn't like it. Cass pulled a knife but fell and cut himself with it.'

Gene squatted beside the bound man. In his hand he held Fitch's rifle. 'Why did you follow us?'

'I don't have to answer that.'

Gene pulled his west aside showing his deputy-sheriff's badge. 'Yes, you do.'

'I was huntin'.'

'What do you know about the death of Harry Forbes?'

'Shot hisself, didn't he?'

'I'm asking *you*.'

Fitch scowled. 'You ain't got a thing on me, lawman.'

Gene stood up. He spoke to Don but looked at Fitch. 'We'll take him back for trial.' He put his hand in his pocket and drew out two cartridges. 'Fitch used your uncle's 30.06 rifle all right, but he forgot that Harry always used hand-loaded cartridges. Fitch's rifle was the same calibre, and he loaded Harry's with his own storebought cartridges. With these and other evidence I picked up in Harry's house we'll bring charges.'

In the bright mountain moonlight Fitch's face showed a spasm of mixed fear and rage.

'Go bring up the horses and let's get started,' Gene said.

As Don tightened the cinches, he asked, 'Will the evidence convict him?'

'A man is innocent until he is proved guilty. But from a detective's point of view, it is more than enough for conviction.'

They pulled Fitch to his feet. He glared at them. 'Maybe I did shoot him,' he growled harshly, 'but 'fore you stick me in jail, just let me lay my eyes on that mine map, will you?'

'Here it is.' Don held up the map in the moonlight. 'We found the Secret of the Guadalupes.' Then he added quietly, 'I'd have traded a hundred like it to hear another of Uncle Harry's stories.'

GRAMMAR VERSUS MODERN
A. Stephen Tring

Frank, Joe and Mickey are three Secondary Modern boys who feel they have a feud with the lads at the local Grammar School. The teams of the two schools are keen rivals at sport, especially in the two Soccer matches played during the Easter term. Told by Frank, who takes part, this is the return match. It is taken from *The Old Gang*, which relates many other adventures enjoyed by the schoolboy trio.

'I tell you one thing,' Joe said.

'What's that?' I asked.

'I'm going into training now for the inter-school sports in the summer, and every single event that Beefy enters for I'm going in for too; and I'm going to beat him in every one.'

Mickey and I thought this was a jolly good idea because Joe was good at pretty well all sports, being a sort of natural athlete, and we thought it would be fun to take Beefy down a peg or two at the summer sports and make him look small.

This inter-school sports day in the summer was looked forward to all the year by the Grammar and the Secondary Modern, and we made all sorts of plans to beat each other. The Grammar had a really good coach called Captain Hodges who had got a double Blue at Cambridge, and usually they beat us on aggregate points, though we always did well on certain things. Joe said he didn't mind this year about aggregate points so long as he didn't let Beefy Marling win anything personally, and Mickey and I had to try to find out what Beefy Marling was going in for. This wasn't too easy at first because it was only March when all this started and there were three months to go till the sports day, but after a bit we discovered that the only events Beefy was going in for were swimming ones; the hundred yards any stroke and the hundred yards crawl stroke.

As a matter of fact it was Margie, my sister, who found this out for us, as she is very friendly with Dolly Hodges, the daughter of the Grammar's coach.

As soon as I told Joe he said, 'All right, then I'll go in for them, too.' When I told him how I had found out he made a face.

'Oh, girls! Now I suppose you'll tell your sister what I'm doing and she'll tell Dolly Hodges; she'll tell her father and he'll tell Beefy.'

I promised him I wouldn't tell anybody, and we made Mickey promise as well.

It was nearly the end of March when we found out about Beefy going in for the swimming and the Easter holidays were due to start in ten days.

Joe said, 'We'll spend the holidays practising at the swimming pool, and then as soon as the summer term starts we'll volunteer for swimming lessons.'

So we agreed to do that, and I was jolly glad to have that sorted out because I had the Grammar-Modern football match to worry about. We always played one another twice each term, and as the Grammar hadn't won a game yet they were naturally anxious to win this one.

In the first game of the Easter term which we played early in February they gave us an awful fright and were actually leading by two goals to none with only twenty minutes to go; then we were given a penalty against them; we scored from that, and they cracked up and we got a couple more goals directly after that, which made us end up all right; but after the match Mr Stewart said we had played the worst game he had seen for ages and didn't really deserve to win.

I didn't get in the first eleven until after that match. Joe was in, of course; he is our goalkeeper, but Mickey was too much of a kid, and he wasn't much good at soccer anyway.

The match was fixed for three days before the end of the term, and as the one in February had been played on our ground, we had to play this one at the Grammar's ground.

I knew Mr Stewart was nervous about the result from the way he spoke to us during the week beforehand, and then the very day before the match he saw Wilkins our centre forward smoking in a cinema in Bulling, and in spite of the fact that he was the best forward we had Mr Stewart wouldn't let him play.

It was perfectly fair really because it was a fixed rule of his, and we all knew it. He told us about a hundred times a term.

'As you are all doubtless aware, smoking is a killer. Furthermore, you boys are supposed to be in strict training and I'm not having any of the ashtray brigade ruining the performance of my team. So if I see anybody smoking during the term I shall take it that he isn't interested in training any more, and doesn't want to be in the team.'

We all knew that, Wilkins included; so there wasn't anything to grumble about. Some of the lads said he might have overlooked it for once, or punished Wilkins in some other way, but I don't see why he shouldn't stick to what he said. We all had fair warning, and anyway everybody knows that Wilkins doesn't really like smoking; he was just showing off because he was taking a girl to the pictures.

Still there's no denying it was a blow to lose Wilkins, who in spite of being a silly fool is really good at centre forward and nearly always manages to score at least one goal during a match.

Freddie Kent, our captain, talked it over with Mr Stewart, and they decided to move Lacey, who usually played inside right, to the centre forward position, and to bring in Page from the second eleven as inside right. The moment I woke on the morning of the match I knew there was something special going to happen that day, and as soon as I remembered what it was I jumped out of bed to see if it was raining. I don't know how it is, but it very nearly always does rain just on the one particular day that you want it not to. Still, it wasn't raining that morning and the sun was as bright as anything. Dad pulled my leg a bit during breakfast about the match, but I didn't mind that. I've noticed that grown-ups have to have their bit of fun about everything, and if you let them crack a joke or two, however silly they are, and laugh at them, they're much happier and it's much better.

Anyway I knew that Dad was quite keen about the game because he and Mum and Margie were all coming to watch it. He usually went up to town directly after breakfast by car, but on this particular day he was staying at home in the morning because somebody from the police was coming to get some information about the value of a car that had been stolen recently from his garage.

The match started at a quarter to three, so Joe and I didn't come home for dinner but had it at Mrs Hunter's with our families. Usually I like being out to a meal as you can have a good tuck-in; but somehow, with the game less than two hours away, I didn't feel like eating much. As a matter of fact, I felt a bit sick, though of course I didn't tell Mum that, or she would have started calling in a doctor or something.

Old Joe ate just as much as ever. I don't believe he ever had nerves. I told him the suet pudding would take away his wind, and he took a second helping of it and said you didn't want wind for a goalkeeper; you wanted width, and suet pudding was good for that.

He was sitting next to Margie and she kept asking him all sorts of questions about the team and the match, which I could have answered just as well. Just like a sister. And after all, I know Joe is better at most sports than I am, but when it comes to footer he is only the goalkeeper and I am the left half, and you can't see as much of the play from the goal as you can from the middle of the field.

Joe's father, Mr Lawley, was the worst, though, because he took up half the meal by telling us about a game he played in when he was at school. Naturally he was the hero of it and scored all the goals and everything like that; but we just didn't want to hear about it that was all. People won't understand that it's what you are doing, or going to do, that matters; not what they did ages and ages ago.

I thought the meal would never finish; but in the end the clock hands got round to two o'clock and we all started to move. Mum said should she buy anything to eat 'in the interval'.

I said, 'For heaven's sake, Mum, do you mean half time?' Women never get technical details right, and fancy anybody wanting to eat anything in the middle of a game! But Joe said, 'Thank you very much, Mrs Dilmot. I think if we had some of these buns it would be lovely,' so Mum bought about a dozen buns, which were tons too many for us anyway, and Margie said she would look after them, and we all got into the two cars.

The Grammar pitch was right in the centre of the town, by the side of the park, and I must say all their playing fields are well laid out. The pitch is a little wider than ours at the Secondary Modern, and Mr Stewart had warned us to remember this especially when putting passes out to the extreme wingers.

They had proper dressing-rooms on the ground in a sort of sports pavilion, and as soon as the cars were parked and we had seen our people in a good position along the touch-line Joe and I went in to change.

Naturally all the Secondary Modern boys were there, and they were all bunched together along one touch-line, and opposite them were the Grammars in their hideous orange and purple caps which looked even worse than ever when you saw so many together.

Mr Stewart was in our dressing-room. He was one linesman, the Grammar sports master was the other, and the referee was a man from the town connected with the Bulling and District Football League in some way.

Mr Stewart smiled at me when we came in and said, 'Feeling all right?'

'Yes, sir — fairly.'

He nodded, 'I know. I always felt exactly the same for half a day before any match, especially an important one, just as though there was a sort of empty space in the middle of my tummy. Never mind. It'll go the moment the game starts. Now don't fool yourselves, boys. It's true the Grammar have never beaten us yet, but today they stand the best chance of doing it they have ever had. They've got a very good forward line, especially that inside right, Pritchard, and they've got a useful defence.'

'Is their goalie good, sir?' somebody asked.

'He won't be good enough to stop shots if you shoot like I've told you to. And half-backs (this meant Freddie Kent, the captain, myself and a boy called Rossi who was right half) remember what I've tried to din into you about feeding your forwards. Wing-halves, get the ball across to the opposite outside men; and all of you keep your passes low. If you want to become pilots you can when you leave school; on the ground will be good enough for this afternoon. Now, keep your heads and do your best.'

Then we all started to strip and change, and Rossi got into a panic because one of the studs had come off his right boot. It was too late to do anything about it, however, and Mr Stewart told him he would just have to make the best of it.

The referee put his head in the door and said, 'All ready?'

Freddie Kent said, 'Coming,' and out we went.

The Moderns were already out kicking about at the far end. I tried to spot where Dad was standing with Mum and Margie, but so many more people had come whilst we were changing that I couldn't see them at first. When I did spot them I nearly had a fit — Margie was actually talking to a Grammar school boy in one of those orange and purple caps. I suppose he was a friend of Dolly Hodges and Margie knew him like that, but it looked pretty bad in front of everybody, and I only hoped Freddie Kent wouldn't notice.

We lost the toss, which didn't matter really because there was hardly any wind; but you don't like losing it because somehow it seems to be one up to the other side.

We had to change ends to kick off, and when we were all in position waiting for the whistle I glanced along our half-back line — Rossi on the right, Freddie Kent in the centre and myself.

The whistle went, Lacey tapped the ball to the inside left, and the game started.

We started off in great style; our passes seemed to go just right all the time and the ball was round the Grammar goal for practically the whole of the first twenty minutes. Joe in our goal had nothing to do, he didn't even get a kick at the ball; but although we had at least six corners we simply couldn't score. Then the Grammar began to find their feet a little and the game evened out. Pritchard, who was their best forward, got the ball more often, and I had a frightfully hard job trying to mark him. Still, they didn't really look as though they would score, and then suddenly, just before half time, they scored twice — once from the only corner they had during the entire first half, and directly afterwards from a scramble in the goal mouth. Half time blew immediately after this second goal and we were two goals down.

Of course the Grammar were chuffed no end and all our lads

looked sick about it. We didn't think we deserved to be two goals behind; but Mr Stewart wasn't very sympathetic. 'If you don't score goals you won't win matches,' was all he said, 'and you had enough chances in the first half to score six times.'

Joe and I drifted off to talk to our people and Margie produced the buns Mums had brought, but Joe wouldn't have one in case Mr Stewart saw him.

Margie said, 'What bad luck. They don't deserve to be leading at all.' I must say that for a girl she has got quite a good idea about soccer.

We got ready to start the second half full of the sort of good spirits you get by talking things over among yourselves. Their centre forward kicked off to Pritchard, who passed the ball back to the centre half; he took a big kick at it and put it right down the field; it went over Rossi's head to the outside left; he took it along a bit, centred it, and there was Pritchard waiting to put it into the net, which he did.

The whole thing only took about a minute and I don't believe one of our blokes even touched the ball! We were absolutely flabbergasted, and I saw poor old Joe fishing the ball out of the back of the net as though it weighed a ton. Of course all the Grammar boys round the touch-line went mad. I suppose it was as much my fault as anybody's because I ought to have been marking Pritchard, but the whole movement had happened so quickly that I was stuck in the middle of the field, and anyway it was no good worrying about it now; we were three down and things looked pretty grim. They looked even grimmer in five minutes' time because Freddie Kent handled the ball in the penalty area, and sure enough the whistle blew and the referee pointed to the spot.

I thought that really was the end, especially when I saw that Pritchard was going to take the shot. When we talked the match over afterwards Mickey said, 'All the time Pritchard was getting ready to take that penalty I was hanging on to my lucky ha'penny like mad.' Maybe it was that that did the trick. Anyway, Pritchard shot hard but straight at Joe, who stopped the ball, gathered it, and just as the Grammar were closing in on him gave it a huge kick right down the field.

One of the tactical points that Mr Stewart has always drilled into us is that when we have a penalty against us, at least two forwards and one half-back must stay well in the centre of the field in case the goalkeeper clears and there is a chance of a break-away.

The Grammar were so worked up about their three-goal lead and so sure of scoring from the penalty that they were all crowded up near our goal except one back who was just about on the halfway line.

When Joe cleared the ball it came straight to me. I saw there was a chance of a breakaway but was scared stiff I was going to do something silly, so as soon as the back came towards me I kicked the ball good and hard over his head.

As a matter of fact it was the best thing I could have done, because Lacey is very fast and he simply shot round the back, trapped the ball as it bounced and made a dash for the Grammar goal.

There just wasn't anybody to stop him except the goalkeeper, who couldn't make up his mind whether to come out or not. He came halfway out, then went back a few paces and never stood a chance with Lacey's shot, which was a beauty, right in the corner.

That made the score 3—1, which was certainly bad enough, but that first goal was worth more than one to us in a way because we had naturally been expecting them to score from the penalty which would have made things pretty hopeless, and instead of that we got the goal and still had a chance.

All our lads started to play up like anything then, and it began to be like the first ten minutes of the match all over again, when we could do everything except score. Only this time we were determined to get the ball into the net, and at last their right back stumbled as he was clearing and Lacey managed to get the ball away from him and just tapped it over the line.

This made us 3—2, so the Grammar were still leading and I knew there couldn't be very much time left.

Freddie Kent asked, 'How much time, sir?' and Mr Stewart called out 'Ten minutes' from the touch-line. So we went at it hammer and tongs and almost immediately forced a corner. We

The shot came back off the crossbar into play

always had hopes of scoring from corners because Freddie Kent is so tall and is really good at heading. He told Rossi to take the corner kick, and for once in his life Rossi put a real beauty in, right in front of the goal and just far enough out not to let the goalie get his hands on it. I saw the sort of look on Freddie Kent's face which meant do or die, and sure enough he managed to get his head to it somehow and nodded it in.

Three all, and five minutes to go! Of course all our blokes along the touch-line went practically mad, and the Grammar shouted too because they still had a good chance of winning, so there was a fantastic row going on all round the field.

It had been a very fast game all the time, and I was longing to hear the final whistle. I kept thinking, 'I can just hang on another half minute and that's all'; but the half minutes went by and that whistle simply *wouldn't* blow.

The Grammar had as much of the play as we did, and Pritchard hit the crossbar with a shot which I felt certain was going to score, so really they had their hard luck as well as us. The shot came back off the crossbar into play, Freddie Kent cleared it to me, and we began to work it up the left wing.

I suppose everybody had been crowding down in our goal like they were when the penalty was taken; anyway, there seemed to be very few defenders about and suddenly was one of those openings which happen sometimes, nobody ever quite knows how or why; the back made a sort of slip in turning, lost a couple of seconds, and one of our blokes was right through on his own with the ball at his feet and nobody at all between him and the goalkeeper.

Worse luck, I was the bloke! I had come well up with the passing movement, and as luck would have it there I was, through on my own and all I had to do, if I could, was to score.

Freddie Kent told me afterwards that I dribbled along quite coolly as though I was at practice. I may have looked cool, but as a matter of fact I could hardly see anything, and I have no idea whether people round the touch-line were yelling their heads off or absolutely silent. I remember that the goal looked about two miles off and that the goalkeeper seemed to fill it up completely, and I was expecting to be tackled from behind all the time.

But I wasn't, and the goal got nearer and I realized that I should have to make up my mind to shoot.

It's a funny thing that when you've got the whole goal to shoot at there's a sort of hypnotism that makes you shoot the ball straight at the goalie.

I was past the stage of being able to mind much where I shot; I just took a terrific boot at the ball and — *missed it completely!* I was in a patch of sticky mud, and as I shot with my left foot (being left-footed naturally) my right went up in the air and I miskicked entirely and sat down on my backside.

As I went down the whistle blew for time.

That was the closest the Grammar ever came to beating us at soccer all the time I was at the Secondary Modern, and it was the only time I had the chance of scoring the winning goal.

When we got back to the dressing-rooms I felt very much like crying my eyes out, but none of the rest of the team seemed to mind, and Mr Stewart said, 'Well, if you had scored, Frank, I think it would have been a bit hard on the Grammar boys; they didn't deserve to lose.'

Dad said, 'Bad luck about that last chance; still you played well all through the game,' and all Mum said was, 'Who was that good-looking man who was umpire?'

'Referee, Mum — referee, for heaven's sake!' Women never do get details about sport right.

THE COPY BOY
David Roberts

Young 'Snow' Thompson was a copy boy employed by the *Daily Chronicle*. He was also a patrol leader in the Scouts and had some quick wits. On one occasion he used them to help his paper get a scoop and for himself earned the gratitude of the senior staff reporter. Not entirely by chance Snow's wits enabled the police to identify a dead man whose past was not what many people thought it.

'Boy!' shouted the night chief sub of the *Daily Chronicle*. He waved a batch of subbed copy in his right hand; his eyes never left his desk. One of the boys standing by the radiator grabbed the copy and 'tinned' it into the tube that shot the story swiftly to hungry machines throbbing below the news room.

The night chief sub never noticed copy boys. He just vetted stories like lightning and yelled 'Boy!' when they were ready for shooting down. His shift was one of the busiest on the *Daily Chronicle*. There were several editions to come out before 3 a.m. and an army of junior and senior subs had to be kept busy. His was a busy life; he might have been forgiven for not noticing 'Snow' Thompson, latest addition to the half-dozen boys who worked in the news room.

Snow's real name was Ralph but only his father and mother called him that! Friends called him Snow because of his very fair hair when he was elected Patrol Leader in the Venture Scouts of the 1st Ryston Scout Troop. He would stick like a leech to any job given to him to do. That is why he was popular in the news room of the *Daily Chronicle*. One of the hardest, toughest jobs in the world lies in the news room of a daily newspaper, where every man has to give of his best until the job is through.

Snow had been on the staff of the *Daily Chronicle* for four months. He found his job most exciting. At sixteen he had certainly had some exciting times in the Venture Scouts, particularly at camp. Last September his Scout Leader suggested that he should apply to the editorial offices of the *Chronicle* for a job. They were advertising for copy boys. He knew Snow's passion for red-hot news was matched by an ability that had already revealed itself in his school magazine, and in reports sent to the editor of the local newspaper.

Snow's reverie was cut short by the strident tones of the night chief sub. Only this time he added 'Come along there, one of you young slackers, this news is burning my fingers!' It was Snow's turn to dash from the radiator, grab the copy and ram it into the tube that was the life-blood of the machines below.

Along the top of the spacious news room ran the long desks of the subs. On the right of them were the desks and phones of the sports department. They always seemed to be feet deep in thin paper tabs that came in at all hours on the tickertape machines, telling the latest news of sport in all parts of the country.

At the other end of the news room were five table-desks belonging to the *Daily Chronicle* staff reporters. They worked in front of the luxuriously fitted office of the news editor. Down the corridor was the library. Snow spent most of his time there when he was on a day-shift. It smelt of printers' ink and paste and gummy scissors that were always snipping something or other from almost every newspaper in the world. When David Dixon, senior staff reporter of the *Chronicle*, showed Snow round on his first night he laughed when he showed him the library and said they called it that because no one could ever find anything there. Snow laughed, too. But later he found that Mr Dixon was only pulling his leg. The untidy library, for all its gumminess, smell of printers' ink and huge teacups on the tables, was regarded as one of the finest newspaper libraries in the country.

Teacups? Yes, that was another thing about the News Room. The reporters and subs drank gallons of tea. Snow and the other boys had to fetch it from the canteen in large enamel jugs. A boy had to edge his way to the front of the canteen drop-counter. Then he shouted, 'Jug of tea, no sugar, Mr Dixon, news room.' The canteen was always full of cheerful machinemen in blue overalls, who seemed to be as fond of tea as the news room staff. The atmosphere reminded Snow of a liner below decks, with the constant hum and throb of machines at work.

Snow dreamed of the day when he would dash down there

through the tobacco smoke and chatter in his shirt sleeves and open collar, like Mr Dixon did when he was hard at work on a big story. He dreamed, too, of Fleet Street, the fabulous home of newspapers, where a thousand ideas are born every day, and most of them die a natural death before a new day dawns.

Snow returned with the tea and was surprised not to find Mr Dixon as usual at his desk in the corner with the large green-shaded light.

'Here, Snow, with that tea,' he heard him shout from the news editor's room.

At eight-twenty on a normal night shift the night news editor sat there at a great walnut desk covered with telephones and type-writers and files and paper. Snow, in fact, rarely saw Mr Could-wood, the night news editor. Sometimes he heard him giving instructions to reporters, or talking at a colossal rate on the phone to correspondents and art editors, and advertising men and compos-ing-room foremen. At midnight, the height of the night-shift, when important editions were going through, it seemed the night news editor was the busiest man in the world. He probably was, but the night chief sub naturally had different views.

'Wait a minute, Snow,' said David Dixon, as he took a mighty gulp of tea. 'Now look here, son. I want you to keep an eye on the phone at my reporters' desk outside. We're already working short-handed, with Joe Grime away, and now Mr Couldwood is down with a filthy cold that looks like flu. Can you do it for me?'

'Certainly, Mr Dixon,' said Snow. 'Would you like me to switch calls through to you in this room?'

'You can do, son,' said David Dixon, grimly. 'But I won't like you for it. There are already two phones in this room. No, just find out who they are and what they want. Switch through if important. Let me know what the others want before you ring off. But if you dare... *if you dare*... miss the most important story of the evening, I'll skin you alive. There won't be much left for that Scout Troop of yours to tear to bits when I've done with you!' He settled back to work, suddenly oblivious of everything except work, like the very good reporter he was.

Snow did not find it an easy job keeping an eye on the phone.

Copy had to be sent spinning post-haste to the composing-room; there were calls for reference books for the subs, and telegrams for the sports department; tea and meals for busy, hungry reporters, a helping hand for one of the other copy boys. There was an odd job to do booking a staff car in the garage for Mr Fildes when he went to cover the paint works fire in Towergate. There were cuttings to find in the library and agency accounts to check over for Mr. Simson. He got through it all, and he loved the urgency of the job.

Then at nine-twenty he took a white slip to Mr Dixon. It had come on the tapes from their London office. In the curious abbreviated language used by newspapers it said that a well-dressed man had been found dead, with suspicions of foul play, according to the police report, in the corridor of a block of flats in South-West London. It was believed he came from Manford district and had Manford office heard anything?

David Dixon tapped a pencil on the walnut desk and looked at the clock. 'H'm. Nine-twenty. And it *might* be a good story. It would happen when I'm up to the eyes with the Russian story.'

'Tell you what,' he said suddenly to Snow. 'Get on to Mr Adams at London office and ask him for further news — if any. Ask him about possible developments. Get all the *facts* absolutely clearly. Bring them to me as soon as you can.' Snow sped to it. He had never had the chance to do anything like this before. He phoned Mr Adams, and saw a new angle on the mysterious discovery in South-West London. The police had been unable to trace the man's identity. There were no traces of identity on the body. The only clue was a tailor's tab inside the jacket. It was an old suit and the name was indistinct. But it seemed the suit was a good quality Cheviot tweed and had been made by a tailor named James. The tab read 'F. and H. James, High Class Tailors, of Seaway.' The word Seaway was very obscure. The name might easily have been Seethay, or Seemay, or S.W.7. The police were sure to be investigating all these possibilities, Mr Adams said.

Snow told all this to Mr Dixon down to the very last and latest detail. David Dixon drummed his nails on the desk and frowned. Was it worth while spending a lot of valuable time on it at such a critical stage of the evening's work? Was it a red herring? Was it a good story? Was it worth following up? Mr Dixon looked at Snow.

'We'll take a chance, son, on this,' he said.

'I'm glad, sir,' said Snow, pleased.

'We'll do the obvious thing for a start. Try Seaway, fifty-two miles from here. Important seaside place. We've a good correspondent there. Compton's his name. Get on to him. Ask... no, I'll ask him myself. I'll see if he's got on to the Seaway police. Keep careful contact with London, they're sure to have some stuff later. With a bit of luck we should have this through in time for the North-Western Edition.'

'What time does that come off?' asked Snow, suddenly feeling very professional.

'One-forty a.m.,' said David Dixon. 'Just giving the vans time to catch the two-seven parcel express. Now go to it. And don't make any mistakes.'

David Dixon informed the Night Chief Sub that Snow was working on the job for him and that it might take some time. So Snow was relieved of other jobs. In less than fifteen minutes he found by telephone that Compton was in at Seaway. A newspaper has correspondents (men who know districts well and live on the spot) in every part of the country, but it can never guarantee that the correspondent will be in when they put the call through to him. Good newspaper correspondents never fail to make arrangements about telephone calls when they go out; now there is an excellent system working for doctors and newspapermen at local telephone exchanges.

Mr Compton replied briefly to Snow. 'I can't say we know of him here. Nor do I know of any tailor here of that name, either. Seaway's a tidy place, you know.'

'Yes,' said Snow, certain Mr Compton must know far more about it than he did. He put him on to Mr Dixon, and thought hard with the aid of a pencil and a pad of paper.

Supposing the man's suit had been made by a Seaway tailor? The tailor might have a note of the suit, the date he made it, and for whom. Or would he? 'Yes, he would,' thought Snow. (He remembered a detective game they had played at a meeting last winter.) No, the name was wrong. It must have been someone else. The police wanted the man's identity too. It would be fine if the *Chronicle* could get an "exclusive". It meant such a lot for a newspaper's prestige when they carried better stories than their rivals. Supposing Seaway wasn't the place? Well, they would have to start on Seathay, a tiny place 38 miles away on the other side of the county. Seemay would be even worse. It was nearly 200 miles away. If it really was S.W.7 (and the man had been found in London) then the police would surely be on to it right away by now.

'Compton's going to see if he can trace the tailor in Seaway,' shouted David Dixon, from the News Editor's room, to Snow. 'Hang on there for London, Snow.'

Snow did hang on. In seven minutes London office were on. They only knew that the police suspected the man was a Londoner and that the tailor's tab was really S.W.7. Meanwhile would Manford office please carry on.

Snow took the latest information to David Dixon.

'This Seaway possibility is not yet a red herring,' Mr Dixon said. 'Suppose the police do carry out their investigations intensively in London? Supposing we find the story we want in Seaway...'

Snow asked a simple question.

'But won't they make enquiries in Seaway at the same time?' he said.

'Of course they will, boy,' said Mr Dixon. 'But we can as well! After all, it's not easy to carry on an investigation at this time of the night.'

Suddenly the phone on David Dixon's desk outside rang, loudly and urgently. Snow dashed to it. The call was from Mrs Compton. Mr Compton had phoned his home to say that there *was* a firm of tailors in Seaway named James. They had a lock-up shop in Devon Street. As it was then twelve-ten no one was there. Mr Compton was trying to trace them... or rather 'him'. There was in fact only one James in the business now. But Compton was on the job. He would ring again.

Snow made a note of the new information.

In fifteen minutes Mr Compton himself rang the news room. He had discovered that Mr Horace James, Tailor of Devon Street, Seaway, lived in Shanklin Heights. But Shanklin Heights was a long road near the end of the promenade. No one knew exactly where James lived. There were many private hotels and a few blocks of flats there. It was going to be a tough job. Mr Compton would try all the houses first, and ring again. He was hot on the trail.

Snow made rapid notes on a pad and took all the latest details to David Dixon.

'Grand,' he said. 'Don't miss *anything*. We want a top-line news splash on this.'

'Can I try an idea of my own?' said Snow, rather nervously.

'Surely you can,' said David Dixon, grinning. 'What is it?'

'Well, it might take Mr Compton a long time to try to find that house, even with directories and local information. Either Mr James isn't on the phone at home or else he lives in a flat. I thought it might be a good idea to try a few of the shops near James in Devon Street and see if they know anything of his movements or his private address.'

'Good for you, Snow,' said David Dixon, obviously pleased. 'Try it out by all means. I shan't be through with this story from New York for a good half-hour or so yet.'

Snow went to the library at once. He quickly found the current section of the directory and traced James's number in the Seaway section in the same way that Compton had, and no doubt the police also. Obviously no one was there and it was no use phoning at all. Snow searched down and along the address columns till he came to others in Devon Street, Seaway. James's number was 456. He found a butcher's shop at 241. Obviously no good. Still he carried on. There was a ladies' wool shop at 780. Devon Street must be a long one. And here was a newsagent at 438! That would be the same side as James. A newsagent usually lives on the premises, and knows everyone in his district. What was the name? Blakey? Good! Snow put a call through to Mr Blakey, Newsagent.

'Difficulty on the line. Trying to connect you,' purred the operator.

'Good,' said Snow, and held on.

At last the ringing tone came. Durr-durr. Durr-durr. Durr-durr. Was no one there then? *Durr—*

'Blakey's, Newsagents, speaking. Can I do anything for you?' said a pleasant voice.

'Rather,' said Snow, enthusiastically, and then remembered suddenly that he had to be very dignified. 'This is the *Daily Chronicle* speaking.' It did not sound like his voice at all, he kept thinking. 'We are anxious to trace the address of Mr Horace James, a tailor, who, I understand, keeps a lock-up shop quite near you. Do you know him — please?'

Mr Blakey was accustomed to calls from newspaper people. He didn't waste any time.

'Why, yes,' he said. 'He's one of my regular customers and a good one, too. Why, I saw him about seven tonight. He'd been working late. He's a tailor, you know.'

'Do you know where he is now?' said Snow, excitedly.

'Well, have you tried his flat?' asked Mr Blakey.

'It's not in the directory. Do you know its number?' said Snow.

'Yes. You might get him. The number is Seaway 72064 and the address is 46F, Shanklin Heights. But he did say he was going to spend the weekend with his daughter.'

Snow realized in dismay that it was Friday night.

'Well, I'll try Shanklin Heights... I think, Mr Blakey,' he said. 'And thank you very much indeed for all your help.'

'Hang on a moment and I'll check the phone number again,' said Mr Blakey. 'I've got the number right here. Yes, 72064, that's it. 'Bye now.'

Snow put the phone call through to the flat and then reported to Mr Dixon. Snow, strangely enough, was wondering exactly how much a year the *Daily Chronicle* spent on phone calls. He soon found himself talking to the letting office at 46F, Shanklin Heights. The porter sounded suspicious when he realized that a daily newspaper was on the hunt for Mr James.

'Yes, he does live here,' he said. 'But what do you want him for?

Mr James is a quiet sort of a man and I know he doesn't like publicity.'

'One moment, please,' said Snow, and put the call through to Mr Dixon. He felt he could handle the porter better. Meanwhile he noted that he had already found out something about Mr James! He was quiet and shunned publicity. In that case he might refuse to say anything at all.

David Dixon dashed from the news editor's room to Snow's desk. 'We'll get something really hot on this,' he said, in the urgent but cheerful way he had when there was real news in the air.

'Now that porter says James left to go and see his daughter in Merrin's about twenty minutes ago. He thought it would take him a good forty minutes to get there, as he's having some trouble with his car. It would be a good idea to get on to Merrin's and see if we can get James for an interview on the phone as soon as he gets there. Probably we'll get him before anyone else does. For the porter tells me no one else has yet been after James at Shanklin Heights.'

Snow was clearly enjoying every minute of it.

'Shall I get him right away at Merrin's, Mr Dixon?' he asked.

'Yes,' said Mr Dixon briefly.

'Oh, and there's another thing that occurred to me, Mr Dixon,' said Snow. 'I don't suppose the porter at Shanklin Heights would have told you so much if the police had already been there to see Mr James, would he? I think he'd have kept pretty mum about the whole business.'

'That's true, son,' said David Dixon, slowly. 'Good for you. Carry on...'

Snow did carry on. He had a brisk talk with the caretaker of Merrin's Super Bungalows Limited. 'No,' said the caretaker. 'There's no Mr James here now. He might have been coming to see his daughter. She lives at *Sunnyside*, I know, but he certainly isn't here and...'

Snow found himself cut off. His brain worked quickly. It was getting late and he knew David Dixon would like the story completed as soon as possible. Perhaps... yes... Snow quickly made a call to Mr James's shop in Devon Street. His bluff call came off. *Mr James himself answered first time.*

It was a strange request, thought Mr James. As a matter of fact his *firm was* F. and H. James. 'F'. was his father, who died many years ago. He, Mr James, was the 'H.' part. It had always been a family tradition to keep a pattern of every hand-tailored suit made by James of Seaway. It would probably take some time to trace but they would certainly have it in the shop; there would also be a sample of the cloth attached to the reference. This would give the name and address of the manufacturer in Scotland, ruminated Mr James. Best thing for the police to do, then, was to compare the cloth underneath the lapels, where it didn't wear so much, with the sample in his possession.

Half an hour later a typed story lay on David Dixon's desk ready for the sub to go through. It told how the *Daily Chronicle* had traced an unknown dead man in London and discovered that he was Henry E. Spergson of Burnham-on-Trent. It told of possible surprising police developments, of Henry Spergson's mysterious activities in the Midlands and North. The story was a very exclusive interview 'By Our Special Correspondent' with Mr James, a Seaway tailor who had made a Cheviot tweed suit for him two years previously, which Spergson was wearing when his body was found. The police report showed that Spergson was only an alias, and that he was known under other names. The *Daily Chronicle* sub made a front-page news splash of it. Told a story of a thrilling chase through the night to catch Mr James, the vital link in the story. No other paper had the story at all, which explained David Dixon's beaming smile.

At last the heavy slog of the night shift eased and soon Snow returned from the canteen with a tray containing Mr Dixon's ample supper. He found him enjoying a quiet pipe, with his chair far back and his feet on his desk. He was looking at a large piece of paper in his hand. David Dixon had to laugh at Snow's astonishment as he unfolded the paper which he gave to him.

It was a handwritten *Daily Chronicle* placard of the stock type used outside every newsagent's shop in Britain. On it were four words, in heavy black splash type: COPY BOY MAKES GOOD.

126

DEATH OF A GANGSTER
Alan C. Jenkins

Here is a nature story with a difference. Deep down in the river was this gangster's domain, where he took his captured prey. He was without mercy, and was to learn in futile flight the terrible ruthlessness of the fate he had brought to others. Yet he did not die because his luck was out, otherwise a boy on the river-bank might have been saved a soaking.

He had many thousands of brothers and sisters; fortunately for the river, few of them had survived. Most of them had perished as eggs; some had hatched out and enjoyed a brief career as young pike, only to be snatched up by kingfisher or heron and even, it must be admitted, by their own relations who, like all their kind, were inveterate cannibals.

This particular pike not only survived but flourished and, by dint of ferocity, cunning, and a certain amount of good fortune, had attained a weight of twenty pounds and a length of something over three feet. His body bore various marks in evidence of his violent past: above his dorsal fin ran a deep furrow where a heron had tried to spear him many seasons before; on his side were sundry little dents where he had been given a volley of Number Five shot...

Nothing could have been more idyllic in appearance than the river he frequented, with its banks of purple loosestrife and brooklime, its nodding willows, the cows wading knee-deep at its edge, and the swallows on the wing dipping to drink.

But the placid surface of the river concealed a jungle in which the death of one creature meant life to another, a jungle over which the pike lorded it, a green monster of a fish whose vicious, undershot jaw, flat brow and cruel, rapacious eyes summed up his character.

Though he patrolled the river constantly, his favourite practice was to lie in ambush, skulking among the streaming waterweeds which camouflaged his olive-green body, with its wavy bands and yellow spots, admirably. Everything was fair game to this gangster — fish, fur or feather — nothing was spurned. The water voles that plied to and fro across the river, the moor-hen fledgelings paddling out for the first time, the sticklebacks guarding their strange nests, all went in danger of their lives. The river was in thrall to this dusky green gangster. The only time the creatures that inhabited it could go their way in peace was when the pike was digesting some particularly gluttonous meal and then he lay comatose among the reeds, his evil jaw half open, his baleful eyes staring blankly.

Obviously, with such a monster holding sway, there was little chance of other fish in that particular stretch of water reaching any considerable proportions. However, it happened that one day a large trout made its way through the pike's territory, a sleek, silvery, fat eight-pounder, himself something of a cannibal at times and always ready to seize whatever came to hand.

The pike, lurking as usual in his vantage-point among the reeds, watched the trout pass, though his menacing eyes betrayed no sign of the eager interest that stirred in him.

The trout was too formidable a prey to be attacked lightly. The pike eyed him cautiously before taking action. Lazily the trout cruised through the dark jungle of the water, a flirt of his tail, a flicker of pelvic fins carrying him on his leisurely course.

When the appropriate moment came, the pike struck hard and swiftly. He knew well the value of the surprise attack. A green, thrusting, menacing shadow, he came sweeping up out of his hideout, hoping to take the trout unawares from beneath. Savage jaws agape, he seized the trout squarely across the body.

Too late the startled fish tried to wrench free. A fearful struggle ensued. The water swirled and boiled, the green weeds waved and shuddered frantically.

Desperately the trout, writhing in agony from the pike's grip, strove gainst his doom. Strong though the pike was, he had to exert all his brutal strength to overpower the trout. He was fighting for a meal; the trout was fighting for his life.

With a terrible effort and at the expense of a great gash of flesh from his belly, the trout contrived to tear himself free. While his life-blood stained the swirling water, he darted down to seek refuge in the reeds.

Relentlessly the pike harried him out, thrusting and jostling him along with his ugly snout until he could seize hold of him again. In despair, the trout turned at bay and tried to defend himself, but though he parried the pike's thrust and nicked him in the gills, he was overborne by sheer weight.

Torn, bleeding, gasping, the trout was hunted up and down, through the reeds, up to the surface, down again to the dark bed of the river.

Again and again the pike seized him in those powerful jaws, only to lose his grip again as the panic-stricken trout, at whatever cost, tore himself free.

For fully half an hour the trout resisted, but he was rapidly becoming exhausted, and presently gaped feebly, incapable of further effort.

The trout was still alive when the pike began to swallow him head-first...

That act of gluttony lasted two days and the pike lay among the reeds in a state of torpor while the river enjoyed a prolonged respite from his gangsterism.

When at last, sluggish and surfeited, he stirred into activity again, he was, like most creatures that have over-eaten, in an extremely irritable mood.

Normally, he was anything but rash, but he was so bemused by the excess he had recently indulged in, that, true to type, he could not resist dashing upon the first prey he set eyes on as he cruised indolently along the river.

It was the most insignificant morsel imaginable, a worm, and could not have been expected to cause any trouble. In point of fact, it was extremely deadly...

Greedily the pike sucked in the worm — and immediately lashed the water in a frenzy of anger and pain and fear, for the worm was impaled on a steel hook, and the steel hook was now firmly embedded in the pike's undershot jaw.

The pike plunged down in fury to the depths of the river, trying to rid himself of this strange, searing enemy that would not let go. He grovelled on the bed, rubbed his jaw along the gravel, twisted, writhed, thrashed the water, all in vain; the hook tore through his jaw as relentlessly as the pike had seized the trout.

Above the surface the reel whirred madly, the line rushed out. The boy who was holding the greenheart rod grinned in incredulous delight as he realized what a monster he had hooked. The grin changed to an expression of grim determination as the battle raged more and more violently.

The pike lunged and darted, crossed to the other side, struggled upstream like a waterhorse. But all his efforts availed him naught. He blundered off powerfully, only to be brought to a halt at the extent of the line. The greenheart curved in a dangerous crescent. The boy was forced to wade out knee-deep, thigh-deep. His arms seemed on the point of parting from their sockets.

Up and down the river the struggle continued. The pike alternately sulked and fought. Had he not been still so satiated from his meal, he could have struggled to much greater effect.

The rod bent and shuddered like a sapling in a gale. The boy gritted his teeth and fought for all he was worth. He could already see that fish in a glass case. He knew that if he held on long enough it would exhaust itself and then he could gaff it.

But it was not to be...

Abruptly the strain on the line ceased; the boy fell back in the water; with a cry of chagrin he scrambled to his feet, soaked through, and cheated of his prey. The trace connecting hook and line had parted, chafed by the frenzied grovelling of the pike against stone and stream-bed.

The pike was free, though the hook still clung viciously to him. For a moment he was so dazed by the battle that he floated aimlessly, a target for the gaff if the boy had been quick enough.

Then he recovered his senses and went flickering away through the rippling water.

He was frantic with anger and terror, for no amount of rubbing against the bank would loosen the hook. Sulkily he settled down in his favourite ambush to recuperate his powers.

The pike sulked in his hiding-place until evening, and when he did bestir himself, it was only at the prompting of his voracious appetite.

He began once more to think in terms of a suitable victim. One came soon enough, a dabchick fledgeling fussily paddling out of the reeds on this ocean of a river as it must have seemed.

The dabchick was a ridiculously easy morsel for this gangster of the river. Beyond a feeble *keek* of protest, it put up no resistance at all. A savage bite, a few convulsive gulps, and the fledgeling, only just out of the floating nest of waterweeds, had gone the way of so many other victims that had contributed to the pike's enormous proportions.

Somehow, in the process of seizing the dabchick, the hook had worked loose and the pike felt better at being rid of that searing barb. He cruised upstream in search of further game, a long, dark, sinister shape, a veritable shark of this quiet river with its wavy ribbons of weed and its kingcups gleaming at the water's edge.

Other hunters were abroad that night. Along the river a bitch otter went hunting. She had only recently come to the river and had borne her three cubs in the roots of a ruined alder struck by lightning many years previously but still dabbling its feet in the water.

The cubs were thriving rapidly and the otter had to hunt far and wide to keep them content. The river-bank showed many signs of her depredations.

She was seized with a terrible excitement at the sight of the pike, for she had never encountered such an immense fish before, and he could only have been a few pounds lighter than herself.

In instant panic, as the fluted waters warned him of the approach of this danger, the pike had turned about and gone streaking downstream as fast as fin and tail would propel him.

Graceful and supple, as if made from water itself rather than flesh and bone and fur, the otter plunged in pursuit, driven by her deft webbed paws, while her long, tapering tail acted as a rudder.

Down through the green underworld of the river fish and animal flickered and curved, while a chain of bubbles told of their progress. In mortal fear, for he realized he was in greater danger than ever before, the pike jinked and dodged, swerved and doubled in an attempt to elude his pursuer.

Lithe and sinuous, every muscle of her body taut, the otter swept down. Under water she could close her nostrils at will; her ears, too, were sealed by folds of skin. She could see several times her own length in front of her, and when she nosed under the sides of boulders and ledges, her sensitive whiskers, longer and stiffer than those of a cat, told her where her prey was hiding.

The pike, bold gangster in his forays against his own victims, skulked cravenly through the fronds and ribbons of weed. He finally sidled into the shadow of a derelict bucket kicked there by tramp or gypsy and backed out furtively, hoping to double behind the questing otter.

But she noticed the faint movement and, turning in her length, fell upon the pike and seized him above the dorsal fin.

He knew terror then, as all his many victims had known it in their time. He lashed clear with the pent-up strength of his powerful body, and the otter, taken by surprise at his weight, lost her grip.

She struck again immediately, however, savage with blood-lust. The pike writhed away and leapt desperately out of the water. She took him again between the pectoral fins as he fell back, and the two long bodies, fur and fish, merged together in a Catherine-wheel of bubbles.

Breathless, the otter was forced to rise to the surface to vent, whereupon the pike sank to the bed and sought shelter in a crevice he knew only too well — ironically, one from which he had ambushed many of his unsuspecting victims...

He would ambush no more: gashed, bleeding, spent, he failed to conceal himself before the otter came weaving down again and drove him out.

Long into the night the pike fought for his life while the im-

The otter plunged in pursuit, driven by her deft webbed paws

passive river flowed like a shroud about him. Above the surface bats flickered in pursuit of moths; the barn owls cried to each other in their hunting; the water voles huddled in their bankside tunnels.

The otter had her quarry firmly across the shoulders now. His ugly jaws gaped in agony. Exerting all her strength now, she endeavoured to drag him bodily out of the river, but the bank was too steep.

Knowing he was spent, she let him go and the river bore him downstream where the bank was shallower. He rolled feebly over so that his pallid belly was exposed, but he could struggle no more, and the otter dragged him out with great difficulty through the rustling reeds and on to the bank among the water avens and the wild flags.

While he stirred and lashed convulsively in his death throes, she crouched there panting and listening anxiously to the sounds of the night.

Then she began to feed eagerly, crunching savagely with her white fangs. Many victims of the gangster were avenged that night.

FUGITIVES IN SANCTUARY
E. K. Seth-Smith

Mun and Jasp, otherwise Edmund and Jasper Tudor, were two brothers taken to the famous Sanctuary of Westminster during the perilous days of the Wars of the Roses. To them comes the man they know as the Whistling Gentleman, Owen Tudor. All three Tudors were to play their part in English history, and Edmund's son Henry was to end the Wars of the Roses and create the new Tudor rose when he eventually became Henry VII. What happens to Mun and Jasp when they leave the Sanctuary is told in *The Black Tower*, from which this story is taken.

Old Noe, as he was called, a nickname given him on account of his likeness to the patriarch Noah as he appeared in mystery plays, had been thirty-seven years in sanctuary, and his real name had been long forgotten. One of Richard the Second's gay young nobles, he had followed the unhappy king until his army had melted away, and then for fear of Henry of Bolingbroke had ridden for days and nights to find safety among the bats and cobwebs of the Sanctuary of Westminster. It had unhinged his wits a little, that disastrous day and despairing ride. Forced at that time to find a bed in one of the ramshackle roof huts, he had chosen to remain there even when room could have been found for him below, for he felt a kind of reassurance in the hanging bell just above him even though it seldom rang. He could sound it, he felt, if Duke Henry were to attack the tower.

It was useless to tell him, as the Tower Warden and Poll and others had told him, that his Duke, King Henry the Fourth, was long ago dead. Sometimes he remembered it, but more often forgot it. Other refugees, taking the air on the roof, had told him of the French War and of the astounding victory of Agincourt, but the impression of such things passed. And that king too was dead, they had told him, but in his lucid moments he remembered that the House of Lancaster was still reigning — and he remained on the roof.

He had always wakened very early. He had clean forgotten the disturbances of the night before, and in the dimness of his hut he noticed nothing unusual about the straw heaped against the farther wall. From time to time folk had slept there and in the other roof sheds, but for a long time now he had been alone, content with the cats and his memories.

This morning, as usual, Old Noe got up, reached for his sanctuary gown — patched and of every shade of grey, brown and purple — with the white keys of St Peter just visible still on the left shoulder, mumbled a Paternoster, felt for his stick, and without changing his nightcap hobbled out to his usual seat, a bench against the parapet. The sun was warm, the birds were chirping, the swarming streets below were still quiet, and the Abbey bells and the bells of St Margaret's and St Stephen's filled the air pleasantly and soothingly. Old Noe closed his eyes as he sat with both hands upon his stick and let himself dream of the days when he was young, and when it seemed always to be summer at King Richard's court — and the King...

'Fair as a maid,' he murmured, talking aloud as do all the old and lonely, 'and dainty in his dress — and the little Queen — so grave of face — lovely gown — and the walls bright-painted — roof with golden stars — and the minstrels and singers — he loved music, the best in Christendom it was, the best in Christendom — always singing, singing there was...'

Half asleep and half awake, he thought he heard it still; the singing in the chapel, was it? He thought he heard the. *Gloria*. But no, they were dancing in the gardens and singing, 'Merry it is while summer lasts.'

He opened his eyes and stared and rubbed them and stared again. He was not at court; he was old and sitting on the leads under the belfry tower. But in front of him two wild elves were dancing, with red curls shaking and shining, two imps in shirts with their hose half down to their ankles, dancing, skipping, and singing snatches of psalms, clear and spontaneous as thrushes.

Mun and Jasp, waking and creeping out of their straw, had found themselves on top of the world, and in the wonder of it they had forgotten the dark steps and all the frights and shocks of yesterday. The light, the space, the sense of adventure, went to their heads like wine.

They saw that the old man was awake and came bounding up to him; then, abashed by his age and oddity, they stood each on one leg, fidgeting, but too well-mannered to speak first.

'So ye came last night. I do remember,' said Old Noe slowly. 'So the Duke was after ye, was he? Never ye fear. This place is the safest. Ye see,' he whispered almost gleefully, 'there's the bell. We could ring it if he came. Was it the Duke, then?'

'Uncle brought us, sir,' said Jasp.

'We don't know why,' said Mun.

'Maybe the swan,' said Jasp cryptically, 'but Parnel didn't hurt it.'

'We didn't mean,' said Mun, 'to offend the King's Majesty.' Then, as though that was, after all, of little account, 'Sir — sir — is this the top of the world?'

'Is it the *whole world?*' demanded Jasper, gazing out over the sea of jutting gables stretching on every side, and Mun, pointing to a long, high roof shining above the mist, added, with some vague recollection of the lessons of Sir Thomas the Rector.

'Is yon Jerusalem? And is that the sea yonder?'

The old man laughed. It was so long since he had laughed that it sounded a little ghostly.

'Neither Jerusalem nor the sea — no, nor even London Town, which is a bigger place, so they tell me. This is but a village, they say, but for the Abbey and the Sanctuary and the Palace. It's Westminster, you see, child. That's the roof of the Abbey Church. Over there,' he waved his stick — 'the King's great hall. The water? That's Thames River, floweth down through London. No, child' — to Jasper, who was running round the parapet and peering over — 'don't look that way. All that side is Sanctuary. Knaves and cheats and naughty folk do live there — nasty — foul places be there.'

'We know — we saw them,' said Edmund, and wrinkled his nose.

'And don't hang over that side,' urged Old Noe. 'All the smells do come up there. It's there all the tower muck is thrown. The fellows paid to clear it are a lazy set of knaves. When the sun is hot, then it's hard to find where to sit.'

'But — the King's great hall?' persisted Edmund. 'Doth the King live there?'

'In the hall? No, child. Who knows where the King may be? Windsor maybe, or Eltham, or Kingston— —'

'But that is his palace?'

'The palace? It's a city in itself. You might wander and wander and lose yourself there, so they do tell me. And there's a little postern,' he rambled on, 'just a little low gate, leads from Sanctuary right into it. Folk tell me, it's like passing from Purgatory to Paradise to go through that little gate. But— —' he pulled himself up and a frightened look came into his eyes— — 'it wouldn't be safe. It wouldn't be safe.'

But Jasper had caught the word "palace".

'Does the monster live there?' he demanded, his eyes large with a half-delicious fear. 'Isbaddaden? Him that calls himself Humphrey on Sundays? Him that folks call the Good Jook because they don't know?'

The old man screwed up his eyes in a vague, puzzled way as though trying to capture some elusive idea.

'Humphrey — Humphrey — it used to be Henry,' he mumbled. 'I grow old and forget names. They talk of him sometimes, the folk from below when they come up to take the air. Duke Humphrey! Yes, that's what they say — in peril of their lives from Duke Humphrey. He's a bad one, did ye say, boy? Hush!' He looked round with a sort of frightened cunning. 'Don't say it! Someone might hear you.'

'There are only the cats,' objected Edmund.

'Ah, but he hath spies, they say. Duke Henry has — or is it Humphrey? And his wife, they say, is a witch and weaves spells against the King's life. Hark! There's the Matin bell. Ye must go down.'

'Down?' they asked blankly.

'Down to the chapel. It's the Abbot's orders. The folk in the tower must hear Matins and Vespers. We are here by favour of the Lord Abbot of Westminster.'

'But down — all those steps? Right down to where we supped last night?' They had grown quite white and pitiful at the very thought. 'They were so dark.'

'Nay, there are two chapels. The upper chapel for Matins, the lower for Vespers. It's only the first steps. Why, before I grew stiff I was up and down those steps as easily as puss here. But now I bide here and say the Matins of Our Lady. Be off now! But best tie up your hosen first.'

'Jasp broke his points, dancing,' said Mun, 'but I think I can tie them,' and he wrestled bravely with the strings that held Jasper's hose to his strong linen shirt. And then at the sound of a second bell they screwed up their courage and began to scramble cautiously through the trap-door.

The darkness was a little less fearsome by day, as a deep, narrow slit here and there in the thickness of the wall let in light enough to guide their feet. Rather breathless, they found themselves on the landing, where a lantern hung and figures, still and ghostly and quiet and all gowned in shadow-colour, were passing from their bedrooms into the upper chapel. It had no window and was lighted only by the red lamp hanging below the pyx. Mun and Jasp crept in with the rest and knelt close together on musty rushes, listening impatiently to the mumbled prayers of the cassocked monk from the abbey whom they had seen pass in with the rest. But Parson at home had drilled them into good behaviour — better, in fact, than that of the people who whispered and sighed and yawned in front of them — and it was soon over. Coming out, they found themselves grabbed by Poll.

'Come down when ye hear the dinner-bell,' she growled. 'But what a work I'm having to find gowns for brats like you!'

Then, as they escaped and began to scramble up the steps, eager to get back to the sunshine and the cats, she said (whether to herself or a fellow servant they didn't see):

'There's great folks mixed up in this — by my Holy Dame there is.'

'Mun,' said Jasper, between his panting breaths, as they forged upward again, 'Mun, when can we go and see all those great houses? I want to go through that little door. I wouldn't be afeared of the monster — would you?'

'There's no monster. It's just a tale,' said his brother.

'But there *is* a jook,' persisted Jasper, 'who calls himself Humphrey. Master Noe said so.'

'We must watch,' said Edmund, 'when they open that great door Maybe dinner-time.'

In the vaulted hall, poorly lit even by day by the only real window in the whole building, two meals were spread daily — meat and bread for dinner, with perhaps a dish of onions or bean porridge; broth and bread for supper, with thin ale. On the farther table such dainties as capons and geese and eel-pies appeared, but they were not for Mun and Jasp. The tower refugees were people of rank who had had the ill-luck to offend the all-powerful Lords of the Council and who felt it safer to be within strong walls than to live like the more ordinary law-breakers in one of the houses outside. The whole tower had been designed as a great double church in which those whose lives were in danger might take shelter under the protection of the Church and of St Peter, eating and sleeping as and where they could, but, as the numbers of those who feared to go outside had increased, parts had been set aside for dining, kitchen, and sleeping quarters, the chapels being screened off by partitions of carved and partially open woodwork. By daylight the place, dingy and chilly as it was, with its odd lights and deep shadows, had a dismal, curious beauty. But the boys preferred the roof and the sunlight.

At dinner-time the great iron-plated door remained shut, to their great disappointment. When was it opened? Mun asked of the ghostly lady beside him, who sat closely wrapped in her lined gown and ate very little. About sunset, she said, when some liked to go forth and take the air. By supper-time the boys were able to face the steps quite boldly, though they stepped cautiously at the bottom for fear of toads. They ate their broth quickly, their eyes upon the door.

'Now,' whispered Edmund, as they saw the door swing open and one or two got up from the table and went towards it.

They slipped out in the shadow of two stout gentlemen, but in a moment Poll's manly strides were after them. Seizing each by the collar, she shook them angrily and threatened that if ever they put their noses outside again she would report them to the Lord Abbot, who would certainly lock them both in their cellars. Not for a moment did they doubt her word as they crept forlornly back.

'Another time,' said Edmund, 'we'll be quicker.'

Vespers in the lower chapel ended their day, muttered as before, but this time there was a quavering attempt to sing the Office-hymn and the boys, who had been taught it by Sir Thomas at home, startled the congregation with their clear, tuneful *Te lucis*. Music could always restore their spirits. Two ladies nodded to one another, and one remarked aloud, 'They'll not sing long here, who-ever they may be.'

The second morning passed somehow with the help of the cats and of the pieces of stone and rubble from the crumbling parapet from which they built a fort. But in the afternoon it rained, and they had to amuse themselves in one of the empty sheds. After a while Edmund tired of playing and sat with his brooding look or, as Aunt Mabily would have said, 'in one of his sulks,' doing nothing at all. And then Jasper, tired of chasing the black cat asked the questions Mun had been dreading, 'Mun, when will someone come to take us home? Will Parnel come, do you think, if Uncle doesn't? I don't think we shall get through that little door, never. Poll is always watching.' Mun only grunted and had nothing to say.

For in the long hours he had had time to realize that Noe had been in Sanctuary more years, many more years than he himself had lived. The thought suggested dreadful possibilities. And if they could slip out and get back to Mere Farm? And what use to go back to Uncle, who said he was no kin to them? For though at first Mun too had felt vaguely that some day, some time, somebody would fetch them away, the frightening thought came again and again that perhaps that would never be. Even if the Whistling Gentleman was somewhere in the Palace they could never find him. There was Parnel, yes — but Parnel had gone away, and perhaps she knew nothing about them. As for going through that little door into the wonderful world of the palace ('like Paradise,' Master Noe had said) in their Sanctuary gowns — for Poll had found some for them and had roughly stitched and shortened them, but yet they were much too large and worried them dreadfully — they would be caught and sent back at once.

145

And therefore Edmund brooded, till his head felt very hot, and when the bell clanged hollowly down below said peevishly that he wanted no supper and was not going down.

'Why? I'm hungry!' protested Jasper.

'I don't like the folk,' said Edmund.

Nor for that matter did Jasper. There was the lady who never spoke, and one that talked all the time to herself in a low gabble, and the man who laughed suddenly and loudly at nothing. The other women gossiped about their children or grumbled at the food; the men discussed old battles or hawking, or the cows and crops on their home manors. Old Noe, with his rambling talk of King Richard's court, was more cheerful company.

'But I want some supper,' pleaded Jasp.

It ended in their sharing the basket of cold scraps that Old Noe had brought up to him once a day by Poll, who had a contemptuous liking for the old man. But Edmund was not hungry. He had eaten very little at dinner-time, a fact that Poll had noted. When the bells of the churches were ringing the curfew she came stumping and grumbling up the stairs with a pot of something black and evil-smelling that she called treacle of Venice, and forced a large spoonful down Edmund's throat. It made him very sick, and he tossed and talked all night.

In the morning Jasper, who had been terribly frightened, was reassured to see him get up, pull on his hose, and go out on to the leads, where he sat himself down rather languidly by Old Noe on one of the logs which earlier refugees had arranged as seats against the parapet. But he wouldn't play, and Jasp had to arrange his bold bowmen, or the sticks which had to serve for them, according to his own fancy on the walls of his castle. As he played he whistled, rather forlornly, partly to show off his new accomplishment and partly to keep up his spirits.

'Don't whistle that tune!' snapped Edmund peevishly. 'Why must you whistle, anyhow?'

Jasp gazed at him.

'But I thought — I thought you had a liking for that tune.'

'No, I haven't. Not — not today.'

He must be in one of his sulks, thought Jasper sadly, and there

146

is nothing to be done about it. He didn't know that that tune was unbearable to Mun because it reminded him that the Whistling Gentleman might come again to Mere Farm, and not find them.

The Matin bell went, but neither boy went down — not that Jasper regretted that. Old Noe and the cats dozed as usual, the yellow one on Old Noe's lap and the black one on Edmund's thin knees. Jasper took to whistling the tune again very softly under his breath.

There were footsteps on the stone stairs below, and Jasp, thinking it might be Poll come to rate them for neglecting morning chapel, squared his shoulders stubbornly and did not turn round. Mun, stroking the cat, took no notice either.

But whoever it was came up through the trap-door with a bound that was quite different from Poll's lumbering movements, and both children looked round, startled, to see a wild figure swooping towards them, both arms outstretched like a windmill, a ragged man who caught them both in a fierce hug, pressing his bearded face against their smooth cheeks. They screamed, kicked and struggled.

At that the man loosed them, but stood holding a shoulder of each, while he poured out words in an unknown tongue, of which they could distinguish only 'Edmund' and 'Jasper.' Then suddenly letting them go he spoke in English, laughing a little unsteadily.

'I frightened ye? Poor imps, it was too bad. Ye didn't know me in these rags — and what wonder? Do ye know me now?'

And then Mun knew his voice, and a weight as heavy as the world slid off him. Rags or no rags, he was the same. The Whistling Gentleman!

After that they were all very comfortable together. He sat on the log with one boy on each of his knees, and they talked and talked till dinner-time. He was sorry he had frightened them, he said, but he would have a barber called in to shave him, and find a gown instead of these rags.

How did he get his coat torn? Jasp asked.

He shrugged his shoulders. He had quick, expressive movements. 'Newgate bars are narrow, and the walls have spikes,' he said.

'What is Newgate?'

'A prison.'

'Who sent you there?' they inquired indignantly.

'Ah! That is a long tale. Let's talk of something else. Where do you sleep?'

They showed him their corner, where the blankets were tossed about the straw-heap; and he examined the other sheds distastefully. 'We will have this one repaired,' he said, looking up at the holes of the least derelict, 'and better beds brought, one for me and one for you. We'll get it fit for princes.'

The children never doubted it. The Whistling Gentleman could do anything; even a prison couldn't hold him.

After a time Old Noe woke up and had to be introduced. He did the honours of the roof very graciously. 'And how may I address you, good sir?' he asked.

'My name,' said the gentleman, 'is Owen.'

'Mine,' said the old man, 'is better not used. Here they call me Old Noe, and sometimes Mathusael, meaning no discourtesy.'

He had come here, he explained, to escape Duke Henry, Henry of Bolingbroke. 'But nowadays folk call him Humphrey, and that confuses me. Perhaps, good Master Owen, you can tell me which name he now calls himself by. Is it Henry or Humphrey?'

Said Master Owen, his expressive face suddenly grim, 'Whatever his name may have been, it is Humphrey now.'

'Humphrey!' echoed Jasp. 'Humphrey. Is that Isbaddaden, the monster, that calls himself Humphrey on Sundays?'

Master Owen looked puzzled; then his face broke into a smile. 'So you remember that tale?'

'But is he, sir?' persisted Jasp.

'It was just a tale, wasn't it, sir?' asked Mun, with a superior air. 'It wasn't true?'

'True — and not true,' said Master Owen.

'And does he live there — there, where the King's Palace is?' went on Jasp excitedly, pointing over towards the straggling palace, of which the gables were rising one by one out of shadow into sunlight.

'He doesn't live there,' was the answer, 'but he lurks about.'

'Ah!' It was a long-drawn 'Ah!' from both boys. 'Is Lord Zacounzel a monster too?' went on Jasper.

They saw a wild figure swooping towards them, both arms
outstretched like a windmill

But this time Master Owen looked completely puzzled and turned to Edmund for an explanation.

'Jasp always remembers names if they be queer ones,' Mun explained. 'Uncle said he wouldn't be mixed up with Lord Zacounzel's matters. We don't know what he meant.'

'I thought p'chance he were another monster,' said Jasp.

'Ah! I see it. The Lords of the Council. It is not one man, Jasp, but several.'

'All — bad — men,' sang out Jasper.

'That is as it may be. All mine enemies, at any rate. But come now, no more talk of monsters and enemies. How got you here? Tell me all the tale.'

They settled themselves by the parapet again, and told him of their midnight wakening, and of the long, stuffy journey when they were not allowed even to peep, and of their coming to the gateway with the faces and hands reaching out over their heads, and of Master Sampson's jokes and questions, and of the very strange behaviour of Uncle Jenks.

'He said we were no kin to him, and then he walked away and didn't look at us any more,' said Edmund.

'What's *kin?*' asked Jasper, who had never really understood Mun's consternation at this particular remark, and then, reminded of other curious things, which had passed between Uncle and the sanctuary official, 'Sir, is it Tidders or Tooders?' he asked.

'What is that you say, Jasper?'

'Is it Tidders or Tooders? The man said he rather thought it was Tooders.'

'Aunt Mabily always said,' explained Edmund, 'that folk called us Tidders because we were little, like the tidling piglets. But what are Tooders? Is it our name, truly, sir?'

Master Owen seemed to think very deeply for a minute. They wondered whether he was going to answer at all. Then he glanced at Old Noe drowsing on his seat, put down the boys from his knees, and took them over to the farther side of the leads.

'It is horrid here,' complained Jasp. 'Sometimes it has a foul smell.'

'But not today. The wind is fresh. Tell me, Edmund and Jasper, can ye keep a secret?'

They assured him solemnly that they could.

'And can ye read?'

'*I* can,' said Edmund, 'but Jasp only knows his criss-cross row.'

'Then can you read this?' And with a piece of stick he drew some letters in the dust. They read TWDWR. Mun tried hard, but had to give it up.

'I can't read it,' he admitted sadly.

'And nor can any Englishman, so be not cast down about that,' said Master Owen. 'See, Edmund, that should be your name and Jasper's for so were your forefathers called, but since it is too hard for English tongues we must needs change it to suit them. Some folk call it Tidder, but for myself I like better the sound of *Tudor*.'

'Tudor,' repeated Edmund slowly, trying to learn it, and 'Tudor,' echoed Jasper.

'Then my name is — Edmund Tudor.'

'Even so, child, but, remember, this is your secret. Call yourselves Edmund and Jasper and, if need be, feign to be simpletons and know no other name. There be many boys in England who have but one name and never miss a second. But one day, when you are grown, you shall use it.'

'Edmund Tudor,' mused Mun again. 'And Uncle is no kin to us.' Then, as they went back to their old seat, his legs feeling rather pleasantly weak after his fever, he settled himself on Master Owen's knee again and laid his head on his broad and comfortable shoulder.'

'I don't care about *kin*,' he said, 'now you have come to take care of us.'

What Master Owen said in reply couldn't quite be heard because he spoke again in his own strange language, but the tone was satisfying and the arm that was round him held him a little tighter.

APACHE DEATH
Gerald Wyatt

Matthew Trent was a soldier's son, so perhaps it was not surprising that he had courage to face Apaches on the warpath.
But what the old scout asked of him required more than courage.
Matthew had to find a way of outwitting the Apaches, and Stub,
the stagecoach driver, did not think such a thing possible. But he
was wrong.

Matthew Trent's alert watch shifted constantly from right to left as the stagecoach rocked through the arid Apacheria. He rested one of the new breechloading rifles across his knees and his blankets. He noted that Stub, the driver, was also armed, but Matthew wondered why he, too, had not been alerted to the peril they faced. He was sure no one had even whispered a warning of the death scourge surging out of the rugged mountains. In retrospect, it seemed they had taken extra care not to alert him. Way back at the last relay station, the exhausted, buckskin-clad army scout had tugged at Matthew's sleeve with a secretive gesture, leading him to an obscure corner.

Matthew's heart pounded anew at the remembrance of the scout's desperate words: 'Here is a sketch of Major Weaver's position, with the hazards of the rugged country noted. Get it to your father!' Then quickly he had affirmed: 'You are General Trent's son?' At Matthew's nod the scout's eyes had lit up with hope as they peered into Matthew's concerned brown ones.

The scout nodded quick approval. 'I was sure, though the last year's stretched your bones, and your skin's faded somewhat. Likely you've been painting overmuch.' He had shoved the crude map with its notations into Matthew's hand and explained: 'The

Mimbreno Apaches are out killing and torturing. They've got Weaver's men boxed. They'll all be slaughtered lest we get help. Take care! You know that—— If you can just get through that box canyon beyond Inscription Spring you'll be safe.'

Matthew stared down at the packet, then, almost reverently, opened the leather case holding his painting materials and placed the map inside. It had seemed so strange to Matthew that the scout should entrust the desperate plea to his guardianship that he had just stared after the man. But a year attending school in the East could hardly change the soldier's deep regard for him. In spite of the weariness, the grime and a weathered bandage swathed around the man's head, Matthew recalled a vague familiarity about the scout. By the time he had rushed to the doorway, the scout had disappeared. Stub was sitting on the box of the coach, his podgy hands holding the reins aloft, ready to snap them on the horses' backs to hurry them on. Matthew glanced from the driver to the station keeper, and was sure the man had gestured silence.

Matthew studied the case beside him, then fingered the rifle. As the miles spun under the wheels, it seemed more and more as if he, all alone, was pitted against the cunning Apaches.

Stub lashed out at the horses with sudden frenzy. The stagecoach lurched, and Matthew was thrown against the side. By the time he righted himself, the four horses were slowing. Matthew stared out of the window at smoke spiralling from the gutted relay station. The stagecoach stopped with a jerk, so close to a heap of tumbled adobes where a timbered door and beams had burned, that Matthew had to push open the opposite door to climb out. Sickened and appalled, he stared about as he clutched his case and rifle. The brutal glare of the high noon sun, the stark, inhospitable land and the savagery of the Apache raid seemed all of the same picture.

'Help me to get these horses inside!' Stub pleaded. His shaking hands fumbled with the harness, as he edged his thick body closer to the ruined gap. 'I got'a get inside with them.'

'Shouldn't we——?' The question choked in Matthew's throat and he jerked his head toward a partially burned stagecoach.

Bodies were sprawled inside grotesquely, and a man was lashed head down to the back wheel where the fire had first been kindled.

'They're past doing fer. They'll get us, 'less we get inside.'

The almost craven panic in Stub's feverish bungling with the lines alerted Matthew to appraise their situation. Other than a few cottonwoods and exposed boulders at the famous Incription Spring, there was nothing but a sandy gravelly soil, studded with sparse cacti. Here and there was a stunted scrubby bush behind which not even a child could secrete himself. 'Our dust would lead——' Matthew broke off.

Stub, his lips working with terror, leaned into the smoky interior, tilting his head to catch the moccasin whisper he so feared.

Now Matthew realized why they had been extra careful at the last relay station not to give any inkling of their peril to Stub. The plea for help had to get through to his father, and the stage was the surest way to carry it. Had Stub known the danger, he would never have driven so hard. Quickly, Matthew placed his case on the rubble, and leaned his heavy rifle beside it. He freed the horses from the stagecoach and turned them toward the gap.

'Here! Take them inside!'

Stub clutched the reins of the horses and hesitated. He was afraid to climb over the tumbled adobes, but equally terrorized at remaining outside.

Matthew smacked the flanks of the horses smartly. They almost leaped over the rubble, dragging Stub along. Matthew picked up his things and followed. The odour of timbers smouldering clung to the interior. Blinking his eyes to rid them of the stinging smoke, Matthew looked about him. Everything was smashed and jumbled up including benches and the table. The two rough bed frames with their rawhide lacings were slashed. He glanced at the door to see if there was anything left of the ticks of wild hay, realizing that the Apaches had fired the building with them. No wonder it was still smouldering, he thought. He could hear the horses stamping in the adjoining stable, and he pushed through the doorway choking and coughing with the smoke.

Matthew hung his case on a harness peg, and then heaved at the door. He was slight for such a task, but with grit and steel-like muscles he wedged the door back into place so they couldn't be stormed by surprise. The next thing was to get the horses down to the spring and water them while they could, he thought, picking up his rifle and heading for the outside stable door, against which Stub was cowering and mumbling to himself. Matthew unbarred the door and threw it open. At the sudden opportunity of fresh air and water, the horses leaped outside. Matthew jerked the reins out of Stub's hands as the driver tried to tug them back. His eyes were pulled to the gutted stagecoach and its gruesome burden as the horses ran down the slight slope to the spring. Unless he could get the message through to his father, Major Weaver's soldiers and all the daring settlers would suffer that very same fate.

Matthew watched the horses plunge their heads into the overflow of the spring. The cottonwoods growing there pushed their roots under the tumbled boulders. It was upon one of these rocks, so legend reported, that the besieged Spaniard had scratched the doom of his pack train, leaving his skeleton to tell of his own fate.

'Look here! Them critters is my lookout,' Stub growled.

Matthew watched Stub as he hesitated, furtively eyeing the distance back to the building he was sure he could make in case they were attacked.

'Why didn't you water them then?' Matthew demanded, sharply. 'You should know this country well enough to realize you can't run horses without water.'

'I don't aim to run 'em. I aim to sit tight right here. Help's bound to come along. I'll wait it out.'

'The Apaches water here, too. They're likely to come first.'

'Well— — Well——' Stub could not bear such a thought. 'We'll hole up in the 'dobes.'

'Without water? Besides, the adobes didn't keep the station keeper safe.' Matthew turned from the putty-like face. He leaned his rifle against one of the boulders, and got down on his knees scooping up handfuls of water, splashing the cooling liquid upon his head and face. He could see Stub fearfully edging closer to the spring; could almost feel the tormenting struggle in the man's mind between greed of the water and his greed of safety. Boy-like, he couldn't resist ladling a palm full of water to his mouth, smacking his lips and commenting: 'It really slakes down that heated dust.'

'Yu watch!' Stub ordered, peremptorily, as he knelt to drink also.

Matthew glanced about him thoughtfully. Buzzards were circling, the only visible movement. His eyes lingered on them as one, more daring than the rest, settled on the body tied to the wheel. His eyes slipped back to Stub. It seemed hopeless to appeal to a man's need of looking out for others, when it was quite obvious he was so selfish he could not comprehend any needs beyond his own. Yes, even if his own safety was dependent upon his consideration of others. But he'd try: 'I have an army dispatch for my father, General Trent, that I have to get through to him.'

Stub raised himself a little and stared with frenzied fear. "Tain't possible to get out. Yu seen what happened up there?'

'I don't think you understand,' Matthew snapped, though he knew it would make no difference to Stub. 'The lives of several troops, settlers and prospectors — — even your own life — — depend upon me getting this through to my father.'

The blob of clay rose up — an ominous threat. 'I ain't going out. I ain't.'

'But I've — —' Matthew broke off, and stared beyond the driver. 'See here! Let me have a horse and I — —'

'You suggesting you might strike out alone?'

'I intend to get word through. I have to. It's right. It's my duty.'

'Duty! Bah! A body's got'a look out fer hisself.'

'If I get word through — —'

'Now look here, yu Eastern Dandy, yu ain't pulling out and leaving me here alone. They'd get me fer sure.'

Matthew tried to breathe back his fury. He studied the horizon, considering his chances of getting through on foot. It would be like walking into the lair of wild beasts.

'Yu jest try skipping out on me, and I'll shoot you first.'

It was so quiet now that the slobbering of the horses sounded mournfully loud, and an ominous rending in the direction of the stagecoach augured their own fate. Matthew picked up an old Spanish spur and scratched into the rock.

'You know they'll come back. This spring —— They'll have to come here for water.' He studied the Spanish spur, and turned it thoughtfully in his hand as if probing its story. 'It will be just like —— Haven't you ever seen the old Spanish inscription here?'

'I ain't never took the time.'

'Well, you know it's here, don't you? That's why they call this Inscription Spring.'

Stub darted furtive glances about him.

It's almost as if he sees the Spanish ghosts, Matthew thought, realizing Stub was well acquainted with the legend. In sheer boyish delight at tormenting, he began: 'I wonder what happened to that old Spanish inscription?' He started searching about, smoothing his hand down over the boulders to detect any carving. 'Two Spaniards, with their Mexican peons loaded with turquoise the Indians held sacred, stopped here to water. Apaches must have trailed them all the way from their mine. For as soon as they began to drink, the Apaches pounced on them.'

Stub frantically caught up the reins and tried to force the horses towards the adobe stable. 'Help me to get them inside!'

Matthew only glanced up, still running his hand over the boulders. 'As soon as they've drunk their fill, they'll —— Here it is! Here's the inscription!' As Stub nervously stepped closer to see, an idea so cunning flashed into Matthew's mind, he kept his head lowered so Stub could spy no inkling of his intent. 'I can't read it all. Some of it's weathered smooth, and there's —— It's like I told you,' he exclaimed, triumphantly. He began to read the Spanish words slowly, as he deciphered the old inscription, and then repeated its meaning in English. Abruptly, Matthew broke off in the middle of a sentence.

'Well?' Stub demanded. 'Read the rest.'

'That's all. The end was written in his mutilated body sprawled over his hand pick. He should have used that energy to think up a way to elude them. That Spaniard knew the Apaches would come back, same as you and I do. Well, they swooped down on him before he could even finish ——'

'Listen!' Stub hissed. 'What's that?' He cowered down behind the inscription boulder.

So vivid had he made the story of the old raid, that for a few seconds Matthew's heart skipped with terror. 'It's the buzzards,' he managed finally. 'They're fighting over them, same as they'll fight over us, unless we get out of here — before they come back.'

'We can't outrun 'em,' Stub cried, hopelessly.

Matthew nodded agreement, warily watching to see that fear held dominant in the putty face. 'So we'll have to outwit them.'

'Apaches? *Outwit Apaches?*' Stub wailed, desperately.

'We can always wait for them to torture and kill us — let them lash us alive head down over a fire, just like — — !' Matthew's sombre gesture drew Stub's terrified eyes toward the gutted stagecoach. 'Just like that!' he whispered. One by one his mind considered methods of running the Apache gauntlet. He remembered, a couple of years before, when a group of warriors had finally surrendered to his father, how they'd come out of the desert almost naked with the scrubby growth tied to their hands and bodies, so that they could stalk their victims beside the trails and yet not be detected. Adept at camouflage themselves, they would spy it out in a flash.

Stub kept mumbling and quarrelling with the horses, trying to urge them back into the stable. As for himself, Matthew dreaded going back into that smoke-filled trap. He'd rather stay here with the ghosts of the Spaniards. A vague legend about a hot spring teased his memory. He scowled, trying to recall the whole story. All he could remember was that the Apaches held it sacred and never attacked any men who stopped there for water. That was no help at all, Matthew decided. Making this spring safe would not aid them; he had to make the trail secure for the stagecoach. It wouldn't take much, he realized, just something to startle the Apaches into wondering and puzzling while the stagecoach rolled ahead. Major Stephen H. Long had managed to awe the savages by his boat, Matthew remembered with despair. How he'd relished Long's report on his explorations, but a lot of good that did! Matthew stared toward the stagecoach, considering again. Was it possible? Long had the bow of his boat shaped like a huge serpent with its gaping jaws belching smoke. Could he — —? He could paint smoke and — — It gave them a chance!

'See here!' Matthew exclaimed. 'Like all savage Indians the Apaches are very superstitious — frightened by what they can't understand. If I contrive — —' He broke off. All he could think of was Long's boat. If it weren't for the horses he might paint the stagecoach up the same way, but — — A sudden gust of hot wind licked at his hair and he brushed it back with a flash of inspiration: Kites! Kites and a sail! He'd take his blankets and rig them up about the stagecoach. He'd paint huge red serpents on them. He'd make it all so fierce that the Apaches would hold back in terror.

Matthew chose his words cautiously: 'Major Long's boat with its bow built like a huge serpent belching smoke frightened the savage Indians back, and thus he explored the Missouri in safety. I'm going to rip up something like that, only it will have to be a sail-like affair. You'll have to help make the frame.'

'I ain't sitting up on that box,' Stub protested.

'I'll sit there,' Matthew uttered in despair. 'Just help fix this up.'

'It jest ain't no use.'

'See here! We've got to work fast. Those Apaches are most likely lurking along the trail waiting for you. They know you're due. If we dally too long, they'll come for us, and then — —' Matthew gestured with finality toward the gutted stagecoach.

In less than an hour the strange stagecoach rolled out on to the trail. Matthew sat on the box, behind the screening blankets which fastened at right angles directly in front of him. The horses were splashed with sky-blue paint to simulate turquoise, and mud was plastered over all the visible area of the coach.

As the stagecoach picked up speed, the wind livened the blankets. On each was painted a huge red serpent on a background of blue. The monsters appeared to writhe forward. Their gaping jaws seemed to move as if swallowing new prey. Above their jaws sailed tiny kites — like puffs of hazy smoke.

'It ain't gonna work. Them Apaches'll get us for sure. I shouldn't 'a listened,' Stub complained. 'Turn about! We got'a get back!'

'I can't,' Matthew yelled.

Stub stuck his head through the front. 'Yu turn back or I'll — —'

The strange stagecoach rolled out on to the trail

'The horses! They're running away!' If the strange rigging only frightened the Apaches as much as it had terrified the horses. Matthew peered through the slit made by the flapping blankets, trying desperately to see ahead — to hold the horses to the trail. Then he glimpsed movement near the rocks; the earth seemed to form into clay figures. His throat tightened. His heart sped in terror. 'Apaches!' he choked out.

Matthew's thoughts raced so that it seemed like an eternity as the horses ran the savage gauntlet wildly. Could he manage to hold them to the trail? Already the sawing reins ripped into his palms, drawing blood. Would the wind-filled blankets tip over the lurching stagecoach? Would Stub remain cowered upon the floor? If he fired on them what happened next? If the Apaches did attack, how could he manage to save the despatch?

The heated dust swirled up and mingled with the odour of fresh paint. The Apaches stared in sudden fear. Matthew darted a glance backwards. Why, it seemed as if they were dissolving back into the earth. Ahead of him he could sight the end of the pass. The only sounds were the wild beat of the hooves and the grind of the iron tyres and the slap-slap of the blankets. The idea was working, Matthew realized, swallowing hard. How soon, he began to reckon the time, could his father get help to Major Weaver?

NO WELCOME
Geoffrey Chelsworth

A puncture resulted in a Londoner touring Cornwall stopping at the Half Moon Hotel. He said his name was Sutherland, and he acted in a very curious fashion when he was left alone. As an outcome he learned about a place called Devil's Cove, on a lonely stretch of coast. He might have visited it had not someone else acted just as curiously as himself.

I was just beginning to wish I hadn't come when the light showed up ahead. It was faint and liquid through the driving rain; but it was a light, and by my reckoning it came from the old inn. All thoughts of the cosy bed I might have had in St Ives vanished. I pressed on, my head bent low, my frozen hands gripping the handlebars of my cycle as I half-walked, half-staggered, leaning on wind and machine, along the coast road.

I tried to quicken my pace. The light grew larger and soon I saw it came from an oil lamp suspended from a ceiling hook. As soon as I drew level with the small bay window I peered in. Except for a man reading a newspaper, the reception hall was empty. Benches lined two of the walls. A fire in the grate was almost out. The place looked cold and uninviting.

I propped the bicycle in the doorway and my attention was jerked upwards by the harsh shrieking of a battered metal sign. As it thrust to and fro in the wind the light from the window glanced across the faint inscription. I could just make out the words "The Half Moon Hotel" and a faded design intended to represent a young moon.

I opened the front door and found myself in a long passage. A small oil lamp on a wall-bracket glimmered at the far end, its badly trimmed wick and broken glass causing the light to flutter in the draught, and send dancing shadows along the walls. A door to my left was ajar; I pushed it open and entered the hall.

The man dropped his newspaper, nodded at me, and slid off an upturned barrel.

'Good evening,' I smiled, tugging off my hat and cape. 'This is a welcome haven after the coast road.' I rubbed my hands over the dying embers of the fire to revive the circulation.

'Aye,' he agreed. ''Tis a terrible night and a very wet autumn. Not a soul's been nigh the whole evenin'.' He picked up a cloth and began to dust an oak chest. He was a middle-aged man with a tough, weather-beaten face. He wore a fisherman's jersey and creased serge trousers.

He began filling a foul-looking pipe.

'What would you be doing in these parts on a night like this?' he inquired, with a meaning glance towards the window.

'I'm touring Cornwall,' I said. 'The hard way — on a bike. I left Penzance this afternoon, had tea at Land's End, and was making for St Ives. I was planning to spend the night there; but the gale blew up and about two miles down the road I had a puncture. I won't make St Ives tonight.' I paused, but he made no comment. 'I was hoping you could let me have a room.'

He looked at me darkly. I had the feeling he was trying to sum me up.

'That ain't easy this time o' the year,' he announced at length. 'The season's just finished. We don't take no visitors in the winter and mighty few in summer. The landlord 'asn't the room or the staff to cope.'

'But it's a filthy night,' I protested. 'You can surely give me shelter for one night?'

The man hesitated.

'Mr 'Ogart will have to decide that,' he declared. 'It makes no odds to me if ye stay; but *he* gives the orders around 'ere.' He stroked his chin and disappeared through a curtained doorway, returning a few moments later followed by a large, corpulent man. His face was large and fleshy. He had managed to get his nose broken at some time and hadn't shaved for a couple of days; a thick, dark stubble covered his heavy jowls. He wore braces over a shirt which had no collar or tie. His sleeves were rolled up, revealing powerful forearms that were dark with hair. I didn't like him; and by the way he was looking at me, I think the feeling was mutual.

A slight incline of his head which I took to be a nod prompted me to wish him good evening.

'Jakes was telling me you want a room for the night,' he announced in a throaty voice. 'But I don't cater for visitors — leastways, very few, and then only in high summer.'

He eyed me suspiciously.

'What's your name and where're you from?' he asked.

'Sutherland, and I'm from London.'

'Bit late in the year for a holiday, isn't it?' he suggested doubtfully.

'I've taken a new job,' I said. 'I was at the bottom of the holiday roster. We often get good weather in October.'

He was silent for a few moments and then came suddenly to a decision.

'All right,' he said. 'I'll fix you up for the night, but we've no facilities for making it a weekend, mind.'

'I'm very grateful,' I said.

He nodded dourly, and went out.

Jakes leaned across and inquired where my bicycle was. When I told him, he said he'd put it in one of the outbuildings at the back. I asked him to bring my cycle panniers with him. He disappeared to get a coat and I was alone again. But only for a moment. The door facing me opened gently and a dark-skinned, delicate girl of about seventeen appeared. Her eyes were large and brown and there was a kind of haunted look about them. It was as if she'd been frightened or expected to be frightened. I smiled at her.

'Would you come thru', Mr Sutherland?' she invited in a steady voice. Her accent was foreign but her English was perfect. I followed her into the passage, along it a few steps and turned right into a small back room. It was furnished sparsely with a long dining table, half a dozen straight-backed chairs and also an old-fashioned dresser on which stood a portable lamp. An oil stove burned on the hearth.

The girl went to the dresser drawer and took out a cloth. She began laying the table for one.

'We have little to offer,' she said, apologetically. 'But I will ask Mrs Bannerjee to do her best.' And she went out of the room.

I stood with my back to the stove and looked towards the door, and it was then I noticed a table in the corner. It was a small table and it had a large book on it. I moved across and found it was the visitors' register. The stiff covers were soft with age but there were many pages without an entry. I took out my pen and was about to write my name on the next line — and then stopped. Someone had written their name on the line already, *and the entry had been erased.* There was no doubt of it at all. A faint smudge ran across the page and the surface of the paper was rough.

Who had stayed at the Half Moon Hotel after August and why was the person's identity rubbed out? Why was Hogart reluctant to put me up? Why was the girl frightened? All these questions seemed somehow to be linked; but I was no nearer the answers when the tread of someone in the passage sent me back to my position near the stove.

A plump woman with lank hair and a greasy overall entered. She nodded at me and set down a tray of coffee and Cornish pasties on the table.

'If you wish for more you will please ring the bell and ask Lily?' She indicated the ancient bell-push in the wall next to the fireplace. I thanked her and said I would.

The girl, Lily, didn't come back again that night, and less than an hour later Jakes showed me up to my room. He gave me my panniers and, leaving me with a half-burned candle, went out and closed the door.

The candle was guttering when I climbed into bed. I snuffed the flame and the room was plunged into blackness. The wind howled outside the window and the rain beat a tattoo on the glass with the noise of a thousand drum-sticks. And there were all the odd creaks which manifest themselves in all old houses. I settled down feeling that nothing was destined to disturb my sleep — but tomorrow night... Hogart had made it quite plain that he did not want me around. Why? What was brewing at the Half Moon? Somehow I had to spend another night at the inn...

Lily served my breakfast next morning. I was looking out of the window at the grey drizzle blowing in from the sea when she entered the room with coffee and cereals.

She looked out of the window.

'The weather is not pleasant for cycling,' she observed. 'But the wind has dropped. I hope you have a nice journey.' Her voice sounded envious.

'Thanks,' I smiled. 'I will if my tyres hold up.' I opened the paper I had picked up at the foot of the stairs, and stopped her as she was about to leave.

'I found this on the table when I came downstairs. It's this morning's paper. Does it usually arrive so early?'

She hesitated momentarily.

'Oh, Mr Dryden brought that with him from Penzance,' she explained. 'He came out by taxi this morning. He often comes here. He is a friend of Mr Hogart.'

'Is he staying here?' I inquired casually.

'I do not know. Sometimes he stays, sometimes not. He travels all over the country.'

'Not much in the news,' I announced, scanning the paper. 'I see another body has been found in the sea. Man drowned in Mount's Bay.'

'Another?' she queried.

'Yes. Wasn't there a man drowned near this coast a few weeks ago?' I was watching her face. 'I remember seeing a paragraph about it in a London paper at the time. Man named Dickson, I believe. Washed up in a cove a mile or two from here. Been in the water some time.'

She avoided my gaze.

'That is so,' she agreed. 'I heard the locals speak of it. They said he was a holiday-maker. The sea is rough and the currents strong here. He must have swum out too far.'

'Do you think he would,' I countered quickly, 'in his clothes? I remeber reading that the body was fully dressed.'

'I was not interested in the details,' she said. 'Death frightens me. If you will excuse me please, Mr Sutherland, I have duties in the kitchen.' She was gone before I could voice the questions in my mind.

After breakfast I found my way to the backyard. The place was cobbled and practically enclosed by the rambling structure of the inn and the outbuildings which adjoined it. I found my cycle in the woodshed, and started to take off the tyre.

When I entered the inn again some thirty minutes later the first person I met was Jakes. He had a piece of paper in his hand.

'Mr 'Ogart left this for 'e, sir.' He handed me my bill.

'You'd better keep that till tomorrow, Jakes,' I smiled, grimly. 'My innertube's rotten. There's a six-inch split in it. If I could get to St Ives or Penzance today, I couldn't buy a new tube. Cycle shops don't open on Sunday.'

Jakes scratched his head, his expression bleak. He didn't know what to say.

So I went on: 'I'm afraid I'll have to ask the genial host for a further night's hospitality. Where is he?'

'Well,' he said at length. 'Mr 'Ogart's out. 'E'll be away for a few hours. 'E'll not be liking it.'

'Why?' I shot at him. 'Why shouldn't he like it? He didn't appear to like it last night but I couldn't see the reason. He had the room.'

'Aye, but tonight it'll be occupied. A friend of 'is arrived this morning.'

'Well, I'm not fussy. I don't mind where he puts me. But I'm certainly not hiking the roads looking for a tube today.'

'It makes no odds to me,' he muttered, shortly. 'Mr 'Ogart's the boss.' And he shuffled away still muttering.

Hogart did not return until early evening. I saw him and a man I took to be Dryden approaching the inn just before dark. I moved away from the bar window from where I had been watching and returned to the dining-room.

I hadn't seen Jakes again since my encounter in the morning. Nor had Lily appeared. Mrs Bannerjee had served my meals but she had not been inclined to conversation. I had been left alone with my thoughts which were now loaded with suspicion. I was convinced that the Half Moon was something more than an ordinary Cornish inn.

When Hogart entered the room a little later I was innocently scanning a copy of the Cornish Guide.

'Good evening, Mr Sutherland,' he said. 'Jakes told me you have a little trouble with your bicycle?'

I nodded. 'My inner-tube's perished. I knew I couldn't do anything about it today; the shops are closed. I thought I could enlist your kindness in putting me up for another night. I don't mind where I sleep,' I added, encouragingly.

He stroked his fleshy chin thoughtfully.

'It is inconvenient,' he volunteered at length. 'But I think we can manage if you don't mind one of the attics. It will be small and not very comfortable...'

'I don't mind a bit,' I said, inwardly relieved.

He went on: 'Every Monday morning a carrier's truck passes on the way to Penzance. The driver usually calls to see if I want anything. He could take you and your cycle into the town.'

I smiled my thanks. 'That would be an excellent arrangement,' I said.

Just before eleven Jakes came in to show me to my room, a small, airless place under the roof. The ceiling sloped almost to the floor and there was a tiny grating in one wall. An iron bedstead, a chair and cupboard composed the sole furnishings. I shuddered inwardly.

'This will do fine,' I said; and with a gruff 'Good night' he went out and closed the door.

I didn't get undressed. Instead I stuffed the bolster and rolled-up blanket between the sheets, shaping them until they somewhat resembled a figure beneath the bedclothes. Then I sat on the chair and waited, listening. The inn was very still, the silence of the night broken only by the low rumble of the surf pounding the cliff base. After a bit I snuffed out the candle and took my torch from the pack. Nothing happened for a long time.

I must have fallen into a light doze for I suddenly came alert to the faint purr of a car engine somewhere close by. I flashed the torch on my watch; it was nearly three o'clock. I crept to the door and listened intently. I thought the sounds came from the back of the inn, a vehicle probably in the yard.

By opening the door carefully I managed to prevent it creaking. Not daring to switch on the torch I felt my way slowly downstairs. I reached the landing and paused, listening. The motor had been shut off but the noise of a van door opening came unmistakably from the yard. I moved blindly along to the window and peered out. The yard was a faint shadow, but in the diffused light of a clouded moon I was able to make out the dark outline of a van. Two figures carried a third figure into the inn. As they disappeared there was a slight movement behind me. I turned instinctively, but before I could switch on the torch a searing pain burned into my head. Coloured lights momentarily seemed to split the darkness and then everything was black.

I came to with the feeling that I was struggling in the sea; but a moment later when I opened my eyes, I found that a jug of water had been splashed in my face. Jakes stood there grinning, with the empty jug in his hand. As my eyes focused, I saw that Hogart and Dryden were present, too. Dryden was holding an automatic; but I couldn't see the reason for I was sitting helplessly in a chair with my wrists and ankles securely bound. Behind them, sitting on a packing case in the corner, was another man I hadn't seen before.

I looked round painfully. We were in what I guessed to be one of the outbuildings. A place used for storage. Barrels and empty crates and boxes were stacked untidily about the floor, and the whitewash on the walls was disfigured and dirty with cobwebs.

'So... our young guest has revived,' Hogart sneered. 'We can get down to business.'

'If you treat all your guests like this,' I retorted, 'it's a wonder you have any business.'

'On the contrary, Mr Sutherland, our kind of business doesn't cater for guests — especially the inquisitive kind. We have kept an eye on you, and when you came out of your room tonight it was necessary to take action. We took the liberty of examining your cycle tube and we found it had been slit with a knife! You would have offered any pretence to stay and spy on us.' He leaned forward, leering. 'You're a danger to our little organization, Mr Sutherland. Who sent you here?' He barked the question at me and cuffed me across the mouth.

'Nobody sent me,' I retorted, furiously. 'I told you I was touring Cornwall. I've spent one or two nights in various places. This is just one of them.'

'And do you usually creep about them at dead of night?' he sneered.

'Not unless I'm disturbed. Something woke me —'

'You *lie!*' he cut in. 'You were not even in bed.'

Dryden spoke for the first time. His voice was guttural.

'Does it matter?' he asked Hogart. 'We're only wasting time. And Leon sails at dawn.'

'Of course,' Hogart assented. He glared at me. 'It wouldn't do for you to miss the boat, Mr Sutherland. We have an excellent shuttle-service between here and Brittany. Passports and false papers, undesirable aliens; any type of cargo that pays good dividends. We've carried some big fish in our fishing boats.' His yellow teeth made his grin even more sinister. 'The service is also useful in other ways,' he went on, slowly. 'Inquisitive people have been known to start the trip but never make the French coast. Leon has a knack of losing such passengers — outside the three mile limit.'

I could feel the beads of sweat on my forehead. I tried to keep calm.

'I see,' I muttered, grimly. 'That's how you murdered Dickson!' But if Hogart heard me he ignored the accusation, for he turned and spoke to the man in the corner, who at once jumped to his feet.

'You know the routine,' Hogart was saying. 'Drive our guest down to Devil's Cove. Give Leon the signal and he will send the dinghy ashore. Don't forget to douse your headlights before you turn off the road.'

The man grinned. 'Aye, aye,' he said. Hogart turned to Dryden.

'You'd better go along too, Max. Keep an eye on him.' He indicated me with a nod. 'We don't want any trouble. I'll go and attend to Wimbeaux. Those French police put a bullet through his thigh and Leon couldn't do much for him on the way over. But he'll recover all right.'

The party then broke up. A rough gag was stuffed in my mouth and Dryden and the driver of the van carried me out into the yard. The van doors were opened and Hogart shone a torch inside.

'What's all that old sacking doing there?' he demanded. I noticed that a thick pile of socks made a carpet on the floor of the van while others were heaped up in a corner.

'We thought we'd make Wimbeaux's journey as comfortable as possible,' the driver explained. 'He didn't want to be shaken up too much and you know how the roads are. But I can throw them out,' he added, quickly.

Hogart looked at me. He was grinning again.

'Leave them,' he said. 'It's his last ride. It might as well be a smooth one.' And with that they threw me on the sacks and slammed the doors.

The canvas division between the driver's cab and the body of the van was about three feet high and when Dryden and the driver were seated I could just see their heads and shoulders. Before we moved off Dryden shone his torch on me to satisfy himself that I was safely stowed, then he faced the front again and I heard him grunt 'O.K.' We moved out on to the road.

We were travelling in the direction from which I had come two nights before — towards Land's End. I didn't know Devil's Cove; but I knew it was somewhere between Land's End and the old mining village of St Just — an isolated stretch of the Atlantic coast. I wondered what my chances of escape might be once we had arrived. If only I could loosen the cords round my wrists! But I might just as well have wished for a police escort! Hogart, or whoever had trussed me up, had made a good job of it, and the knots refused to yield.

It was while I was thus engaged that I suddenly became acutely aware of the heap of sacking in the corner. *It was moving.* Not through the jerking of the van, but by means of some other agency. It moved slowly towards me. Suddenly a hand appeared and gently drew aside one of the rough bags and a dusky face

She put a finger to her lips

was revealed. It was Lily! She wriggled forward, her body still hidden by the sacks, until she was level with my ankles. She put a finger to her lips warning me to be quiet while she worked on the knots.

A few minutes later my ankles and hands were free. Lily remained hidden beneath the sacks; but as a final accomplishment she handed me a small shifting spanner.

I moved slowly towards the partition. I took up a crouching stance, stepped forward and pressed the end of the spanner in the driver's back.

'Take it easy, both of you!' I ordered, sharply. 'Keep driving and we'll let you live.' They thought I was holding a gun and the driver kept driving. I turned to Lily.

'Get Dryden's gun,' I said. 'It's probably in his pocket.' She shook off the sacks and reached over the partition and eventually held up the automatic. I kept them both covered with the real gun, and 'persuaded' Dryden into the back where his hands were firmly tied behind his back.

'Now for his mate!' I said and ordered him to stop the van. Within five minutes we were off again. I was driving and Lily kept the two trussed men covered with the automatic.

I drove fast in St Harran and pulled up with a shrieking of brakes outside the small police house. A sleepy-eyed constable was soon wide awake when he heard my story. He struggled into his uniform while I talked and then went out to get our prisoners. While he was doing so I got through to Penzance on the telephone and spoke to Superintendent Manning.

When I came off the phone I found Lily in the small sitting-room. She told me the constable's wife was making coffee and that Dryden and the driver were in the police office safely handcuffed.

'I haven't had a chance yet,' I began, simply, 'to tell you how grateful I am for your brave action tonight. You've saved my life.'

'I might have saved the man, Dickson, if I had been alert enough,' she declared, miserably.

'Then he did stay at the inn — *his* name was removed from the register? You knew what was happening?'

'I knew the kind of business Hogart was running; but I did not guess what had happened to Dickson until he was found. When I heard that he had been in the water three days I suddenly remembered the night I was locked in my bedroom. I remembered the van being in the yard and the light coming from the outhouse. It was just the same tonight. But I got out of my room, listened at the door of the outhouse and then hid myself in the van.'

'It was a brave thing to do. But why didn't you go to the police before or tell me all you knew yesterday?'

'I was terrified of Hogart,' she said, fearfully. 'If we did not obey him he threatened to send me and Mrs Bannerjee back.'

'Back?' I echoed.

'Back to Pakistan. We were refugees and we wanted to get to England. We escaped from a camp. We had no papers. Then we met Wimbeaux, the Frenchman they brought to the inn tonight. He made arrangements with Hogart and we were smuggled to France and across the Channel in a fishing boat. The condition was that we should work for Hogart at the Half Moon. We did not know, but we might have guessed, the inn was a cover for smuggling.' She leaned forward. 'The police — they will not send us both back?' she exclaimed, anxiously.

'With all the evidence you have against Hogart, you'll be all right,' I assured her.

'Poor Mr Dickson was on holiday,' she said suddenly. 'But he was a detective, was he not? That was why, when he stumbled across Hogart's activities, he continued investigating... You are from the police?' she asked slyly.

'Not exactly,' I said, and turned my attention to the coffee the constable's wife had brought in.

Two hours later, back at the inn, Manning came out to the woodshed and found me.

He was grinning. 'You didn't come all the way from London on that?' he suggested, sweeping the machine with a contemptuous glance.

'No.' I smiled. 'I hired it in Penzance.'

He scratched his ear and frowned. 'You know, Sutherland,' he declared, 'you're a bit of a mystery to me. When you mentioned Scotland Yard and Inspector Trevors on the phone an hour ago, I got through to him. All he told me was that you had kind of wangled his unofficial permission to investigate what you thought was a mystery surrounding the accidental death of one of his men. Just what did he mean?'

'Well,' I said. 'It really all began when I got the news that my cousin had been drowned. I couldn't believe it was an accident —'

'Your *cousin?*' he exclaimed in surprise.

'Yes, on my father's side,' I said, slowly. 'You see, my name isn't really Sutherland. It's Dickson...'

LOST CANYON TRAIL
Joseph E. Chipperfield

Kirk Merrett is bent on finding the stallion known as Dark Fury.
When he catches sight of him, the stallion is leading a herd of
wild mustangs, and the trail leads to the fabulous Lost Canyon,
an almost legendary place, where the wild horses found strange
sanctuary. This is one of the many stories told in *Dark Fury*, from
which it is taken.

On that same day when Kirk Merrett passed up the trail west of Saddle Mountain, Dark Fury was penetrating well up the valley, and by late afternoon was within a mile or so of the place where the wild horses were peaceably grazing.

The stallion was in no great hurry to press on up the valley. He knew he was back in his old familiar surroundings. More than that, he sensed in the wind that the herd — his herd — was not far away.

A bear was moving up amidst a copse of juniper. Dark Fury watched the animal's progress with interest, disclosing no sign of alarm, only recognizing in the huge, lumbering shape something that had always belonged to this land of mountain and canyon.

He whinnied approvingly, then glanced back along the trail to where the huge swell of cliffs buttressed the red-domed peak of Saddle Mountain. A drift of cloud was trailing gossamer-like across the ridge; northwards, another, more distant ridge, glowed in the crimson flare-path of the westering sun.

Then two very large-pinioned birds held his attention. They came gliding up the valley on a strong current of air, and Dark Fury knew them to be Grookah and Grannah — the two golden eagles who dwelt on an ancient eyrie set high up on Grouse Creek Mountain overlooking Lost Canyon.

Again the stallion whinnied, and closely watched the two birds as they flew in low, seeming to hover for a brief moment over the spot where he stood gazing upwards.

Suddenly he heard them bark one to the other, and the stallion knew that he had been recognized.

A second later they had gone — travelling the air lanes of the sky to Lost Canyon.

Dark Fury shook himself and heaved a long sigh. For the first time in many months he was aware of a rare contentment. His long journey was practically at an end. There were no enemies in the Valley of Little Lost that he did not know and, if necessary, could not subdue.

Almost instinctively he sought out a scattering of larch and juniper encircling a shallow lake; and there, as dusk came encroaching up the valley, he stood relaxed until he felt the need for sleep. Lying down on the pine needles, he dozed, his nose set in a northerly direction so that it caught every trickle of air that came down to him from the ravine where the wild horses were.

When the cold clear light of the new day stood firmly in the Valley of Little Lost, Dark Fury moved on; and, not far behind, came Kirk.

Never before had Kirk seen such a remarkable labyrinth of rock. Sage had put in an appearance on some of the nearby slopes, and brush and juniper straggled everywhere. The enormous rock formations marked the way from peak to peak, and all along the main ridges, so high above him, was the sharp gleam of frozen snow, with an occasional upheaval of red rock where the snow had melted away.

Then, when he least expected it, he found himself travelling a downward course, and in less than an hour was approaching an amphitheatre that was vividly green, but completely hemmed in by bulging cliffs that zig-zagged up and up until they were lost to sight amidst the moving panorama of the sky.

Perhaps he was absolutely unprepared for what he saw next; perhaps he was still living in a dream-like state of wonder; but when the whole significance of the sight burst upon him, he could only hold in his trembling horse and stare open-mouthed.

Less than half a mile away there was a wild milling of animals, all racing and screaming and scattering from north to south, and out-running them all was the black stallion that had once been a circus attraction back in Utah.

Dark Fury was rounding up his herd!

In moments, the entire band was hidden behind some monstrous rock formation; then the first of the mares would appear, running wild-eyed and with threshing hooves, closely pursued by some of the younger animals. Backwards and forwards the band went, first one way, then another; and always behind them, seeking to drive them into a closely packed mass, was the snaking shape of the black stallion.

Tireless and determined, he continued his task, separating the young stallions from the mares. He seemed to be in all places at once — a black lightning flash that was relentless in its striking, that gave no respite and yet somehow was bringing order out of chaos and serenity out of turmoil.

At one stage of the proceedings, Dark Fury trumpeted like an enraged moose bull, and Kirk, concealed behind an overspill of boulders, felt his horse tremble violently at the sound. He patted the animal gently as if to reassure him, and then stared out across the arena in time to see Dark Fury driving in at another animal as black as himself. The mares packed themselves tightly together as if for protection, and as if aware that Dark Fury was about to exercise his right to leadership, they froze into a stillness that brought complete silence to the amphitheatre.

In a matter of seconds, the two black horses stood facing each other, less than twenty paces apart.

Once again Dark Fury uttered that queer trumpeting cry, and snaking forward, reared up and brought his forefeet crashing down upon his enemy. Dark Fury's attack was made with a suddenness that took the other horse by surprise. The next moment, however, both stallions were whirling and striking at each other, Dark Fury gaining an advantage by suddenly locking his forelegs around the other's neck.

Both beasts staggered like wrestlers, until the younger horse broke away, and with ears closely pressed against his skull, fled northwards, leaving Dark Fury the victor.

In that moment of achievement, the stallion uttered no cry of triumph. He stood like a statue at the head of the amphitheatre, surveying the herd.

Kirk, watching him, knew then that, whether or not he found Lost Canyon, what he had just witnessed had made the long journey he had undertaken more than worthwhile. He had seen the real Dark Fury in action, and it was the experience of a life-time!

All was quiet in the Valley of the Little Lost River for the rest of that day. The herd did not attempt any breakaway, most of the animals having recognized Dark Fury as their old leader.

Following the hasty departure of the over-impetuous horse that had challenged Dark Fury's right to assume control after so long an absence, most of the mares had gone back to their grazing. Even the young yearling stallions, which Dark Fury had segregated from the main herd, had accepted the position. Many of them, when still inexperienced colts, had been brought down from Lost Canyon for the spring grazing in the Valley of Little Lost, and they had vivid memories of the stallion's exploits during the trek. The huge black horse was, as well they knew, an exceedingly hard taskmaster when the occasion demanded it of him.

As for Kirk, no more beautiful day could he remember having spent in such ideal surroundings. The few clouds that passed high over the Valley of Little Lost sent an ever-changing pattern of sunlight and shadow sweeping from one end of the glen to the other. Bluebirds continually called way up in the junipers, and a lone mocking bird kept up a shrill whistle from the copse beside the shallow lake where Dark Fury had slept the night.

Twice that afternoon the two eagles Grookah and Grannah from Grouse Creek Mountain came sailing leisurely overhead, and each time Dark Fury marked their passage with a steady eye. It was not until the sun began to go down behind the Little Lost Range and the shadows started to drop quickly over the valley that Dark Fury made his last patrol of the day. He went at an even trot around the amphitheatre, pausing only at the southern end when he discerned the smoke from Kirk's camp-fire rising upwards.

Now, more than ever, did Dark Fury accept Kirk Merrett's presence as something closely allied to his own existence; and so, satisfied that all was well with the herd, the stallion took up a position on a low ridge, the better to gaze down upon the valley and watch the spiral of smoke with peaceful eyes.

Even as it had been a truly lovely day, so too, was it a lovely night. The first star shone direct over the distant northern peak which the stallion would have readily recognized as Grouse Creek Mountain. Soon, in the paling evening sky, there appeared other stars, all twinkling like lamps lit way up in the air lanes of the sky which only the eagles knew... and low down, where the red dome of Saddle Mountain was but a dark smudge on the horizon, came the slow uplifting of a silver boat... the new moon!

Kirk beheld the rising of the ship of night, and a sudden catch in his heart reminded him of Washakie's words... 'We meet again when the full moon rises over the Valley of Little Lost...'

As he lay on his back, with his hands clasped under his head, he pondered carefully over the Indian's words. Washakie had known that when once the stallion joined up with the herd he would probably remain in the valley for many days... possibly much longer than the sixteen days that must pass before the moon was at the full.

The more he considered the matter, the more did he realize how frail now was his chance of ever discovering Lost Canyon. Without the aid of Dark Fury to lead him to it, he knew he could never find it.

But, as sleep came stealing over him and the silver ship of the moon rose high over Saddle Mountain, his mind relinquished its hold on the hope of visiting Lost Canyon, and he only knew that the night breeze was cool on his cheeks, and that a long way up the valley a night bird was calling, sharp and clear, but tenderly musical.

Perhaps he fell asleep dreaming of the night bird's song, and the soaring ship of the moon; perhaps it was all a dream too — that rocky mountain he thought he could see so clearly... and the deep valley that lay beyond. Maybe, too, no more than a dream the pine tree as big as any pine could be... and a waterfall that fell tossing from off a mountain ledge... and a rainbow that fell in an arc of loveliness towards the sunset.

All dreams, maybe; but certainly no dream that distant clamour breaking in upon his subconscious meanderings... a clamour of hooves beating a tattoo away off in the fastnesses of the valley, and a high, sustained trumpeting like a bugle note winding up to bid him awake and follow.

Kirk awoke and saw no more of the moon high over Saddle Mountain, and heard no more the night bird's song. All he could see was the morning sky with the last stars fading, and he heard, hard and sharp in his ears, the steady echoes of feet tramping away from him... a hundred, hundred feet, and one last call floating up to him... the call of a stallion who had set out in the golden light of dawn to trek to Lost Canyon!

Ten minutes later, he had broken camp, and was riding quickly down the valley, following that distant line of horses that moved slowly between the towering walls of the mountains to that immense peak that rose many miles to the north... Grouse Creek Mountain!

A warm wind came blowing from off the very high hills. Way over against Borah Peak on the Little Lost River Range was a flight of wild geese. Soon their honking echoed down the valley. For a moment or two the sunlight quivered with their passing, then a stillness closely akin to austerity possessed the whole glen from north to south. Not a sound disturbed the quietness. It was almost uncanny. There was not even an echo ringing out from the hooves of the many moving feet as the wild horse herd, driven by Dark Fury, went steadily up along the fertile river basin, slowly approaching an even greater frown of mountains which, in their soaring, seemed to shut out the day.

All that bright day, and the next, the great trek continued, with Kirk Merrett, full of wonder at what was taking place, following as close as he dared on the very heels of the magnificent black stallion.

About the middle of the afternoon on the third day, the band of horses began to ascend a clearly defined gulley that struck upwards north-west of a narrow lake like a finger pointing the way to some hidden break in the mountain chain.

Kirk's heart beat high with hope. This surely was the trail that led direct to Lost Canyon. He could see it mounting higher and higher above the brink of the little lake, ascending very steeply indeed at one point until, like a piece of string, frayed out and done, it disappeared into what seemed a fissure in the mountain wall.

Yet there was something decidedly odd about that track. It was so deeply scored in the hillside, and in places full of debris and boulders. There were also great hollows in it, some as much as three feet in depth.

At last Kirk understood. He was travelling what had once been a river bed, possibly that of the Little Lost River itself.

His excitement grew.

Throughout the whole of that afternoon and well into the slow gathering evening the trek went on and then as the silver slip of the moon began to rise once again over the now far distant dome of Saddle Mountain, Kirk discovered that the herd ahead of him was no longer on the move but grazing on a small plateau between the uprising walls of the mountain.

He was hard put to find a suitable place to set up his camp in such a desolate neighbourhood. Although he had not been aware of the fact, the boulder-strewn trail had ascended farther up the slope than he had thought possible, and he was not too far from what, way down, had been the frayed end of the track. Nevertheless, he managed to discover an ancient cedar, dwarfed and very old, set high up on a bank, and close to it, a patch of grass suitable for his horse.

Soon he was snugly wrapped in his blankets, and the sight of the towering hills now steeped in darkness brought a sharp stab of dread to his mind. Supposing in the night the band of horses returned and stampeded at sight of him? What then would be the end for both himself and the horse who had carried him so faithfully for all these past weeks?

As if in answer to his strange forebodings, up amidst the hidden peaks the wind moaned and cried loudly in the cedars that clung to them with the desperation of living things whose day was nigh over and who so soon would be tossed into eternity.

Kirk snuggled deeper into his blankets. He could hear the munching of his horse. Then, a while later, the far-off barking of a hill-fox. After that, nothing, for sleep came, deep and profound, until at daybreak he was awakened by the cold.

Sunrise from his high spot above the valley was a thing of incredible beauty. Far down the trail, the slope slipped away towards that narrow finger of the lake, and stretching out beyond it, the entire scene was a widening basin fringed here and there with cedars and junipers, with the surrounding hills breaking into small creeks and canyons. At the very head of the valley, Saddle Mountain dominated the scene, snow-clad above the skyline, with only the red dome of its summit glinting in the morning light. Then the outline of the mountain became more clearly seen, the snow on the ridge holding the yellow of gold poured in a running stream from some giant cauldron in the sky.

Not long afterwards, Kirk was once more in the saddle, and following again that slow-moving herd of horses that, an hour before, had started on the last stage of the trek to Lost Canyon.

The day seemed endless, each mile of the upward thrusting trail becoming interminable as the gorge narrowed. Only once that day did he get a glimpse of Dark Fury, now quite three miles ahead of him. Not many minutes later, as the sun glowed redly above the western line of hills, he realized that he could no longer see the stallion, or the herd. The frowning mountains had taken them as surely as if they had never been.

Kirk spent a very restless night, once again painfully aware of the cold at such a high altitude. He was only too glad to kindle an early fire and prepare a hot meal. Then, as on the previous day, the sun was scarcely above the horizon when he again set off up the trail, entering now a shallow depression flanked high up on either side by dwarf cedars. He noticed that the farther he travelled along the ever-narrowing gorge, the gloomier it became. Then he found himself approaching what was an enormous cavern set in the wall of the mountain, and the trail vanished into it, filling Kirk with a measure of uncertainty as to its ultimate destination.

Nevertheless, it was obvious that the band of wild horses, driven by Dark Fury, had gone through into the darkness to some pre-destined point.

Dismounting to examine the debris-covered track the more thoroughly, he got a shock when he discovered, close against the cavern wall, a cask of the type used to transport gunpowder.

Kirk was not long in finding that the cask did indeed contain explosive powder, sufficient, he calculated, to cause a considerable landslide.

His next thought brought a wave of excitement. Perhaps the tunnel led to Lost Canyon, and the stories he had heard about the wealth it contained were not only true, but others also knew the Canyon's secret and were intent on mining the area. There could be no other explanation for the presence of the powder cask.

In addition, he discovered some specially prepared brushwood bundles, clearly intended to be used as torches. This lent support to the idea that mining activities were contemplated by somebody or other.

Taking as many of the bundles as could be conveniently placed in the saddle packs, he lit one for his immediate use, and holding it aloft, grasped his horse by the bridle and started the laborious journey through the cavern. The very instant he entered the darkness, he experienced a strong current of air blowing through from some distant opening.

He felt encouraged, and his heart beat high. The lighted brand disclosed that the tunnel retained an even height, and that the floor was composed of small pebbles with here and there a clear run of sand. More strongly than ever was the fact impressed upon him that he was traversing an ancient river course.

It was a little after high noon when he entered the cavern. At times, the cold stream of air was sharp against his face, so sharp in fact that he was forced to close his eyes and gasp for breath.

After a while, the floor became more sandy than otherwise, and his footfalls and those of his horse were completely silenced. Kirk could see, however, from the fitful glow of the torch, that the sand was broken and churned as if by countless feet having passed over it, and he knew that the feet had been the hooves of the band of wild horses, and their leader, Dark Fury.

Suddenly his horse tugged against the bridle, forcing Kirk to come to a halt. He heard the animal whistling through his nostrils with fear. Glancing down, he gave a gasp of horror. A few feet away was a deep crevasse in the floor of the cavern. Cold sweat trickled down his forehead. But for his horse, and the uncanny sense animals have of approaching danger, he might have plunged headlong into it, for it was in the very centre of the track.

He noticed that the left-hand wall of the cavern thrust away a little from the crevasse, and judging from some firmly made hoof marks, the wild horses had passed the spot in single file, and quite clearly without mishap, for there was no sign of violently disturbed sand or gravel.

Kirk summoned up all his reserves of courage. Stroking his horse gently and speaking reassuringly to him, he proceeded forward with care, keeping close to that widening bulge in the wall, and making doubly sure that the animal was well on the inside and as far from the crevasse as possible.

In a couple of minutes the danger spot was passed, and pausing, Kirk peered into that awesome break in the tunnel floor. He kindled another torch of brushwood, casting the remains of the old one into the gap.

It fell out of sight, the flame flickering then suddenly sweeping up before spluttering into nothingness. In that brief flickering, however, Kirk had seen enough. He had glimpsed the fissure disappearing into a void that was too terrifying to contemplate. He wondered no longer why rivers seemed to be forever disappearing in this strange country. Before him was a plain answer. The crevasse was yet another sink.

The air was cleaner as he advanced, with a fragrance in it. That was it! A fragrance such as one might find in a breeze blowing from off a lofty mountain range covered with larch and pine. Then Kirk knew! Resin! That was the fragrance. Resin!

He hurried on, his excitement rising and his heart beating wildly. He was so engrossed in moving steadily into the wind that

Suddenly his horse tugged against the bridle

he failed to notice another tunnel branching off from the right. Even had he seen it, he would not have considered following it, for the hoof prints still lay thick in the trail at his feet.

Despite the darkness and the limitations imposed on his vision by the feeble glow of the torch, he had lost his sense of fear. He knew that he was following what had once been a water course, whose age was perhaps a million years or more. He knew, too, that the horrifying darkness was as impenetrable as any he had ever known, and that the silence, save for the fall of his feet and those of the horse in the soft sand, was a silence fraught with danger. But Dark Fury and his herd of wild horses had passed this way, and the end of the grim underground trail could not be too far off. The wind told him that. The wind...

As it increased in force, a sudden surge of panic rose to match it. Fear clutched at his heart. He thought chaotically: Now I am in the very bowels of the earth... under a mountain. There might be other crevasses. There might be the sudden rising of a river...

He heard a voice—his own voice strangely distorted, saying: 'Take care! Have a grip on yourself. Dark Fury and the herd came this way. It's the way to Lost Canyon... Lost Canyon...'

He found himself laughing mirthlessly, then was aware of tears dimming his eyes and his tongue cleaving heavy and thick to his mouth.

The grip on his heart tightened, and silence and solitude were no more, for reaching out to him from some place not far off came an ominous sound, the muffled roar of falling water...

He paused in his tracks, gasping, but his horse nudged him on; the beast was wiser than he. There was no danger for him in that distant roar of water. More important, the horse could sniff not only the scent of resin, but grass also——rich grass, and he was impatient to reach it.

The rush of wind against Kirk's face was colder and stronger than ever. The roar of the water was a part of it. Another wave of fear swept over him, turning into absolute panic as the torch flickered, the flame suddenly rising and throwing distorted shadows on the walls of the cavern. He glimpsed for a fleeting second the roof above him from which stalactites, like tusks, gleamed ominously, then were lost in darkness as the torch flickered and went out.

From a moment of seeing to a moment of blindness was eternity in that terrible underworld of wind and sound. He stumbled forward, and suddenly the darkness was not the same darkness; light filtered through from some place ahead——grey light. As Kirk moved forward, it changed to golden. A minute... two perhaps... three... even... four... He did not know. He couldn't tell. All he knew was that the opening came steadily nearer, and framed against it, a silvery fall that was water tumbling from a great height; and beyond the water and the gold, mountains and trees... and way up, beyond both... the sky... a blue sky... a very blue sky...

'Oh, thank God! Thank God!' and while the words still echoed like a prayer in his mind, he found himself standing on a grassy plateau close to the spumy fall of water. Then with eyes dazed with wonder, he gazed down at long last upon Lost Canyon——the last remaining sanctuary of the wild horse herds and the many wild animals who sought to live in peace away from man—the destroyer of their kind!

VENGEANCE CAN WAIT
Ford Whitaker

The man had sworn vengeance against the she-wolf who had dragged her claws across his cheek and earned him the nickname of Scarface. He told himself his vengeance could wait. But he did not expect the day would dawn when he would look upon his she-wolf enemy as a friend. However, a man learns how to discard old notions and come to grips with grim reality when his days are spent against a background of Arctic snow. It was such a lesson that changed Dave Bowman's mind.

'That old she-wolf sure carved up your chops, Scarface!'

'You weren't no beauty before, boy, but by gosh, I wouldn't like to meet you on a dark night now!'

In the saloon at Fort Macgregor, Dave Bowman fingered the puckered scar on his cheek and smiled grimly as he settled down to his coffee and sausages. In the past two years he had grown used to the friendly jibes, for everyone in Sagwa Territory knew his story.

'Don't worry,' he grinned over the rim of his steaming cup. 'I'll get that she-wolf in my own good time.' The friendly light went from his blue eyes and his jaw set, making the scar tense perceptibly, almost as if it were capable of coming to life by itself. It was a strange thing, which everyone noticed, that when the she-wolf was mentioned, the scar on Dave's cheek seemed to grow more livid, though this, no doubt, was caused by the fact that in his anger the blood mantled into his cheeks and made the scar stand out more vividly at the same time.

Scarface Dave had sworn vengeance on that wolf for the injury she had caused him. One day two winters ago, making the round of his traplines, he had come across a large she-wolf caught by a paw in one of his traps. Evidently she had only recently been caught, for she was merely held by the toe of one hindpaw and would doubtless have soon dragged her way out, albeit painfully.

For a moment or two Dave — he wasn't Scarface yet! — stood eyeing the crouching wolf as she stared back at him, her muzzle crinkling in a snarl, her slanting eyes watching the man intently.

'You ain't worth a bullet,' Dave muttered. When you have to sledge a hundred miles for your supplies, including cartridges, you learn to be sparing! He took the wood-axe from his belt and cut a sizable, cudgelly branch from a near-by tree. He figured to parry the wolf with this and deal her a deathblow with the axe.

The she-wolf savaged the cudgel as he poked it at her. Cautiously but swiftly he manoeuvred round at arm's length, axe at the ready. But at the very moment he lunged forward to bring the axe crushing down on the animal's skull, one of his snowshoes broke through a crust of the snow and he slipped. Desperate, the she-wolf leapt. A big, heavy animal, she fell across Dave as he floundered in the snow. He had a momentary vision of flashing eyes and white fangs. A pain like flame ripped across his cheek, narrowly missing one eye. Lashing out with the axe he struck at the wolf. In a frenzy of snarling she tore herself from the trap and went limping away, leaving a trail of blood on the snow. Blood was streaming down Dave's face, too. There was a hideous wound where the wolf had ripped him and the pain was agonizing.

Nevertheless, Dave set off in pursuit of the she-wolf, unslinging his rifle as he went. But despite her injured foot she had got away and in the intense cold Dave dared not leave his own wound too long. Presently, he gave up the chase. He must get back home as quickly as possible and have his partner, Joe Gilson, doctor him up as best he could.

If Dave had gone to hospital the doctors would have put half a dozen stitches in the wound. Joe contented himself with two, and Dave's knuckles stood out white as he gripped the sides of the chair he was sitting on. Joe's work was crude but it was effective. But Scarface was Dave's inevitable nickname thereafter.

Grimly he swore vengeance on that she-wolf. His thirst for revenge became almost an obsession. Any news of the wolf would send him miles off his beat. Nor was it particularly difficult to get news of her. She was phenomenally large, even for a timber-wolf, and since being caught in the trap she had a distinctive trail, for her mutilated paw left an unmistakable spoor.

'Hiya, Scarface! Made it quits with that she-wolf girl-friend of yours yet?' the boys would rib him whenever he trekked into the trading post. 'What are you waitin' for? Gettin' fond of her?'

'Shucks, don't you get it? Scarface is gonna turn the other cheek when he meets her!'

Scarface smiled at the jests, but he was grimly determined sooner or later to even up the score with the limping she-wolf. There was only one other living creature he hated more and that was a human being. Some time back, through no fault of his own, he had been embroiled with a get-rich-quick type named Jackson, who had badly done down a Megaleep Indian, Kondiaronk. Dave had innocently been responsible for Jackson's gaining the confidence of the Megaleeps and they had never forgiven him, even though Jackson himself had been dealt with by the Mounties. Kondiaronk and his people still had it in for Dave.

Scarface had hit the trail of a bull moose. He had cashed the result of his latest round of the traplines and was looking forward to a brew-up when he happened upon tell-tale signs where the shoots of various trees had been stripped. Only a moose could have browsed like that; only a moose could have churned up the surrounding snow like that.

Scarface's eyes quickened with satisfaction. A sizable moose would keep him and Joe in meat for several weeks. He searched through the grove of trees and came across droppings that were still fresh. The moose could not be more than half an hour ahead of him.

The going was just right. It was early winter, with not too much snow, and what there was had been made crisp by the frost. The trail was plain to read, the great splayed hoof-marks of an animal weighing around half a ton. Keeping an instinctive check on the wind Scarface began to follow, swiftly but cautiously. The bark scraped off overhanging boughs told him that his quarry was a bull that had not yet lost its huge antlers.

The moose was apparently in no hurry. Browsing here and there on any deciduous trees it came across, it made its way upwind through the forest and Scarface followed expectantly, rifle in hand. The snow glittered with untold gems of frost which had packed it down iron-hard, so that even the heavy moose was able to move freely.

It was not going to be as short a hunt as Scarface had at first hoped. But he was not going to give up now and he pressed on steadily at a tireless lope. The growing freshness of the trail convinced him that he was overtaking the moose and also that his quarry had not grown aware of his presence. Pulling out from the trail, he circled to one side of it. He knew only too well the moose's habit of standing aside from its path and pausing for signs of danger. Tensely, Scarface kept his eyes skinned for his quarry.

Then, abruptly, all thought of the moose was forgotten.

He came to a halt, staring at the snow. His eyes narrowed, his nostrils flared. His jaws tensed and the scar on his cheekbone stood out vivid and angry at the edge of his fur-lined hood.

There, imprinted on the snow as clearly as words in a book, was an unmistakable trail: three sound paws and a dragging fourth. Like morse code spelling out a message those paw-marks studded the snow. It was the trail of the she-wolf. Involuntarily Dave put a mittened hand up to the throbbing scar. He wasn't going to let an opportunity like this pass by. The trail was older than that of the moose, but it wasn't that old. If he pressed on now he might make up the start the wolf had on him.

He shouldered his gun again, for he knew it would be some time before he needed it. The wolf's tracks led roughly eastwards, almost at right angles to those of the moose. Unhurriedly, but with burning determination, Scarface set out to get his revenge. The ugly cicatrice on his cheek hurt him as if the wound had been inflicted afresh.

On through the short winter day, Scarface pursued his quarry. He took his time. As long as the trail was going steadily he was content to press on evenly, relentlessly, certain that this time he was going to succeed. Nobody was a more even-tempered, likable person than Dave Bowman. As all the Territory knew, he was as straight as a die, always ready to lend a helping hand. But he was obsessed with the thought of avenging himself on the she-wolf that had ripped his cheek. For nearly two years now he had brooded on it, schemed about it, hiked miles on false trails, risked blizzards. He had even neglected his trapping at times because of some rumour that the she-wolf had been seen. One or two trappers had taken shots at her but missed. It seemed as if fate was preserving that grey beast so that Scarface could wreak his vengeance in person.

Onward the trail ran, the she-wolf was hunting on her own, and by the look of it she wasn't having much luck, for little game was moving about at that time. Mile after mile the limping trail continued, with scarcely a check. Mile after mile Scarface followed on his snowshoes. Any thought of hunger or tiredness was forgotten in that one all-powerful motive that drummed through his brain as insistently as an Indian drum. Vengeance! He had sworn to get that she-wolf and get her he would, at whatever cost.

The trail led down to the Sumach River and turned along it. Scarface followed. Some way along the frozen river he came to a beaver dam. He saw that the wolf had been scraping hopefully at the roofs of the beaver lodges, trying to break into them, but the mud with which the beavers had coated their well-made homes had frozen hard, and the wolf had spent a long time without result.

Scarface nodded with satisfaction as he inspected the extensive efforts of the wolf. She had spent a long time at the beaver lodges. This was his chance to gain ground on her. Without further delay he scouted round and picked up the trail again.

He quickened his pace. The trail was that much fresher now. He braced himself against his mounting weariness. On he went, while the livid scar still burnt as if intent on strengthening his resolve.

Some distance from the river the wolf tracks halted momentarily. The wolf had circled round irresolutely before going on.

'Winded something, has she?' Scarface speculated. 'Hare, maybe? Hazel-grouse?'

No, it didn't seem to be like that. The wolf was uneasy. Her trail went off at an angle and further on she had halted again. Frowning, Scarface followed. The further he went, the more broken the wolf trail became. It was no longer holding straight on into the wind. Now it broke back again, paused, circled. He could envisage the she-wolf halting, hesitating.

With a sudden tightening of the heart Scarface realized what had happened. Someone else was hunting the she-wolf.

Someone else?

He unslung his rifle and stared watchfully into the trees. A worried look had come into his keen eyes. He rubbed his nose reflectively with a mittened hand. Someone else was trailing the she-wolf. Of that Scarface was certain. But he was puzzled by the animal's behaviour. Why had she zigzagged like that instead of merely changing direction when she realized she was being hunted? He tried to reconstruct what had happened. The she-wolf had winded someone; turned away from him...

'Okay,' he muttered to himself, chewing his lip. 'But what made her turn again...'

Suddenly it dawned on him. There were several men hunting the wolf. Three or four maybe; even half a dozen. They were surrounding her in a huge circle and she had realized it. That was why her trail had become so irresolute.

Scarface glanced about him. By chance he himself had broken into that circle, unbeknown to the other pursuers of the wolf. Somewhere in that circle, which was maybe as much as a mile across, was his quarry, the limping she-wolf, and somewhere else, watchful in the trees, moving steadily in on her, were the men who were hunting her.

He had no difficulty guessing who they were. Megaleep Indians. Nobody else could be there. He had travelled many miles from his home ground. He was very near Megaleep territory. Until now he had not given the matter a moment's thought, so obsessed was he with the pursuit of his enemy.

'You've walked right into it, bud,' he murmured. 'It's Megaleeps for certain. Kondiaronk's own bunch. If they find you here they'll skin you as well as the wolf.'

It took a lot to scare Dave Bowman. All the same, he knew he was in a tough spot. Kondiaronk would not hesitate to shoot him down after that Jackson affair. The Megaleeps had a deep-down grudge against him. It was a chance in a million that they had happened across the wolf while they were out hunting and had managed to throw a circle round her, skilled hunters that they were. How many men? Dave wondered. His guess was six at the most. They might be a quarter of a mile apart. It depended how far into the circle he had gone as to whether he could extricate himself without being discovered.

Once he had got over the shock of realizing what had happened, he was riled at the thought of being cheated of his quarry at this last moment. Cautiously he pushed on into the silent trees awhile, every nerve alert. He might well be walking into a death-trap. He came to a tangle of storm-felled trees that had crashed on top of each other. He crouched down in the angle the branches had formed and stared out watchfully at the snowy terrain in front of him.

The whole arctic forest seemed to be watching and listening. The silence became so profound that it was almost audible. Scar-face could hear his heart hammering away. With an effort he suppressed an impulse to turn and get out.

Somewhere a hawk-owl uttered its cry, startlingly sharp on the frost-lashed air.

'You're wasting your time, bud,' Scarface told himself. 'Best make yourself scarce before them Megaleeps tread on your tail.' But he continued to crouch there behind the angled tree trunks. He was beginning to feel cold after the steady exercise of the pursuit.

All at once he tensed. He had caught sight of a faint movement seventy yards away across the snow. The slightest stirring on that white background showed up instantly. It was the wolf. She emerged from a clump of snow-hung bushes and headed slowly in Scarface's direction. Even if it hadn't been for the limp he would have recognized that wolf a mile off. Her almost black fur noticeably grizzled round the neck, she was a fine beast. She'd stretch out every inch of six feet when she was skinned, he wouldn't wonder.

She had come to a halt now in a little hollow which completely screened her from one side. She was plainly on edge. Ears cocked, tongue lolling, she stood there vigilantly, testing the air with ear and nose for any sign to guide her. She was hemmed in and knew it. At key points somewhere in the trees half a dozen Indians were moving silently in on her.

Scarface's hands tightened on his rifle. He eased the weapon up through the branches that sheltered him. The scar on his cheek throbbed painfully. This was the moment he had waited two years for. He was on the point of avenging himself on the animal, that had obsessed him all that time as crazily as Moby Dick had obsessed Captain Ahab. She was in his sights. There, stark against the snow, oblivious to his presence, the limping she-wolf stood, an easy target.

As he was on the very point of squeezing the trigger, Scarface caught sight of another movement out of the corner of his eye. He hesitated. Imperceptibly he swivelled his gaze to the right. What he saw made him grunt in dismay. Scarcely any further from him than the wolf was, an Indian had appeared, rifle in hand, heading straight for the tangle of tree trunks behind which Scarface crouched.

Clearly the Megaleep could not yet see the wolf. His vision was obscured by the undulating ground. As it happened, Scarface could see both man and wolf. The wolf glanced about her. She could not fail to be aware of the approach of the Indian. But she knew also there were men somewhere behind her. Her dilemma was equalled by that of the white man. He still had her in his sights. One squeeze of the trigger and the wolf would be stretched out on the snow. At the same time that avenging shot would assuredly spell Dave's fate. Even if he were prepared to try to fight off the Megaleeps he would most certainly finish up stretched out on the snow, riddled with the bullets of Kondiaronk's men.

But he was bound to be discovered in any case, whether or not he fired. Slowly, intently, lithely, the Indian advanced, gun at the ready. He was less than twenty paces from Scarface's hide-out. Despite the cold Scarface found himself sweating as he crouched there. What was he to do? Shoot the Megaleep before he himself was shot down? He knew he had not got it in him to shoot a man in cold blood. Besides, if he did that he knew Kondiaronk would run him down, sooner or later.

206

As it happened, Scarface could see both man and wolf

Steadily the Indian came on towards the fallen trees. He was so close now Scarface could hear the sound of his breathing. At any moment now the Indian must grow aware of the white man's presence. If he did not catch sight of him he was bound to notice the tracks leading to the trees.

Every muscle quivering with the effort of keeping still, Dave crouched there, unable to think or act. He knew his nerve was on the point of snapping. The breaking strain was not far off. But in the end it was not his own nerve that went. It was the she-wolf's. All at once she could stand the suspense no longer. Abruptly she broke cover, went loping away back into the trees. There might be other men lurking somewhere, but she *knew* that one man was there and that was enough for her.

With a cry of triumphant warning to his hidden companions, the Indian turned instantly as he caught sight of the wolf emerging from the hollow. He fired as he ran but the shot ploughed up the snow. The she-wolf loped on, scrambled up the rising ground and vanished from Scarface's view. Another shot rang out further away. An angry shout made it evident that the Indians had failed to stop the wolf.

Scarface came to his senses. He peered carefully through the branches. Then he got to his feet and went swiftly on his way, following much of the trail he had broken in his pursuit of the wolf.

'Good luck, old girl,' he muttered, as he slogged along on his snowshoes. He grinned wryly to himself as he realized the irony of his words. Never had he even remotely imagined there would come a day when he felt indebted to the she-wolf that had scarred his face for life. Yet undoubtedly if it had not been for her he would be a dead man by now. One pace more and the Megaleep brave could not have failed to discover him.

'Reckon we'll call it quits,' he said to himself as he trudged wearily through the darkening forest. Vengeance would have to wait!

BAAL CHIMNEY
Arthur Catherall

Two friends on holiday in the Lake District decide to climb Baal Chimney and by so doing impress the son of their employer. But climbing the chimney proved more than an arduous outdoor exercise. Before the friends reached safety they had discovered the meaning of both cowardice and heroism.

The thing had happened so swiftly, yet so casually, that Bob and Allan scarcely realized, until it was too late, the extent of the difficulty which had swooped out of a clear sky and now threatened their short Easter holiday.

As the door of the climbing hut closed behind the athletic young man who had just been talking to the seventeen-year-old pair, Bob turned accusing eyes on Allan Thompson.

'You're crazy, Allan. You've dropped us in the soup and no mistake. What are we going to do?'

Allan scratched his head, and grinned sheepishly. It was his fault, there was no doubt about that. He and Bob Jones had begun a short tramping holiday the previous day, intending to walk through part of the Lake District, staying at various youth hostels. A chance encounter with a ditched motorist had made it impossible for them to get to the first hostel, and the grateful motorist had taken them to the climbing club hut, where he was staying. He found a couple of bunks for them and arranged supper. Still the perfect host, he had seen they had a good breakfast, and had then gone out with two climbing companions.

Bob and Allan, sitting unobtrusively at a corner table, had disposed of their porridge and were tackling fried bread and sausages, listening with keen interest to the talk going on among the climbers. They had thrilled to the talk of Napes Needle, Gimmer Crag, Doe Buttress, Baal Rock, Eagle's Nest — places they had heard of, but never thought to climb. These keen-faced men were going out to climb the difficult rocks. The two youths were absorbing it all until a man came into the hut, walked to a corner and picked up a coil of climbing-rope. As he was turning to leave the room again he chanced to look across at the two youths. He stopped, stared, then came over... there was a smile on his face.

'Well, this is a surprise. I never expected to see you here. Don't you work for me?'

Bob and Allan had started to rise, recognizing this young man as their employer's son, the new manager of Watson and Watson Ltd. He waved them back to their seats.

'I didn't know I'd two rock climbers on my staff,' he went on. 'I thought I knew most of the members of this club. How long...' He was interrupted then by a voice from outside yelling:

'Come along, John, we're waiting.'

'Yes, yes... I'll not be a minute,' John Watson cried, and turned again to the two youths. 'What are you doing today? Doe Crag, the Buttress, Eagle's Nest?' There was a quizzical smile on his face, for he was naming some of the most difficult climbs.

Bob was trying to find words to tell Mr Watson that he and Allan were not really rock climbers at all, that they were not even members of the Climbing Club, but Allan forestalled him. Allan was quick-witted. Allan thought he saw a chance of impressing the young 'chief'.

'We haven't really made up our minds, yet,' he confessed. 'We thought we might try Baal Chimney.'

'*Watson!*' The man outside was growing very impatient, and John Watson hitched his coil of rope more comfortably across his shoulder.

'I'll have to go... let me see... Thompson, isn't it? Thompson, and Jones?'

'Yes, sir,' Allan said brightly, feeling chuffed at the interest shown. 'I hope you have a good day, sir.'

'Thanks, I hope you do. Are your boots well nailed? You need good boots on Baal Chimney.'

Allan thrust a boot out. Allan was very proud of his boots. They were a present from his cousin, and they were nailed for rock climbing with side-nails and tricounis.

'Good enough. Well... I must be off. I'll see you here tonight. You must tell me what you've done... and perhaps we can have a climb together, tomorrow. Cheerio!... and don't take any risks.'

Then he was gone, and the two lads stared at each other, suddenly realizing what had happened. Mr John Watson thought they were members of the climbing club. Allan had stupidly allowed him to think so... they *were* going over the screes of Baal Buttress, but had no intention of climbing the Chimney. Worst of all, however, was the fact that Mr Watson, who knew them by name, had said he wanted to have a chat with them that evening... and that was impossible. They could not come back to spend another night there. They had been found bunks solely and simply because they had helped the stranded motorist.

'I thought it might be useful... to sort of impress him,' Allan said, lamely. 'It is a good thing, you know, Bob, to be known to the boss. Sometimes it helps a lot.'

'It's... oh, let's get out into the fresh air,' Bob snapped. 'We'll perhaps be able to think of some way out of the mess. He's got to be told, Allan. If he's just left to find out for himself he'll have a very poor impression of us, very poor indeed.'

Their kits were soon packed, and they went out into the crisp spring air of Easter Saturday. The sun was shining, and some of their gloom left them. It was impossible to be downhearted on such a lovely morning. The hills towered above them, green-clad part way, and then grey-brown rock. The air was alive with the music of the rills. The sheep were out again. Winter was ending, and there was promise of life on every side.

By half-past ten they were crossing the screes on Lammamoor, and needed all their breath for the task. Up above them towered the gaunt rock face on which several men were clinging like limpets. In the bright sunshine it was just possible to make out the rope which connected them. It looked like a thread from a spider's web.

Up and up the two youths went, the sheer muscle-cracking fatigue making them forget the unpleasantness of their attempt to impress Mr Watson.

Coming to the foot of the rock face they paused for a rest. Bob produced some sweets and raisins and they chewed gratefully. Looking back they could see the valley and the lake. The houses, dotted here and there, were little more than blobs of white. A car on the road was like a tiny beetle.

Just as they were about to start off again, skirting the grim grey-brown rock, they heard a faint yell from somewhere up above. Looking up, Bob and Allan instinctively cringed as something came whirling down towards them. It passed them, turning over and over, hit the scree about fifty yards below, and rolled for a few feet before lodging against a stone. It was a felt hat, with a bright little feather in the band!

Something else came down a few seconds later. A small rucksack!

They looked up, and both caught their breath in horror-stricken gasps. Up above, just visible round the ledge against which they stood, they saw the figure of a man roll gently off a ledge and drop ten or fifteen feet to another ledge.

In breathless silence they waited for him to fall again, but he remained still. One leg dangled in space. They could see his head and shoulders. The ledge was small. It must be very small. If he moved... Bob swallowed the lump which had come into his throat... there was nothing below the man now but space — a drop of about seventy or eighty feet, with the cruelly sharp screes waiting for him.

After a moment Bob and Allan turned to look at the rucksack. It had burst when it hit the scree first of all. There was a woollen scarf and a paper packet that had contained sandwiches. They were lying about. A man falling would be broken, just as surely.

'What... I wonder... can you see the others?' Allan asked, and his face was as white as the paper in which the sandwiches had been wrapped.

Bob could not answer. He was staring, staring, waiting for someone to go to the man's aid. A minute passed... another minute... still no sign nor sound from the fallen climber's companions.

'Could we... ought we to...' Bob looked up, then at Allan. The scree, going steeper and narrower, went up another forty feet. Then it ended in the beginning of the Chimney. Only experienced men climbed Baal Chimney. It needed stout nerves, strong hands, good boots, and — most essential — experience.

Without answering the unfinished question Allan started to climb. Bob followed. It took them five minutes to scramble to the end of the scree, and they were breathless when they leaned against the rock face and looked up. The man was still there, limp, a few inches of rocky ledge between him and death — if he *was* still alive.

'Well, what can we do now?' Bob gasped, his lungs labouring, his throat feeling as if it were being rasped with red-hot barbed wire.

'We... can't do... anything,' Allan replied. 'Look... look at that rock, smooth as... it's too smooth for us. If we slipped...'

Bob stared upwards, stared until his eyes ached. He thought he had seen a faint movement of the man's head. If he did move... when recovering consciousness... Bob closed his eyes at the thought and shuddered.

Opening his eyes again he looked upwards once more, and this time his heart contracted. The man *was* moving. He was trying to turn over, and coming nearer to the edge. In a minute he would be off.

'Stop where you are,' Bob shouted. 'Don't move... *Don't move!*'

Whether the admonition was heard or not, the movement ceased. Bob turned to Allan.

'Give me a hand.'

Allan stared at him, his throat worked convulsively, but for a few seconds no coherent words came. He looked at Bob, he looked at the perpendicular rock face, so smooth, so few ridges or crevices. The nearest seemed to be eight feet high, at least.

'Don't be... don't be a fool, Bob,' he gulped. 'It's a... you need experience, and a rope, for that job. If you fell...'

He did not finish the sentence, but looked at the sharp rocks at his feet. The scree was a pitiless thing to fall on, and it was so steep at this point that a body would just roll and roll, bruising, tearing all the time.

'Give me a leg-up,' Bob ordered. His face was white. There was a queer, sickish feeling in the pit of his stomach. It was the same feeling he had experienced once when swimming in the sea. He had chanced to look back towards the shore. The sand had seemed so far away, and an instant of panic had struck him, a terrible feeling that he could not swim back. He remembered that feeling now. He looked up again. One arm was over the ledge now and the fingers seemed to be clawing. The man must be slowly regaining consciousness.

'Come on,' he said harshly, and Allan cupped his hands, braced himself, while Bob put a foot in the support and forced himself up the rock face.

From across the valley three men stood at the top of another climb, and one of them looked across the valley through a pair of powerful binoculars. They had been watching their fellow-climbers and had seen the man fall when his rope broke.

The man with the glasses could see three men coming down the Baal Chimney, coming down cautiously, but they had still the better part of a hundred feet to come. He could see two others, and saw they wore khaki shorts; he judged them to be two youths who had been in the climbing club hut that morning.

'One of 'em is having a go, Watson,' the man with the glasses said. 'It's going to be touch and go. The ledge the climber is on is so small. Don't you remember that ledge? It's the first "rest" on the Chimney climb. If that fellow moves the least little bit, one way or the other, he'll be off.'

Tensely he reported Bob's progress for several minutes. Twice he found himself making suggestions, telling Bob, though a mile separated them, where the best fingerholds were. Then he gasped, lowered his glasses, then lifted them to his eyes again.

'He's fallen!'

John Watson, who had been standing impatiently by, snatched the glasses and clapped them to his eyes.

Bob's boots had betrayed him. They were nailed, but only with

'He's fallen!'

ordinary hob-nails on the bottom. Had there been side-nails or
tricounis in the soles, he could have found, and held, a better
grip. As it was, one boot slipped, he clawed frantically, put extra
weight on his aching fingers, trying to hold himself, and failed.
Two fingers came out of the small crack in the rock. He kicked
desperately, took the skin from his right knee trying to gain a
fresh hold, then went down, yelling a warning to Allan some
sixteen feet below.

Allan broke his fall, and prevented what might have been a
deadly roll down the steep scree. Bob had a gash across his cheek,
and he was gasping for breath when Allan helped him to his feet.
Allan whipped out a handkerchief, eyes wide at the blood pouring
from the cut cheek.

'No... no,' Bob gulped, and jerked a thumb upwards. 'He's...
he's moving. I saw him. He's opened his... eyes. He'll start...
moving... in a... minute. Give me... a... leg-up.'

'You can't climb like that,' Allan snapped. 'You're bleeding
badly. Have some sense, Bob. If you fall again...' Allan stopped,
then, for Bob, his chest heaving convulsively, had turned and
looked at him. Bob had never been the leader. Allan had always
been the one to say what should be done next, he had always
been the planner, the spokesman. Bob did not speak, even in this
emergency — he looked at his friend, then he looked up at the
tiny ledge, at the injured man.

Allan looked up at the rock face, then turned to Bob.

'Give—give me a leg-up.' His face was white, lips a thin line.

Allan had well-shod climbing boots, but no experience, yet he
went up the thirty-odd feet of rock as quickly as any experienced
man, though the risks he took would have made a seasoned rock
climber close his eyes in dismay.

It was not fear for the injured man which made Allan go up so
quickly, cling so desperately, take the skin off his knees and forget
even to wince. Allan was angry — angry and afraid. He was afraid
of the rock, afraid of what might happen if he fell, but he was
even more angry than afraid. He had seen something in Bob
Jones' eyes he would never forget. He knew himself to be just
a little quicker than Bob in most things. More daring, quicker off

the mark mentally and physically, yet there had been contempt in the eyes of his friend a few minutes earlier. Bob, without speaking, had branded him a coward. That hurt. That made Allan angry. He was talking to himself, talking to Bob, arguing with him, and climbing — always climbing.

He reached the injured climber just as the man was beginning to try to get to his knees. Allan stopped him. Allan clung to the rock like the proverbial limpet, half on the tiny ledge, half off, keeping his position by means of his right boot jammed against the rock face, his right hand clinging desperately to a little crack in the rock just above the injured climber. He clung thus, holding the man on the ledge long after his arms and legs had started to tremble violently with fatigue.

The strain became so bad that he found himself whispering: 'I can't hold on any longer... it isn't any use, Bob, I just can't.' Bob could not hear him, and so did not answer but Allan hung on just the same. He hung on until, with a clatter of nailed boots and encouraging cries, a climber was lowered down to where he clung so desperately. The rest was relatively simple.

It was mid-afternoon before they got down to the rough road in the valley bottom. There they found John Watson and his two friends. That trio had broken records getting down and fetching help. An ambulance was waiting, and several cars. Bob, his face hidden in a rough dressing, was taken to hospital along with the injured climber, the others returned to the climbing club hut.

Little was said until they had drunk many cups of hot, sweet tea and tackled piles of sandwiches which the Hut Warden put before them; then tongues were loosened. Congratulations and praise were showered on Allan. The club members knew that the injured climber owed his life to the youngster who had held him on that narrow ledge. The man would live; but had he slipped off that last ledge, death would have been certain.

Allan said little. He looked white and shaken, and John Watson finally persuaded him to have a hot bath and go to his bunk for a rest. Before he went he turned to the men sprawling before the log fire.

'I... I want you to know something,' he began, and there was a strained look about his eyes. 'You've said a lot of nice things that I... didn't deserve. I... didn't really save that man. Bob saved him.'

There was a moment of expectant silence. Then one man laughed:

'Well... you climbed up and held him on the ledge, didn't you?'

'I wouldn't have done,' Allan admitted, 'if it hadn't been for Bob. He went up first. He fell down, cut his face, and would have gone up again, and fallen again... you see, Bob's like that. I went up... because... well, I went up.

'He didn't actually say I was a coward,' Allan whispered. 'Bob wouldn't do that. He just... looked at me, that's all. I... felt you ought to know that... if there was a hero, it wasn't me: it was Bob.' Then he turned and walked to the bathroom. It was not easy to confess his feelings.

John Watson came into the bathroom a few minutes later, bringing well-warmed towels. Through the cloud of steam he spoke to Allan.

'It takes a good man, Thompson, to say what you said a few minutes ago. A very good man. It would have been so easy just to take the plaudits of the crowd. Don't worry about how you felt. We're all cowards when we face danger. I ought to know... They gave me an M.C. and a "mention" while I was in the army. I know what being afraid is.'

'If you had not given your friend credit, Thompson, for being the driving-force behind the rescue, I'm afraid I should have had a poor opinion of you. You see, I watched the rescue through powerful glasses. The man who climbs when he is scared stiff is not a coward. He's a hero.'

He leaned his left hand on the edge of the bath, took Allan's wet right hand and shook it firmly.

'I think we are going to be good friends. And I am going to propose that you are elected members of the club.'

Allan's jaw dropped.

'Then you knew this morning that we weren't members? Knew that I was acting a... a sort of lie?'

Watson laughed, merrily.

'I'm the secretary of the club. Forget it. It doesn't matter a great deal... so long as we come up to scratch at the vital moment. You and Jones did that. Would you like to become members?'

Allan nodded. The Easter holiday was a success, even though Bob did have stitches in his cheek and had to walk about like a wounded hero!

A STRANGE SAMARITAN
John Newton Chance

Audacious Cotterell is assuredly the most eccentric of all inventors, but he has in the ever-buoyant Bunst a youthful assistant to match his own unique quality. When a certain rogue named Marston Gulliver tries to learn the secret of the Flying Eye it is only in the nature of things for the unexpected to happen — and to go on happening. This story is from *Bunst and the Flying Eye*.

The room was very dark. The only light was the glowing oblong of a television screen, which looked like a ghostly bubble floating in nothing.

The glow shed a faint light before it and showed the gleaming metal edges of a film camera, staring with its single eye at the empty white screen. The hum of its motor was all that could be heard. By the side of the camera a big man was standing, staring almost fiercely at the screen, as if silently challenging it to show more than the blank white light. Close by, a small man watched with the alertness of a sparrow.

'Ah!' The big man gave a sigh like a gale roaring in winter trees. 'Here it is!'

The sparrow man cocked his head on one side and looked at the picture that had suddenly appeared on the screen.

'He's just switched on, guv'nor,' he twittered excitedly. 'Here's the outside door!'

A large carved door appeared on the screen and grew bigger, as if the whole dark room was going quickly towards it. A hand appeared in the picture, holding a key which was thrust towards the door-lock.

'Not so fast!' bellowed the big man, as if the unseen actor could hear him.

The key plunged into the lock and turned. The door opened, and the watchers seemed to be drawn into the broad stone hall of an ancient house.

'So far—excellent!' boomed the big man. 'I doubt if I could do better myself.'

'It don't need to be better, Gulliver,' said the sparrow man. 'This is the job all right, I'm telling you!'

Enthusiastically now, the big man bent closer to the screen and heard the motor of the film camera humming in his ear. Upon the screen appeared another door, and once again a hand came into view, holding a second key of different shape. The second door was opened.

'The door to a fortune, Barnaby!' cried Gulliver. Watch it closely, man. Gad! I can hear the gold clinking in my pockets already.'

The picture vanished, leaving a white blank.

'Thermie's being careful with the batteries,' remarked Gulliver's companion.

'Sensible fellow!' cried Gulliver, in a voice that sounded like somebody shouting into an empty dustbin. 'Excellent chap! I've a mind, almost, to give him more than his share of the treasure, Barnaby!' And he laughed heartily, in a way which made the sparrow man shrink into himself. He was frightened of Gulliver. The brightness of his eyes showed it.

'He'll be lucky if he gets any share out of you at all,' he muttered, but not loudly enough for Gulliver to hear. 'And that goes for me too,' he added.

'Wait for this,' cautioned Gulliver, still watching the screen. 'The third door is coming.'

Until now, the loudspeaker of the television set had been silent. The transmission they were watching had been quite soundless. But now they heard the familiar hiss that precedes sound transmission. Gulliver and his companion exchanged glances, as if wondering what the sound could be. Then a gigantic voice proclaimed:

'I never heard of sausages in pancakes!'

Gulliver started up to his full height, astounded by this remark.

'By heaven!' he snarled. 'What's that?' The first shock past, his eyes narrowed suspiciously and he said, very slowly, 'I—seem—to—know—that—VOICE!'

In another minute his suspicions were confirmed, for a second voice rang through the room. It said:

'It does not matter whether or not you have heard of sausages in pancakes, boy. This is the first time they have ever been cooked by television.'

'Well, be careful you don't burn 'em,' replied the first voice in a shrill tone of caution.

'Thunder and lightning!' bawled Gulliver, raising a great fist and shaking it in the air. 'Audacious Cotterell! And that boy! Bunst and Cotterell! What does this mean?'

Suddenly the screen flicked into life again, but not with the expected picture of a door. Instead there was a frying-pan, with sausages and some sort of stuff that might have been pancake mixture in it. It was beginning to make a sizzling noise. Then the well-known face of Audacious Cotterell, battered hat askew on his head and white moustache trembling with excitement, appeared right in the middle of the frying-pan and the sausages, and began to turn slowly round like a gramophone record.

'Thunder and blinkers!' roared Gulliver. 'What is this?'

'It's terrible,' said the sparrow man. 'They must have got all their cameras mixed up. And look — there's the door. All mixed up in the mess.'

The blurred image of another door appeared, and a hand and a key, but it was all so confused with sausages, Audacious and the frying-pan that it was difficult to sort anything out.

'We're being jammed!' cried Gulliver furiously.

Audacious, now upside down in the frying-pan with a key coming out of his nose, said: 'Have you got me in the sights, Bunst?'

'Goodness knows what I've got,' said Bunst. 'It all seems to be mixed up. I'll just change the switches over.'

There was a loud crack in the speaker, then silence. Bunst's transmission ended abruptly, leaving just the picture of an opening door. That, too, vanished, and the screen was blank.

'Spoilt!' twittered the sparrow man. 'Ruined'!

Gulliver switched off the film camera with an angry gesture.

'Spoilt all right,' he said between his teeth. 'But—by hokey, Smokey, that's not all! Those two—those two—'

He sat down in a chair, brought a battered cigar from his pocket, and began to bite it.

'Smokey, we must take care,' he said suddenly. 'The pictures may be all right. We cannot tell till you develop them. But Audacious Cotterell will not be all right. If I had known he was around here, I should have got rid of him first.'

'Why? Who is he?' Smokey asked, going to the camera to take out the film.

'Mortal enemy, boy,' said Gulliver. 'They found me out once before. He had a boy called Bunst. Wretches.'

'That's bad,' said Smokey, taking out the drum. 'They can't be more than five miles away. That's about the maximum range for amateur transmissions.'

Slowly Gulliver got up. Smokey switched on the lights in the small room. Gulliver seemed even larger now that he was more than a shadow. He wore a cloak that hung in folds like a bat's wings, and carried a stick in his right hand. As he turned towards the door he took a big furry top hat from the top of the film camera and jammed it rakishly on his head.

'Develop the film, Smokey,' he said, flicking his stick at the small man.

'Where are you going?' Smokey asked.

'I'm going to find out where Audacious Cotterell is,' said Gulliver. 'I don't want him stumbling into our affairs again.'

'Rough stuff?' asked Smokey, cocking his head sharply.

'My stuff is never rough,' said Gulliver grandly. 'Out of the way, Peahead. Away!'

He swept the small man aside with his left arm, opened the door and left the room. Smokey remained leaning against the wall, gasping to get his breath back.

'I don't like the look of him like that,' he said, after a while.

Upon the hill overlooking the village was a white-walled cottage with a flat straw roof. In a meadow by its side there was a huge barn with crooked, bulging timbers and tiles which sprouted aerials like barebranched Christmas trees.

If you were looking for the source of amateur radio or television transmission, this seemed a likely place.

On this sunny morning Audacious Cotterell stood outside the open door of his barn wiping his brow with a handkerchief. By his side stood Bunst, short and round, eating a large hunk of bread-and-cheese and looking rather like a ball wearing overalls.

'You spoilt the sosses, after all,' said Bunst contemptuously.

'It's difficult to work out the proportion of ultraviolet rays to the pound, boy,' said Audacious.

'They wizened into cinders,' said Bunst accusingly.

'We'll get some more,' said Audacious. 'Pop down to the butcher, boy, and get another pound.'

'Not if you're going to spoil 'em,' said Bunst solemnly, and shut one eye.

'I won't. Not this time,' promised Audacious. 'We'll soon get the hang of it. It's a new idea, this invention of cooking by short waves.'

'Perhaps you should have learnt to cook by the ordinary way first,' said Bunst. 'I shouldn't be surprised if you didn't frizzle up the bangers on a long-wave open fire.'

'That's sarcasm, boy,' said Audacious sternly. 'Away now, and get some more bangers. Take the Rocket.'

The Rocket was Audacious' new jet-driven motorcycle.

'No fear,' said Bunst placidly. 'You haven't tested it yet. I'll take the Jumbo. It's safer.'

The Jumbo was a kind of motor-scooter, which Bunst rode like an expert. Now he got it out of the garage and purred away into the lane and down towards the village.

'No confidence, these youngsters,' said Audacious to himself as he wheeled the Rocket out of the garage.

The garage was by the side of the cottage garden, and the flowers and bushes were looking very bright that fine day.

The Rocket had the frame of a powerful motorcycle, but in the middle, where the engine should have been, was a contraption of cans and cylinders studded with bolts, sprayed with wires and pipes, and ending in enormous exhaust-pipes that looked like guns pointing backwards. Audacious swung into the saddle, set the controls on the top of the tank, and switched on.

For a second or two nothing disturbed the placid loveliness of the morning; then there was a sound as if a pair of gigantic trousers had been ripped on a barbed-wire fence.

The motorcycle shot away across the meadow. Audacious remained standing where he was, legs wide apart, like a human croquet arch. Behind, there was a great envelope of flame and red smoke lying right across the garden Roses, pieces of bush, leaves and a few sticks were flying about in the volcanic cloud of exhaust until they vanished in small bursts of flame.

The machine swerved round, fell over, skidded and came to rest some distance away. The flame and smoke subsided, leaving only a black, chemical column winding up towards the bright blue sky.

'What a very extraordinary thing!' gasped Audacious. 'There must have been a wrong connection somewhere.'

Then he started violently.

The smoke had cleared from the garden, and he saw a dreadful figure from another world standing amid the wreckage.

It was big, and black all over. It wore a cloak, tattered and blown full of holes as it whirled in the uneasy draught of the explosion. It held a broad top hat on its head with one great hand, and as Audacious watched, the whole apparition shuddered.

'Thunder and blitzkrieg!' it said, and collapsed in a sooty heap on the ground.

Audacious stood quite still.

'Good gracious!' he cried. 'This looks like trouble.'

He was right.

Gulliver lay on the ground, waiting for Audacious to run to his assistance, and inwardly chuckling now that he had recovered from the shock.

'It could not be better—for me!' he murmured, and tried to look as if he were dead.

Gulliver groaned. It was a terrifying noise. He had been a travelling actor, a barn-stormer, and there was no noise he could

He saw a dreadful figure from another world standing amid the wreckage

not make that might strike terror into the hearts of his audience.

'I am dying!' he declared in powerful but sepulchral tones.

'Oh dear,' snorted Audacious, galloping up. 'I hope not. What a ghastly affair! Accept my apologies, sir. Where are you broken?'

He went down on his knees beside the blackened, fallen colossus, and began to search for broken bones.

'Don't do that,' cried Gulliver sharply. 'It hurts!'

'My dear sir! I am so sorry,' said Audacious. Then, with a curious, startled frown on his face, he said: 'I seem to know you, sir.'

'Long ago, long ago. When I was alive, sir,' groaned Gulliver. 'Now I am scorched, blackened, burnt and blotched. No one will know me any more. Oh, if only I had a bed, with a view of the trees and the sky from a window, so that I could pass on peacefully!'

These lines were part of a play he had acted in years before, and they went down very well just now. Audacious looked quite upset.

'My poor fellow,' he said anxiously. 'You do sound bad.'

'I am bad,' said the black-faced sufferer. 'I have been fried with flamethrowers—'

'Marston Gulliver!' shouted Audacious, his eyes popping. 'By gad, I knew I knew that voice!'

'Ah—ah!' groaned Gulliver. 'The pain is terrible!' He kept his eyes shut and made fearful faces. 'Is there no one to help me in my agony?'

Audacious forgot his surprise. The man on the ground was quite likely in pain, for he was black from head to foot, and might be badly burnt somewhere. And though he thought, privately, that Marston Gulliver deserved to be badly burnt—for in their previous encounters the ex-actor had proved himself to be a rogue of the blackest dye—Audacious could not bear to see anybody in pain.

'Can you walk?' he said. 'You may lean on me. I'll get you to a bed and fetch a doctor.'

'You are a Samaritan, Cotterell,' murmured Gulliver, opening his eyes as if for the last time. 'I knew you were a fine man at heart. Yes. Yes, I might manage to walk.'

Audacious helped him up. Gulliver leant so heavily on him to start with that the pair of them almost ran sideways across the flower-beds. Slowly they went towards the cottage, with Gulliver groaning all the way.

'Thank you, thank you indeed, dear fellow,' he moaned from time to time. 'I shall never forget this, I promise you.'

'It was an accident,' said Audacious.

The cottage was full of gadgets, for Audacious had invented mechanisms to do everything he could think of, and some things he couldn't. The room into which he brought the groaning Gulliver was a nice sunny bedroom, but it was hung about with wires like jungle-vines. Monkeys could have swung about on them. And there was a whole panel of buttons and switches by the bedside.

How Audacious managed to get Gulliver cleaned and into bed he did not quite know, but it was achieved in the end, and the huge man closed his eyes and groaned rather louder.

'I'll ring up the doctor,' said Audacious.

'Not now!' cried Gulliver suddenly. 'Let me sleep first. I am too wrought with racking pains to see strangers just now.'

He waved a big hand rather feebly in the air.

'Leave me, Cotterell, dear fellow! I shall be better by and by.'

Audacious went out frowning. As he reached the small hall of the cottage, Bunst came in at the front door, hugging a parcel to his chest and peering about as if looking for burglars.

'Oh!' said Bunst. 'There you are, sir.'

'Yes, Bunst, here I am,' said Audacious briskly, but keeping his voice low. 'There has been an accident.'

Then he told Bunst what had happened.

'Gulliver!' said Bunst, and looked as if he had swallowed a dozen raw sausages. 'What a foonorious thing to happen!'

'I don't know what that means,' said Audacious, 'but yes indeed.'

'Is he hurt?' Bunst asked.

'I can't make that out,' Audacious admitted. 'But it must have given him a shock. It gave me a shock, I confess.'

Bunst put the packet of sausages to one ear and closed one eye.

'He's come to spy,' he whispered.

'On what?' gasped Audacious.

'On us. The new invention,' hissed Bunst.

Now, although some of Audacious' inventions were what Bunst

called "a bit cracked", others were valuable. Audacious had invented quite a few things that had been worth money.

'You mean the cooker?' whispered Audacious.

'No! Who wants a microwave cooker, when you can just put the pot on the fire?' said Bunst contemptuously, and then corrected himself. 'I mean, sir—well, you know what I mean, sir.'

'The Flying Eye!' said Audacious, staring.

'That's the one,' Bunst agreed, nodding. 'I bet my boots he's after the Flying Eye.'

Audacious looked across the little hall to the bedroom door that hid Marston Gulliver.

'By gad, Bunst,' he breathed, 'I shouldn't be surprised if you're right!'

'After all,' said Bunst, 'what did he come for? Did he tell you that?'

'I didn't ask him,' Audacious confessed. 'Really, he was making such a noise groaning that I didn't like to interrupt.'

'He must have been spying in the garden,' said Bunst fiercely.

Audacious thought about this.

'Perhaps you're right,' he said. 'In fact, I can't think why else he should come here.'

Bunst did not like Gulliver, and he was excited at the very idea of having a spy about the place.

'Keep him here,' he whispered. 'Keep him here in bed. Then he won't be able to do anything without us knowing.'

Audacious opened his eyes wide in surprise, and then nodded his approval.

'Bunst, you're fairly bursting with brains today,' he chuckled. 'By gad, sir! It's the very notion.'

He laughed and looked towards the bedroom door again.

'We'll keep him here,' he promised, and then rushed to the front door and out into the garden so that he could laugh out loud.

Meanwhile Marston Gulliver was crouching at the bedroom door, bent almost double to get his ear to the keyhole. He heard very little for his trouble.

'Whispering, confound it!' he muttered. 'That proves that they are up to something. Thunder and lightning, I was wise to come here.'

He straightened up and made a dive for the bed, for he could hear Bunst crossing the hall outside. But because he was so bulky, he tripped on a wire by the corner of the bed and fell face downward.

He did not know which switch he touched, but his hand hit the wall somewhere, and almost at once something began to whirr. Then the bed tilted and the floor opened, showing a shallow bath beneath. Gulliver was tipped off the bed into the bath, and from above a shower of water descended on him. He struggled to get out through the artificial rain-storm, but before he could do so the shower stopped, the bath emptied with a rushing sound and great waves of hot air suddenly blew at him from somewhere in the floor around the bath. At the same moment a large hot towel flew out of a hole in the wall and struck him in the face, knocking him back into the bath again.

'Great thunderbolts!' he roared through the thick folds of the towel. 'Murder! Slaughter! Fire and mayhem!'

He struggled up again and managed to step on to the solid edge of the floor round the bath. At once, the hole in the floor shut up and all signs of the bath disappeared. He unwound the towel from his head and fell on to the bed just as it righted itself.

'Merciful heavens!' gasped the unhappy man.

And at that moment a hole appeared in the wall by the bed and a shelf slid out bearing a cup of hot tea. Gulliver was too exhausted to take it.

Bunst, attracted by the noise, opened the door and looked in. 'Hello!' he said. 'Having a bath?'

Gulliver said something that sounded like Dutch. Very cross Dutch.

'This is a MADHOUSE!' he shouted finally.

'You must have touched the wrong button,' said Bunst mildly.

'I touched nothing!' roared Gulliver, sitting up in the soaked envelope of one of Audacious' nightshirts. 'I fell—that is to say, I turned over in the bed, like this, when —'

He stopped. With another whirr a hole appeared in the ceiling and revealed a television screen. Both Gulliver and Bunst stared up at it, for the screen was not blank.

Audacious must have left his television camera on when he put it in the barn, for the picture on the screen showed the inside of their workshop, and right in the forefront of the articles on view a curious-looking flying machine. It was rather like a big flatfish, and pinned to a board behind it was a large plan of some electrical circuits.

'The Flying Eye!' gasped Bunst, and, diving across the bed, he thrust his finger against a button.

The screen blanked out and the hole in the ceiling closed with a click. Gulliver, his head on one side, watched the boy suspiciously.

'Flying Eye, boy?' he asked very smoothly. 'What exactly do you mean by that, eh?'

'Oh nothing,' said Bunst, turning red to his ears. 'It's just an old model that Mr Cotterell made.'

But Marston Gulliver was too old and cunning a man to be fooled by Bunst's pretending. He lay back on the bed as if exhausted by the day's affairs.

'Fetch me a dry nightshirt, boy,' he said. 'I shall freeze to death in this.'

Bunst went. Gulliver sat up on the bed and looked at the faint cracks in the ceiling that marked the position of the television screen.

'Flying Eye, eh?' he muttered. 'I must look into this while I'm here.'

Bunst came back with another of Audacious' nightshirts.

'Would you be so good, boy, as to inform my Company of my plight?' asked Gulliver.

'Company?' echoed Bunst, surprised.

'Indeed yes. I control a film company which is at present making pictures in the district. Mayfield two-four-seven is the number. I thank you, boy.'

Smokey came out of the darkroom with a cigarette dangling from his mouth. It made it hard for him to see because of the smoke in his eyes, but he did not take it out, because he had a coil of film like a snake in his two hands.

Next to the darkroom was the room where the television set stood. That, the camera and two chairs were the only furnishings, unless you counted the old army blanket that hung over the window to keep out the daylight.

A tall, thin man in a grey suit was sitting there staring at nothing. He turned his head as Smokey came in.

'Has it come out, brother?' he asked.

Smokey shook his head until the cigarette almost fell out of his mouth.

'First two doors—clear as daylight,' he said. 'Keys fine! Every detail. Third door—biffo! It's all sausages, and this guy Cotterell's face mixed up in a frying-pan, and the key goes into his nose somehow. Can't fix the thing at all.'

'So I wasted my time,' said the thin man bitterly. 'After all that risk and personal danger.'

'Parcel, you worry about yourself too much,' said Smokey. 'There's two keys clear as daylight.'

'But what's the good of the two without the three? And that third key is the most important one. It opens the door that leads right into the laboratory itself, with a time-lock on it.'

'No good. I agree. You'll have to go there again.'

'Not me,' said Parcel, shaking his head. 'I had the feeling I was going to be shot in the back all the time I was there.'

'They didn't suspect anything?'

'No. They didn't,' said Parcel. 'But I only had to drop my bowler hat and they'd have seen the TV camera inside it. Then I should have been shot dead.'

'You wouldn't,' said Smokey. 'They'd have been jailed for life if they'd shot you.'

'That's a comfort,' said Parcel sarcastically. 'I should have laughed in my little cell.'

He relapsed into silence.

A telephone bell rang, and Smokey put down the coils of film on the second chair and went to the instrument, which stood on the dusty floorboards over in one corner of the room.

'Hello,' he said. 'Gigantic Films speaking.'

He listened for a moment.

237

'What did you say your name was? Bun? Bunch? Oh, Bunst. Well, that's a queer one, eh? What!'

Whatever Bunst had said had startled Smokey, for the cigarette fell out of his mouth.

'Is that so? Well, well. Thanks for the gen, lad. Thanks.'

He put down the telephone, straightened up, retrieved his cigarette and looked at Parcel.

Nothing ever made Parcel excited.

'I know,' said Parcel in a bored sort of way, 'Gulliver's burst. With pride,' he added, and grinned slowly.

'No,' said Smokey. 'He's been blown up by a rocket.'

'Who's been letting off fireworks so early in the year?'

'I don't know,' said Smokey. 'But I'm going to see him. You stay here, Parcel. And if anybody comes, tell 'em you're out. They won't know the difference.'

Smokey laughed and walked to the door. Parcel stretched out a leisurely leg and tripped him. Smokey went flat on his face and remained lying on the floor for a moment.

'Anybody would think you were a school kid,' he grumbled, and got up.

'They were the best days of my life,' said Parcel, and started to polish his nails.

TIME FACTOR
Geoffrey Morgan

When Alan Hart chartered the five-ton sloop *Dolphin* for his fortnight's holiday he set off along a part of the coast with which he was familiar. But before that holiday was over he was to find not only adventure, but a mystery which he helped Inspector Raymond to solve.

When Alan Hart arrived at Leeman's Point he wasn't surprised to find that the Muller-Shane affair was still the topic of conversation, although the police inquiry into the case had been closed nearly a fortnight. And it was just Alan's misfortune that the first person he ran foul of, when he sailed into the river, was Nick Muller himself.

Alan had heard a little about the case in London. He knew Muller and Derek Shane had been partners in a small charter boat business, that they had broken up, and that Shane had started on his own and prospered while Muller's fortunes had declined, and that this was followed by the climax in which Shane's magnificent new boat had been mysteriously destroyed by fire. Alan had acquired some knowledge of the affair and it intrigued him. That was why, when he chartered the *Dolphin*, a five-ton sloop at Peggleswick, ten miles along the coast, for a fortnight's holiday, his first port of call was Leeman's Point.

He was not familiar with that part of the coast. The Point from which the village derived its name ran out into the sea in the shape of a muddy sand-spit, forming an underwater bar just beyond the river mouth. On the other side of the entrance were mud flats, uncovered at low water, which stretched to the low-lying eastern shore of the river. The main channel followed close to the curve of the bank on the western side, forming a sheltered harbour for deep water moorings, and the village itself sprawled up from the waterfront in haphazard style, its brick and timbered cottages snuggled against the wooded hillside. The hinterland undulating from the river valley was clothed in rich shades of green, gold and brown — a floral pattern of trees, shrubs and arable land.

Alan thought there were few prettier places as he coasted into the river under a mild breeze and a lazy swell that kept the bar buoy tolling mournfully. He steered towards the mooring trots, but decided that the only vacant buoy off the club jetty was too far in, and he altered course for the moorings just below the small boat yard further upstream. He selected the nearest buoy, rounded up and fished it out with the boat hook. He snapped the chain over the bitts and stowed the sails.

He was slipping on the mainsail cover when the small, black motor-boat came in. She was an old but well-designed craft with a varnished superstructure. She wasn't much longer than the *Dolphin*, with a raised fore-cabin ending in a windscreen and shelter partly covering a spacious cockpit. There was only the helmsman aboard, a burly dark-bearded figure in a fisherman's jersey. Alan was ready to pass the time of day with him but before he could do so, the boat throttled down and swept in close and the man leaned out.

'I'll thank you to take yourself off my mooring,' he said rudely. 'Visitors moor up off the yacht club. These are private.'

Alan was taken aback but he recovered quickly.

'There'll certainly be more of a welcome there,' he said. 'These were easier to pick up, that's all. But I'll push on—'

'I'm in a hurry to get ashore,' the man cut in arrogantly; and to drown any reply Alan might have made, he throttled up the engine and swung round in a wide curve, watching the *Dolphin* with dark angry eyes. Alan shrugged and ignored the man, leisurely starting the auxiliary and dropping the mooring buoy. He obviously didn't belong to the fellowship of the sea and was not worth further attention. He motored down river and moored up off the jetty.

Ten minutes later he had forgotten his unpleasant encounter and was rowing ashore in the dinghy. He was a powerfully built youth, with the natural rugged look of the outdoor man about him, although he spent most of the year cooped up in an office. He regretted the tedious routine and circumstances that forced him to spend the greater part of his time at a desk in the heart of the City, but he liked his job, and with the prospect of promotion to the new department, he could look forward to a freer existence in which his duties would take him about the country. Meantime, he managed to snatch a breath of sea air at weekends and holidays following his other great interest in life — sailing.

Although Alan couldn't afford a cruiser of his own, he kept a dinghy on the Thames. This wasn't ambitious enough for a fortnight's holiday, however, and he had, late in the season, managed to book the *Dolphin* at Peggleswick.

Alan tied up the dinghy at the jetty and, collecting his petrol can, methylated bottle and canvas hold-all for the various bits of shopping he'd been too early to obtain before leaving Peggleswick, he made his way to the club house.

The small but attractive building was deserted save for the steward, a round-featured, middle-aged man, who immediately made him welcome.

'It's a little early, sir, but you could probably do with some tea?' the steward suggested thoughtfully.

Alan accepted gratefully. Having been under way since daybreak that morning with little inside him apart from breakfast but some barley sugar, he was ready for a cooked meal. But his intention was a light tea ashore and a good solid evening meal on board a couple of hours before turning in.

Alan sat in a deep chair alongside one of the long observation windows in the club lounge, and filled his pipe. Before he had the tobacco burning evenly the steward reappeared and set a tray of tea on the table in front of the window. After Alan had inquired the whereabouts of the petrol station, the post office and the general store, he mentioned his disappointing introduction to the river with the burly motor-boat owner.

The steward looked sympathetic but he didn't seem surprised.

'Sounds like Nick Muller,' he said. 'Big, dark-bearded man, black boat?' He pointed up river towards the moorings.

243

'Yes,' said Alan.

'That's him,' the steward confirmed. 'Nasty bit of work, though maybe it's not for me to say so. Rude, crude and tough, that's Muller. Thought he'd improved a bit since he'd cleared himself over the arson business; but a leopard can't change its spots.' The steward reflected for a moment and then: 'I expect you heard about the mysterious fire that burnt out Mr Shane's new boat. Or maybe it didn't get into your papers?'

'There was a paragraph or two about it, but it was soon lost in the international news,' Alan said. 'What happened exactly?'

The steward glanced round the lounge and out of the windows, then leaned forward, supporting himself on a chair back.

'Well, maybe it's not my business to gossip,' he began, 'but since it's still on the tongue of most folk in Leeman's Point and you'll hear the whole story sooner or later, I may as well tell you now.' He paused to straighten the collar of his white jacket. 'Derek Shane and Nick Muller were partners in a little charter boat fishing business. They had a boat apiece and used to take clients out to fish in Cobber's Channel for blue shark. They didn't do so badly, but Muller wasn't satisfied. Whether he began to cheat the clients a bit or played some other crooked game no one can say, but Shane didn't like his methods. Wouldn't accept them. There were quarrels, so it was said, and finally, a scrap. No one knows for certain what happened except that Shane packed in, took his boat and moved over to Cobber's Island to start up on his own.'

'Cobber's Island?' repeated Alan. 'That's just a few miles off the coast, opposite here.' He had seen the low-lying shape from the *Dolphin* that afternoon, and he knew its position from the chart.

'Six miles to be exact, sir,' the steward confirmed.

'If Muller was going to be such an unpleasant rival what made Shane start up so near?' Alan suddenly realized the reason. 'The fishing's so good in these parts, I suppose?'

'Perfect. The shark are plentiful in season and the best fishing grounds are closer to the island than they are to the mainland. There's snug harbour at the western end. Since Oldport has been developed, the rail link from London and other parts has greatly improved — it's easier for clients to get there than it is here. Shane meets them at Oldport and takes them across to the island, accommodating them in an old farmhouse he converted. With these advantages and Shane's friendly and helpful manner, it wasn't surprising that most of the old clients went back to him, and for the last two seasons he's been booked solid, and had a waiting list of new customers. When he bought his new boat less than a month ago it was common knowledge he'd invested every penny in her. She was a magnificent craft — fast, with roomy accommodation and all the latest equipment in her aft cockpit for fishing. She cost over three thousand, and when she was destroyed by fire a few nights after berthing in Cobber's harbour Shane hadn't got her fully covered by insurance.' The man paused, a sympathetic gleam in his eye. 'I don't know what the hitch was exactly, but it appears it was Shane's own fault. It seems the Universal Marine Insurance are not legally bound to pay out, though negotiations are still going on'. He spread has hands in a helpless gesture. 'Of course, it'll ruin Shane if the claim falls through.'

Alan nodded thoughtfully.

'And that was what the fire-raiser intended?' he murmured.

'Shane and everyone else thinks so.'

'Naturally Shane suspected Muller, but he had a good alibi?'

'We all suspected Muller, including the police. But you could trust Muller to cover himself.' A sardonic smile flickered over the steward's lips. 'No one could raise a scrap of proof. It was perfectly planned — even to the sea mist.'

'But if the police think that Muller did it, why can't they break his alibi?' Alan frowned.

'It's the time factor,' the steward explained. 'Muller proved he was unable to cover the distance in the time.'

'You mean going out to the island, committing the crime, and getting back here again?'

'That's it. And he had responsible witnesses to support it, and although they were reluctant to back him up, they had to agree to his evidence because it was the truth.'

Alan felt himself drawn more and more into the intriguing puzzle of the affair. Having already had a brush with Muller he felt the man quite capable of removing any obstacle that stood in his way, and if it meant committing sabotage or arson to ruin his late partner, whom he obviously hated, then he had the spur of his own declining business to push him on. Obviously he had cunning, too, or how else could he have devised a way of smashing his successful rival, knowing he would be suspected yet so certain that no part of it could be held against him?

Alan fingered the ash in the bowl of his pipe.

'What was the evidence? How did the time factor come into it?'

The steward hesitated, uncertain where or how to begin explaining it.

'Well, sir,' he said at length, 'it is officially recorded that Mr Shane's boat was seen to be on fire a few minutes after midnight. Harry Fox, the coastguard, was on night duty and he saw Muller leave the river in his boat at 11.30 that night. Muller turned down along the coast and then the mist rolled in, and he was lost from sight. But at 12.25 Fox saw him appear out of the mist and enter the river again.'

'Where was he supposed to have been at that time of night?'

'Checking his bait lines.' The steward paused reflectively. 'You see, during the day we'd had a moderate gale. No one went out. But it dropped by the evening and a sea mist came up. Muller said he went out to check his lines. It was a fair enough reason, because one or two of the local fishermen did the same. But when next day we heard that Shane's boat had been destroyed by someone around midnight, Muller was suspected. There were inquiries. Shane must have told the police whom he suspected. They questioned Muller, but didn't get anywhere. Muller could prove that he couldn't get out to Cobber and back in the time. And, of course, he had Fox to confirm that he was out only fifty-five minutes. You see, the maximum speed of Muller's boat is twelve miles an hour.'

Alan nodded. 'What was the state of the tide?'

'Low water.'

'The island is six miles away, and it would take him an hour if he only went straight there and back at slack water.' Alan's eyes narrowed as he stared out of the window.

'Exactly,' agreed the steward. 'So you see, what case there was against him collapsed.'

'Did the police check his engine?'

'They made every check there was. Muller invited them to go ahead. They timed the speed of his boat over a measured distance. At full revs it made twelve miles an hour. So, there it was... They were stumped.' The steward turned, as a member entered the lounge, and then politely excused himself, leaving Alan to finish his tea and draw at his pipe in silence.

It was a curious business. In spite of the evidence the steward and, according to him, everyone else in Leeman's Point were convinced that Muller had been responsible for the act of sabotage — yet if Muller had done it, how had he accomplished it in the time?

Half an hour later Alan left the club, dropped the petrol can at the village garage, bought the methylated and groceries from the stores, and wandered the longest way back to the garage and the waterfront. But there wasn't much to see in Leeman's Point except, as far as Alan was concerned, Muller's place. It was in a narrow road that ran between a line of derelict boarded cottages and a row of tarred waterfront sheds. Through the gaps in the sheds he could see some of the fishermen's moorings and in line with Muller's boat he found the man's place of business. A small, grimy office window overlooked the narrow thoroughfare, and alongside the office door was the entrance to a low shed that extended into the mud beyond the tide line. Over the doorway in faded lettering was Muller's name.

It was getting dark by the time Alan boarded the *Dolphin* again. He lit the oil lamp in the cabin and stowed away his purchases, then he spread the chart out on the folding table and sat down to study it. It covered the river mouth and part of the coast, taking in Cobber's Island. He had gone over it before on the sail down to Leeman's Point, but in the light of the steward's story he learned nothing new from his careful scrutiny now. The distance, the tides flowing up and down the channel between the island and the mainland, the depth in the harbour at the western tip of the island; none of these things helped in the solution of the sinister operation he was sure Muller had undertaken.

Alan lay back, his head against the cushion, drawing at his pipe. The police had tested Muller's boat but had they examined her?

He sat up again, slowly. Why not take a look at her himself? Of course, the affair wasn't his business; but he couldn't resist a challenge, especially if it meant putting right a wrong. And there would be a sense of achievement if he succeeded where the police had failed. It would be a pleasure, too, to cut a man like Muller down to size. And if anything came of it it might even help his expected promotion. So why not?

He went up into the cockpit and stared over the stern to the dark shape of Muller's motor-boat riding to her mooring a hundred and fifty yards up river. He considered the swim. It would be cold, but with the tide to help him each way he could do it comfortably. It was high water soon after midnight. If he slipped over towards the end of the flood he'd be practically carried to the boat. Half an hour or so aboard would be sufficient and he could swim back to the *Dolphin* on the beginning of the ebb. At that time, too, everyone in the village would be safely tucked up in bed.

To the sound of faint midnight chimes from the church clock Alan, complete with watertight torch attached to the belt lacing his swimming trunks, stepped down the short accommodation ladder and slipped quietly into the water. He swam effortlessly with the tide, steering himself towards his objective. In less than ten minutes his hands were groping alongside the hull as he guided himself to the stern. There he paused, glancing across the water at the dark open-ended shed which hid Muller's little office. Nothing disturbed the shadows.

Alan gripped the rudder trunk, his feet feeling for the blade. Once he was on this he hauled himself quickly over the transom to the deck. He crawled across towards the cockpit, his hand scraping over an uneven patch in the deck. He paused, lying flat, and unhitched his torch. Holding the glass just above the deck and shielding the light between his hand and the cockpit coaming, he switched it on.

There was a round mark in the canvas so faint it would pass unnoticed to the casual eye. Although it had been painted over the minute edge had not been rubbed down, and it was this Alan had felt as his hand slid over it. He pressed the patch with his finger. It was quite hard, but neither wood nor canvas. About a foot further along the side deck and in line with it between the coaming and the toe rail, was another, of roughly the same size. He switched off the torch and climbed over into the cockpit. Feeling the deck on the opposite side he found a similar pair of patches parallel to the first pair.

He crouched down and fumbled for the locker lid under the side deck. Inside was a long narrow roll of new canvas. It was the type used for decking. Alan realized that if Muller wanted to obliterate all trace of those circular patches he would need to re-canvas the decks. The prepared tool-tray and the tin of copper tacks under the canvas suggested that this was his intention.

Alan felt inside the locker, his fingers scraping the underside of the deck, seeking the hole he knew must be there, when the creak of rowlocks and splash of oars froze him rigid. He closed the locker quickly and peered over the coaming towards the shore.

A dinghy was pulling out from the sheds, heading in his direction. For a tense moment he watched the dark figure at the oars, and in that moment the man turned his head. The pale moon faintly lit the distant face and Alan knew for certain what until then he had only feared.

It was Muller...

There was no time to slip over the side. No time to seek concealment in the cockpit. No choice but the cabin, and is he crawled across to the doors, Alan prayed they were unlocked.

The latch yielded silently to his touch, and with some relief he pulled back the narrow panels and his bare feet found the short companion ladder inside. As he reached the cabin and closed the doors again he heard Muller's dinghy bump alongside. Alan paused, listening until he heard the man clamber aboard, then he turned and moved for'ard through the cabin, colliding with the folding table, but reaching the sliding door in the bulkhead that gave entry to the fo'c's'le without further sound or mishap. The door slid back in its channel with a faint creak and, bending low, he stepped into the fo'c's'le.

It was a confined, uncomfortable place. There was no headroom and he was forced to crouch until he found the chain-locker. Half-sitting on the edge of this allowed him to straighten his back, but the damp, rusty chair rasped his bare legs. A faint light filtered through the opaque glass roundel in the fore-hatch outlining the navigation lamps, coils of line and other loose gear on the fiddled shelves around him. There was a smell of rope and rust and the musty atmosphere of the bilge in the almost airless compartment.

Alan felt cold with the salt water still drying on his body, and it was no comfort to realize that he might have to spend the night under the conditions in which his curiosity had placed him. His only consolation was that he could not be trapped. If Muller came through, then the hatch and the river was Alan's escape route. But that was the last resort. The last thing he wanted was to alarm Muller by revealing himself.

The faint sounds of the owner moving about the cockpit continued for a short interval and then Alan heard the motor started. A few seconds later rubber-soled shoes padded on the deck just above him. There was the rattle of the chain and then the loud splash as the mooring buoy was dropped overboard. The feet padded aft and then he felt the boat moving slowly, the chuckle of the bow wave rippling away from the planking just outside.

Alan wondered where they were heading. He had no sense of direction in the close confine of the fo'c's'le, and it was not until he heard the sudden high-pitched revs of the reverse gear and felt the slight shudder as the keel scraped the mud, that he guessed Muller's reason for the midnight expedition. He was taking the boat ashore on the top of the tide.

Before the reverse gear could bring the boat to a standstill it was disengaged; Alan felt the craft glide forward a few feet, then the faint light from the hatch port-hole was suddenly blotted out and he was in complete darkness. He knew then they were in Muller's boatshed.

Alan remained still, listening as Muller moved about the deck and eventually splashed about in the water around the bow. The boat began to settle in her berth and soon she was motionless, lying at a slight angle on her port bilge strake. He waited, straining his ears for the slightest sound, but the silence was complete.

It seemed a long time before he ventured the return journey to the cockpit, although it was in fact no more than two minutes, but the shed was silent and deserted. Muller had brought the boat in, no doubt ready to begin work on her in the morning. Under cover. That's how he'd want to work if he were re-canvassing decks that didn't really require new canvas. In the shed he'd be out of the way, covering up the clues he'd been forced to leave behind. Concealing the tell-tale punctures in the deck for all time.

Alan moved across to the locker opening above the seat. He knelt down and, pushing his torch inside, switched it on. He found the two parallel holes in the underside of the deck which had been roughly plugged from above. When he had cleared away the new roll of canvas and the tools and the other odds and ends of gear, he found directly beneath each hole a faint narrow impression on the floor of the locker, at either end of which were two shallow penetrations of the wood. The impressions had been made by a short strip of metal screwed at each end into the locker floor. Each had the outline of a small cleat; but Alan knew that a cleat or a fairlead would serve no purpose there.

He crawled across to the other side of the cockpit and found directly beneath the holes in the deck an identical pair of impressions in the locker floor. These were fainter but no less visible to one looking for them. But there was nothing to show their meaning. He switched off the torch and silently returned the gear to its original position, his mind grappling with the mystery his discovery presented. And it was while he was thus engaged that he heard the creak of the shed door and saw a splash of light beyond the bows of the boat.

Alan moved swiftly to the side and saw a figure moving towards him, weaving the beam of light over the boat. Muller had either returned for something he'd forgotten or has seen a reflection of light from Alan's torch.

'Who's there?' The gruff demand was unmistakably Muller's voice. He advanced slowly, warily, and for a panic-stricken moment Alan wondered how he could escape without being recognized. Then he saw the mooring line. In the moving torch-light he saw the rope lying across the muddy surface hitched to a ring at the side of the shed. The line came up over the side deck to the cockpit. In that second of observation Alan's fingers were groping for the end of the line somewhere beside him. Muller paused, uncertain, as Alan's hands clenched the coarse rope. He waited, breathlessly.

'Who's there?' Muller rasped again. 'Come out — or, by thunder, I'll come and get you!'

The torchlight splashed over the windshield of the boat and Alan could see that no more than a few paces would take Muller to the line lying harmlessly across the surface. He knew if his ruse was to succeed he would have to encourage the man to move quickly towards him. He let out a low grunt. Muller's head jerked up and then he began a rush towards the cockpit. Calmly timing his operation, Alan suddenly pulled the line in. It rose taut from the ground as Muller reached it and with an oath he tripped across it and fell heavily in the mud beside the boat, his torch crashing against the hull and plunging the shed into darkness.

Alan took full advantage of his success. He leaped over the other side of the cockpit to the sound of Muller's spluttering curses, and within seconds he was out of the open end of the shed and running along the foreshore. A fifty yard sprint brought him in the shadow of another timbered building. He moved round the end of this and paused, getting his breath back and watching for some movement at Muller's shed. A few moments later Muller appeared, staring along the foreshore, obviously puzzled by the sudden disappearance of his visitor. He stood there, gazing around him for a full ten minutes before finally giving up, and going back into the shed. Alan waited a little longer, and then moved off along the edge of the mud, hidden in the shadow of the fishermen's sheds that reached down to the high-water mark.

He reached the yacht club jetty unobserved, slipped into the water and swam out to the *Dolphin*. He was relieved to get below and give his body a vigorous towelling. He pulled on a thick sweater and slacks, made a steaming mug of coffee and sat on the top step of the companion gazing out over the *Dolphin's* cockpit while the moon slid silently down the sky.

Alan's eyes fastened pensively on the low, dark shadow of Muller's boatshed. Muller had not seen him but the encounter

Alan suddenly pulled the line in

must have disturbed any man with a conscience as guilty as Alan thought Muller must possess. But how to prove the guilt when he could not even understand the significance of the holes on either side of Muller's boat? He knew they were not for stanchions; no one would put them in the middle of the deck and, anyway, stanchions were usually slotted into holders. Alan suddenly stared at the stanchions on the *Dolphin*, and realized that the metal fittings that had made the impressions in the locker floor of Muller's boat could have been temporary holders. In which case they had supported two rails or rods on either side... Having decided on the objects, Alan could reason no further. He could not see what object Muller could have had in inserting two pairs of rods through his side decks; but that there had been some dark reason for it was obvious from the fact that the holders had been removed and the holes in the deck covered to deceive the casual eye.

And now he was preparing to re-canvas the deck. Muller was still afraid these clues, vague as they were, might be detected and followed up, leading to the tracing of his temporary equipment. When did he make the alterations? On the night Shane's new boat was destroyed? Could the tell-tale marks *prove*, after all, that Muller was guilty?

Alan closed the companion doors, pulled the hatch half-way, and began to undress. He thought he was probing at the beginning of the riddle that, once solved, would smash Muller's alibi to pieces; but there was a long way to go yet. He decided to continue the lead first thing in the morning.

After breakfast he rowed ashore and made his way to the coast-guard cottage set on the shallow cliff above the village. He did not go direct. He decided his meeting with Harry Fox must be casual. He turned off a narrow road on to a footpath and sat down in the long grass at a point where the cottage and its garden were under observation. He filled his pipe and waited.

It was nearly an hour before he saw any movement from the house. Then an elderly man appeared at the door and went into the vegetable garden. He began forking the soil. Alan decided that he must be Harry Fox, and near the verge of retirement by his appearance. But according to the club steward he hadn't lost his powers of observation.

Alan followed the footpath to the hedge on the further side. He skirted this to the end which brought him out on a track that passed the cottage gate. He walked slowly towards it as if he were making for the narrow road, then eased up at the garden boundary. He thought he was giving the impression he was out for a stroll, and the coastguard needed no excuse for a talk once they had exchanged morning greetings.

'You're a stranger in these parts,' Harry Fox said in a low, kindly voice. It was more a statement of fact than a question. 'But I recognize the boat.' His blue eyes twinkled down over the river to the distant *Dolphin*. 'Saw you come up yesterday. She's one of the charter fleet from Peggleswick.'

'That's right,' Alan said agreeably. 'Wouldn't have got such a sweet little ship at the height of the season.' He smiled at the old man. 'That's one advantage of being a junior in the firm — have to take a late holiday; but you get the best attention when the crowds have gone home. Best weather, too.' His gaze swept the arc of blue sky. 'I hear the fishing's very good here — especially the shark.'

'Aye,' Fox nodded. 'The blue shark's been mighty plentiful this season. But Shane's the man you want to talk to about shark. Over on Cobber. He had a good summer — 'cept that there disaster to his boat robbed him of everything at the end.'

'Yes, I've heard about that affair,' Alan said with cool interest. 'Suspected arson, wasn't it?'

'That's what everyone reckons.'

'The police haven't traced the fire-raiser?'

'Not as yet — well —' Fox hesitated. 'Leastways, most folk reckon it was Shane's former partner — Nick Muller, though mebbe one shouldn't repeat the gossip.'

'Muller — eh? I heard he wasn't a particularly pleasant character. What happened exactly?' Alan listened patiently to a repeat of the strange facts the club steward had told him the afternoon before, and in addition he had Fox's own personal story of what he himself had observed on the night in question.

'And if Muller did it, as they reckon, nobody knows how,' the coastguard ended wondrously. 'You can't get away from the time and the distance; but Muller has. Mind you, he had a sea mist to help him; but that still don't solve the mystery.'

'It sounds an extraordinary business,' Alan said slowly. 'Did anyone else see him leave and return that night apart from yourself?'

'Only Alf Davis,' Fox said. 'Leastways, Davis saw him return. That's what he told the police. I saw him come in at the time. He'd been out tending his lines, and suddenly came out of the mist and found himself close to Muller near the bar buoy.'

'He didn't see or hear anything unusual?' Alan persisted gently.

'No? Nothing to speak of. The only thing he told me he heard, just before he saw Muller's boat, which alerted him to the fact that he must be dangerously close to another vessel, was a loud splash.'

'A splash?' Alan repeated slowly. 'Which side of the buoy?'

'Seaward side, I think it was. But there's nothing important in that. There was quite a swell running. They were near the buoy. It could have been an extra large wave breaking against it, or the bow wave of Muller's boat.'

'Or the gash-pail emptied overboard,' suggested Alan with a smile, recalling the number of times he had shot the bucket of empty tins and other rubbish over the side.

'Aye,' agreed Fox, his eyes a-twinkle again. 'If Davis mentioned it to them the police didn't make much of it, anyway.'

Alan smiled.

'Understandable,' he said. 'Nothing unusual in that.'

A few minutes later Alan left Harry Fox to his garden and went back to the yacht club. He asked the steward where Alf Davis lived, but when he had the address he decided against going to interview the man. Alan was a stranger in the district, and if he began asking Davis questions the man would immediately become suspicious. If, by any chance, he was on speaking terms with Muller he might report that Alan had been asking questions — or let the fact out accidentally. So Alan went to the yacht chandlers instead and bought a drag-hook. He stuffed this in his canvas shopping bag and returned to the *Dolphin*.

He made some coffee and filled his pipe, and as he drank and smoked he pored over the chart. He found the spit of sandy mud running out to the bar buoy. At low water ordinary times the buoy floated in eighteen feet of water, and for a distance of about half a cable around it the depth varied between eighteen feet and twenty. On the seaward side it was eighteen, gradually shelving down to thirty and dropping sharply away into Cobber's Channel to depths of seventy and eighty feet.

The more Alan considered it the more certain he was that the splash Davis had heard in the mist was caused by no natural movement sea or boat. Neither did he think it was the refuse from the gash-bucket. He was sure it had some bearing on Muller's alibi.

The rest of the morning Alan prepared himself and the boat for the dragging operation. He reeved and knotted on to the hook nine fathoms of terylene rope stored in the aft locker, and left it stored neatly out of sight under the starboard bunk. He shackled the C.Q.R. anchor to its chain and filled the petrol tank. Then he checked the time of low water in the tidal almanac. With preparations complete, he cooked a light lunch and settled down to lounge the rest of the day and most of the night away.

The *Dolphin* was under way before the first streaks of dawn tinted the sky next morning. Alan had no wish to advertise his departure, and he had purposely kept himself aboard to avoid another encounter with Muller. Now, while Leeman's Point still slept peacefully in the hour before dawn, Alan sailed out silently on the last of the ebb.

The breeze was light and fickle, but the tide took him in the direction he wanted to go. Once clear of the river mouth he started the engine and lowered the sails, heading out towards the bar buoy over a gentle swell.

He rounded the buoy to seaward and shut down the engine until the throttle was sufficient to give the boat way; then he lowered the drag-hook. He had timed it perfectly. It was slack water and he had no tides to contend with; his only concern was as it grew lighter, his action might be seen from the shore. From the distance someone might think he was fishing; but if Muller heard about it or saw him, he'd know what he was fishing for. Alan didn't want to attract interest or curiosity. After all, he could be wrong.

As he continued to and fro over the bar, his hook dragging slowly across the bottom and the sky growing lighter with every run, he began to wonder if he was wrong. Soon the sun would be up and the *Dolphin* would be recognized from shore or boat and he would have to call it a day, forced to wait another twenty-four hours or try his experiment in the dark that night.

Alan turned the boat and went back once more over the unseen bar eighteen feet below, and it was as he decided it must be his last run that morning that the hook stuck and held fast. With mounting excitement he let the rope slip through his hands while he kicked the engine out of gear. He dared not pull on the rope for fear of dislodging the hook. With the engine idling, he ran for'ard and dropped the anchor. Next, he shut off the engine and pulled gently on the drag rope. The hook held, and he decided that whatever the object was it was robust and weighty. Slowly he pulled on the rope and brought the *Dolphin* back stern first until she was riding almost directly over the spot. He set the anchor chain round the bitts on the fore-deck and returned to the cockpit. When he had secured the drag rope to a cleat he stripped down to his swimming trunks and lowered himself over the side. He held on to the rope, took a deep breath and dived down, following the rope with his hands.

Before Alan could distinguish the soft grey matter that was the seabed he saw the object that had trapped his hook. Through the greenish, murky light he recognized the broken outline of weed-covered metal half-embedded in the silt. He had no need to touch bottom and already his lungs were urging him back. He turned and sped towards the surface. He climbed aboard and sat in the cockpit, gasping but triumphant. His hunch had proved correct. He had found the evidence that would break Muller's alibi wide open...

Inspector Raymond's car stopped outside Muller's office. Alan followed the Inspector and Sergeant Loader out on to the narrow street. It was getting dark; but to Alan the time since dawn that morning seemed no more than a few quickly passing minutes. So much had happened since he had made his discovery near the bar buoy fifteen hours before. He had reported his findings to the police, the local sergeant had contacted the Divisional Inspector, a frogman had been engaged and the salvage operations completed before mid-day. Now, as one of the plainclothes detective-constables raised the bootlid of the car, Alan could see the glaring evidence, lightly covered with a sheet of canvas.

Inspector Raymond detailed his two plainclothes assistants to await his word at the car, and he led Alan and Sergeant Loader into Muller's office. There was no one there, but they could hear a faint hammering going on in the boatshed adjoining. The Inspector rang the hand-bell on the untidy desk, and the three stood waiting. Presently, the door giving entrance to the shed opened and Muller appeared. He stood on the threshold eyeing his visitors with a half-curious, half-arrogant look, then he crossed to his desk and sat down.

'What can I do for you, gentlemen?' he inquired casually.

'We're already known to each other over the Shane boat fire, Muller,' Raymond said calmly. 'So we won't waste time on preliminaries. We'd like to question you further about that affair.'

'I thought that case was closed,' Muller said, his dark eyes flashing in challenge.

'We never close an unsolved case,' the Inspector returned gently. 'And some fresh evidence has come to light concerning your alibi.'

Muller said nothing, but Alan noticed his face had paled.

'The one important factor proving your case was the time and the distance. You couldn't get to Cobber's Island on the night of the fire in the time the coastguard saw you leave and return within the normal capabilities of your boat.'

'But we've been through all that,' Muller protested.

'I know,' Raymond nodded patiently. 'What we failed to understand was the possibility that for one occasion your boat might possess abnormal capabilities.'

'What d'you mean by that?'

'I'll show you.' The Inspector suddenly called to the officers outside, and they came in carrying the canvas bundle. Raymond whipped the covering away and it revealed the rusty metal of a powerful outboard motor. 'This provided the extra power.'

Muller stared at it horrified; but he was too astonished to speak.

Raymond pointed to the distributor's nameplate still on the petrol tank.

'We verified with the firm who supplied this motor a week before Mr Shane's boat was destroyed, that it would increase the speed of your boat by an extra eight miles an hour,' the Inspector went on, 'thus giving you ample time to do the journey to Cobber both ways and set fire to Shane's vessel.'

'We took this engine to the distributors' at Oldport this afternoon and they identified from the number that it was sold to you a week before the crime. We salvaged it from close to the bar buoy at the spot where Alfred Davis heard you drop it over the side when you returned from Cobber's Island on the night of the fire. You fitted the engine on a special metal bracket fixed through two holes in the decks either side of the cockpit. And,' the Inspector glanced towards the boatshed, 'I'll hazard a guess you are now busy covering them up by re-canvassing your deck.'

Muller looked ghastly. He sat there, staring open-mouthed at the Inspector.

'But — how did you get all this —?'

Raymond half-turned and smiled at Alan.

'We have to thank this young gentleman for the lead,' he said modestly. 'His knowledge of boats, and his initiative, have broken your alibi, Muller, and it will go better with you if you make a full statement here and now.'

'We have met a couple of times, Mr Muller,' Alan said. 'The second time, I had the pleasure of tripping you next door, in the shed. I thought I owed it to you for your unpleasant welcome when I first came into the river.'

Muller stared at Alan, a beaten, vicious glitter in his eyes.

'Who the heck are you, anyway?' he demanded.

'Just an insurance man on holiday,' Alan smiled, and dropped a plain business card on the desk.

'Universal Marine,' he said.

CAVE OF THE DEAD
Jack Cox

Redskins were known by early settlers in the West to respect the antics of men who had gone crazy in the wilderness. Less well known was the fact that many Indians feared the dead. In this story, two youngsters who were cornered by a Ute war-party used their knowledge of Indian superstitions to win their way out to freedom and safety.

Ward didn't have time even to snatch up his rifle when the Utes cut them off from their hunting party. It was just the two boys, without arms, running only a few paces ahead of the savage Indians, taking the only direction open to them. When he realized they'd run into a rockstrewn canyon, Ward felt they were doomed. At first it had seemed sheltered and cool out of the grilling mid-day sun. Now the cliffs rose sheer on either side. They could not turn back.

Bart, struggling to keep at Ward's side, made an odd choking noise that was half sob and half gasp. Ward jerked his hand out for silence, then caught hold of the boy's homespun sleeve to help him along. Chipmunks and squirrels scurried from their path. Ward darted a backward glance to judge how far they were ahead of the Indians.

When his eyes flashed to the front again, the canyon walls seemed to merge. Fear strangled his throat until he noted that the pinon and juniper trees which were rooted precariously into the layers of rock appeared to be stunted on the left wall, therefore he knew the canyon only turned. It just might be possible, he realized, for Bart and himself to work their way up the canyon wall by clutching the trees and creeping along the ledges. If this were a box canyon, they would be trapped if they went into it. Perhaps there, where the canyon turned, at the first break — —

Something flew by so close to his ear he thought he felt its movement. His eyelids blinked down to shut out his terror. Then Ward steeled himself to look back. The twisted junipers, the pinons and the tumbled rocks gave no hint of any movement. It was a bird, he tried to reason.

Still clutching at Bart's arm, Ward ran straight ahead to the left cliff, leading the way, and at times almost hoisting the younger boy. They began an arduous zigzag ascent, climbing out of the canyon. A fusillade of arrows darted up, reaching for them. Ward yanked Bart down and for a while huddled behind a twisted juniper while he loosened rocks and sent them crashing downward.

Climbing again, they reached a thickened slab of sandstone that seemed unscalable. Ward darted along the ledge, but he found no way to climb up. We're trapped, he thought, pushing his back tight against the rock to stare downward. He could spy no sign of the Utes.

A scurrying whisper from overhead caused Ward to glance up in alarm. A rock squirrel had almost reached his head before catching his scent or movement and darted back up the thick slab of rock. Ward stared in amazement. There were notches climbing up the rock as if they were hewn by hand. Motioning Bart to do likewise, Ward jerked off his shoes and stuffing his socks inside he knotted the thongs and slung them about his neck. He tried to boost Bart up, but the younger boy hung back. Ward took the lead, his hands and feet reaching the slight depressions as he scaled the rock precariously. Twice only was he able to reach down and help the smaller boy up.

Ward had heard vague, almost legendary, rumours of this, but still he could hardly believe his eyes as Bart choked out:

'Ward, what is it?'

'A cave, a huge cave with — —' Ward whispered. He flicked a glance at the boy. Many times Ward had been annoyed at Bart's trailing after him. He sighed wearily.

'But — —but look!' Bart quavered.

Ward ventured along the smooth cave floor, staring in wonder. 'It's an old stone building. Imagine building a huge stone house in a cave! Why, it must be centuries since——'

Bart, too terrified not to stay by Ward's side, suddenly grabbed at him. 'Look! There!'

'It's just a—— It's a very old and dusty skeleton.' Ward was more sure than before that no one had been there for ages. Even so, in imitation of the hunters the two had been cut off from, he studied the dust of the cave floor for tracks. In this dust, accumulated through the ages, there was no imprint other than that made by tiny animals. 'It's just as if it had been untouched for centuries,' he puzzled.

Bart shivered. 'I don't like it here, Ward. Let's get out of——' He edged away from the ruins, then noting how close he was to the lip of the cave, he moved back again quickly.

Ward's baffled eyes swept over the old masonry walls curiously, before they settled on Bart. 'I don't know——' Cautiously, he stepped to the cliff and lay flat so only his head was exposed as he stared downward. For several minutes he studied the canyon floor. Suddenly, his body tensed. Far down on the canyon floor he spied a brown body moving from behind a rock to a screening juniper. 'Get me a rock!' Other Utes slunk from shelter to shelter before Ward tossed the rock down. There was no doubt of it. The Indians were now retreating. But why? Ward wondered with a baffled feeling, as he rose slowly to his feet and looked up.

Bart tugged at his sleeve. 'Ward, let's get out of this—this trap!' he whispered, urgently.

'It's strange they didn't follow us up.' Ward's eyes strayed back to the ancient masonry walls. They were so old that even in the shelter of the dry cave some of the dressed rocks had tumbled down in ruin. Could it be that the Utes were leaving some warriors to watch in the canyon below, while others went around to the top to guard against their escape? No, some of them would have followed us up, he thought. Nervously, Ward ran his fingers through his straw-coloured hair. 'No doubt they'll have warriors on top to catch us, if we——'

'You mean——we're trapped in here?'

Ward considered Bart, his eyelids narrowing. 'I'd say we'd found a haven. Maybe it's only temporary. But at least——well, those old Utes do seem sort of set against getting very close to this.' He made a sweeping gesture that indicated the cave, the ruins, and lingered on the ancient skeleton.

'Well——' Bart's voice quavered, his frightened eyes darting about.

Ward slipped on his shoes. 'Look! There're just those two trails reaching in here. The way we climbed in, and those notches up there.' He pointed to the toe holds little more than etched into the sandstone ledge rising sheer from the cave roof to the mesa. 'Both are so chancy, I don't think—— If you sit here, you can guard them both. I'm going in and look about.'

'Ward!' Bart protested in a strangled voice.

'I know,' the older boy agreed, with a rare hint of kindliness. 'I'm afraid, too. But I've just got to look about and make sure how we're situated. You know, I've never been so thirsty in my whole life.' His feet stirred up the dust as he moved slowly toward the nearest tiny doorway.

Cobwebs festooned the aperture, and he brushed them aside to look in, losing some of his fear as curiosity surged up, prodded a little by the vague rumours he'd heard of these strange, un-peopled dwellings perched high in the cliffs. It was very murky inside when Ward climbed through the entrance. He could spy nothing at all, only the dust of centuries, some plaster crumbled in a heap, and finally, in a far corner, a polished stone digging stick, its wooden handle still intact. He picked it up, thinking it might make a reasonable weapon.

Ward entered one room after another, climbing ancient ladders for entry into upper storeys, and treading along the cave floor through a narrow passage. It was here that he found parts of more skeletons. In the half-dark, he probed a skull with the digging stick. Suddenly, there was a whirr of wings past his head. It's only an owl, was the thought that passed through his mind. I have nothing to fear in these ruins, he forced himself to reason.

Methodically, he searched from chamber to chamber until he reached the back, where the cave roof closed into the floor. In hopes of finding a spring, or at the very least a water seep at the back, he'd picked up an ancient pottery mug. But it was dark and apparently dry at the back and filled with trash. If we have to stay here, he thought, I'll make a torch and come back and probe about. Since its abandonment, it appeared quite evident that no human had ever ventured into this ruin. Too many ancient tools and too much beautiful pottery lay about. Why? he wondered, realizing if he could guess the answer it would assure Bart's and his safety in getting out of the area.

Ward moved back thoughtfully to the opening of the cave. The floor slanted to the front, and to his right, and he walked to the edge, still hopeful of finding water. About a foot below, he spied a tiny trickle of water. He lay flat and, reaching down, brushed out the loose shale to form a catchment basin. As the water gathered he splashed it out with his hand, to wash the dust from the ancient mug. He hadn't realized how thirsty he was. It must be the hard run and climb through the grilling sun and the centuries of dust. He gulped down the liquid and refilled the mug for Bart, studying the black design on the white background of the cup. If he only knew!

'Ward!' Bart hissed.

Ward gathered up the digging stick and rushed to Bart's side. 'What is it?'

'Down there! I saw something move.'

Finally, Ward chuckled softly and said: 'It's only an elk. Those old Utes have really high-tailed it away from here. But why?'

'I don't know, Ward. Don't you know?' Suddenly, he added brightly: 'If the Utes have gone, why can't we leave, too?'

'They'll be waiting. Fanned out through the brush and trees, they'll wait just in case we do escape the little people.'

'What little people?'

'Look at those doorways! They must have been little. It's so strange. Those Utes knew this ruin was here, or they would have followed us up. And they're in mortal terror of the place, else they'd have carried off the pottery, and especially the necklaces and the tools and the other——' Ward's voice subsided into an awed silence as he smoothed his hand over the polished stone of the ancient digging stick. It was of exquisite workmanship, just as the other objects lying about were. Why hadn't the Utes looted the place?

'What kind of necklaces?' Bart managed to overcome his fear enough to ask quaveringly.

'Oh, all sorts! Bone and shell, and— There's a beautiful turquoise one all tangled about the bones of a skeleton back there.'

'I'd rather have your rifle,' Bart judged, then as if afraid Ward might think he was complaining, he added placatingly: 'But you'll get us out of this.'

Ward swallowed uneasily. 'I'm going to fix a torch and get back in there and look again. If the Utes are so terrified of this place they wouldn't follow us in— —well, all we've got to do is take enough of this place along with us to frighten them back so we can get through them.'

'Like— —like that skeleton?' Bart asked, dubiously.

'Maybe,' Ward studied the scattered bones. 'It would probably work. Only— —how could we make them know it came from here?'

Ward climbed down the toe holds far enough to break off a branch and to strip the fibrous bark from a juniper. Back on the cave floor he thoughtfully twisted the hairy bark about the stick to make a torch. Bart held it while he lit its tip. Ward took it and his digging stick and hurried back into the ruins. Now and then, he probed the light into a tiny doorway, not sure what would aid them, but alert for anything which might serve their needs. When he came to the turquoise necklace, he shifted the bones so he could pick it up. They clanked dismally in the tomb-like silence. His fingers clasped the turquoise necklace, and the blue stones felt chilled and cold as from the sepulchre. Shivering, he slid the icy pellets hastily into his pocket. Holding the torch out, he studied the skulls. After a moment he shook his head, and moved on reluctantly.

The further he penetrated into the cave, the more eerie the ruins appeared in the flickering torchlight. Timbers, protruding from the ancient masonry walls, grew distorted, and seemed to be tentacles grasping for him. He held his breath in terror as he listened, imagining he heard the shuffling of ghostly feet beside him. Cobwebs flared into nothingness, just like the people, Ward thought, oppressed. He, too, knew the awe and the superstitious dread the Utes held for the place.

Ward's eyes swept over the centuries of debris heaped across the back. He longed with his whole being to hurry out into the open. The thought that alone he might be able to slip through the cordon of savage Utes teased at his mind. They'd make it together, or not at all, he determined, forcing the temptation back. His face wrinkled over such a disloyal thought. Why, he was letting fear make him a craven, inhuman being!

Ward crawled up on the refuse and stuck the torch into the loose matter. Having no idea what might be secreted in the trash, his mind dwelt hopefully on clothing, or some sort of regalia which would create the illusion the mysteriously vanished people had returned. So that he wouldn't cast shadows with his probing, he crept backward facing the torch. He jabbed the stone spade in and out of the dehydrated rubbish. Ancient corn husks crackled into bits, and cobs rolled to the side. Pottery shards and old bones offered no barrier to the stone spade, other than a dull grating as it slid on down.

Acrid dust swirled up into Ward's nostrils. He'd have to be more careful, he realized, coughing a little as he turned his head towards the mouth of the cave, and waited for the dust to settle back. After a little, Ward began again, now easing the stone spade into the accumulation with care until his gripping fist touched the debris. In and out he forced it, until the ancient tool seemed to be held for a moment, then broke through and slid on down.

Ward pulled the stone digger out and stared at it. It seemed as if it had caught on clothing, he thought excitedly. He shoved the spade in again and found it was barred by a solid object. Oblivious to the dust, he began scooping the debris aside with both hands. Soon the fingers of his right hand tangled in some matting. He tugged at it gently, then again with more force. The matting held securely.

His heart thumping wildly, Ward pushed more of the debris out of the depression he'd dug, until he could see the matting was wrapped around a fair-sized bundle. What had he unearthed? he pondered, shivering, as he tugged and lifted it out. The dust choked him until he could hardly breathe. An ominous dread shook him; he had to get out of the cave. Clutching the stone spade, the torch and the bulky package, he stumbled through the narrow corridor and out in front of the masonry ruins.

'Have you found something?' Bart exclaimed, rushing over to Ward's side.

Still coughing. Ward could only nod his head. He placed the bundle on the cave floor and beside it the stone spade. He started to roll the blazing torch in the dust to extinguish the fire, then, thinking they might need it again, he propped it against a fallen stone.

'What do you think it is?' Bart asked excitedly.

Ward shook his head slowly. 'Maybe something we can drape about us,' he finally managed to gasp. Reluctantly, Ward moved to the lip of the cave and dipped the pottery mug into the water basin. He rinsed the dust from his mouth, then let the soothing liquid wash down his throat.

'It's horribly dirty,' Bart protested when Ward came back to stare down at his find.

'It was buried.'

'Really! Ward, you don't suppose it's——it's—?'

'If it can get us through the Utes, it will be a rich treasure, all right.' He reached down to tug at the matting. He brushed away the clinging dirt, and turned the bundle over before finding an end to peel back.

'It's just feathers,' Bart complained with disappointment.

'It's feathers woven into a sort of cloth. There's something inside as hard as stone,' Ward explained, as he rolled the bundle over to unwrap it.

'Is that a blanket?'

Ward nodded. He shuddered as he felt the chilling outlines of the object shrouded inside. His hands hovered just above the cotton material, not daring to reveal its secret.

'Well, aren't you going to open it?' Bart urged.

Ward swallowed uneasily. He looked at the younger boy soberly and managed a slight downward jerk of his head.

A mummy stared up at him

'Well, go on!'

Ward grasped the edge of the ancient blanket. Closing his eyes against the sight, he tugged back the cloth.

'No!' Bart shrieked. 'Cover it up!'

Ward opened his eyes. A mummy stared up at him! Quickly he replaced the shroud. He could still feel the probe of its dark eyes, see its long black hair, its browned gaunt cheeks, and teeth bared by the dried lips.

'Put it back,' Bart cried out. 'Take it back before it——before something horrible happens to us.'

'It's only a mummy,' Ward managed to say, gaining a little courage himself as he tried to calm Bart.

'Only?'

'Sure! It's dead as——' Ward pulled back the covering and stared curiously at the dried body. 'I just can't imagine anything being——well, just any deader. He can't hurt you.'

'What about curses?'

'Curses?'

'If you disturb a mummy, aren't you horribly cursed? Ward, you're not listening.'

Ward looked aside at the skeleton they'd first seen, then back at the trussed-up brown mummy at his feet. 'I just bet that's it. I just bet that's why they're so—— We're taking him with us.'

Bart backed away, horrified. 'We can't——I just can't——'

'Would you rather be holed in here with more of them, starving while we try to outwait the Utes? Try to escape and get scalped? Or get through them by carrying him along?'

'You mean—— How do you know he can—— I mean, will it work?' Bart cried, despairingly.

'I'm not really sure. Only—— They've just got to be terrified of these ancient ones, else they'd have followed us in, and they'd have looted the ruins, too. Here we've found one of these old—— Well, we can carry him along to scare them back.'

'Do you really think he——it will scare them off?' Bart extended his hands in a pleading gesture, as if to say he placed his life in Ward's care. 'If you think——'

Ward nodded soberly. 'I'd say we should start now, while we

have the sun to light us through. Besides——' Ward gestured toward the ruins and shrugged with distaste. 'It just seems a trap of death. He isn't too heavy. I think I can lash him to my back with that matting. When we get down we'll sort of hoist him up between us — carry him on our shoulders. We want the Utes to get a real good look at him.' He smiled encouragingly at Bart.

'Can't we climb out up there?'

'I think it's better to get back the way we came in. Besides, it will give these old Utes more of a shock. Come on! Let's get ready! Let's get started!'

Deep shadows stretched across the canyon when they reached its floor. 'Be jaunty!' Ward had cautioned him. 'Make them think this fellow returned to protect us!'

At the base of the cliff, they slipped on their shoes and carefully adjusted the burial wrappings about the neck of the trussed-up mummy. When they lifted the ancient one up on their shoulders, the wind caught the long black hair and it writhed about on the feather robe and across the boys' heads.

Ward and Bart neither saw nor heard the Utes as they made their way to safety. Neither did they spy any wild animals. They knew that the Indians were close to them — silent and terrified as the mummy's eyes leered at them with ageless mockery.

THE LEAGUE OF THE SCORPION
Leonard Gribble

Here is a story of the future, of a time when the peoples of the world are united. Even in such a nuclear-space age trouble rears its head, and a bandit appears in the skies. But courage and determination to win are still qualities that bring success, as Roke Dorsey, youngest pilot at Space Base No. 3, proved against grim odds.

Tiki Rostin, the senior pilot at Space Base No. 3, lifted his eyes from the control panel of the north radar tower and stared across the yellow waste of the Sahara's sands.

'The circuit's broken,' he announced. 'We can't make contact. We can't send or receive.'

Roke Dorsey, the post's youngest pilot, who not long before had received his commission in the Astro-Wardens, said slowly. 'You mean we're isolated, Tiki?'

The Finnish senior pilot brought his eyes back from the flying-field stretching beyond the control pylons, between which, curved in the fashion of an enormous igloo of transparent polar ice, extended the wide hangar of welded crystal plastics that housed the base's space shuttles

'Yes, I mean that,' he said gravely.

'But what of the auxiliary circuits?'

The question was levelled by a dark, slender man who lounged against a curved wall. Juan Martinez was a Brazilian and in every way the opposite of his fair-haired, broad-shouldered leader.

'Nothing doing, Juan,' said the Finn. 'I should have said that it was impossible for us to be cut off in this way. But I should have been wrong. The impossible's happened.'

'When the impossible happens the sky isn't even a limit,' said a short, mild-mannered man with slant eyes that only slightly betrayed his oriental ancestors.

Charlie Lay was a Canadian of Chinese extraction. In fact, he had claimed upon more than one notable occasion that there were so many nationalities mixed up in his family tree that he was the finest example of a Unified Person on earth. And in the early years of the twenty-first century, with the World State of the Unified Peoples about to enter upon the most momentous period of its development, that was quite a claim, even for Charlie Lay, one of the oldest pilots at Space Base No. 3.

'Where are you going, Charlie?' asked Rostin, as the other walked to the door.

'To get a drink.' Charlie Lay's flat face broke into a knowing smile. 'The impossible always did give me a thirst.'

The door, controlled by an electronic eye, closed silently.

Roke Dorsey spoke. He said, 'You'll have to make the alarm circuit to the Corrective Council, Tiki.'

The Finn nodded gravely. 'Orders are very clear,' he muttered. 'The Corrective Council alarm circuit is only to be used in a case of dire necessity.'

'Well, that about covers an impossibility, doesn't it?' said the Brazilian, with a questioning smile.

Rostin nodded. 'Very well, here goes,' he muttered, and turned down a scarlet button beside the radar receiving screen. At once light flowed across the screen, glowed, then faded.

'What the——'

The base's senior pilot didn't complete his exclamation of surprise. Out of the greyness of the screen an image appeared, flickered for a moment, as the circuit flow achieved maximum strength, and the watchers in the tower room stood staring at a repellent, wriggling image.

'What is it?' asked Roke Dorsey.

Martinez' face had lost its smile. 'A scorpion,' he told his companions, 'and a symbol of evil.'

A voice that came as clearly to them as though the speaker were in the room said, 'Rather a symbol of power. The League of the Scorpion has taken over the World State.'

Rostin stretched out a hand and depressed the scarlet plunger. Voice and scorpion vanished. The screen stared back at them with a dead eye.

'Hell, I forgot the circuit,' muttered Martinez. 'But this League of the Scorpion, Tiki. I thought that stuff was only talk.'

'You mean the underground movement?' said Roke Dorsey.

'That circuit was on to the action chamber of the Corrective Council,' said the Finn gravely. 'It couldn't have sent that message unless the followers of the Scorpion have taken over world control. You know what that means. The other bases are either captured or out of action.'

His listeners received his words in silence. They looked grave. Six space bases spanned the world, manned by Astro-Wardens with special space vehicles armed with ato-guns. Base 1 was in Greenland, Base 2 in the Andes, Base 4 in Iraq, Base 5 in Tibet, and Base 6 in Northern Australia. If Tiki Rostin was right, only they, Base 3 the Sahara, the nearest post to the European mainland, remained in action and capable of offering resistance to this menace to world security.

From time to time, since each could remember, there had been talk of uprisings against the World State, but the talk had always been idle words.

'So it's come at last,' said young Dorsey. 'The history books record that every century has had its dictators who tried to control man's destiny. Napoleon in the nineteenth, Hitler in the twentieth, and now it's the turn of the twenty-first century.'

'But who is the leader of the Scorpion League?' asked the Brazilian.

'I've heard a dozen tales,' said Rostin. 'He's a German scientist or a mad American. Next he's a descendant of the African Zulus, or a Jap with a secret factory. Oh, one just took it for more talk. But it's real enough.' The Finn's voice changed, hardened with resolve. 'Well, they've done their work well. The Director-in-Chief and the rest of the Corrective Council must be prisoners. The other five air posts can't operate. That leaves us.'

'But why?' urged Martinez. 'Even now we shouldn't have known the truth unless you'd switched on to the alarm circuit, Tiki.'

The Finn moved towards the entrance, paused.

'We happen to have the new Charnex space shuttle in our underground hangar. I'd already received secret instructions to put it through a number of special tests without making normal reports. I've got to make sure that shuttle's safe.'

The others had heard more than enough to hurry their steps in the wake of their leader. They had served in the grim operation against Pacific Island P/X7, when Professor Feodor had attempted to hold the World State to ransom. They knew from experience what flying through the higher stratosphere and fighting with laser guns meant. They had trained their slim lasers on targets of concrete and steel that had melted like ice in the flame of a blowlamp when the atom-charged rays found a positive focus. The rays from those guns split molecular tension. Nothing constructed by human hands could remain in a solid state when under direct positive focus from them. The Astro-Wardens, with their terrible and swift means of total destruction, had been the front-line troops of the World State. They were under the direct orders of the Corrective Council of the Unified Peoples, which dealt with all major crimes and attempts at insurrection against world authority. Bernard Wallines, the popular and genial Belgian Director-in-Chief, was the one person who could counter any order from the Corrective Council. English was the universal language, had been for several decades, and the correlated radar circuits linking cities and townships throughout the world allowed the entire world community, so far as was practical, to live as neighbours.

Young Roke Dorsey, still able to take a personal pleasure in the spacesuit of an Astro-Warden, and the gold wings of an Astro-Warden, first class, realized that for the first time the basic security of the World State was threatened.

The fact that this underground menace had grown to such proportions that the other bases could be put out of active operation, the world circuits cut, the alarm circuit of the Corrective

Council itself captured, could only mean that already a new power had taken possession of the entire world. Simply, easily, by capturing the centres of authority. There were no armies or navies to fight back as in the old days he had read about. Modern, twenty-first century methods of warfare were efficient and direct, but they were not varied. Punishment and retribution was something that came from the skies on the wings of the Astro-Warden's space shuttles.

Roke knew that if danger threatened Space Base No. 3 it would strike from the air.

They reached the mid-field control tower, descended to the underground hangar, and Rostin threw the switch that operated the doors. Young Roke Dorsey caught his breath. The silver-blue shuttle anchored to the linear magnetic ramp was something that made his heart leap. It was smaller, more slender than the standardized craft of the Astro-Wardens. Its power outlets were tapered back from short, sweptback wings.

'Roke,' said Rostin, 'get in. You're taking off.'

The youngster stared at his leader.

'But, Tiki——' he started to protest, only to be stopped by a peremptory gesture from the Finn.

'I can't take off. I must remain here, so must Charlie and Juan. Our reserve pilot,' Rostin said, with a slight smile, 'will not be missed when we get visitors. You can fly the shuttle, Roke. I wouldn't send you otherwise. There is one thing to remember, however. The jets are concentric. That multiplies the boost. The ampoule belts are loaded. Now, in with you, and stay aloft till I get word to you on the indigo circuit. I can do that from down here. Then attack, my boy. Beat up everything on this base.'

Roke Dorsey froze as his leader's hand fell from his shoulder, and he stared back into the steady blue eyes of the Finn. He knew what Rostin's words meant. He would have to kill his companions, unless...

'The Charnex suits,' he muttered.

Rostin nodded, a trifle impatiently. 'We'll see,' he said. 'Perhaps—perhaps not. Now, hurry!'

A couple of quick hand-shakes, and Roke was climbing into the space shuttle. The self-sealing doors locked. He depressed the automatic air-pressure control, and a violet light winked above his head. He threw the switch of the muted turbines, depressed the power-feed lever, and the belt fed with lozenge-shaped ampoules of thoranium moved on its S circuit. He had no further time for thinking about being alone. A green glare glowed ahead. Current ceased to flow through the magnetized chocks and the holding-ramps. The trigger arm of his graphometer trembled, and as the craft moved slowly forward recorded a thread of scarlet on the electromagnetic chart as it revolved slowly on its polarized spindle.

The green flare died. Bright sunlight rushed to meet him. The violet gleam above his head turned to pale amber and he fingered the air-pressure lock. The automatic flow device changed the gleam back to violet, and Roke was rushing to meet the burning desert sun.

He fingered the boost lever, trimmed the cabin gyroscopes that counteracted the flow of speed in relation to a varying gravitational value. He waited until he passed the 100,000 feet hairline on the altimeter and a blue pilot light came on over the electromagnetic chart. Then, for ten breathless minutes he put the new craft through her paces. The thoranium pellets clicked in and out of the turbines as the shutt screamed through the thin air. At first Roke felt confined, but gradually he became used to the cabin layout. At 125,000 feet the tachometer was hovering on the 1500 line. Roke fed his boosts, put the plane on a helical circuit, and the speed crept beyond 1900. With a thrill he knew he could reach 2000, always beyond the attainable limit of the standardized shuttles, with their jets working in parallel.

Suddenly a deep blue glow burned under the screen level with his right ear.

'Tiki!' he muttered to himself excitedly, and switched on the indigo home station circuit. He spun the alternating control device, and the light deepened. 'Come in, Tiki,' he said.

But it was not the familiar voice of Tiki Rostin that answered his invitation.

'This is Sardo Zarotti,' said the voice of a stranger. 'Return to base at once, and obey the command of the Scorpion.'

Roke was climbing into the space shuttle

Roke, his mind filled with dismay, cut out the helical circuit. He reduced speed by bringing in the reserve power cut-out flaps. He fingered the indigo circuit marker, and the deep blue glow winked mockingly at him.

'I ordered come in if you value the lives of your fellow-pilots,' said the harsh, strident voice.

Roke recalled Tiki Rostin's last order. 'Attack... beat up everything...'

It came to him in a split moment of time that the amazing events of past minutes had swept him into a position unequalled in the long history of mankind. He alone had the means of combating the League of the Scorpion. He alone could save the entire world. He felt suddenly full of wild exultation. He threw the master circuit switch that enabled his words to be picked up on all space base and Corrective Council circuits. The indigo light faded and changed to bright crimson.

'Sardo Zarotti,' he announced, 'I am attacking you and your illegal League of the Scorpion. I, Roke Dorsey, Astro-Warden of Base Number Three, am attacking in the name of the Unified Peoples.'

He cut out all circuits, blanketed his approach, and gave himself to watching the magnetic indicator that crept over a gently rocking map of the world, showing his position. Now that he had flung out his challenge he felt that he had been foolish. He could strike the base in the Sahara sands, but he could remain operative only so long as his supply of thoranium ampoules lasted. It was a question of time.

Time. ...

It seemed that in the space of a few breathtaking moments he had aged several years. This was what he had been trained for, why he wore his Astro-Warden's wings. Death no longer mattered, neither his nor his companions'. What mattered was that an evil force that would enslave mankind was resisted.

Tiki Rostin had known that.

Tiki — Juan — Charlie...

He was young. His friends and fellow-pilots had filled his life. Now he was elected to be their executioner, because he could not attack without killing them as well as the Scorpion Leaguers. And afterwards...

He thrust that from his mind.

The marker crawled across the width of Africa as he swung on to his magnetic meridian and adjusted the terminals of his Laser gun.

He became an automaton, without feeling and conscious thought, obeying only impulses that lived on a mental screen as the violet light of the air-pressure indicator lived — a symbol only.

He searched the stratosphere through his telescopic sights, shielded by ultrared screens, and he was down to 80,000 feet when he saw the enemy craft hunting for him. He was within their magnetic field. Soon their guns would be turned on him. That would be the test of the new Charnex insulation. If his smaller plane did not crumple and disintegrate it would be his turn.

It took all the courage of which he was capable to remain steadily watching the approach of those searching black specks. He counted four. As they grew larger in his telescopic sights he made out the design of a scorpion on their close-trimmed wings.

He saw one dip and come up at him and purposely fed his cut-out flanges. He gauged that he entered the magnetic field of the other planes' laser guns when he was down to a little over 600 miles an hour.

He felt his craft shudder. The violet light again changed to amber, and he was gasping for air as he fumbled with the gyroscopes. Then the violet light came on, and the wobbling electromagnetic chart steadied on its polarized spindle.

Again a feeling of intense elation filled him. He had come within the field of that attacking craft's laser gun. The destructive element of uranium had been powerless against this new wonder plane he flew. Without thinking, he threw down the switch of the master circuit again and announced to the world:

'Scorpion planes are attacking me. I shall now attack in turn. Stand by for my next announcement. In the name of the Unified Peoples!'

He locked the terminals of his own laser, spun its vernier disc, and went to meet the second approaching black speck. He set his teeth, emptied his mind of thought, and turned on the ray. Almost immediately, as he watched the defiant shape of the painted scorpion grow larger in his sights, the shuttle disappeared behind a black spiral of cloud shot through with an orange flash. Then the air was transparent again.

He turned after the next plane, feeding his power boosts. Another flame-shot dark cloud that evaporated like steam, and he was hunting another enemy.

But the other two were in full flight. Their only hope was to reach the Base No. 3. He knew that. He fed his boosts until the tachometer needle quivered on the 2000 hairline. He lost count of the passing minutes. He went down, checked his speed, circled the familiar field at just under 50,000 feet, and waited for his prey to come in.

He caught the first within the field of his gun before either of them was aware that he had outpaced them. A black puff-ball that hovered in the air, and the fourth bandit went streaking down, alone. As he turned his plane to follow it down Roke saw another black patch leave the base.

The fools!

Didn't they realize by now that...

He levelled off quickly as the craft he was chasing dissolved into another tell-tale cloud that dispersed like a puff of spent breath. He found he was talking rapidly, describing what he had seen, and only when the alternating control clicked on his master circuit and he heard Tiki Rostin's voice did he realize that he had raced beyond the air post and was heading straight for the distant Atlantic.

'Take it easy, Roke,' said the Finn. 'You've let the whole world now by this time. Switch on your indigo.'

Roke's hands and face were moist with perspiration as he obeyed.

'Tiki,' he said, 'what's happened? I thought— —'

'I'm in the crew shuttle,' Rostin told him. 'I've got Juan with me. Charlie — remember he went to get a drink? Well, he did, and he wasn't available when Sardo Zarotti and his thugs jumped us — oh, very neatly, with all circuits jammed. But Charlie tumbled to the truth before he could be rounded up and reached one of our craft. He turned his gun on the north tower. It wasn't pretty, Roke. We had time to get our Charnex suits before Zarotti's four shuttles took off. Zarotti wanted your vehicle. Because you had it he had to jump before he was ready. Now——'

Tiki Rostin's voice faded.

The indigo light throbbed, and Charlie Lay's voice came in on the home circuit.

'Watch yourselves up there!' he warned. 'There will be another wave of Scorpion bandits. I've got friend Sardo in a real state. Seems his pals are coming if they don't get a code signal on our circuit. They'll be coming from Tripoli.'

The indigo light dipped and glowed bright again, and Tiki Rostin's voice came over strong and earnest.

'All right, it's your show, Roke,' he said. 'We can't leg it with you, youngster. Go in and carve them up. But keep off the master circuit. What you tell the world you also tell Zarotti's pals. Good luck.'

'Good hunting, Roke boy,' came Juan Martinez' soft tones, and then the indicator light died.

Roke fed his boosts and made an about turn that swung him three hundred miles north. He climbed, levelled at 100,000 feet and cruised at slightly over 1000 miles an hour. He caught the bandits in his screen, swung in to intercept, and when he could use his telescopic sights got ready for action.

The bandits jumped him. There were six of them. Too late, he realized that their leader had worked a trap. They had got him into their combined field power and would turn their lasers on him simultaneously. It was something he hadn't allowed for. There was a chance his craft could not stand the combined weight of their bombardment. His one sure hope seemed to lie in outranging them.

He closed his own laser circuit. A bandit blew up, and then Roke felt his own craft tremble and falter. It turned turtle and fell like a rock out of control.

The five bandits were torn from his sights, whirled off the teleradar screen. He was numbed with shock. It was something he should have foreseen, he told himself, and realized that he was growing angry.

He worked the gyroscopes, fed the boost of the cut-out flanges. The space shuttle swung around unsteadily on an even keel and the rate of fall was reduced. He was down to below 50,000 feet, he saw. The craft responded, but not with its earlier alacrity. One of the primary magnetic fields had been fractured. Power was going to waste, and wasted power in such a vehicle was a source of grave danger.

He cut the central of the two concentric jets, and flew on half power, slowly boosted this single jet, and then let in the central jet again. That was when he made the discovery that power was leaking to the gyroscopic control circuit. He would have to land if he was to save the plane. There must be a flaw in the insulating Charnex material, and unless he could out-manoeuvre the bandits he would merely be a sitting target for their combined power, and with it safe to fly on only one jet his chances were slim.

But if he could lure them down...

They came into his radar screen again, all five. He plummeted. They were sponged off the screen like fly specks.

Then he let all the power he could leak to the cut-out flanges. He watched the moving needle on the tachometer: 450 — 300 — 175...

The ground was coming up to him and the horizon below was flattening out. There were palm trees and a glint of silver water and a transit strip picked out with luminous paint that absorbed the sun's rays. There was a cross-continental commercial land-freighter, large, ungainly, blunt-ended, crawling like one of the old-fashioned locomotives of an earlier age.

He went down over it, flattened out, swept towards the palms and dipped over the transit strip. Twice in the past he had made emergency landings on the magnetic transit strips, which ran in geometrical straight lines for thousands of miles. Once during his training as an Astro-Warden. But he had never tried landing such a plane as the one he flew now on any field without landing strips. He cut all circuits, touched the strip, and ground to a swaying stop.

He waited for the bandits to follow. He was gambling on the hope that they would wish to take his craft intact. They swept out of the sky, circled him, and the master circuit hummed, but, he kept it cut off in the hope that they would consider him unable to answer because his circuit was damaged. They came low, swinging wide. Perspiration streamed down his face, soaked into his clothes. This was the hardest part of his ordeal.

He had to wait until — until...

He rose with his extra power boost, like a rocket, and was beyond them and above before they were aware of his intention. Then he threw his space shuttle into a power dive, with the bandits circling below him, their laser guns untrained.

He locked his gun terminals. Laser rays jetted at the black shapes.

Two dissolved into the familiar black clouds. Then the three others were coming for him. This time if he went out of control he had no chance to go back towards earth. The earth was close enough to wreck him like a crashing meteorite.

Then he was within the field of their united fire. The gyroscopes juddered, but he kept flying, got another bandit in his own gun-field, and the juddering stopped abruptly as another black cloud slipped earthwards.

He had beaten the bandits!

There was a painful hammering at his temples as he realized the truth. Their fire-power couldn't harm him now. Almost as realization came to him he was aware that the two remaining bandits were flying with a single purpose. He had kept his circuits switched off purposely, and so had not heard their cross-talk.

Too late to do anything about that now. They were above him and diving. They were going to ram him!

It was madness. The same brand of madness that made power-frenzied men try to conquer a world for their own selfish ends. They were about to destroy him because he had frustrated them.

He had no chance to boost his speed sufficiently at the lower altitude. He caught a climpse of the lumbering transit freighter in the distance. It could not be making more than 140 miles an hour. There was already talk of doing away with such ancient methods of transport.

Well, he wouldn't...

His head went back as the bandits smote his silver-blue craft. Almost at the instant of impact he turned the nose up. He was almost beyond their frantic clutch, but not quite. One hit his tail unit. The other grazed a wing and the central jet died. He saw the two assassins crash, and then he was trying to put his crippled space shuttle into a glide, only the gyroscopes would not work and he could not breathe, because the amber light had come on above his head and there was a strange singing in his ears, and it felt as though a million red-hot needles were pricking his skin, while the roof of this head was rising like a balloon.

Rising... rising...

He came to in a hospital ward in Paris, and a cheerful nurse dressed in a yellow silk, germ-proofed uniform was doing something to his chin with a shiny pencil-slim instrument that made his face feel pleasantly cool.

'I think you can see them now,' she said, and smiled when be looked puzzled.

'Them?'

She nodded, and walked to the arched entrance. In came Tiki Rostin, Juan Martinez, and Charlie Lay as she opened the door. She said something to them in a whisper, and they glanced at Roke and nodded.

She went out and the three came towards the draught-proof hospital crib that was sunk below floor level.

'How's the hero?' grinned the irrepressible Charlie, his slant eyes crinkling with genuine affection.

'How's the thirst?' countered Roke. 'And drop the gagging, fellows.'

'Charlie isn't gagging,' Tiki Rostin said, swallowing hard. 'You just about pulled everybody's chestnut out of the fire, Roke boy.'

'All the same, you were lucky, Roke, that the crew of that transit freighter broke a record and reached you,' said the slim Brazilian.

Piece by piece, he heard the story of how he had been rescued and flown by Tiki to Paris, where Bernard Wallines himself had announced the immediate award of the Valour Cross, the highest honour the Unified Peoples could bestow on anyone who risked his life for the common good.

The story of the insurrection of the Scorpion League was now history. Sardo Zarotti and his fanatical dupes were repenting at leisure on a prison fish farm in the Antarctic. They had tried to capture the entire world on a bold bluff, first by jamming the primary radar circuits with the help of quisling members of their underground organization, then by pumping Space Base No. 3 and capturing the new single-seat shuttle before the other bases could make contact with the rest of the world. Any who did merely got the Scorpion warning on their screens.

Had the bandits secured the plane and been able to put the other bases out of action, then a period of twelve hours might have seen the peoples of the earth pass under the control of the first dictator of the twenty-first century.

'But it wasn't to be, Roke,' Tiki Rostin said. 'There was an Astro-Warden named Dorsey who was around to do something about it — and in the old-time lingo of what the history books call the Second World War he did plenty!'

They remained until the yellow-clad nurse came and beckoned to them to leave. She returned when they had gone, and ran the ice-cold tip of her bright pencil round his face.

She was pretty, he saw, and her small even teeth shone like matched pearls in the filtered artificial daylight.

'Soon you'll sleep, Astro-Warden Dorsey,' she said, in a voice that already sounded distant, 'and you won't dream. No dreams,' she smiled, and the touch of the faintly buzzing pencil in her slim fingers became colder.

Roke tried to stir himself. There were things he wanted to know, questions he felt he had to ask, about — oh, about a score of things.

But he didn't ask them.

The sopho needle, probably the greatest gift science had made to mankind, soothed his ragged, shocked nerves into smooth peace under the firm, competent hand of the nurse, and when she went off duty and a nurse in pale blue took over, Roke still slept, finding his way back to health, while all over the world people from Mongolia to Mexico, from New Zealand to Islamabad, stared into the screens of their television receivers and heard the latest proposals for a fitting reception planned to do justice to the occasion when Bernard Wallines, in their name, presented the coveted Valour Award to the youngest of the Astro-Wardens at Space Base No. 3.

THE HONOUR OF THE REGIMENT
George Charles

Tommy Dunn was a bugler in one of Wellington's hard-pressed line regiments during the Peninsular War. When he was reported missing it was thought he had deserted, but Tommy was on a secret mission of his own, and when the truth was finally told Tommy heard the Iron Duke himself say he was proud of the 95th Regiment's boy bugler.

The survivors of the 95th Regiment of the Line were in desperate straits, but Captain Mervyn, his green pelisse hanging in rags from his shoulder, the plume of his shako trimmed by a French dragoon's sword, was still a martinet.

Bugler Tommy Dunn, now on two hours' knapsack drill in double-quick time for breaking ranks after a Spanish pig, had other names for him.

The 95th, separated from Wellington's main force, had been hunted and harried through the Spanish mountains. They were now at bay in a valley, every path in the saw-edged mountains blocked against them by redoubts, and the surrounding slopes seething with Marmont's troops.

' 'Bout turn! Jump to it, ye young limb of Satan,' roared the corporal, who would have been resting but for Tommy's misdemeanour.

Wearily, Tommy lifted his blistered feet and squared his aching shoulders. But what hurt most was the thought that ten thousand amused enemy eyes could witness his shame, and he hated Captain Mervyn whole-heartedly. Such a man would be capable of anything.

Whichever way he turned at the corporal's command he saw white tents on the surrounding slopes, light sparkling on muskets and lances and the cones of helmets, breastplates turned to gold by the sun and French Eagles tipped with fire. Snatches of laughter and song hung on the still air. The French were taking it easy, their prey at their mercy; the chase had been long that day;

morning would be time enough to strike, after the hated British had suffered another sleepless night.

Vultures wheeled overhead and, in the lavender shadows, wolves licked their muzzles over the coming feast.

' 'Shun! Dismiss!' the corporal ordered thankfully.

'Cheer up, Tommy,' grinned a dirty bearded soldier whose feet were swathed in bloody rags. 'War's mainly lice and blisters. Here's your supper.'

He handed Tommy a small knob of tough meat toasted on the end of a sword. Chewing it painfully, Tommy looked about him. Men were sprawled in every attitude of exhaustion, accoutrements in shreds, many without boots, the powder of bitten-off cartridges still on their lips. Among them, like a tribe of gypsies, were a few soldiers' wives, as ragged as the men, bare-legged, men's greatcoats over their heads, for they, too, shared all the rigours of war except the actual fighting. All were without shelter, for the baggage had long since been abandoned.

The only tent was that used by Colonel Barker as an orderly room. It had been brought on the last pack-horse, which had just provided the last meal.

'Bugler Dunn!' came a yell from the tent.

Tommy groaned.

'Skip to it, Tommy, lest you want more pack-drill,' a bandaged soldier advised.

'Make up my bed,' the Colonel ordered when Tommy entered and saluted.

Captain Mervyn and the Colonel were talking quietly. Tommy, busy with his task, ignored them until he heard the Colonel remark, 'These may be the last despatches I shall ever write, but, if they are acted upon, the French are in for a shock.'

His gaze fell upon Tommy.

'You'd better get some sleep now, Dunn,' he said kindly. 'You'll need all your breath in the morning for your bugle. Pity we hadn't time to let you catch that pig this afternoon.'

'Yessir,' said Tommy, drooling at the thought of it.

The Colonel nodded towards the untasted meal laid out on his case. 'I'm not hungry tonight. You'll know what to do with it,'

'Yessir.' Tommy said eagerly, disappearing with the food before the Colonel could change his mind.

'He's a good lad,' Mervyn smiled when Tommy had gone. 'I'm sorry I had to punish him, but discipline breaks easily under these stresses. I couldn't risk it spreading to the men.'

'Quite,' said the Colonel. 'He's a chip off the old block. We lost a fine soldier when his father was killed. Tommy will take after him — if he survives,' he added softly. Then, after a brief pause: 'We haven't a dog's chance unless you pull this off. If you don't, I shall send out the women under a white flag in the morning, and we shall fight to a finish. The 95th don't surrender.'

'No, sir,' said Mervyn. 'I understand.'

'It's a hard role for you, Mervyn, and it is fortunate you speak French fluently. The enemy must be made to believe that you are a deserter. Our situation is so desperate that the Duke would surely forgive me for forging his signature to these despatches. Nothing else could induce Marshal Marmont to withdraw his forces to the Heights of Bardos, and if he is deceived into believing that Wellington is about to occupy them he'll strain every sinew to get there first. Your life won't be worth much when he discovers his mistake.'

'I realize that, sir.'

'But it's our only chance. You must get those plans to Marmont quickly. If they bluff him, he won't waste time on us and we might slip from this trap. All depends upon you.'

'He shall have them, sir.'

'Wait until it's dark — I shall myself instruct the sentries to pass you through the lines — then collect the despatches from my tent. And now ensure that the men stamp out their fires. We don't want to present enemy snipers with night targets.'

The lavender shadows deepened to violet, then to blue, and from blue to the purple of the bruised bodies warming themselves at the flickering bivouacs.

'It ain't 'uman,' a soldier grumbled to Tommy when, on Captain Mervyn's command, he extinguished his fire. 'This perishin' cold 'ud kill a Spanish goat. Whose side is he on, anyways?'

'Just what I say,' agreed Tommy.

'Where's our Arthur?' the cry rose from other bivouacs, for the British soldiers believed that there was no situation so bad from which the Iron Duke could not extricate them.

But no one could possibly have known that at that very moment Wellington was considering the transfer of his main force to the very place where Colonel Barker was hoping to draw the forces of Marshal Marmont, and, if the enemy reached it first, the British would march into a trap that would result in complete and utter disaster.

Doomed to discomfort, the 95th shivered in the darkness, encircled by the French fires on the slopes.

Tommy could not sleep for the cold, his legs thrust into the sleeves of an old watch-coat tied at the cuffs, the rest of the coat under him as a blanket.

Finally, he crept behind the Colonel's tent which served as a windbreak. The sky was powdered with stars and a young moon floated amid clouds as he lay listening to the groans of the wounded and the muttering of men in their sleep. Gradually the sounds of the French army died away, except for the regular calls of their sentries.

Suddenly Tommy was alert as a tall figure approached the tent. He pretended to be asleep as it halted a moment by his side, but through half-closed eyes he recognized the shorn plume in the shako of Captain Mervyn. The Captain entered the tent. Tommy changed his position so that he could see what was happening, for he heard no voices. Then the Captain came out, stuffing a document inside his green tunic.

Why was he there at this time of night? His movements were stealthy. Tommy's dislike of the Captain hardened with suspicion as he recalled the words he had overheard in the Colonel's tent: 'If these despatches are acted upon, the French are in for a shock.' Did Captain Mervyn intend to desert to the enemy with these very despatches? It was unthinkable that any member of the 95th could fall so low. Yet the Captain was heading for the perimeter of the camp. Tommy crept after him. The Captain slipped past a sentry, apparently unobserved, for there was no challenge. Tommy felt sick at heart. What should he do? If he raised a false alarm he might well be flogged for another bad practical joke. It was not fear that deterred him, but pride in the regiment, a pride that had been strengthened by his father's death on the grapnel-swept *glacis* at the siege of Badajoz.

The honour of the regiment was a vital thing to him. If the men knew that an officer had deserted they would lose heart, and the 95th would be the mock of every unit in the Peninsula. Tommy hesitated no longer. The men slept by their arms in case of a night attack. Tommy quietly took one of the newly invented rifles with which the 95th had been equipped and crawled after his captain.

Fortunately, Captain Mervyn travelled slowly, using every scrap of cover. Tommy waited until the nearest sentry turned his back, then slipped through the lines and hid behind a clump of bushes. For a few moments he lost his quarry, then he saw a shadow move and went after it. When they were some distance from the British camp Captain Mervyn proceeded more quickly. Once he turned, and Tommy dropped down, his heart pounding.

From the foothills, the valley was a lake of blackness. Tommy now realized the wisdom of showing no lights, for the French could not be sure that the 95th had not moved, and they would be unlikely to risk an attack in which they might suffer frightful losses; daybreak would be soon enough, when they could bombard the enemy before finishing him off with one overwhelming wave of fire and steel. But Captain Mervyn might after all be attempting to pierce the French lines and deliver the despatches to Wellington. If so, he was a brave man, and Tommy just a fool who would be posted as a deserter. Yet he must be sure.

It was harder to follow the suspect as they began to climb. They must be near the French outposts; enemy fires were bigger and brighter; a mule brayed, disturbing other beasts; sharp voices quietened them, and he heard the jangle of accoutrements.

'*Qui v'la?*'

Captain Mervyn stopped at the challenge and replied in French.

In the bright starlight Tommy saw the Captain produce the despatches at the point of the French sentry's bayonet.

Tommy's worst fears were confirmed. So the Captain was a traitor. At any price he must be prevented from handing over the despatches. If the sentry signalled for his guard commander it would be too late. Tommy was so close behind the sentry that he could see over his hairy goatskin knapsack the strained face of the Captain. The two men were deep in conversation as the butt of Tommy's rifle caught the sentry between jaw and shoulder, dropping him instantly. Captain Mervyn had not time to move before Tommy had him covered.

'Dunn! What are you doing?' the Captain exclaimed furiously.

'Taking you back with those despatches,' Tommy said grimly. 'The regiment must never know of this.'

'You young ass! You may have ruined everything. You'll destroy the regiment.' Captain Mervyn took a step forward.

'Back!' Tommy snapped. 'I shall shoot if I must. Return those despatches and I promise no one shall hear a word of it.'

'Fool! I am obeying orders.'

'The Colonel is no traitor,' Tommy asserted. 'About turn, or I fire.'

'You don't know what you are doing,' the Captain urged desperately. 'For the love of heaven, keep out of this unless you want a massacre in the morning.'

'I shall count three. One — two —'

Captain Mervyn saw that Tommy was in earnest, and turned. But below them was another outpost.

'Left wheel,' Tommy ordered, 'and no noise.'

It occurred to Captain Mervyn that even if Tommy killed him the plan might still succeed if the shot guided the enemy to his body and they found the despatches. But Tommy might escape with them, and even if he failed to do so the extra delay might render the plan useless. He would have to take the boy into his confidence.

'Let me explain,' he begged.

Tommy had been so intent upon the chase that he was no longer certain where the 95th lay, except they were somewhere below them in the valley. A halt would enable him to get his bearings.

300

'Treachery can't be explained,' he said curtly.

'You must believe me, Dunn. These are false despatches intended to deceive the French. If the Colonel's plan succeeds they will be on the move before dawn, and our boys may win their way out. It's our only chance. Even you must see that.'

'Tell that to the Colonel,' Tommy snapped, angered by the last sneer. 'Get moving.'

'You'll be court-martialled for this,' Captain Mervyn exploded.

Tommy hoped that the direction they were taking was the right one, but when they climbed from another fold of the hills he knew, by lights below and above, that they were in the French lines.

'You should have stuck to your bugle,' Captain Mervyn mocked him.

'Try to escape and I shall shoot you,' Tommy threatened him, picking out a break in the line of fires below through which they might steal. 'Right wheel.'

As they descended the hillside, Captain Mervyn fell. 'My ankle,' he groaned.

'You'll walk if it's broken,' Tommy said coldly.

He relaxed his caution for a moment as he stood over the fallen man. With a lightning movement Captain Mervyn jerked his ankle. The rifle exploded; cries broke out all around them, and as Tommy and the Captain struggled on the ground French hands dragged them apart and hauled them to their feet.

Captain Mervyn's rapid French was meaningless to Tommy.

'What has your stupidity served now?' Captain Mervyn said bitterly. 'They don't believe me, and we may be shot as spies; in any case, the delay may wreck the Colonel's plan, and you will be responsible for the destruction of your comrades.'

'There is no need to pretend longer,' Tommy said wearily. 'You have disgraced the Regiment.'

Captain Mervyn did not answer, and they were hurried along by mustachioed men with red shoulder-knots who wore French eagles in their caps. Captain Mervyn was interrogated in a well-guarded tent. Though he felt that Tommy's misguided zeal had ruined everything, he still clung to the faint hope that it might not yet be too late. He spoke so plausibly that at last suspicion yielded to doubt, and a messenger was hurriedly despatched to inform Marshal Marmont of an important capture. Another hour was lost before their examination was renewed in the Marshal's headquarters.

'The signature might be a forgery,' Marmont said at last, looking up from the despatches spread before him, 'though it looks genuine to me. It is the boy's behaviour that has convinced me you are not acting a part, Captain Mervyn. He could not have simulated such anger and contempt. When we have occupied the Heights of Bardos and the British have walked into the trap, you shall be free to serve the Emperor as you say you wish. Meanwhile you are my prisoner. Does that satisfy you?'

'Perfectly, sir,' Captain Mervyn answered, though he knew there could be only one end for him.

'Then we will leave your ex-comrades of the 95th for another day,' Marmont said. 'One does not hunt jackals when the tiger is abroad.'

'And the boy?' asked Captain Mervyn. 'He was doing his duty as he saw it. I bear him no ill-will. He is of no use to you. Can he be set free?'

'No, but use him as a servant if you can tame him,' Marmont smiled sardonically, 'and remember that you are both under arrest until further orders.'

Captain Mervyn scarcely expected obedience from Tommy, and he was not surprised when the boy stoutly declared: 'You can have me flogged, but I won't clean the boots of a traitor.'

'In your place, I hope I should react in the same way,' Captain Mervyn said unexpectedly. 'Nevertheless, you will be disgusted to know that but for your behaviour the Marshal would not have moved to Bardos. Your insolence to me convinced him that I am a traitor '

'If... if you had been alone, he would have had you shot as a spy?' Tommy stuttered.

'In all probability.'

'Then all I have done is help the enemy,' Tommy cried despairingly.

'That is the alternative to believing me,' Captain Mervyn said gently.

He would have been horrified had he known that even then the vanguard of Wellington's army was marching to its new position. Disaster awaited the forces that should be last to reach the fatal Heights.

All that night and the following day they trudged by forced marches in the dust of a French baggage wagon behind the splendid army, unaware if the 95th had escaped from their trap. Through green valleys and forests of pine and over ridges covered with dwarf oaks the army wound like a brilliantly coloured serpent — cavalry in the van, dragoons in bear-skin helmets, chasseurs in green and purple and yellow, hussars with dolmans and shakos every colour of the rainbow — behind them the six-horse gun-teams, then the blue-coated infantry keeping step to the pulse-beats of drums, and last of all, powdered with yellow dust, the baggage-train.

Tommy's anger burned fiercely against his Captain. Unwittingly, he aided the Colonel's plan, for Marmont's spies reported that he refused to speak to his superior, thus confirming the Marshal's opinion that he could not have been acting a part the previous night.

At last the proud army entered the pass through the frowning hills they were to occupy, colours flying, bugles playing, the sun glinting on their Eagles, when the slopes on either side burst into flame. The French reeled beneath the shock; the cavalry halted; the artillery drove into them; the infantry were flung into disarray. All was confusion. Bugles sounded above the din — the English one for the Charge, the French for the Retreat.

Back down the valley streamed the shattered host, order and discipline lost. The gun-teams wheeled about, their drivers standing in the stirrups and lashing the wild-eyed horses that scattered the infantry in their mad flight. The cavalry pounded past the rocking gun-carriages. Dead and wounded sprawled among the abandoned litter of a defeated army. Cheer after British cheer rang from the deadly slopes.

Captain Mervyn struggled to Tommy's side as they were swept

along by the tidal wave of fugitives, seized his arm and dragged him down behind an overturned wagon.

The tide of battle streamed around them as the British poured down the slopes in a red flood.

'Now!' Captain Mervyn shouted as the fleeing mob thinned. 'Run for it!'

But he had reckoned without the Marshal and his staff who were struggling to rally an improvised rear-guard and hold up the enemy so as to let his battered forces withdraw.

Marmont's roving eye lit upon the two Englishmen, and his face was suffused with fury.

'Seize those men,' he roared. 'Shoot them if they resist. I will deal with them personally when we are out of this cauldron.'

Neither Captain Mervyn nor Tommy had any means of defence. Frantic soldiers pricked them along at the bayonet's point, and they became part of the flight that ended only when darkness stopped the pursuit.

Though the French Marshal had plenty of matters to occupy his mind, foremost was the thirst for revenge upon those who had engineered his humiliation. Upon Captain Mervyn and Tommy he poured all the vials of his wrath.

'Sir,' Captain Mervyn protested, fighting for their lives, 'the despatches clearly said that the British intended to occupy the Heights. How could I know what delay would occur before you moved?'

His excuse, casting blame for the defeat upon the Marshal, merely augmented his anger.

'According to the despatches,' the Marshal screamed. 'Wellington should not have marched for another twenty-four hours. You deceived me deliberately. My army is broken. Yet I shall act according to the rules of war. You shall have a drum-head court-martial, and if you are found guilty, as you will be, you will be shot as spies.'

'The boy had no part in this, as you well know,' Captain Mervyn insisted.

'Liars, both of you,' the infuriated Marshal shouted.

'Then, sir,' said Captain Mervyn, 'as you are so punctilious about the rules of war, may I observe that we both wear British uniforms, and should therefore be treated as prisoners of war, not as spies.'

'*Nom de chien!* You would teach me my profession,' the Marshal bawled. 'Remove them before I lose my temper. Convene a court-martial immediately, Captain Brabont. You know my wishes. The sentence is to be carried out at dawn.'

'The Marshal sounded in a bit of a wax,' said Tommy as they were marched away, curiosity forcing him to speak to Captain Mervyn. 'What happened, sir?'

'Bad news, Tommy. We are to receive the farce of a court-martial and to be shot at daybreak. It is what I expected for myself, but it is a crime that he should include you in his revenge.'

Tommy's heart stopped momentarily, and he shivered as with cold. Then he pulled himself together.

'You'd have been shot by the Duke if not by Marmont,' he said. 'As for me, I'd rather have died in battle like my father, but by tomorrow it won't matter.'

'I wish you could believe me,' Captain Mervyn sighed. 'Neither I nor the Colonel knew of the Duke's change of plans. I sweat with fright when I consider what would have happened had he not reached the Heights first.'

'That's as it may be,' Tommy said non-committally. 'I'm only a bugler, and I don't understand these things, but if, by a miracle, we were both saved, I should tell what I knew and leave our Arthur to sort it out.'

'Silence!' growled a guard, jabbing his rifle-butt between Tommy's shoulder-blades.

Captain Brabont acted quickly. The court-martial was convened— a few questions, replies roughly interrupted and ignored, a unanimous verdict of guilty, sentence of death, and the prisoners were marched away, their feet and arms bound, and an armed sentry placed over them.

It was a lovely night. Never had the stars looked so bright and beautiful to the two men gazing upon them for the last time. With so few remaining hours of life, they could not sleep, though the ground was covered with men in the sleep of utter exhaustion.

When Captain Mervyn spoke to Tommy, the sentry snarled at him to be silent, and Tommy pretended to be asleep, for he was still convinced that Captain Mervyn was a traitor with whom conversation would be an insult to his dead father.

All too quickly the hours raced by, marked by the changing of the haggard sentries. Tommy felt a sneaking sympathy for the last to arrive, so fatigued that he seemed on the point of collapse. He examined their bonds, and then stood guard over them. Tommy saw him reel with weariness; then the man looked round to ensure that no officer was on his rounds, and sat down. Soon his chin sank on his breast, and shortly afterwards Tommy, too, must have slept, for he next felt a hand on his shoulder, and Captain Mervyn was whispering in his ear; he caught the gleam of starlight on a French bayonet in the Captain's hand.

'It's a forlorn hope,' hissed the Captain as he severed Tommy's bonds, 'but you might make it. I'll look after the guard. Good luck.'

The thought flashed through Tommy's mind that it was another trick, but it was no worse to be killed escaping than to face a firing-squad. He massaged his wrists and ankles, feeling the returning blood stab like a myriad needles.

'There's no time to lose,' the Captain urged. 'Off with you.'

Tommy inched away without a word of thanks or farewell. Why didn't the Captain come, too, if he were innocent? But he could not argue that out now. He wormed his way through a multitude of twisted bodies, freezing into immobility if one stirred, then crawling on again. He was on the fringe of the army when he heard the clink of accoutrements as the sentries were relieved. Now his flight would be discovered. Panic seized him; he stood up and ran; someone shouted, and the quiet camp broke into uproar. He dodged a hand that tried to catch him; bullets whizzed past in the night. He reached open country seamed with the dry beds of streams into one of which he jumped so that his silhouette would not appear against the starry sky. Crouching, he hurried along its course. After a time he scrambled out and began to run again.

He stopped to listen for sounds of pursuit, but was breathing so heavily that at first he could not be sure there was no one behind him. He rested for a time to regain his breath, then set off again doggedly, uncertain of his direction, but jubilant to be still alive and free, and more kindly disposed towards Captain Mervyn.

He did not stop until the mud wall of a village loomed before him. There was no sound, not even the barking of a dog. Then he noticed the wall was broken in places, and through a gap saw heaps of rubble and roofless houses, though the great church that dwarfed the surrounding buildings looked to be undamaged by war.

He needed rest and shelter. Perhaps there was still some Spaniard left to help him. Cautiously he climbed the rubble left by a cannon-ball and began to explore the deserted village.

Two or three flat-roofed houses, close together, seemed to have escaped material damage. He knocked softly on a door, then, as there was no reply, he pressed against it. The door swung open. There were two rooms downstairs and two above, one of which gave access to the roof. From the roof he looked about him. All was quiet, so he went down again and was soon asleep.

Like an animal he was wide awake at an unusual noise, and the sound that alerted him was a stealthy movement outside. Through a crack in the shuttered window he saw beyond the smashed fountain in the dusty square a dozen or more soldiers searching with lanterns amid the broken columns of the arcade. Two more were near the house. Opposite the arcade the great dome of the church towered over the square, and in its black shadow a horse whinnied, while others restlessly stamped the cobbles and champed their bits.

Someone passed the window and stopped at the door. Tommy had reached the top of the stairs and had opened the door to the flat roof wide enough to let him slip through as the door below creaked open. In that fraction of time he heard the quick indrawn breath of the intruder. He flattened himself on the roof. Peering over, he watched six French soldiers, one with a lantern, run round the corner of the adjacent house. Four more entered the house he was in — that would make five of them, including the one who had disturbed him. Two more passed directly beneath him to search the next house.

He was angry with himself now for having fallen asleep instead of pressing on his way. He could not think how they had followed his trail, nor did he know how long he had been asleep. But dawn must be near, the hour when he was to have died.

On the roof of the neighbouring house a soldier appeared with a lantern. He held it above him, then spoke to his unseen companions, and they all descended and joined the soldiers who were still searching the rooms below him. Maybe they had not yet visited the roof where he lay because they had found food or wine, but it could only be a matter of time before he was discovered.

A hand clapped over his mouth prevented him from crying out at the unexpected movement beside him.

'I didn't expect to find you here,' Captain Mervyn whispered. 'I seem to be unlucky to you, Tommy. They'll be highly delighted to capture the two of us.' He listened to the voices below. 'They're coming up now. One of them says he saw someone here from the next roof. Fools! They could have picked us off nicely from there. They must want to produce us alive and kicking to the Marshal.' He stood up and looked round, gazing thoughtfully at the space between the two roofs. Then he said cheerfully, 'Come on, Tommy. We'll give them a run for their money.'

He took a short run and landed as light as a cat on the other roof, turning in time to steady Tommy who followed him.

'Their horses are outside the church door,' said Tommy. 'If we could...'

'Good boy,' said Captain Mervyn, guessing his thoughts.

They were half way down the stone steps alongside the outside wall as the French soldiers reached the roof they had just left. Keeping to the shadows they hurried towards the church.

'Someone is sure to have been left in charge of the horses.' Tommy panted. 'If we can enter the church by the side door we might take him by surprise.'

'You'll be a General yet, Tommy,' the Captain laughed.

The church, like the houses, had been hurriedly abandoned, and its doors were open. The smell of incense still lingered in its chill interior; it was dark there, but the great main doors framed a velvet-blue arch of night.

The search was still in progress when they reached the top of

*The discomfited soldier sent a musket ball whistling harmlessly
after them*

the steps leading down to the *plaza*. Below, a knot of horses stood head to head, a soldier in their midst holding their reins.

'He'll raise the alarm before we can snatch a couple,' whispered Captain Mervyn.

'I'll find a way to let you get among them,' said Tommy, and, leaving Captain Mervyn no time to reply, he crept down the steps. Hidden from the soldier's view by the horses, he approached him, then stepped boldly into sight.

'Who are you?' the soldier asked in French, as he pushed aside the horses for a better view, not expecting to see a boy.

Captain Mervyn's steps were muffled by the stamping of the horses. His fist sent the soldier sprawling, and released from his grip the horses started away, but not before Tommy had scrambled into the saddle of one and Captain Mervyn had mounted another.

They clattered away as the discomfited soldier struggled to his feet and sent a musket ball whistling harmlessly after them. Behind them, hubbub broke out among the searchers. Tommy followed the Captain through a gap in the crumbling wall, and they were in open country.

In silence they tore through the night until the horses began to flag, when Captain Mervyn turned aside into a wood to rest them.

'There's little chance of those fellows finding us now,' he said. 'I wonder if you have changed your mind about me yet?' As Tommy did not answer, he continued, 'You're a hard chap to convince. It seems that the Duke must decide this between us after all.'

Dawn was breaking as they reached the British outposts. An officer conducted them to a small house of wood and stone where the Duke had his headquarters.

At Captain Mervyn's request they were escorted in together, and soon they faced a neat slender man, quietly dressed, whose deep violet-blue eyes flashed with fire.

'Why is the boy here?' He turned to someone behind him. 'He's one of yours, too, by his green coat and black buttons.'

Tommy followed the Duke's gaze. In a corner of the room stood Colonel Barker, battle-stained and subdued.

'This is Bugler Dunn, sir,' said the Colonel. 'He was missing yesterday. I thought he had deserted.'

'Captain Mervyn is the deserter, sir,' Tommy said boldly. 'I saw him sneaking out of camp with papers he had stolen from the Colonel's tent. So I went after him to force him back. But it didn't work out that way and I was captured.'

'Wait till you are addressed,' the Duke snapped. 'You certainly haven't taught him discipline, Colonel.'

'I seem to have taught him something more valuable, sir,' the Colonel spoke up, realizing what had happened.

'You take the unpardonable liberty of forging my name to false despatches, the boy breaks camp at a critical moment, Captain Mervyn fails to carry out his orders promptly. Is this discipline? You have told me your story, Colonel. Now I will hear theirs.'

Nothing made sense to Tommy. Was the Colonel, too, a traitor? And had he abandoned his men to save his own life? Captain Mervyn told his story and Tommy's part in it, and he told it fairly.

'Well, Bugler Dunn?' the Duke growled when Captain Mervyn had finished. 'What have you to say?'

'Sir,' Tommy asked. 'Did the 95th get away?'

'Look through the window,' said the Duke.

There, among the red coats, he saw the green uniforms of the 95th.

'I'm sorry, sir,' Tommy stammered. 'I've made a fool of myself.'

The Duke ran a hand through his crisp dark hair, and wrinkles of laughter creased his eye-corners.

'Individually,' he said, 'you might have had me kicked out of Spain, but between you, you have enabled me to give Marmont the shock of his life. My congratulations, Colonel.' His hand fell on Tommy's shoulder. 'Bugler Dunn,' he said gravely. 'Your father would have been proud of you — as I am.'

'Nice work, Tommy,' the Captain smiled when they were outside, and Tommy knew that his Captain was a man he could follow now through fire and flood.

MR SNOOKS FORGETS HIS SPECTACLES
Fielden Hughes

Bill Holmes liked nothing better than playing detective, a fact that was well known to Inspector Quilta. But he had no idea that within a short while he would be meeting the Inspector when he set out on his cycle to collect the spectacles forgotten by Mr Snooks, his form-master. Bill's adventures after calling for the spectacles are related in *Bill Holmes and the Fortune-Teller*, from which this story is taken.

Bill Holmes, the boy detective of Wimbledon, was not a prime favourite with Mr Snooks, his form-master.

There were many reasons for this. Mr Snooks' special subject was English, and at that subject Bill was not very strong. His spelling was erratic, and his powers in the matter of essay-writing were small indeed, unless the topic had something to do with the technique of detection, in which subject Mr Snooks felt only the most passing interest.

Then, all too often, when the master was dealing with some very important aspect of English Language and Literature, Bill's mind was far away from the matter in hand. Time after time Mr Snooks had been obliged to punish Bill by giving him extra work because the boy detective had been scrutinizing documents having to do with one of his many cases instead of paying attention to his teacher.

Unfortunately, though Mr Snooks knew about Bill's interest in crime detection, and had even, on previous occasions, been made aware of Bill's skill in clearing up mysteries which had baffled other and older investigators, he still persisted in the pathetic belief that the boy would be better employed in learning English.

So the two often clashed, and there was not that affection between them that there ought to have been.

One morning in the summer term, Mr Snooks came into the form-room, and instead of plunging with his customary horrible relish into the morning's work, he felt in his pockets, looked first into his briefcase and then into his desk, and finally beckoned to Bill to come out. This was where Bill got his surprise, for as we have said he knew he was no favourite with the master.

'Holmes,' said Mr Snooks in a low voice, 'I am greatly annoyed.'

That, reflected Bill, was nothing new. What could he have done to annoy his form-master anew?

'I have left my spectacles at home,' went on Mr Snooks, 'and I cannot be without them. You have a bicycle, I believe.'

'Yes, sir,' said Bill. Could it be that Snooker was going to send him to get the missing glasses and so give him a little respite from the English lesson? That was exactly it, and Bill wondered why one of the more able members in the form was not to have this treat. There was, however, a sting in the tail of all Mr Snooks' remarks.

'You have it here, I trust? In the bicycle shed?'

'Oh yes, sir,' replied Bill joyously. 'I can get it right away, sir.'

'I have no doubt of your willingness to lose class time, or of your speed in business other than your own,' said Mr Snooks ungratefully. 'I want you to go to my house. Do you know where I live?'

'It's in Gratton Road, isn't it, sir?'

'Yes. Fifteen is the number. If you forget that, the house is called Birch Lodge. That, I feel sure, you will not forget.'

Bill grinned a receipt of this grim jest. Just right for Snooker's house, he thought.

Mr Snooks produced a key and held it out to Bill.

'There is no one at home,' he said. 'Mrs Snooks has not yet returned from her weekend in the country, and my daughter will have gone to work. This is the front-door key. Let yourself in carefully, and go into the front room. The door is the first on your left. You will find my glasses in their case — a red one — on my bureau. Close the door carefully as you come out of the room. I do not wish the cat to get in and ruin the furniture by scratching. Then bang the front door — not too hard — but hard enough to make the lock click. It is, as you notice, a Yale lock, and only requires you to shut the door. And *please* do not leave this key inside, otherwise I shall be unable to enter on my return home tonight.'

As Mr Snooks gave all these directions, Bill groaned inwardly. What *did* Snooker think he was? As soon as Bill saw the key, he knew what to do. As for the cat, Bill would have left everything as he found it, anyway. What a tedious bore Snooker was. Still, one must not grumble. Here was half an hour out of school. Bill pocketed the key.

'I'll look after it, sir,' he said.

'In case the thought should have occurred to your mind,' said Mr Snooks, 'I must apologize for putting you to this trouble, and for robbing you of time better spent in school.'

'Oh, that's quite all right, sir,' replied Bill magnanimously. 'I don't mind.'

'That,' said Mr Snooks, 'it what troubles me. But I console myself with the thought that, as I shall be obliged to set the class to private study till I have my glasses, and as you, Holmes, never by any chance do any private study, I shall inflict least damage on myself, the class and you, by letting you go on this errand.'

'I see, sir,' said Bill gloomily.

Mr Snooks looked at his watch.

'It is now half-past nine,' he said. 'The journey from home to school takes me fifteen minutes. Allowing that you are no more expeditious than I am, and adding five minutes for the search, you will be back at, say, ten minutes past ten at the very latest.'

'Yes, sir,' agreed Bill. 'I'll try.'

'Ten minutes past ten,' repeated Mr Snooks.

'It's nine thirty-one now, sir,' said Bill.

'Begone, boy,' said Mr Snooks sharply. Bill went swiftly to the door and vanished. The master turned to the class.

'Take out Firnham's *English Grammar and Composition*,' he ordered. 'Turn to Chapter Thirteen, which is on Metaphor and Simile. Study the text, and consider the questions at the end of the chapter.

I shall require you to answer them a little later in the week. If in doubt, ask me any questions you wish.'

The boys obeyed, the minds of many going after Bill on his pleasant ride in the morning sunshine. Meanwhile, Bill Holmes had taken his bicycle from the shed and was riding down the road with a jaunty air, his mouth puckered up to whistle joyfully as he tasted his lawful liberty.

As he approached the police station, his old friend, Detective-Inspector Quilta came briskly out. The policeman's sharp glance fell on the lordly Bill riding along the road in a leisurely fashion.

'Well, young Sherlock,' he cried, 'and where are you going?'

Bill grinned at him cheerily.

'Is that an official question, or a friendly one?' he asked.

Mr Quilta beckoned with one finger.

'Come here,' he commanded.

Bill made a big swoop with his bicycle and stood supporting the machine with one toe on the ground.

'Don't do that, either,' said Mr Quilta. 'Have you read the Highway Code?'

'Yes, sir,' said Bill. 'Several times.'

'Well, then. You didn't look behind or make a proper signal. There might have been a car behind you. But why aren't you at school?'

'I'm out on an errand for my form-master,' replied Bill.

'Oh! That's it, is it?'

'Yes.' Bill looked at Mr Quilta demurely. 'Don't you want to know what the errand is?'

'Why should I?'

'I thought detectives were like that.'

'What you want,' said Mr Quilta, 'is a little bit of the cane.'

'Now I,' said Bill, ignoring this coarse remark, 'am only an amateur detective. But I can tell where you've been and where you're going without asking.'

'Indeed?' said Mr Quilta. 'And where might that be?'

'You were up very late last night,' replied Bill. 'In fact, I shouldn't be surprised to hear you never got to bed at all. You've had a quick breakfast, probably standing up, you took time to fill your lighter, and now you're going to arrest somebody, but not before you've been to Colley's.'

Bill pointed to the barber's shop — Colley's — just across the road. Mr Quilta looked sarcastically at the young detective.

'All because I haven't had a shave,' he remarked. 'Not very clever, young Holmes.'

'But quite correct, isn't it?' asked Bill.

'Yes. As a matter of fact it is. But you can congratulate yourself on a run of lucky guesses.'

Bill shook his head sadly.

'Maybe you do your work by guess, Mr Quilta,' he said. 'But other people have better methods. Deduction. That's what I was doing.'

'Really?' said Mr Quilta. 'Then how do you know I ate standing up?'

Bill stooped and took a corner of the policeman's overcoat in his fingers. He showed it to its owner.

'A spot of egg,' he said. 'Quite fresh. If you'd been sitting down, it couldn't have got there. Mind,' he added, 'some folks don't spill at all, sitting or standing. It's just a matter of being careful.' He dodged the playful clout Mr Quilta aimed at him. 'And — just to help you — there's a reek of lighter fuel coming from your pocket. No — not that one — that's the one where the handcuffs bulge.'

Mr Quilta wagged a finger towards Bill's bicycle.

'I can tell you what you're going to do next?' he said.

'Yes?' said Bill, with interest. 'What's that?'

Mr Quilta's voice rose to a roar.

'You're going to get on your way,' he cried, 'and be double quick about it. Be off!'

Laughing, Bill pressed down on his pedals and went off along the road, leaving the policeman glaring after him.

Gratton Road, where Mr Snooks lived, is a turning off the main road to Kingston, where all the buses run and there is a great deal of traffic. Gratton Road itself is a cul-de-sac, pleasant and quiet, tree-lined and as Bill thought just the kind of respectable road where a schoolmaster might very well be found to live.

Bill approached the turning, giving the correct hand-signal, and as he rode into the entrance to Gratton Road he observed a dark, sturdily built man of about thirty just turning out of the quiet road into the busy main thoroughfare. The only thing worthy of remark about the man, apart from the fact that he was walking along in a very leisurely way, was his blue suit. Even in the quick glance that Bill gave him, it was noticeable that he seemed to have grown out of the coat and trousers. They were a little too small for him, so that he looked like an overgrown boy who was still having to make do with last year's suit. He looked rather comical and Bill gave a little grin at the sight. In another moment the man had turned the corner and was out of sight. Bill rode on along Gratton Road, where no one stirred except a milkman whose truck stood beside the kerb farther along. A black cat nipped across the road in front of Bill's wheels and he swerved to avoid it, forgetting in a moment the man in the blue suit.

Number fifteen, Mr Snooks' house, was a small, modern place standing back some way from the road, and screened from the view of passers-by behind a tall hedge. The number was painted on the gatepost, and the name, *Birch Lodge*, appeared in Gothic lettering on a tablet of wood nailed to the gate itself. Bill reached it, jumped off his bicycle, leaned it against the kerb, and decided he need not padlock his wheel in such a respectable neighbourhood.

'I'll bet no burglar would have a got at Snooker's house,' he thought with an inward smile. 'Not if he knew Snooker.'

He walked up the path to the front door, feeling the kind of interest in seeing where his form-master lived, moved, and had his being that an explorer might experience in coming upon the lair of the King of the Beasts; or that a civilized man might feel on entering the palace of some jungle potentate. He was going to see at what points Mr Snooks was human and fallible like all the rest of us.

With a certain diffidence he inserted the key in the lock, turned it and opened the door. As he stepped inside he noticed, as he had often observed before, that every house has its own smell, quite different from other houses. In the atmosphere of the master's house there was a dry refined smell, not like, but just as clean as, a hospital. There was the smell of floor polish, and there was a faint perfume of flowers. Besides these odours, there was the scent of books, reminiscent of a bookseller's shop. Bill took a deep breath and gave a little grin at the suitability of the smell of Mr Snooks' home. But then he saw something that surprised him. The door of the front room was, as the master had told him, on the left. But, in spite of what had been said, the door stood open.

'Well, I'm blowed,' said Bill to himself disgustedly. 'All that yap about shutting the door and not letting the cat in... and he left it wide open himself.'

Even as Bill looked, a black cat, well-fed and with great moon-like eyes, strolled complacently out into the hall, and seeing Bill, opened its mouth to miaow, but no sound came out The fancy came into Bill's head that the cat knew he was one of its master's pupils and was behaving accordingly in a condescending manner. He would hardly have been astonished if it had spoken and said to him: 'Get me a saucer of milk, lad, and hurry up about it.'

However, it never said a word, but stalked in a dignified manner towards what looked like the kitchen door, also open, and vanished into the room beyond.

Bill went into the front room, and there was the bureau, with the red spectacle-case resting on the top. But Bill's gaze was arrested by something else. The bureau had a front which could be pulled down to make a writing surface. That front should have been shut, if Bill knew anything about Snooker's habits. But it wasn't shut. It was open, and the papers within were in disorder. The bureau also had six drawers, and these too were pulled open and their contents disarranged. His heart beating fast with excitement, Bill went over to the bureau, absently pocketed the glasses, and stared at the disordered papers. There was no other sign that anyone had been into the room in its owner's absence, but to Bill's eyes there was no doubt about what had happened.

He left that room and went down the hall and into the kitchen The cat was at a saucer under the table lapping milk, but Bill took no notice of her. He stared around him at the evidences of intrusion. On the table lay the rude remains of a hasty feed — a crust of cheese, some cold meat, an empty milk-jug, the crust of a loaf.

Crumbs and fragments had fallen to the floor, and some were trodden into the floor-covering. An attempt to find money had been made, for here too drawers were open, and the intruder had ranged about the shelves looking for stray cash hidden under jugs or tins.

'My goodness,' thought Bill, grinning joyously, 'what a mess. Poor old Snooker.'

There was a small scullery behind the kitchen, from which the food had been taken, but what interested Bill most was how the thief had made his entry. The front door had been all right when Bill unlocked it. The kitchen door was firmly locked, with its key inside and apparently untouched. He glanced into the scullery, which had a tiny window with a gauze covering to keep out the flies. This gauze in its wooden frame was open inwards, but the window opening was so small that Bill himself could not have got through it.

He raced upstairs and satisfied himself that all the windows there were safely closed. Then he ran down the stairs and stood for a few moments in the hall. It was very baffling. There had been a thief inside the house since Mr Snooks left home that morning. But unless he was a tiny child, how did he get in? Well, Bill knew what he had to do next. The telephone stood on a small table in the hall. With gloating joy, he picked up the receiver and dialled 999.

A deep voice answered and Bill spoke excitedly.

'I'm speaking from Number Fifteen Gratton Road and...'

'Police, fire or ambulance?'

'I beg your pardon?'

'Do you want police, fire-brigade or ambulance?'

'Why, the police,' said Bill. 'Why should I want...'

'Hold on.'

A new voice spoke.

'Police.'

'I'm speaking from Number Fifteen Gratton Road,' said Bill. 'There's been a thief in the house this morning. He hasn't taken a lot, I don't think, but...'

'Fifteen Gratton Road where?'

'Why, Wimbledon, of course.'

'Very well. Are you the householder?'

'No.' Bill was stumped for a moment and then replied with a grin. 'I'm just a friend.'

'Very well. We'll send someone round.'

'Will they be long?'

'A few minutes only,' replied the voice, and Bill heard a click.

He blew out breath. He could hardly believe his good luck. Not that he wanted poor old Snooker to be robbed, but if he had to be, what better chance than that Bill should be right in on it like this? Now Bill knew full well what his next step ought to be. He ought to telephone the school and inform Mr Snooks of his misfortune in being the victim of a thief. He looked at the telephone and hesitated. He knew equally well that if he did ring, Snooker would order him back to school, which would be intolerably dull in view of the exciting happenings now due to take place. No, he couldn't possibly take the risk of being excluded before the fun began. Besides, he reflected with a self-righteous air, he couldn't leave the house to look after itself. No, no. He must stay on guard till the householder, as the police called Snooker, reached home in person.

In an incredibly short time he heard a car draw up outside, and then quick footsteps came up the path. The bell rang sharply and authoritatively. Bill went to the door and opened it. There stood two police officers, an inspector and a sergeant. For a moment the men stared at Bill and he at them.

'Well, blow me down,' said Inspector Quilta, 'it's that boy again.'

'Good morning, Inspector,' said Bill demurely.

'Did you put the call through?' demanded Quilta.

Bill nodded. 'Thought I'd better let you in on it,' he said, 'as it looks like a case of breaking and entering.'

'It had better be,' replied Quilta grimly. 'Let's take a look, George. I know this young gentleman very well. He's quite a humorist, but if this turns out to be one of his jokes, it'll be his last laugh.'

'Well, I like that,' said Bill indignantly. 'I do my duty as a citizen and all I get...'

323

'We'll talk of what you'll get later,' said Mr Quilta. 'Meanwhile, what are you doing here anyway?'

Bill explained patiently.

'As you're so good at telephoning,' said Mr Quilta, 'no doubt you've rung up your school and told your teacher?'

'No, not yet. I thought I'd better ring you first.'

Mr Quilta nodded at Bill and addressed his companion.

'You want to watch him, George,' he said. 'He knows all the answers. He's a bit of a detective himself, you know.' Then he returned his stern gaze to Bill. 'No doubt you've had a look round, eh?'

'Yes. I have,' agreed Bill.

'And perhaps you have a pretty good notion of how the job was done... maybe you even know who did it.'

'No. Not yet,' replied Bill. 'But it looks a straightforward job. I'm sure you'll manage very well.'

'Thank you. Thank you indeed,' said Mr Quilta. Then with a sudden ferocity, 'You didn't touch anything, did you?'

Bill looked at him pityingly.

'No, of course not,' said Mr Quilta hastily. 'I forgot. You're first-class on theory. It's practice that fogs you, isn't it?'

'Would you like me to show you round?' asked Bill politely.

'No. We wouldn't,' replied Mr Quilta. 'You get on that telephone and report yourself to your teacher. He'd better come home right away. We shall want to see him.'

The policemen went into the front room, and Bill dialled the number of his school. The secretary answered.

'Bill Holmes here, speaking from Mr Snooks' house. I must speak to him. It's urgent.'

'He's in class,'said the secretary, Miss Grubb, an elderly woman who thought schools would be fine places if there were no boys in them to spoil everything. 'I can't disturb him now. You must tell me what you want.'

'Miss Grubb,' said Bill desperately. 'I know he's in class. But I must speak to him.'

'What about?' said Miss Grubb crossly.

'I don't mean to be rude,' replied Bill, 'but I can't tell anyone but Mr Snooks.'

'Good gracious me,' said Miss Grubb, 'I don't know what boys are coming to. Perhaps you might condescend to tell the Headmaster?'

'Miss Grubb,' said Bill earnestly, 'I must speak to Mr Snooks. I can't even tell the Headmaster.'

'Wait there,' said Miss Grubb, as if Bill would have gone down the road for an ice-cream when she wasn't looking. 'I'll tell Mr Snooks what you say, and I only hope for your sake that the matter seems as important to him as it does to you.'

'It will,' said Bill, 'only more so.'

Miss Grubb put down the receiver with a sound like a secretive tortoise walking about her desk.

While Bill was waiting, the policemen came into the hall from the kitchen, and began to ascend the stairs.

'How did *he* get in?' Bill heard George say to Mr Quilta.

'We'll talk to him later,' replied Mr Quilta.

Bill couldn't believe his ears. Surely they didn't believe for even one moment that he was the guilty party? How wonderful it would be, he thought, to be wrongly arrested, and to have all the fun of... but no; on second thoughts he would prefer to be at liberty, especially if the police failed to solve the mystery. He jumped as a voice rasped in his ear.

'Holmes!'

'Yes, sir,' he gasped into the mouthpiece. It sounded as if Mr Snooks had suddenly materialized out of the empty air and was standing right beside him. But the master was for the moment safely far away at the school, holding the telephone.

'What do you want? Why are you not back at school?'

'There's been a thief in your house, sir.'

'A what?'

'A thief, sir. When I got in, I found your bureau opened, and whoever it was had had a meal in the kitchen.'

'Good heavens, boy. Do you mean I've been burgled?'

'No, sir. Burglary is a crime that has to take place at night. This was breaking and entering.'

'Don't bandy words with me, boy. What have you done about it?'

'I dialled 999, sir. The police are here. They want you to come home.'

'What, immediately?'

'Yes, sir.'

'I can't do that. I'll see them during lunch hour. At the moment your classmates are engaged upon important work.'

The policemen were coming downstairs. Bill looked at Mr Quilta and pointed vigorously into the mouthpiece as if he had Mr Snooks, in the shape of a fierce lion, imprisoned there, and likely to leap out at any moment and devour everybody in sight. Mr Quilta stared.

'Who've you got?' he demanded.

Bill covered the mouthpiece with his hand.

'Mr Snooks,' he whispered.

Mr Quilta held out his hand for the telephone, and as soon as Bill removed his covering hand, Mr Snooks seemed to come to life.

'Hullo, hullo,' came his voice angrily into the air. 'What on earth are you doing, lad? Answer, will you?'

George stirred and grinned.

'A bit of a tartar, that one, isn't he?' he said.

'And how,' Bill said with feeling.

'Inspector Quilta here,' said the detective into the telephone.

'Who?' It sounded as if Mr Snooks thought Bill was playing tricks with his voice.

'Inspector Quilta. The police.'

'Oh. Well?'

'Your house has been entered. I must ask you to come home at once, if you please, sir.'

'Won't it do if I meet you later?'

'I'm afraid not. You see, we need you to check on what has been taken.'

'But I'm very busy at the moment.'

'So are we, sir. I'm afraid I must ask you to join us at once.'

'Oh very well,' said Mr Snooks impatiently. 'I'll be there in a quarter of an hour. But it's a great nuisance.'

There was a click as the master hung up. Mr Quilta put down his receiver.

'Well,' he remarked in a more leisurely tone, 'we've just got to wait for him. There isn't much we can do till he's checked his belongings.'

George took out a packet of cigarettes. Mr Quilta put out his hand automatically and took one. The sergeant followed suit and held out the packet to Bill.

'No, thanks,' said Bill, shaking his head. 'I don't smoke.'

'Not when we're about, maybe,' he said.

'Not at all,' said Bill sharply.

The sergeant felt in his pocket again and produced a bag of sweets.

'Try a toffee,' he said.

'Beware of the Greeks,' replied Bill, 'when they come bearing gifts.'

The sergeant bent forward and inclined his ear towards Bill.

'Come again,' he said humorously.

'Nothing,' said Bill. 'It's only a thing Mr Snooks says sometimes.'

'You mentioned the Greeks?' said George.

Bill drew a long breath.

'If you turn it into police English,' he explained, 'it means that if a copper offers you anything, you want to be on your guard.'

'It's wonderful that they teach 'em in school nowadays,' said George. 'Did you ever hear of Greek coppers when you were at school, Mr Quilta?'

'No,' replied Mr Quilta, 'I didn't. But I've heard a lot about smart alicks and what happens to them.'

Quite casually, and as if it followed naturally on the conversation, George addressed Bill again.

'When you came in through that front door, what was the first thing you noticed?'

'The smell,' replied Bill promptly.

There was a moment's dead silence.

'What smell?'

'The smell of the house. All houses have their own smell.'

'And what was this smell?'

'Flowers and furniture polish.'

'Hm. What did you observe next?'

'That the doors were open.'

'Didn't you expect them to be open?'

'Mr Snooks said they'd be shut.'

'And then?'

'I saw the cat come out of the front room.'

'What did you do then?'

Bill gave a full account of what he had seen and done.

'Wait a minute,' said Mr Quilta. 'You say that the kitchen door and all the windows were securely fastened?'

'They were. I checked them all.'

'Did you notice anything in the pantry?'

'Yes. That little window was open.'

'It is little, isn't it?'

'Yes.'

'A man could hardly have got through, could he?'

'He'd have a job.'

'Could a boy, do you think?'

'A small boy might. But I doubt it.'

'Would you object to trying?'

Bill stared.

'What... now?'

'Yes. Now.'

'I don't mind.'

'Come on, then.'

Bill and the policemen went out of the front door and round the side of the house into the garden. Below the tiny window there was a square of concrete, and the aperture of the window was just above Bill's head. He looked around and saw a wooden packing-case. He nodded at it.

'I'll have to stand on that,' he said.

The sergeant brought it to him and placed it just below the window. Bill climbed on top of it and tried all ways to get his body through the window, head and shoulders, one leg and then the other, but it was impossible. He gave it up and turned to look at his companions.

'I can't do it,' he said.

As he spoke, another voice was heard. It was Mr Snooks, who

had taken a taxi from school and had come round to the back of the house. He looked sternly at the group.

'And what, may I ask,' he demanded, 'is that mountebank trying to do?'

'Good morning, sir,' said Mr Quilta, touching his hat. 'It's just a small experiment to see if entry by that window would be possible.'

'I gather,' said Mr Snooks grimly, 'that it is not.'

'That would appear to be so, sir.'

'I can assure you,' said Mr Snooks, 'that if a hole is too small for that boy to get through, it's too small for anyone. He's a slippery customer if ever there was one. Isn't that so, Holmes? I trust you don't feel I am being too harsh in saying so.'

'Your spectacles, sir,' said Bill, fishing them out of his pocket and handing them over.

'Thank you,' said Mr Snooks, taking them. 'Now, unless these gentlemen require your services for any further experiments, such as ascending a chimney or crawling, perhaps, through a drain...'

Mr Quilta shook his head.

'Then I suggest that you return to school, Holmes, with all possible speed,' said Mr Snooks. 'With all possible speed. The morning is nearly gone. You must try, when you reach the form-room, to redeem the time.'

'Thank you, sir,' said Bill.

Mr Snooks waved his hand.

'Not at all,' he said. 'You have done your duty by me. The least I can do to show my gratitude — which is sincere, Holmes, don't mistake me — is to perform my duty by you. Good morning.'

A grin rested upon the face of George, the sergeant. Mr Quilta stood as impassive and solemn as a mourner at a funeral.

'Good morning, sir,' said Bill, and went disconsolately round the side of the house, got on his bicycle, and rode slowly down the street.

MOHAWK AMBUSH
Eric Leyland

Six Gun Gauntlet, a frontiersman named Swift as Light by the
Redskins, was hunted by the Mohawks. He might have fallen
victim to a cunning ambush had not Little Bear, son of a murdered
Mohawk chief, arrived in time to save him. Little Bear was his
friend, which was why he helped the scout prepare another ambush
for the Mohawks led by Roaring Bull, who had killed Little Bear's
father. This is one of the many adventures shared by the friends in
Six Gun Gauntlet Rides Again.

Six Gun Gauntlet, most famous of all the lone frontier scouts, squatted on his heels by the small fire he had built close to the tinkling stream. Near at hand was Silver Streak, his white horse.

Six Gun's name and his deeds were common talk amongst the warrior tribes of the sunset trail. Stories of his skill and courage were told in the lodges of the distant Ojibways and Kickapoos of the far north; they held spellbound the braves of the Cheyennes, the Blackfeet and the Mohawks of the south. And Silver Streak was as famous as Six Gun Gauntlet, whose name amongst the Indians was Swift as Light.

Now, as the scout ate his pemmican ration by the fire so cunningly built that not a wisp of smoke rose above the trees of the forest to betray his presence, Streak suddenly raised her head, nostrils wide, ears pricked. She turned her head away from the stream which tumbled over its rocky bed. She whinnied once, very softly.

Instantly Six Gun was on his feet, one of his shooters in his hand. There was no man in all this vast wilderness of forest, plain and mountain as quick on the draw.

As he moved he stamped out the glowing fire, for even here, within two hours' ride of Fort Lloyd, there could be danger. Six Gun had been born and bred to danger.

Streak was as experienced in scenting trouble as her master. Now she had heard or smelled something unusual. Although Six Gun himself could as yet neither see nor hear anything, he trusted Streak.

He stroked her sleek, arched neck gently, while he stood tensely, his gun ready.

'Take it easy lass,' he whispered, as though she could understand.

He waited, listening... and then he picked up the sound which Streak had heard or perhaps only sensed, moments earlier. Somebody was moving through the forest, moving stealthily.

Six Gun shifted his grip on the shooter. The sounds were not approaching but neither were they fading. Whoever was creeping so stealthily through the forest was moving from left to right and perhaps a quarter of a mile ahead.

This district had been conquered from the Indians many years before. Not for a long time had it been the scene of savage battles between white man and red. Fort Lloyd, the headquarters of the U.S. 19th Cavalry, lay only twenty miles away. Yet although the area was peaceful, the Indian tribes friendly, danger could always rear its head, as Six Gun knew.

'Stay around, Streak,' he murmured. 'I'll be back after I've had a look-see.'

Streak remained motionless as her master moved into the forest. Not even Thunder Cloud, the lone hunter, the most expert of the Blackfoot scouts, could give him points when it came to treading silently. Six Gun Gauntlet vanished amongst the trees like a shadow. Not a sound betrayed him.

Every now and again he halted to listen. The wind was blowing towards him. It carried not only the slight sounds of movement, now drawing closer, but also something else. After so many years of riding the trail, for a long time alone, but during the last three years often with a companion, Six Gun could smell Indian. Indian there was in the forest and very close at hand.

This was Blackfoot country. The Blackfeet did not hunt in this district, however. Their hunting grounds were much further north. Here, as Great Elk their chief had once told Six Gun, the white men were too near. There were too many white settlements, not in the forest itself but scattered from its edge to Fort Lloyd.

'Wa, Swift as Light, when the paleface comes the game flees,' Great Elk had said. 'Like some of the tribes who hate and fear the white men,' he added. 'Fear rides with hate. The Blackfeet neither hate nor fear, Swift as Light. Thus do we live in peace, not as do the Mohawks, beyond the Indian River, plotting revenge and dreaming of scalps.'

At this moment Six Gun wasn't thinking of the hostile Mohawks, who three years before had caused bad trouble along the frontier; but he did realize that no Blackfoot hunter was treading stealthily after game.

Some sixth sense deep inside Six Gun warned him of danger. What danger he didn't know and couldn't guess, but he never disregarded his instinct. He pushed on, still silently.

Within ten minutes he came back to the trail which he and Streak had been following when he had halted for food and water by the stream. But now Six Gun was half a mile from the stream, and within sight of the trail that led towards the edge of the forest and the distant Fort Lloyd.

He halted, crouching behind the bole of a mighty tree. He saw ahead of him, nearer to the trail, an Indian behind a bush, a short knife in his hand. He was staring through the leaves, staring along the trail towards the edge of the forest. He did not move.

Six Gun watched from behind his tree fifty yards away. The sun, which had been shining strongly a little earlier, had slid behind clouds, so that he could see the figure of the Indian only dimly. He strove to make out the markings on the blanket slung Indian-fashion across the naked shoulders. What manner of man was this who crouched close to the trail? Was he a Blackfoot... or perhaps a wandering redskin attached to one of the bands which roamed sometimes as close as this to Fort Lloyd seeking to plunder a settlement swiftly, and ride before the cavalry could be called?

And why was he waiting here by the trail, knife in hand? He was surely no brave, for he carried no tomahawk, spear or bow. No feathers adorned his head, not even the single feather of the ordinary fighting member of a tribe. Had Six Gun come upon him at Fort Lloyd, and in other circumstances, he would not have wondered, for there were Indians at the fort, serving the white troops. These did not wear tribal feathers. Now, all his suspicions were aroused.

Faintly in the distance, but approaching from the direction of the forest edge, Six Gun heard the clop-clop of horse's hooves. Somebody was riding down the trail, and making straight for the Indian.

Six Gun saw the man tense. He knew then that he awaited the rider, who could surely not know that he was riding into danger. The Indian brought his knife up. Six Gun saw him finger the keen edge. There could be no doubt that he meant to attack whoever was approaching. Why he lay in ambush for him, Six Gun could not know. At this moment it mattered nothing.

The white scout smiled grimly. The Indian did not suspect that he was being watched. He had no idea that Six Gun was so close behind him. He would shortly discover that interesting fact!

Six Gun could have shot him where he crouched, but simple as this would have been, he did not use his gun. Instead he slid it back into its holster. To prevent a killing was not enough. Six Gun wanted to know what lay behind the ambush, what reason there was for an attack. It might be that the redskin sought only plunder, but it was unlikely, for it was not the Indian way to kill and steal single-handed. Either the red men operated in tribes or in roving bands, never alone.

Six Gun was vastly interested. With his gun in its holster both hands were now free. He snaked his way from behind the tree. He reckoned to get much closer to the redskin. Judging by the speed of the approaching rider, he had time to do it. The horse was not being ridden hard but was only trotting.

As he moved, the sun came out from the clouds. A shaft of bright light slanted down through the branches of the trees and fell across the Indian's blanket. Six Gun's eyes narrowed as for the first time he saw the design clearly.

Every tribe had its own blanket patterns. This one was Mohawk! Three years before the Mohawks had revolted against their chief Black Eagle, had placed Roaring Bull in his tepee as chief and had attempted to begin a full-scale Indian war against the whites.

They had failed and had been driven back to their own country beyond Indian River, far to the north. Since then they had remained there, savagely hostile but not recrossing the boundary river to kill and plunder. Now here was a Mohawk, far from his own country, crouching with drawn knife by the edge of the trail.

Six Gun moved on. There was plenty of cover between the tree and the bush where the Mohawk waited. Six Gun made skilful use of it. Silently he drew nearer and nearer to the redskin. Now more than ever did he need to take the man alive.

The trail made a sharp bend only a few yards from the Mohawk. The horseman was close to the bend, as Six Gun could hear. Then the Mohawk shifted his grip on the knife. He took it by the tip of the blade and poised it ready to throw.

Six Gun had to act swiftly, for it was evident that the man meant to throw the knife as soon as the rider appeared round the bend. Six Gun had seen Indian knife-throwing before often enough. He had watched brave after brave, round the camp-fire, split a hazel wand at two hundred paces.

He wasn't as close to the Mohawk as he intended to be before attacking, but there was no time to waste. At any moment the rider would round the bend... and he would be a dead man if Six Gun didn't act. Yet even now he aimed to take the Indian alive. He reckoned he could still do it.

He broke cover and flung himself forward, arms outstretched, hands ready to grip the Mohawk round the legs.

Even as he sprang, the rider came into view round the bend in the trail. The Mohawk threw the keen-edged knife...

It flicked through the air deadly, death-dealing, the sun glinting on the steel. As swift as an arrow it sped, silently, from dappled shade into full sunlight.

A fraction of a second before the knife left the Mohawk's hand, Six Gun's clutching hands gripped him below the knees. The knife flew on its way, but Six Gun had acted in time. The redskin reeled back even as he threw the deadly knife. His aim disturbed, he missed his target. The weapon flicked between the head and shoulder of the rider who had come round the bend in the trail. It passed on to bury itself, haft quivering, in the trunk of a tree on the other side of the track.

337

This Six Gun realized as the enemy crashed back, his legs jerked from under him. Something else did Six Gun realize... the one brief glimpse he had of the rider before he was fighting for his life with the Mohawk was enough. It was Little Bear, son of the murdered Black Eagle, chief of the Mohawks, who had ridden round the bend. For three years Six Gun had ridden the trails with Little Bear. If he hadn't been here in the forest at this moment, however, they would not have ridden together again.

Just the one brief glimpse he had of the Indian boy and then the Mohawk was on him. Six Gun had been unlucky, for in jerking the Indian off his feet he himself had tripped over a tree root and had fallen. The Mohawk was on top of him.

A second knife appeared in the man's hand. It flashed up... and down, in a killing stroke. Once again the redskin missed. Six Gun twisted to one side. The blade of the knife pierced the dressed skin of his hunting shirt. It grazed the flesh underneath but that was all.

Six Gun, however, as he twisted, crashed his head against a boulder. As his senses swam and pain seared through his skull, he heard a shout from the trail. Little Bear had swung lithely from his mustang.

The Mohawk leaped away, leaving Six Gun where he lay, the knife caught in the tough skin of his hunting shirt. As Little Bear ran across the trail into the forest, the Mohawk fled.

None of this did Six Gun know until some little time later, when he came to himself, to find Little Bear kneeling by his side. The Mohawk's knife lay on the ground. Six Gun's shirt had been opened to reveal the scratch on his upper arm, a scratch which so easily might have been much more than that.

The Mohawk who had lain in ambush for Little Bear had escaped into the thick forest. Little Bear had not followed him.

'I thought you were dead, Swift as Light,' he said simply. 'I stayed with you.'

Six Gun came slowly to his feet. His head still ached agonizingly from the blow above the temple, but he was tough and in good condition.

He smiled at Little Bear. 'Your courage is the courage inherited from your father, Black Eagle, the white man's friend and blood-brother of Swift as Light,' he said.

He was remembering how he had rescued Little Bear from death at the hands of Roaring Bull, who had broken the Mohawk treaty with the white men and led the tribe on the war-path against the palefaces. Now for a long time the two had ridden the trails together.

'It's okay, son, I'm not dead yet,' he murmured. Then, as his mind began to work smoothly again, he added, 'But maybe it's an idea not to let on about that.'

Little Bear's brown eyes searched his face. Little Bear was still Indian for all that he had ridden with Six Gun for three years and through him had come into contact with many other white men. Yet he was not so Indian as he had been.

He had learned from the white men to show something of his thoughts in his face. Now a flicker of bewilderment, plain to see, was revealed in his eyes. When he had lived with his father amongst the Mohawks, neither curiosity, fear, hope nor any other emotion was ever revealed, for the true Indian keeps a poker-face.

'I do not understand,' he said, speaking in English. Then, still watching Six Gun's face, 'I saw a Mohawk blanket pattern. Is that why you would have him believe you dead?'

Six Gun was buttoning up his shirt. The scratch was nothing and had nearly stopped bleeding.

'Partly, son, but I guess next time our friend is on view he won't be wearing a Mohawk blanket...'

Little Bear did not understand, but said nothing, knowing that Six Gun would explain more fully if he wanted to, and that if he didn't, nothing would persuade him to.

Six Gun, however, did explain, although first he wanted to know how Little Bear came to be riding the trail. The two had been scouting together but had separated two days before. They had arranged to meet at Ford Lloyd, yet Little Bear was here, two hours from the fort and riding away from it.

'I came to the fort early,' was the boy's answer.

'I rode to meet you, for I knew you would take this trail.'

'Right, Little Bear... then I reckon you were spotted some way back. That Mohawk planned to kill you. Does that mean anything?'

Little Bear's lean face grew grim. Yes, it meant much to him. Roaring Bull had murdered his father, Black Eagle, and had seized chieftainship. Little Bear had sworn to seek his revenge, and he had sworn, too, that one day he would be chief of the Mohawks, as his father had been before him.

'Roaring Bull fears that some of the tribe will support me,' said the boy slowly. 'Now only two Months of the Falling Leaves must pass before I am of age to become chief. Roaring Bull would have me dead.'

Six Gun agreed that this was likely. Two autumns only must pass before Little Bear was eighteen. There might well be reasons why Roaring Bull feared the boy. There might be trouble within the tribe. Some might wish the son of Black Eagle to rule them when he came of age.

'Most likely you're right,' said Six Gun. 'We'll get back to Streak. I've got something else to tell you.'

As they made their way back to Silver Streak, Six Gun told Little Bear what was in his mind.

'I reckon you didn't see that varmint's face, son, but I did. I've seen him before — at Fort Lloyd. He's Wabeno, always made out he's a Comanche, but that doesn't hold water now. He's a Mohawk and I reckon he was planted at the fort to watch for a chance to get you... and me, too, maybe. Roaring Bull doesn't love either of us.'

Little Bear shook his head slowly, which in an Indian meant that he agreed. Roaring Bull was a dangerous man and a clever one, strong and cunning. Friendly Indians were employed at the fort. Wabeno, not a Comanche but a Mohawk, had been sent there by Roaring Bull.

'Wa, that must be the truth, Swift as Light. That is why you would pretend to be dead?' His brown hand rested lightly on the stout neck of his mustang.

'Sure, that's why. If you thought I'd handed in my checks, then I guess he thinks the same. I looked dead when you found me?'

'I thought you were dead and my heart grieved,' was the reply.

That suited Six Gun. If Wabeno thought he was dead then he

would probably return to the fort, knowing that he hadn't killed Little Bear but hoping for another chance. He would know that Little Bear hadn't seen him closely enough to recognize him. Six Gun had, but he would believe him dead. Dead men tell no tales.

'We'll hope it works out that way and he goes back to the fort,' added the scout. 'If so, then we can grab him so long as he doesn't see me first. He's go to be told I'm dead. I shan't show up until I know he's back there.'

'Swift as Light has the cunning of the fox,' answered Little Bear, the ghost of a smile at his lips. 'My people believe that he can work magic, but I...'

'Sure, you know that it's just cunning!' broke in Six Gun. 'I guess we'd best get along and make for home.'

Home to them was Fort Lloyd, where both were always welcomed by white men, quite apart from the fact that Six Gun's tracking skill was at the disposal of the troops; Little Bear because he was Six Gun's buddy.

Six Gun found Streak unharmed and still tethered by the stream. Pretty soon the two were on their way, Little Bear vaulting easily on to his pony's back.

For half an hour they rode, Six Gun working out his plan of action against Wabeno, now known to be a Mohawk. Then, as they entered another spur of the forest, having ridden for some distance across open ground, without any warning an attack was launched on them.

Had it been launched from ground level, they might have had a chance, but as it was the assault came from above. Six Gun reeled from the saddle as a half-naked figure dropped on him from the overhanging bough of a tree. At the same instant another figure leaped on Little Bear.

As Six Gun crashed to the ground, he glimpsed other brown-skinned figures dropping from the trees. A war-cry rose, blood-curdling, the war-cry of the fighting Mohawks!

'Aiee! Aiee!'

Wabeno was not the only Mohawk at large in this territory so near to Fort Lloyd. Others had left their fastness beyond Indian

341

River and had ridden into Blackfoot country. They had come seeking prey, but not as the wandering bands of Cheyennes, the Prairie Dogs, hoping for any plunder, any scalps. The Mohawks must have ridden with an object... the life of Little Bear, son of Black Eagle!

Even as he fell, this thought flashed across Six Gun's mind. Then he was fighting for his life. The redskin who had brought him to the ground was snarling with triumph. In his hand gleamed his tomahawk, upraised, as he knelt on his victim.

'Death to Swift as Light!' he screeched in the Mohawk tongue which Six Gun knew so well. 'Death to the paleface... Aiee!'

Six Gun saved his energy for action. It would have paid the Mohawk to do the same, but it was ever the way of the tribe to howl triumph before victory was won.

The Indians had named Swift as Light well. He could indeed move swiftly... and did so now. As the gleaming tomahawk was raised, Six Gun brought up his knee with the force of a sledge-hammer. It struck the Mohawk brave in the stomach and he reeled back. As he did so, Six Gun's hand flashed out and, gripping the enemy's wrist, twisted it so that the weapon fell to the ground.

The next instant he was on his feet. His gun appeared in his hand like magic.

One glance was enough to show him the exact position under the overhanging trees. Six Mohawks had dropped from ambush. One Six Gun had accounted for, the brave who had attacked him was now lying motionless. Another lay crumpled against a tree, evidently Little Bear's victim.

That left four. And they were now attacking the Indian boy, who had backed against the trunk of a tree and was fighting desperately.

Six Gun fired and a third Mohawk joined his comrades on the ground. The gun couldn't be used again, however, for the other three Mohawks were bunched too close to Little Bear. Even Six Gun, expert shot though he was, dared not risk another shot for fear of hitting Little Bear.

The shooter went back into its holster. One of the enemy swung round, as his comrade fell, and Six Gun was on him. He ducked under the swinging stroke of a tomahawk, straightened, and then his fist hit the redskin under the jaw. There was a sharp click, the enemy's head snapped back and he crumpled to the ground.

Now there were only two braves left. The odds were even. A few short moments had almost turned the tables on those sent into Blackfoot country by Roaring Bull.

One of the braves still attacking Little Bear turned, his killing spear thrusting. Six Gun dodged the vicious cutting head, grabbed the wooden shaft and pulled with all his strength. The redskin stumbled forward, staggered, and as he did so, Six Gun swung the heavy shaft round. It hit the Mohawk across the head and he fell.

Little Bear was fighting silently. There was no need for Six Gun to assist him any more, for as the fifth enemy crashed to the ground, the boy settled accounts with the remaining brave.

As Six Gun grabbed Streak's bridle and Little Bear swung round towards his own well-trained mustang, which was now coming towards his master, one enemy crawled away into the forest. Six Gun fired after him but the bullet went wide, the enemy finding cover. Then, in the distance, could be heard war-cries and the trampling of horses.

'Out of here, quick!' snapped Six Gun, leaping into Streak's saddle. 'These boys weren't alone, I guess!'

He was right, for the war-cries, drawing nearer, were Mohawk. Wabeno had been thwarted earlier in his attempt on Little Bear's life. Now the trap laid by the Mohawks had failed — but yet more enemies were coming into the attack.

There was no sort of sense in taking on maybe a dozen or more redskins. Six Gun was all for getting out of the trap as quickly as he could.

Little Bear swung astride his mustang. The two thundered up the trail. Behind them, but well behind, they could hear the war-cries and the sounds of pursuit.

The enemy gained ground. Little Bear's mustang was limping, having been injured in the fight. The boy couldn't obtain the speed he needed. The war-cries grew louder.

Six Gun thought quickly. He remembered Saddle Pass, lying

away to the left. Very soon a minor trail turned off the one they were now following and, reaching the foothills of the mountains beyond the forest, passed through a deep cut defile.

This was Saddle Pass, so named because the trail rose sharply up hill and then dropped just as sharply beyond a ridge in the centre of the defile.

Six Gun rapped out an order.

'We'll make for Saddle Pass... follow me, son!'

He knew that they could never outdistance the enemy. He himself could ride on and escape, for it was a certainty that no Mohawk would catch him mounted on Streak. But Six Gun wasn't leaving Little Bear to his fate, and the boy's mustang was now limping badly. He reckoned that Saddle Pass would offer a means of settling with the Mohawks, provided that there were not too many of them. It was unlikely that Roaring Bull would send a large party across Indian River, for murder, not wholesale war, was evidently the object. A small party could move fast and stealthily.

The two reached the fork in the trail and swung left. Very soon the forest dropped away as the rugged foothills were reached. Open, broken ground stretched ahead, gaunt hills rising higher and higher until the mountains were reached, blue in the far distance.

Saddle Pass lay within half a mile as the fugitives broke from the forest. The trail ran straight for it. Six Gun, however, now left the trail. The ground rose sharply on either side of the trail, rose until a cliff more than a hundred feet high was formed, the trail running below it and between the cliff face and another fringing the other side. The rising ground to the right of the trail was covered with trees, a spur of the forest.

Six Gun led the way through the trees, making for the top of the cliff. Reaching a hollow, he reined in and dismounted. Little Bear did the same.

Then they climbed up through the trees on foot, as swiftly as they could. The trees began to thin as the top of the cliff approached, but there was plenty of scrub and undergrowth, which provided good cover.

The sounds of pursuit grew louder and louder. The Mohawks had discovered that their quarry had turned off the main trail.

He and Little Bear crouched behind a mass of boulders

Now Roaring Bull's braves were speeding along the minor trail, making for Saddle Pass.

Six Gun reckoned he had time to reach a position to deal with them as they passed through the narrow defile, toiled up the sharp slope of the trail, and then over the saddle-back ridge. Of necessity, they must move slowly.

The fugitives reached the top of the cliff dead above the saddle-back ridge a hundred feet below. The trees had thinned considerably by now and there was also far less undergrowth and scrub. Instead the ground was rocky and littered with boulders, many of them close to the lip of the sheer cliff. Six Gun had remembered this when he had been casting round for some way of settling with the Mohawks.

He and Little Bear crouched behind a mass of boulders and watched the trail winding far below. They had a perfect view.

They saw the Mohawks break from the forest. They did not swerve to right or left but continued along the trail, taking the slope which led to the defile. Had they been in less haste they must have seen the signs which Six Gun and the boy had been unable to conceal — signs which revealed that they had left the trail and taken to the tree-covered slope leading to the top of the cliff. But the Mohawks did not draw rein. Evidently they believed that their quarry had kept to the trail and were now out of sight beyond the saddleback ridge halfway through the defile.

This was exactly what Six Gun had aimed they should believe. He counted them as they emerged from the forest. There were fourteen; that made a total force of twenty dispatched by Roaring Bull to seek the life of Little Bear! That was just about the number Six Gun had expected. The Mohawks had lost six of their original force.

'I reckon we can settle with this lot,' he said grimly, turning to the boy. 'You know what to do... get busy, but don't finish the job before these guys are underneath.'

He had briefed Little Bear during the climb up the slope. The boy knew what to do and now made his stealthy way to another group of boulders some yards away. Like the first this group was poised on the very edge of the cliff.

The Mohawks, mounted on their fast, wiry ponies, were now halfway up the slope. The cliffs were closing in on the trail. The slope was becoming steeper and the enemy were forced to drop speed.

Six Gun, behind the first group of boulders and nearer the oncoming braves than Little Bear, waited tensely. The braves were riding into a trap. He hoped nothing would happen to halt them before they reached the ridge in the centre of the defile.

Motionless Six Gun Gauntlet waited and watched. Now, far below, the Mohawks, bunched closely together, had entered the defile itself, where the cliffs drew very close together. There was room for four to ride abreast. The enemy were toiling up the slope in closed ranks. The white, alkali dust rose in clouds as they urged on their sweating ponies, convinced that the fugitives had passed this way and were not far beyond the saddle-back ridge ahead.

It was surely too late now for anything to hinder Six Gun's plan. The Mohawks were nearly at the ridge. Once there, they would expect to see their quarry riding down the slope on the other side. Then they would set their ponies down the hill and give swift chase.

The leaders passed under the spot where Six Gun was crouching. They moved on and came nearly to the top of the ridge. High above them Little Bear was ready for action behind the loose boulders.

Now the moment had come... the entire party was massed between Six Gun and Little Bear, although a hundred feet below and with no suspicions that they had entered the trap.

Six Gun raised his hand in a signal. If this wasn't the end of fourteen of Roaring Bull's murderous braves, then he would never ride the sunset trail again!

Little Bear, watching for the signal, set his shoulder to the first of the loose boulders. Six Gun did the same. Both boulders went over the edge of the cliff together... they were followed by others, hurtling down a hundred feet to the narrow trail below, smashing down upon the enemy closely grouped in the defile.

THE GAUCHO GOES TO TOWN
Charles Sydney

Mateo, a young gaucho from the *pampas* of South America, forsakes the plains for the life of a town, and is quickly disillusioned. But adventure dogs his spurs and he is forced to demonstrate that his skill with the *bolas* is something more than a circus trick. By that time he is glad to ride back to the life he had forsaken.

The young gaucho on the roan stallion wondered why traffic had suddenly stopped in Bahia Blanca's busiest thoroughfare.

His long *revenque*, the riding whip with flat, leather thong and heavy handle, dangled loosely from the wrist of a slender hand. A slight pressure with his knees halted the roan. Like a piece of statuary, man and horse were motionless in the glaring sunshine.

The gaucho was sixteen. A wisp of black hair fell from his *sombrero* over a high cheekbone; he had a thin nose and sensitive nostrils, tight lips, dark eyes narrowed as though gazing over the wide *pampas*, and the proud bearing of his Spanish and Indian ancestors. He wore his best outfit: short embroidered jacket, snowy nylon shirt and yellow scarf, long knife thrust through a belt stiff with dollars, and baggy trousers tucked into soft silver-spurred top-boots. A *poncho* hung over his left shoulder; a lasso lay on his horse's crupper, and his *bolas*, with its rawhide-covered stones, was to hand.

His roan's leather glowed with the glossy warmth of a newly shelled chestnut; buckles and stirrups winked in the white light.

They looked as though they had stepped straight from the town's circus; in fact, an impudent citizen had jeeringly said so, and

Serafino, Mateo's father, had bribed a *milico* to look the other way until an abject man had apologized through his remaining teeth.

Mateo had seen many queer things in the city, but the strangest was this sudden emptying of a busy street. Then a wave of screaming people approached, some pausing to beat frantically and vainly on bolted doors before rushing on again. Gaucho and horse stood rocklike as the crowd swirled round them and passed by. There, glaring up with baleful yellow eyes and ready to spring, crouched the same puma that Mateo had seen in the circus. The roan trembled, but stood firm. From windows facing the street, hundreds of eyes watched the unfolding drama.

Discontent had brought Mateo there from an *estancia* in the far south of the province, while a neglectful owner was responsible for the escape of the puma from its cage.

'Life's not what it was,' Mateo's father was always complaining. 'The modern world has no room for gauchos.'

American cars and the petrol engine had certainly changed things. Serafino had snorted indignantly when he heard a man boasting on the radio that he had saved the expense of twenty gauchos by rounding up a herd of cattle in a helicopter. The radio itself was a grievance. What chance had the *guiterero* — the guitar troubadour — against a professional jazz-band? It was easier to listen than to perform. The old songs of adventure on the *pampas* were forgotten. The gaucho himself was dying out.

That was how Serafino used to talk when he caught Mateo humming the latest 'song-hit', for young Mateo believed that the new was better than the old. He liked motor cars, and radio, and all they represented. He preferred crowds to herds of cattle, cities to open plains, a tame car to a wild horse, and a town sparrow to an Andes condor — or, so he imagined when he argued with Serafino.

Of course, they were both wrong, for while there are wild horses and herds of cattle there will be gauchos, and youth always values the new above the old until experience proves which is better. Serafino had forgotten that he once talked like Mateo; moreover he was prejudiced, for he had never lived in a town. So they both talked hotly about things they only partly understood, and

352

annoyed each other, but Serafino always had the last word because he was Mateo's father.

Mateo had been born in the saddle, as they say, and he was a horseman of whom even Serafino was proud. He used the lasso and threw the *bolas* as well as the next man. He had a good voice, too, for a gaucho song, and when he was happy, which was not infrequently, he could not imagine himself in any other occupation. But the more Serafino decried towns, the more ardently Mateo longed for them.

Finally, Mateo's mother so wearied of their constant bickering that she advised Serafino: 'The boy has never been away from us. The next time you visit town, take him with you, and let him stay for a month, and if he finds himself a job don't put obstacles in his way. There are times when a horse must be given its head, as you well know, and a high-spirited lad must not be ridden on too tight a rein.'

'Or a high-spirited lass,' Serafino grinned, remembering the days of his youth when his wife had sighed for the excitement of a town.

'I was cured,' she said. 'Let Mateo be cured in the same way.'

So when the cattle had to be driven into the Puerto Galvin yards at Bahia Blanca, Mateo accompanied his father on the roan stallion that he had himself caught and tamed.

At night under the stars, the eight men of the party leaned against their saddles round a wood fire, singing the old songs to a mournful guitar, and by day they kept the cattle moving, vying in tricks of horsemanship to enliven the slow journey, though Mateo found time pass too quickly. He was half sorry when the journey ended, still more regretful not to be returning with such good companions. But the town captured his imagination. The people, the houses, the traffic, the garish cinemas, the smell of the sea and his first sight of ships — everything excited him, and he had a whole month in which to find work.

They had changed into their finery before entering the town, and bore themselves proudly, imagining that every eye in Bahia Blanca was upon them.

When they had disposed of the cattle and found accommodation for themselves and for their horses, the gauchos began to spend their savings. Serafino had a list of things to take back with him, so he and Mateo would have a few days together before parting. Mateo was glad of this, for he felt lost in the city where the gaucho dress, his former pride, made him feel self-conscious. His feet ached on the hard pavements, and the busy streets were equally unkind to a horse. After the first few rides in buses and taxis — for a gaucho never walks when he can ride — he longed for the feel of the roan between his knees, though he would not admit it to his father.

Serafino, who knew the city slightly, was happy because it was a complete change, he would soon be returning to the ranch, and it is always enjoyable to air one's knowledge. But doubts began to trouble Mateo as to the wisdom of living in a town when one was so ignorant. However, he reassured himself that when he had to fend for himself he would soon learn its ways.

Serafino, in fact, was far more excited about everything than Mateo, and he was somewhat disappointed that his son showed such little enthusiasm.

'It is because Mateo feels at home here,' he sighed to himself. 'Maybe he was right, and the *pampas* can no longer hold a lad of mettle.'

'But that's something we don't see down on the *estancia*,' he enthused after a visit to a cinema.

'I have a headache,' Mateo blinked in the dazzling daylight. 'One couldn't breathe in there.'

'Ah-ah!' chuckled Serafino. 'So there's something to be said for the country after all.'

'Just as one gets saddle-sore after being away from horses too long, so one must also learn to breathe the air of a city,' said Mateo sourly.

'Well, there are other ways of amusing ourselves,' countered Serafino cheerfully. 'There is a circus outside the town on the river-bank. I saw one when I was a boy. The riding there will make us gauchos look like townies.'

But it was a poor show, and the worst horseman on the *estancia* could have beaten the finest trick riders in the circus. Disillusioned,

Serafino and Mateo ended their visit with an inspection of the dejected animals in the small menagerie behind the Big Top.

The old cages looked insecure and smelt abominably. Mateo had hunted many of the animals in their wild state, but he pitied them now. He had felt trapped like them in the cinema, and the stone canyons of the town stifled him, though he kept it from Serafino.

The puma shocked him most. It rarely attacked man, though it had been necessary to hunt this killer of sheep and calves and foals. It crouched in a corner, its small head between its paws. Its eyes were lustreless, and the gloss had gone from its tawny skin, yet, to Mateo, it recalled vividly the fresh winds of the *sierras*. As it returned Mateo's stare, the puma's eyes filled with life and fire; perhaps it conjured up in that animal brain visions of freedom and of the age-old enmity between gaucho and mountain lion. Its muscles rippled again as man and beast held each other's gaze, and then the puma launched itself like an arrow, so that Mateo instinctively shielded his face as the animal crashed against the bars and fell back. For a few moments it went mad, spitting and snarling as it tore round the cage, hurling itself frenziedly at the bars, and straining the rusty hinges of the ancient door.

'Better dead,' Mateo murmured.

'The brute would be all right if fools would leave it alone,' an attendant snapped, imagining that Mateo had been teasing it. As Mateo looked at him, he added uncomfortably, 'Not meaning you, of course, señor.'

'You should replace those hinges,' Mateo said, coldly.

'That's up to the boss,' said the man, carelessly. 'My pay doesn't run to it.'

Mateo's depression deepened when, the following day, he rode a league out of town with the returning gauchos.

Like boys released from school the gauchos began an impromptu race down the dusty road. Serafino turned once and waved.

'Travel with God,' Mateo called in farewell.

Then he rode slowly back to town.

After stabling his horse he felt lonelier than ever. It was still early in the morning, and a long empty day lay ahead. Looking for work would fill in time, but disillusion was swift. His experience was useless here; no one was interested in horses either, except a cinema manager who, because of his gaucho dress, offered him temporary employment distributing hand-outs of a forthcoming cowboy picture. Mateo withdrew politely, but with growing dismay. Then he remembered the cattle-yards.

He was directed to a burly unshaven foreman who obviously considered himself tough. A stained scarf encircled his corded neck, and he toyed with a short iron bar as he contemptuously eyed Mateo's elegance. Mateo disliked him at sight, but swallowed his pride, begged humbly for a chance, and was taken on with a sneer.

Before lunch, Mateo had sickened of the work — not because of its arduous nature; he had expected that. And he had corralled cattle often enough, and had killed when killing was necessary. But he had not anticipated the cruel treatment they received here, or that such brutes as the foreman would be responsible for them.

At last he made his protest.

A red river of dazed beasts was being diverted into a pen when the leading steer turned aside. Knowing that the rest would follow, the foreman leapt forward. His iron bar crashed on the defenceless skull, breaking off one of the wretched animal's horns, and a second savage blow sank to the bone above its muzzle. The terrified beast dashed into the corral, and the others passed in a bellowing stream between Mateo and the foreman, so that he had to shout.

'Don't try that again while I work for you,' he yelled above the pandemonium.

The foreman stared incredulously, then pushed through the cattle, and, before Mateo could defend himself, a hamlike fist knocked him down. He was up again like a cat, hissing with fury. But the press of moving animals had taken care of the foreman. Galloping after their leader, their sheer weight had borne him along with them. Mateo watched the iron bar fall desperately and repeatedly as the foreman tried to clear a space around himself. Then, as he went down among the trampling hooves, he screamed, and Mateo waited no longer.

The cattle were jammed tightly together in the corral as Mateo leapt the rail and scrambled from back to back until he glimpsed a coloured scarf among the forest of legs. Then he dropped astride a beast and, merciless now, sank his spur deep into the flank of the adjacent animal and thrust. Pressure and pain drove it those few inches which let Mateo stoop and yank the foreman upright by his scarf.

Fortunately the man still had the wit to clamber from immediate danger before the gap closed again. Helped by Mateo he reached the rails, bruised and bleeding, slipped over, and fainted.

Mateo stood aside and let others attend to him. He very soon recovered.

'Those brutes would have trodden me to a pulp. I give you a job; you save my life. It is justice,' he gasped by way of thanks.

'Señor,' Mateo replied quietly, 'had justice been done, I should not have interfered with Divine Providence.'

Then he returned to the city, for those few words, he knew, had ended his career in the cattle-yards. Then he began to reproach himself for his impatience. This was the first day he had sought work, and, up to a point, he had been successful. But at the back of his mind lay an uneasy dread of the city and its ways, and he felt an unexpected longing for the *adobe* home of his parents, with its untidy comfort and its sun-bleached oxskulls for chairs. The city spoke a different language; its words were the same, but cold and impersonal, like these many-storeyed buildings of chromium and glass. He glanced up at them now, distastefully, the bleeding steer with its smashed horn fresh in mind. He would ride into the country for a while to get matters into proper perspective.

Astride his horse, on the way out of town, he felt much better. He saw in his mind drifting herds of cattle on the quiet *pampas*, wild horses, tails and manes streaming in furious flight, the gauchos thundering after them, and the old *adobe rancho* where horsemen dropped from the rail on plunging stallions released from the corral.

And then he became aware of the city again, blinking like a man rising from heavy sleep to consciousness. The street was different. A yelling mob of frightened people rushed towards him, filling the sidewalks and the road itself, and from its fringes people beat frantically upon closed doors before renewing their wild flight.

357

They yelled incoherently as they streamed past, and then he was alone, and, for the second time, man and puma, both aliens, held each other's hostile gaze.

Anticipating the beast's spring, Mateo flicked up the reins, brought the roan on its hind legs and neck-reined it to the right. The scared but disciplined stallion whirled round, its plunging forelegs crashing on the airborne puma's neck and striking it down. Instantly the snarling cat was on its feet again, belly down for another spring.

Mateo had no gun; the puma, mad with pain, would scarcely feel the heavy handle of his *revenque*. His only hope lay in thwarting its spring. The old gaucho trick came to his aid. He whirled his horse again. At every half-turn the stallion thrust itself into the air with a foreleg that barely touched the ground. Again the deadly hooves of the stallion struck its enemy aside. At the third spring, as the claws of one paw left bloody streaks on the stallion's flank, Mateo leaned from the saddle and the full force of his *revenque* caught the puma on its tender muzzle.

The beaten puma twisted away in flight. The wounded stallion, screaming with rage and pain, responded to the touch of Mateo's spurs. The spectators at the windows saw the two balls of Mateo's *bolas* circling round his head, and the flying weapon twist round the puma's hind legs.

The puma fell, but, after one savage bite at the *bolas*, made a desperate attempt to bound away, its hind legs still clamped by the twisted rawhide thongs. The drama was not yet over. In one smooth movement Mateo rose in his stirrups as he whipped the lasso from behind him. Its noose fell over the puma's head, half strangling it as the stallion reared back and took the strain. Before the puma could turn, coil after coil of rope rendered it helpless, and then the beast's keeper ran from a doorway, clapped a pistol to its head, and fired. The tawny body jerked convulsively, and the head fell back, and the limbs were still.

Instantly the street filled with people again. The carcass was dragged into the gutter. Traffic began to flow. Mateo was surrounded. A reporter struggled to his side.

'Before anything else, my horse needs attention,' Mateo said.

358

Its noose fell over the puma's head

A large crowd followed them, chattering excitedly. Down a side-street the roan received attention. The pain allayed, the stallion was less restive. Mateo relaxed, and, somewhat surprised — for the gaucho loves admiration — discovered that he was not universally popular.

'It was a put-up job, I tell you,' an angry man was addressing the crowd. 'I see through him. Anyone can tell he's from the circus. Just another publicity stunt to pull in the public.'

Murmurs of assent rose from the fickle crowd. Mateo turned to the speaker, a tall man with a long raw neck emerging from a grubby white collar who reminded Mateo so much of a vulture that he addressed him with silky insolence: 'What, *Señor Condor*, did the *vaquiano* (big-head) see through the *vaquero*?'

The mob guffawed, tickled by Mateo's crude wit, and their favour swung towards him again.

The man, stung by ridicule, saw only an insolent boy and grinned as he removed his coat. Other countries; other ways. From time immemorial the gaucho has fought with a knife, his *poncho* wrapped for protection around his left arm.

'Well, *Señor Condor*?' Mateo awaited him coolly.

The man licked his dry lips as he eyed the keen edge of the long *facon*. The he turned a sickly yellow, gulped, and fled from the jeers of the crowd.

They would have acclaimed Mateo now, but he was done with them. Easily he swung himself into the saddle.

'My story!' the reporter called feverishly.

'*Adios, señor*, and many thanks,' Mateo said courteously with a slight inclination of his slender body

With any luck he should overtake his father before noon of the following day. Already his heart was light again.